D0774182

PRAISE FOR *UNHINGED*

'Superb Nordic Noir. Dark, intricate and extremely compelling. Contemporary Scandinavian fiction at its best' Will Dean

'Blending a gripping storytelling structure with thrilling tension and heartfelt moments that may bring tears to your eyes, *Unhinged* is a standout instalment in an already excellent series. The Blix and Ramm series is one of my favourite Nordic Noir "hidden gems" and if you're a fan of writers like Lars Kepler, Stefan Ahnhem and Søren Sveistrup you won't want to miss this thrilling crime-fiction series' Crime by the Book

'The Blix and Ramm series could be the perfect basis for a movie or a TV show ... this is, hands down, the best book in the series so far, and it will satisfy even the most demanding readers. It has a little bit of everything: action, drama, suspense, mystery, and a strong whodunit element' *Tap the Line Magazine*

'Fraught with tension, packed with nerve-wracking moments that keep you completely on edge, *Unhinged* has one of those jaw-dropping, "what did you just do" kind of conclusions that will leave fans of the series reeling ... With flawless translation that brings the story to life in such vivid tones, it's a book that really leaves a mark, and one that will take some time to forget' Jen Med's Book Reviews

'The stunning conclusion left me reeling, but so too did the preceding pages, all of which thrilled, moved and shocked me as only the most exceptional fiction can. If you've not yet discovered Blix and Ramm, then make it your New Year resolution. I adored *Unhinged* more than I can put into words. Intense, dark, emotional and utterly outstanding!' Hair Past a Freckle

'Best one yet in the Blix and Ramm series. A thrill ride but also unexpectedly emotional. I can't wait for the next one. There will be a next one, right, guys?' Sandra Amor

'The opening chapter had me gripped! In a storyline that was utterly explosive with shocking twists, it was easy to read *Unhinged* in a matter of days ... The plot is not revealed at the beginning, it's a twisty, melting pot of sumptuous prose, and the character of Alexander Blix must surely be one of THE best in Nordic Noir, we feel everything he does so deeply. Only writers with extreme talent can write books like *Unhinged* – that shock you, that make you gasp, that make you hurt – just like Blix!' Jude's Book Worm Blog

WHAT THE READERS ARE SAYING

'Enger and Horst step up again and conceive an exciting thriller with a touch of emotion!'

'The story was tough but well written. The characters were believable. I hope there is another book in the series'

'An absolute page-turner'

'Exciting, with some unexpected events'

'Opaque, emotional, exciting, and tragic. A real pleasure to read'

'A great addition to a fantastic series from two exceptionally talented writers'

'Absolutely brilliant'

'An enjoyable read with a great cliff-hanger of an ending'

'An exciting thriller from Enger and Horst'

'By far the best book in the series ... I'm already looking forward to part four'

PRAISE FOR THE BLIX AND RAMM SERIES

'An exercise in literary tag-teaming from two of Norway's biggest crime writers with a bold new take ... a series with potential' *Sunday Times*

'Grim, gory and filled with plenty of dark twists ... There's definitely a Scandinavian chill in the air with this fascinating read' *Sun*

'This tale often surprises or shifts in subtle ways that are pleasing and avoid cliché. As the opener for a new series this is a cracker – long live the marriage of Horst and Enger' *New Books Magazine*

'A fast-moving, punchy, serial-killer investigative novel with a whammy of an ending. If this is the first in the Blix and Ramm series, then here's to many more!' LoveReading

'A stunningly excellent collaboration from Thomas Enger and Jørn Lier Horst ... It's a brutal tale of fame, murder and reality TV that gets the pulse racing' Russel McLean

'After the case mushrooms into a succession of eerily planned and executed homicides of amoral celebrities, Blix and Emma concoct a brilliant but dangerous scheme to catch the culprit. A devilishly complex plot, convincing red herrings and well-rounded characters help make this a winner. Scandinavian noir fans will eagerly await the sequel' *Publishers Weekly*

ABOUT THE AUTHORS

Jørn Lier Horst and Thomas Enger are both internationally bestselling Norwegian authors. Jørn Lier Horst first rose to literary fame with his No. 1 bestselling William Wisting series. A former investigator in the Norwegian police, Horst imbues all his works with an unparalleled realism and suspense. Thomas Enger is the journalist-turned-author behind the internationally acclaimed Henning Juul series. Enger's trademark is his dark, gritty voice paired with key social messages and tight plotting. Besides writing fiction for both adults and young adults, Enger also works as a music composer.

Death Deserved, the first book in the bestselling Blix and Ramm series, was Jørn Lier Horst and Thomas Enger's first co-written thriller and was followed by *Smoke Screen*.

Follow Jørn Lier and Thomas on Twitter @LierHorst and @EngerThomas, and their websites: jlhorst.com and thomasenger.com.

ABOUT THE TRANSLATOR

Megan Turney is originally from the West Midlands, and after spending several years moving back and forth between the UK and Norway, she is now based in Edinburgh, working as a commercial and literary translator and editor. She was the recipient of the National Centre for Writing's 2019 Emerging Translator Mentorship, and holds an MA(Hons) in Scandinavian Studies and English Literature from the University of Edinburgh and an MA in Translation and Interpreting Studies from the University of Manchester. She has previously translated *Smoke Screen* by Jørn Lier Horst and Thomas Enger. Follow Megan on www.meganeturney.com.

The Blix and Ramm Series – available from Orenda Books:
Death Deserved
Smoke Screen
Unhinged

UNHINGED

JØRN LIER HORST & THOMAS ENGER

TRANSLATED BY MEGAN TURNEY

ORENDA
BOOKS

Orenda Books
16 Carson Road
West Dulwich
London SE21 8HU
www.orendabooks.co.uk

First published in the United Kingdom by Orenda Books, 2022
First published in Norwegian as *Slagside* by Capitana Forlag, 2020
Copyright © Jørn Lier Horst & Thomas Enger, 2020
English translation copyright © Megan Turney, 2022

A catalogue record for this book is available from the British Library.

ISBN 978-1-914585-00-5
eISBN 978-1-914585-01-2

This book has been translated with financial support from NORLA

NORLA
NORWEGIAN LITERATURE ABROAD

Typeset in Garamond by www.typesetter.org.uk

Printed and bound by CPI Group (UK) Ltd, Croydon CR0 4YY

For sales and distribution, please contact *info@orendabooks.co.uk* or visit
www.orendabooks.co.uk.

UNHINGED

1

There were no windows in the interrogation room – just four grey walls, three chairs and a table. The air was warm. Stifling.

Alexander Blix had spent many hours in various interview and interrogation rooms, but never here, at Kripos – Norway's National Crime Investigation Service. And certainly never on this side of the table.

He raised his hand to inspect his forehead. The bandage. The skin around the stitches stung.

He thought of Iselin and a pain far more intense tore through him, shooting up from the pit of his stomach and settling in his chest. His beautiful little girl. The terrified look in her eye, her motionless body. It had all happened so fast. He hadn't even had time to think.

The door to the interrogation room opened.

'Sorry for making you wait,' the man apologised as he entered. 'There's a lot going on just now.'

Bjarne Brogeland was a tall man, just over six foot. Always well groomed and meticulously dressed, and, even though he was now in his late forties, he still had a rather muscular build. His dark hair was shaved into a buzz cut. Recently, by the looks of it. Brogeland's powerful cologne permeated the heavy air around them. It made Blix's stomach churn.

With a few careful steps, Brogeland crossed the space between the table and the door, letting it close automatically behind him. He had a glass of water in one hand, and a bundle of papers and a pen in the other. He sat on the opposite side of the table. Shuffling the papers into a pile, he studied Blix, scanning him up and down, as if taking a mental note of his injuries, and, judging by the look on his face, making no effort to disguise his thoughts about them either.

Blix and Brogeland used to work in the same department, and had done so for years. Rarely together, for the simple reason that they'd never really got along. Blix had been pleased when he found out that Brogeland was leaving to start a new role as a specialist investigator for Kripos.

'How is your daughter doing?' Brogeland asked.

Blix took a deep breath. The images of what happened crashed over him, chilling him to the bone. He could see the rope as clearly as if he were still there – the fall, the lifeless body on the filthy concrete floor. The blood. The way she was sprawled on the ground, her limbs contorted in that unnatural position.

'I don't know,' he said, exhaling heavily, fighting to hold back the tears. 'I was told I'll be updated as soon as they're done in the operating room. But ... you've got my phone, so...'

'You know how it is,' Brogeland said.

Blix looked down. 'I do.'

'I've told them to come and get me as soon as they hear anything,' Brogeland informed him.

'Who are *they*?'' Blix asked.

'Ah, the others here at the station. The people sat through there, watching and listening in.'

He nodded up at the camera in the top left-hand corner of the room.

Blix didn't follow the movement. Instead, he asked: 'Are you questioning Emma as well?'

'I ... can't answer that,' Brogeland answered. 'You know...'

'Yes, I know. Interrogation tactics,' Blix said.

Brogeland smiled in confirmation, but didn't elaborate.

'You're sure you don't want a lawyer present?'

'I'm sure.'

'And you're definitely going to be able to do this? Now, while—?'

'I want to get it over and done with,' Blix interrupted. 'So I can be with Iselin.'

Brogeland frowned at him, as if he were unsure whether Blix would be allowed to leave the station at all.

Blix held his gaze. The specialist investigator shuffled slightly in his chair and looked away. Took a sip from the glass of water in front of him. Checked that the camera was on and recording, before announcing who was in the room, what the time was, and which case the questioning concerned.

'You know the drill, Blix,' Brogeland said. 'We need to go through everything.'

'Fine by me.'

'Grand. Age?'

'Forty-eight.'

'Civil status?'

'Divorced. I live alone.'

'Address?'

'Tøyengata 13, Oslo.'

'Profession?'

'Detective chief inspector. Homicide, Oslo Police District.'

'How long have you been in that role?'

'Eight years.'

'And how long have you worked for the police overall?'

'Coming up to twenty-one years and seven months.'

Blix answered without hesitation, all the while fixated on one specific spot on the floor. The warmth of the room had become oppressive. He started to sweat, but didn't bother wiping it away.

'Timo Polmar,' Brogeland pressed on. 'Who is he?'

'He...' Blix clasped his hands together, intertwining his fingers. 'I don't know.'

'You don't know?'

'No.'

'But ... you shot and killed him, did you not?'

Blix grimaced. That cologne...

'I believe so,' he answered. 'But I can't say for sure.'

'Why not?'

'Because I ... I'd never met him before today. And I didn't check his ID after I...'

Brogeland furrowed his brow. He jotted something down on one of the sheets of paper he had resting on his lap.

'You shot him four times?'

'Sounds about right.'

'Why four?'

'Because…' Blix took a deep breath. 'Because that was what needed to be done, to stop him.'

Brogeland studied his face.

'I did what I thought was necessary,' Blix said. 'Then and there, in that moment, it made sense to shoot. They were four *justified* shots.'

Brogeland didn't respond.

'Can you tell me how we ended up here?' he asked after a short silence. 'Can you explain how exactly it came to be that you wound up shooting and killing a man earlier this evening?'

Blix straightened up and released his fingers, forming a triangle with his hands instead.

'I can certainly try.'

THIRTY-TWO HOURS EARLIER

2

'...And I know how trivial this is going to sound, what I'm about to say, but the *absolute* most important thing you can do, as the family of a victim or as survivors yourself, is to allow yourselves to acknowledge how you really feel. You are *allowed* to be angry, to be depressed, especially considering what all of you in this room have been through, the things you've experienced. And you're allowed to take a step back from everything, and only think of yourselves for a while.'

Blix's gaze swept across the audience. The organisers had said there would be around sixty people attending his talk today, but there couldn't have been more than forty in the room. But forty people meant forty lives that had been cut short. Each and every one of the audience members looking up at him now had experienced a great personal tragedy. They had felt what it was like to lose a loved one as a result of an accident or a criminal act.

Emma Ramm was one of them.

She was in the front row, notebook balanced on her lap, listening intently, as she had done throughout the entire event. Not that she needed to take on board anything he had to say; she'd heard it all before. If anyone knew how to cope with losing someone close to them, it was her. Blix had suggested she come anyway, seeing as she was writing a book on the subject. It could prove useful for her; the speakers and attendees might be able to contribute to her project.

He felt his phone vibrate in his trouser pocket. It must be something important. That was the seventh or eighth time it had gone off now. He considered glancing at the screen to see who had been calling, but resisted the urge.

'The second most important thing is to remember that feelings are facts,' he continued. 'It's tempting to put a lid on your emotions. But what you're feeling is not wrong. Your emotions aren't something you should ignore or try to bottle up. It can be tempting to do the exact opposite as well – only focus on the emotions you recognise, emotions you've felt before. Hatred, for example. And you are *allowed* to feel that hate. It's only natural – of course you're going to feel a gnawing, over-whelming desire to seek revenge.'

His phone stopped ringing. He had a quick look down at his notes, skipping over the personal anecdote he'd planned on including, and carried on.

'The main difference,' he continued, 'lies in what you choose to *do* with those emotions. If you do choose to seek revenge, then you're not really dealing with what's actually driving your actions, the emotions *behind* them. The other problem with that is that you'd be breaking the law. And if you did that,' he said with a grin, 'you'd have the likes of me coming to stop you.'

Timid laughter spread around the room.

'Preferably before you get that far, though,' he added, taking a moment before turning solemn again.

'But grief takes many forms. And everyone mourns in different ways. A lot of people find it hard to deal with, once the media have lost inter-est. It's at that point the emptiness sets in, and maybe even a bitterness too, because you feel like people have stopped caring about what hap-pened. People don't realise that, for you, the pain is just as fucking excruciating as it was that first day – all day, every single day.'

Blix always liked to emphasise the swear-word a bit. It usually had an effect on the audience.

He didn't particularly enjoy giving these talks, but he'd had a steady increase in requests over the last few years. He was glad this one was nearly over. And it wasn't long until the weekend. He only hoped that the calls he'd been getting weren't to ask him to do overtime. He just wanted to get home as soon as he was done here. Crack open a can of beer or two and do absolutely nothing, other than wait for the evening and weekend to roll in.

He started to wrap up, encouraging everyone to stay and mingle.

'It's the greatest cliché of them all, I know, but in the absence of a magic formula to instruct you on how to get through this, how to deal with what each and every one of you are currently going through, the best thing you can do might actually be the simplest. And that's to talk to each other, arrange to meet, family to family. Share your experiences. *Help* each other. You are stronger together. You can process the pain, survive this, together.'

He felt a vibration in his pocket again. Two short buzzes against his thigh. A text.

Blix glanced at the clock on the lectern. He still had a few minutes left, but strictly speaking, he had said all he'd wanted to say.

'Thank you for listening,' he said, gathering up his notes.

He stood there, papers in hand for a moment, taking in the audience's polite applause, smiling and nodding his appreciation a few times.

One of the organisers walked onto the stage, holding a bouquet of autumnal flowers. She said a few words about how grateful they were that he had taken the time to come talk to them today. Blix shook her hand, smiled and nodded one last time, before removing the microphone from his shirt collar and handing it back to the sound engineer.

He walked to the side of the stage and pulled his phone out.

Nine missed calls.

His finger slid across the screen, unlocking it. Kovic had called twice. As had Fosse, just a few minutes ago. The notifications that caught his eye, however, were the four missed calls from Iselin. They had come through in quick succession, each immediately after the other.

He swiped up on the call log and opened his texts. Fosse had told him to ring him back as soon as he received his message. Blix felt a growing sense of uneasiness. He tapped on his boss's number and lifted the phone to his ear.

'Have you heard?' Fosse asked, answering on the first ring, as if he had been sitting with his phone in his hand, waiting for Blix to call.

'Heard what?' Blix asked, catching the eye of one of the audience members and sending them a brief smile, before laying a finger over his other ear to block out the din of the room behind him.

'We've dispatched all our units to Kovic's flat,' Fosse answered. 'A suspected intruder. And reported gunfire. Where are you?'

Blix didn't answer the question.

'Have you heard from Kovic?' he asked instead.

'She's not picking up.'

Blix's stomach clenched. His thoughts went straight to Iselin, who rented a room in Kovic's flat for when she was back in Oslo during the weekends. She had tried calling him four times.

'Are you there?' Fosse asked.

'I'll call you back.'

Blix could hear Fosse protesting, but he hung up and called Iselin.

No answer.

Blix cursed inwardly and opened his unread messages. Iselin had left a voicemail after her last attempt to call him.

He opened his inbox, first listening to a recording of Fosse, basically telling him the exact same thing he had told him a moment ago, but with the addition of:

'Another woman rang for an ambulance, but she didn't identify herself. Iselin lives with Kovic, right? Not that that necessarily means anything, of course, let me stress that, but call me anyway. The moment you get this.'

Blix pressed the button to hear the next message. The sound of movement, ragged breathing, fast footsteps slamming against asphalt.

And then:

'Dad!'

Blix had seen and heard his daughter in moments of fear in the past, but there was a primal panic in her voice this time, one he had never heard before. She was running, trying to talk at the same time.

'I ... think he shot her!' she yelled.

More fumbling, erratic breathing. The sound of a car driving by. Rustling, as if she were pushing her way through a bush, snapping its branches.

'I think ... he might be ... chasing me. Dad, you have to—'

The recording ended.

'Shit,' Blix swore to himself, checking when the call had been made. Twenty-one minutes ago.

He tried calling her again. A woman at the edge of the crowd was trying to catch his attention. Blix turned his back to the room as he waited for Iselin to pick up. With his free hand, he opened his satchel and shoved his notes inside, all the time listening as the phone rang. And rang. And rang.

He noticed Emma standing a few metres away too, watching him. She mouthed: *What's going on?* Blix didn't respond. The ringing continued.

And then, finally, an answer:

'Dad...' Iselin, whispering. Trembling. It sounded as if she were struggling to breathe, taking in short, sharp gasps.

'Iselin,' Blix exclaimed. 'Where are you? What's happened?'

'I'm ... hiding,' she said.

'Iselin, listen to me: where are you?' he urged.

'I'm...'

He could tell she was exhausted. That she couldn't think straight. He repeated the question.

'St. Hanshaugen,' she told him at last. 'In the park.'

'Is someone following you?'

Again, he had to ask her twice.

'I don't know.' It came out as a sob.

'Kovic, she...'

She couldn't finish the sentence.

'Have you called the police?'

She took a few seconds, before replying: yes.

'You didn't pick up.'

It sounded like an accusation – it felt like one too.

'Did you tell them where you were?'

She wept. 'I ... don't remember.'

'Call them again, get them to come and find you. Tell them exactly where you are, they'll send a patrol car to pick you up.'

'Can't you come?'

'I'm still twenty minutes away,' he answered, knowing it could be more. 'The patrol car will get to you faster.'

Iselin didn't respond.

'Are you in pain?' Blix asked. 'Are you injured?'

'He missed.'

'Missed? What do you...?'

'He shot at me, Dad!' The words came out staccato – as if she were shivering. Another sob escaped her.

Blix ran his hand over his head. 'Okay, stay where you are, but call the police again,' he ordered. 'Now. And then call me back immediately after. I will be there as soon as I can.'

3

Brogeland lifted his chin, scrutinising Blix, who sat a little more upright, pushing his shoulders back.

'So at this point, you had no idea what had happened in Kovic's flat?'

'No, I just knew that *something* had happened. I tried to call her – Kovic, I mean – after I'd spoken to Iselin, but her phone was off. Or ... I couldn't get through to her anyway.'

'You...' Brogeland flipped through the stack of documents on his lap. 'You called her at ... 16:42?'

'If that's what it says there, then yes,' Blix said, nodding at the papers. 'I wasn't really paying attention to the time.'

'Was Emma Ramm with you already at that point?'

'No, I left the event by myself.'

'And you didn't talk to her before leaving?'

Blix hesitated for a second before shaking his head. 'I just told her I had to go.'

'You didn't tell her that something had happened?'

'No, but I think she realised.'

Brogeland jotted something down. Blix was expecting him to ask what kind of relationship he and Emma had. Wondered how much Brogeland knew.

'Okay,' the Kripos investigator said. 'You left the talk and drove back to Oslo. What happened then?'

❄

The other motorists obediently pulled onto the hard-shoulder at the sight of the flashing blue light on Blix's car roof. He adjusted his headset to try and hear more clearly. He had made Iselin stay on the line as he got back into his car, but the communication had been almost solely one-sided. He'd tried getting her to explain what had happened, what she'd seen, but she had answered absent-mindedly, offering monosyllabic responses.

Pulling off the motorway at the exit to Smestad, Blix asked if she could see the patrol car yet.

'They're here.'

'Can you see them?'

No answer.

'Get up. Go to them,' Blix insisted.

He had spent the drive trying to reassure her that whoever had tried to shoot her would most likely have wanted to flee the scene afterwards, and that they wouldn't be running around the entire borough of St. Hanshaugen, trying to track her down. But he wasn't sure she had taken any of it in.

'Just focus on the police car,' he said, overtaking a taxi. 'Make yourself visible.'

Nothing.

'Iselin,' he said sternly. 'Make sure they can see you. Wave. Let them know it's you they're looking for.'

Iselin took a deep breath, as if she were trying to talk herself into getting up.

Voices in the background. Whose they were, Blix couldn't tell, but plenty of officers had met Iselin at the station over the years, and even if they hadn't, most of them would recognise her face. If she couldn't bring herself to wave or say anything, there was a good chance that they would find her and help her themselves.

The call cut off.

Blix stared at the screen, afraid that Iselin's fears had come true. He was in the process of calling her back when a message from an unknown number popped up on the display:

Your daughter is safe – Eriksen.

Blix had no idea who Eriksen was, but it didn't matter. All that mattered was that Iselin was safe. He could relax his shoulders.

Approaching the city centre, he headed towards the Majorstua district, grateful for the fact that the blue lights served as a plough through the traffic. He was soon on the street where Kovic had been living for the last eleven months – Geitmyrsveien. Blix had visited her there a few times, the first time being for the housewarming party. He had felt so old among her friends. Out of place beside their younger colleagues. He'd left early, as he always did with parties. Kovic had been a bit disappointed.

His stomach lurched at the sight of more blue, flashing lights a few hundred metres up the road. He could see the uniformed officers assembled on the pavement outside, the spectators who had gathered on the other side of the police tape, filming and taking photos. Exchanging worried glances.

A first-responder's car pulled off the pavement and drove off. Blix parked in the empty space and was out of the driver's seat before the engine had even stopped. He could hear the blades of the police helicopter oscillating in the air above him.

He pulled his ID card out, presented it to the officer as he approached the barrier, ducked underneath and hurried towards the open door.

The sound of his own footsteps reverberated around the stairwell as he stormed up the steps, taking three at a time. Another uniformed officer was standing guard at the door to Kovic's flat, but moved aside at the sight of Blix, handing him a pair of plastic shoe covers to put on before going in.

Blix stopped on the threshold and took a deep breath. Tried to prepare himself for what he was about to see, readying himself as he always did when entering a crime scene. This wouldn't be the first time that the home of someone he knew, or knew of, had become the location of a crime. But this was different.

He dragged the plastic covers over his boots and took a step inside. Then another. Blix kept his gaze fixed to the floor. He couldn't bring himself to look up. Not yet.

He closed his eyes, kept them shut tight. Inhaled through his nose. Opened his eyes again. Then gradually raised them, like the lens of a camera in a slow-motion film, and found himself staring down the hallway.

He blinked a few times, unable to focus. Yet, between the officers who had arrived before him, he could see a body. Back to the ground, head tilted, one arm cast out to the side, the other raised above her head. As if she had her hand up to ask a question.

There was a bullet hole on the left side of her forehead. She was lying in a pool of her own blood. Her eyes were wide open. Blix swallowed. Once. Then again.

'Jesus,' he whispered to himself.

Sofia Kovic had been executed.

4

'What was the nature of your relationship with Kovic?'

Blix raised his head to look directly at Brogeland.

'What do you mean?'

'I mean – what was the nature of your relationship with Kovic?'

Blix stared at him in silence for a few seconds.

'I was her superior,' he said eventually, a little more aggressively than he'd meant it to sound. 'From the very first day she joined Homicide. I kind of took on the role of her mentor.'

'And that was all?'

'What do you mean by that?'

Brogeland didn't react. Just waited patiently for Blix to answer.

'Are you trying to insinuate that I had a relationship with her?'

'I'm not insinuating anything, I'm just asking.'

'We were colleagues,' Blix answered. 'I'm old enough to be her father.'

'That doesn't necessarily mean anything.'

'No, maybe it's never meant anything to *you*.'

Brogeland smirked. 'Your fingerprints were all over her flat.'

'My daughter lived there,' Blix said. 'I've been there several times. And they can't have been *everywhere*, seeing as I've never been in Kovic's bedroom, for example.'

'And you're sure of that?'

'I'm sure,' Blix replied. 'There was never anything like that between us.'

Regardless, Brogeland's question made him uneasy. As if Kripos had found something that would prove otherwise. He racked his brain, trying to remember if he had ever wandered into Kovic's room at any point, maybe when they were being shown around the flat during her housewarming party, but he distinctly remembered having waited in the doorway.

He sat up slightly in the chair. 'Has someone claimed otherwise?' he enquired.

Brogeland didn't respond.

'When was the last time you were in the flat?' he asked instead.

Blix tried to recollect when that would've been. 'A couple of weeks ago, maybe?'

'And your fingerprints were still there from a few weeks ago, were they?'

'I don't know how regularly they cleaned,' he said, his patience wearing thin now. 'You think I killed her? Is that what you're trying to get out of me? Are you trying to figure out if I had a motive to murder her?'

He didn't give Brogeland a chance to answer:

'I was in Sandvika when she was murdered, giving a talk, just in case you've already forgotten. There were forty attendees. And anyway, do you think I'd then try and kill my own daughter afterwards?'

Brogeland continued, unfazed: 'Do you usually spend much time in your colleagues' homes?'

'Well I've never been to *your* house, Brogeland, but that's because you've always been a dickhead.'

Silence. Blix could feel the anger coursing through his body. It felt like they were wasting time, but he knew he was only dragging out the process even more by rising to Brogeland's provocations.

He took a sip from the glass of water on the table in front of him. Wiped the sweat from his forehead.

'Sorry,' he said. 'That last bit was unnecessary.'

'It's fine,' Brogeland replied. 'I know I'm a bit of a dickhead.'

He sent him an amiable smile. Blix appreciated it.

'Do you want to take a break?'

Blix shook his head. Deciding to try and be as cooperative as possible, so he could get out of there sooner rather than later.

'To answer your question – no, I don't make a habit of visiting colleagues at home. But Kovic was special, that I'll gladly admit. We had a good relationship. But there was never even the hint of an amorous moment between us, just pure collegial empathy and respect, as it should be.'

'She was special, you say. In what way?'

'She...'

Blix stopped to consider his words.

'It's hard to explain,' he said at last. 'But she was talented. A real hard worker. Genuinely committed to the job. She never left a stone unturned, was always ready to lend a hand. She was obviously the youngest in the department too, and for those of us who are getting on a bit, she brought this infectious energy to work with her. Everyone liked her.' He shook his head, let out a long sigh. 'It sounds like I'm giving her a reference.'

Brogeland wrote something on his notepad. Blix couldn't see what exactly.

'Emma Ramm's fingerprints were also found in Kovic's flat,' Brogeland went on.

'Emma and Kovic had become good friends over the last few years,' Blix explained. 'They spent a lot of time together, would work out together. Cycling and that kind of thing, every now and then, as far as I'm aware. Emma knew – knows – my daughter well too.'

He stopped himself. His thoughts returned to Iselin. Her lifeless body. Her unresponsive eyes. He had to trust that the surgeons knew what they were doing.

Brogeland studied him for a moment.

'What did you do after entering Kovic's flat?'

Blix thought back.

'I went up to Iselin's room.'

5

Blix pulled on a pair of latex gloves and made his way carefully up the stairs to Iselin's loft room. Almost as if he was afraid of waking someone who might be asleep up there. The door was ajar. He used his elbow to nudge it open and stood there, looking in.

It was obvious a fight had taken place. Shards of glass from the mirror that had once hung on the wall were now scattered across the floor. The desk chair had been overturned and was lying on its back. Textbooks and various toiletries had been strewn about the room. One of the curtains had been torn down, while the other fluttered out of the open window.

Blix made his way cautiously through the mess.

There was something lodged in the windowsill.

A bullet.

He stepped quickly but lightly back to the landing and shouted down to the hallway below, requesting one of the forensic technicians come up and secure the evidence.

Someone had entered the flat, Blix thought, shot Kovic, and had then come upstairs to get rid of Iselin.

Because he'd heard her?

Or had he known she was home?

Blix looked around for places the perpetrator might have left traces of himself. He was soon joined by someone from the forensics team. Blix knew the man's face, but not his name. Tall, rather thin, with a big brown beard he had tied up with an elastic band to keep it out of the way as he worked.

Blix pointed out what he'd found, taking a moment to peer out the window. Scaffolding. That must've been how Iselin had managed to escape. The front of the building was being renovated.

The police presence outside had grown enormously. There were blue flashing lights down the length of the street. Through the scaffolding, he spotted his fellow homicide investigators: Tine Abelvik, Nicolai Wibe and Petter Falkum. A police car pulled up alongside them. Abelvik leant down to talk to the driver.

'You'll need to leave in a minute,' the forensics technician told Blix. 'We need to examine this floor, seeing as it looks like the perpetrator was up here too.'

'Of course,' Blix said.

On the way back downstairs, he tried to summarise in his mind everything he knew about Kovic's personal life. Not a lot, he realised – Kovic had never really been one to share much about her life outside of work. All he knew was that she was taking this week off in lieu of overtime, but he didn't know what she'd had planned. Blix had been tempted to call her a few times over the last few days, but he hadn't been able to remember the last time he had a single day, let alone a whole week, off without someone from the office calling about something or other, so he had decided against it. It was one of the worst parts of the job – you never really had time off. Exactly why he had chosen to leave Kovic in peace.

He found Abelvik and Falkum waiting for him in the kitchen. It only took a few seconds before Abelvik's face crumpled and she burst into tears. Blix felt his own eyes prickle as he embraced his colleague, stroking her back a few times as she wept.

'Unbelievable,' he said. 'Just ... unbelievable.'

Abelvik pulled away, dabbing at her eyes. 'Iselin's waiting downstairs in one of the cars,' she said, followed by a sniff. 'They're taking her to A&E before she gives her statement.'

Blix automatically took a step back towards the door.

'How is she?'

'She sustained an injury to the face, and she's got a pretty bad cut on the bottom of her foot. She'll need stitches. It's from the scaffolding, I'd imagine. She climbed down it barefoot. She'll probably need to get an x-ray as well. Looks like she may have a few broken ribs.'

'Broken...?'

'Yes, she fought the perpetrator, before getting away.'

Blix tried to swallow away the shock. 'How did she seem to you?'

Abelvik hesitated. 'I think she'll be okay, but she's going to need some help,' she answered. 'Talk to someone, process the thoughts that will inevitably crop up, considering what she's just been through.'

'I'll call Neumann,' Blix said immediately. 'He's usually made time outside of office hours before. Maybe he can see her tomorrow.'

'I think that'd be best.'

Blix took another few steps back into the hallway. 'I'll go with her to the hospital,' he said on his way out. 'Have you got everything in hand here? Forensics have already started, but we need to start knocking on doors.'

Abelvik nodded.

Petter Falkum started to usher him out. 'We've got this,' he said, with a nod back into the flat. 'Go be with your daughter. And let us know if there's anything we can do.'

Blix nodded instead of saying thank you.

By the time he was back on the pavement, the patrol car with Iselin had pulled away and was now moving down the road. The flashing blue lights blinded the journalists and spectators standing nearby, forcing them to look away. Blix ran after the car for a few metres, before giving up and hurrying back to his own to follow behind instead.

The police helicopter was still hovering overhead. Another car pulled up with two young officers sat in the front seats. Gard Fosse climbed out from the back, in full uniform as always, donning his police cap with its traditional, gold oak-leaf embroidering. Some of the photographers standing nearby turned to take photos.

He spotted Blix.

'Status?' he asked, approaching him.

Blix clenched his jaw and shook his head.

'She's dead,' he eventually managed to say. 'Shot in the head at close range.'

Fosse tried to speak, but stopped to compose himself first.

'And the perpetrator?'

'No leads thus far,' Blix answered, going on to describe how Iselin had escaped. 'She's on the way to A&E. I'm heading there now.' He opened the car door. 'Abelvik and Falkum are upstairs,' he said with a nod back up to the flat.

Fosse responded with a brief nod in return and headed towards the building. An officer lifted the barrier tape and escorted him inside.

Blix dropped down into the driver's seat. Put both hands on the steering wheel and took a few deep breaths before starting the engine. Using one hand to manoeuvre out onto the road, he unlocked his phone with the other, found Emma's number and called her.

'Blix?' she said the second she answered. 'What's going on?'

He couldn't bring himself to say anything at first.

Then: 'I...'

A siren started wailing in the background.

'Are you in St. Hanshaugen?' she asked. 'I've just had some news alerts come through.'

'Yes,' he replied, clearing his throat. 'And it's awful, what I have to tell you, but ... Kovic is dead.'

'*What?*'

'Kovic's dead,' Blix repeated. 'She was shot and killed at close range. Less than an hour ago.'

'But...'

'I know you two were close,' Blix continued. 'So I wanted to let you know. Before you heard it elsewhere.'

Emma didn't say anything for quite some time.

'Thanks ... for letting me know,' she said eventually. 'Who ... Has anyone been arrested?'

'Not yet. Iselin was home at the time too. She escaped.'

'God,' Emma exhaled. 'That's...'

Blix had to stop for a red light. He moved the phone to his other ear.

'When did you last talk to Kovic?' he asked.

'I ... I saw her yesterday,' Emma answered. 'We went on a long bike ride. Down to Tusenfryd and back.'

'How did she seem to you?'

'I mean ... like her usual self.'

'There wasn't anything about her behaviour that may have indicated she was having problems with anyone at all?'

'Nothing that I noticed,' Emma said. 'We had a good time, had a laugh, the usual really. But ... now that I think about it, she was maybe a bit ... distant.'

'Distant?'

'Yeah, like her mind was elsewhere. Like she was thinking about something. Not the whole time though, just ... every now and then.'

The light changed from red to green. He pressed his foot down on the accelerator.

'You didn't ask what was on her mind?'

'No. I thought if it was something important, she would've brought it up.'

'Did she usually do that?' Blix asked. 'Talk through things with you?'

'It'd depend,' Emma replied. 'I think I was the first person she told when she ended it with the plumber.'

Blix frowned. 'The plumber?'

'She was dating a plumber for a while. Jo Inge Fjellvik, or at least I think that was his name. It's not been that long since they broke up.'

Blix made a mental note to talk to him as soon as possible.

'How's Iselin doing?' Emma asked.

He told her all he knew.

'I'm on my way to the hospital now,' he added.

'Let me know if there's anything I can do,' Emma offered. 'I can help. I can come and keep her company, just be there with her.'

'Thanks for offering,' Blix replied. 'But I think I should look after her myself tonight.'

'What about tomorrow, though? You'll have work, won't you?'

'I haven't thought that far ahead yet,' he answered, followed by a long exhale. 'I've got to go, anyway. But keep everything I've said between us for the time being. We've not informed Kovic's mother yet.'

'Of course,' Emma responded. 'Bloody hell. This is just ... horrific news.'

'I know,' Blix sighed. And that was putting it mildly, he thought.

They ended the call. The sudden silence filled the car. Blix reached across to the dashboard and turned on the police radio. The operations centre had set up a specific channel for the investigation. He caught the tail end of a bulletin. Something about a burglary in the same area the day before – a man wearing a hoodie, jeans and military boots. The report included several potential witness statements, evidence of a glove that the dog patrol had tracked down the road and found outside the local school, and information that the covert policing unit had arrested someone they had been pursuing in a surveillance operation just a few minutes away, in the square at Alexander Kiellands plass. It was difficult to decide what was actually relevant to the case, and what was just coming to light in their intensive efforts to find the person responsible.

Blix detached the portable radio and took it into the A&E department with him. He approached the desk and was guided into the private waiting room reserved for victims of assault and other patients who had been involved in criminal cases.

Iselin was sitting in a corner, beside a table piled high with old magazines. She had a blanket wrapped around her shoulders. Other than that, all she had on was a white bra and pyjama bottoms.

She looked worse than he had been prepared for. Her lip had been split open and her chin was coated in dark, congealed blood. There were scratches all over her face. One of her eyes was swollen. She had a bandage wrapped around one of the deeper cuts on her arm, and some of the smaller wounds looked like they had stopped bleeding. She had nothing on her feet, which were filthy. There was a loose bandage tied around her right foot, which the blood had soaked right through.

He wasn't sure whether she had registered his arrival. She was staring at the floor, a distant look in her eye. Sitting down in the chair next to her, he gently laid his hand on top of hers. Only when she felt the warmth of his skin on her own did she turn to look at him.

'My darling,' Blix said in a low, soothing voice. Again, he had to fight to keep the tears back.

Iselin didn't say a word. Blix moved his hand to her face, her forehead, swept her fringe aside, out of her eyes. She was so pale. Her eyes were bloodshot. He pulled her in close.

'Is she dead?' Iselin whispered.

Blix waited for a moment before answering:

'I'm afraid so.'

He had expected Iselin to break down, but she didn't say anything, didn't respond to his embrace. When he let go, it was as if her body were there, but her mind was elsewhere.

A female police officer who had been standing guard at the door cleared her throat. 'We're waiting on the doctor,' she informed him. 'And one of the forensic technicians is on their way to document her injuries and secure any evidence and DNA traces.'

Blix looked up at her and nodded, taking it as a given that she knew who he was. He turned back to his daughter.

'Iselin,' he began. 'We need to know what you saw. If you can describe the perpetrator.'

He tried to get eye contact with her. Still nothing.

'Did you talk to Kovic today?'

Iselin didn't respond. There was nothing behind her eyes. Her lips were dry, cracked.

A door opened and a nurse entered. 'Iselin Skaar?'

Iselin didn't respond.

'You can come through for your x-ray and MRI scan now,' the nurse told her. 'Do you think you can manage?'

Blix pushed himself up from the chair. His knees cracked. Iselin pulled the blanket tight around her shoulders and stood up.

'I can get you a wheelchair if you want?' the nurse offered.

Iselin shook her head and trudged towards her. Blix followed them into a new waiting room. Another nurse arrived, and they took Iselin into a separate room for her examination.

'Should I come with you?' Blix asked.

Iselin shook her head.

'You can wait in here,' the nurse told him. 'There's a coffee machine out in the hallway.'

Blix took a seat. He couldn't stomach anything. The police radio crackled as an update came through. Several patrol units had assembled outside an apartment building. They were waiting for the police tactical unit, Delta, to arrive. The rest of the message cut out.

'I imagine this will take a couple of hours,' the officer who had been waiting with Iselin said. 'After that, we'll drive her to the station to get her statement.'

Blix's phone rang. Abelvik.

'We have a suspect,' she said.

'Who?'

'A thirty-three-year-old man named Martin Hikes. Known to police for various misdemeanours. He's barricaded himself into a flat in Iladalen. We're evacuating the other tenants. Delta are outside, ready to go in.'

Blix stood up, sent a quick glance to the door of the room Iselin was in.

'I'm on my way,' he said.

6

'So you left Iselin at the hospital?'

Blix could feel his anger rising at Brogeland's long-winded approach to interrogation. His questions were rhetorical. His repetitions had no other function than to provoke him. It was like Brogeland took pleasure in emphasising and pointing out the things Blix did wrong. It felt like he was purposefully wasting time.

'Yes,' Blix answered promptly, not wanting to spend any more time explaining his thought processes.

'This Hikes...' Brogeland continued. 'How did he become a suspect?'

'It was a combination of things,' Blix answered, stretching his legs out under the table. 'There had been several cases in the same neighbourhood over the last few weeks, where an intruder had climbed up the scaffolding, looking for open windows and letting themselves in. Martin Hikes came up as a potential suspect, seeing as he's known to police as a local thief and had been convicted in a serious assault case. On top of that, he lives in the same area and happened to be seen in a nearby street not long before the murder. Could've been a break-in that went wrong.'

'And you were there when Delta stormed the flat?'

Blix nodded at the pile of documents resting on Brogeland's lap.

'I imagine you've already got the answer to that in those reports of yours.'

❄

It was getting dark out. The beam of the police helicopter's searchlight guided the way. The flashing lights atop the police cars coloured the old brick apartment buildings blue. Curious neighbours stood in their windows, watching the events unfold.

Blix drove right up to the barrier, got out and ducked underneath. He strode over to the building entrance, where Petter Falkum was already stood waiting beside two uniformed officers.

'We can't get a hold of him,' Falkum explained. 'He's not answering the doorbell or his phone.'

'Are we sure he's even in?'

'His neighbour said he came home about an hour ago.'

One hour. Blix tried to calculate whether that would fit into the timeline. Possibly.

Two black vans rolled up and mounted the edge of the pavement. Six Delta officers jumped out. Black coveralls, helmets, shields, weapons. One of them had a battering ram perched on their shoulder. A few brief commands were given before they entered the building in one swift, well-rehearsed manoeuvre.

Martin Hike's flat was on the second floor. Blix and Falkum waited on the landing below.

One of the officers hammered his fist against the door. 'Police!' he roared. 'Open the door or we'll break it down.'

Whoever was inside was told that they had ten seconds to comply. The officer with the battering ram positioned himself in front of the door, holding it with both hands, ready. When Hikes's ten seconds were up, the officer hurled it at the door. The wood splintered. The door caved in, with part of the frame left hanging on the hinge. The unit charged inside, weapons held out steady in front of them.

Blix stayed where he was on the landing below – he could tell what was happening in the flat from the sound of the commands directly above them.

'Armed police! Stay where you are!' Followed by: 'Get on the floor! Arms at your side.'

A few seconds passed by, and then a message was issued over the police radio.

'Suspect arrested. All clear.'

Blix ascended the last few steps and entered the flat alongside Falkum. They stepped over various bits of computer equipment piled up on the floor in the hallway and headed into the living room. Several of the Delta officers had removed their helmets.

Martin Hikes was lying on the floor in a pair of grubby jeans and a black hoodie, arms handcuffed behind his back. Two of the officers lifted him up and sat him in an armchair. His hair was draped over his face. He wore a thick pair of glasses that had been knocked askew in the arrest. He seemed indifferent.

'What's this about?' he stuttered.

'A shooting on Geitmyrsveien,' he was told.

'A shooting?' Martin Hikes shook his head. 'Nothing to do with me. Don't even like guns.'

The Delta unit leader approached Blix. 'Do you want to talk to him here, or shall we take him in?'

'Take him in,' Falkum answered instead, and turned to Blix: 'I'll see to this.'

Two of the men pulled Hikes up onto his feet and steered him out of the flat. Blix stood there watching as they practically dragged the gaunt man away. Something told him they were on the wrong track. That what happened to Kovic wasn't the result of a botched burglary. Something else was behind Kovic's execution.

7

'Martin Hikes was ruled out then?' Brogeland asked, using the top of the ballpoint pen he had in his hand to scratch his forehead.

'Eventually,' Blix nodded.

'How so?'

'We searched his flat. Found plenty of stolen goods, but no guns. Brought in all his shoes for testing, but none of them matched the print we lifted from Kovic's flat. He had no trace of gunpowder on him or his clothes. No blood either. He didn't fit the profile anyway. He's not a murderer.

'But Timo Polmar was?' Brogeland asked.

'I don't know.'

A deep crease appeared on Brogeland's forehead. 'You don't know?'

'No. As I said, I don't know if he was the one who killed Kovic or not. There's a lot that would point to it being him, but I'm not convinced. Something doesn't add up.'

'What doesn't add up?'

'I can't figure out his motive,' Blix answered. 'We've gone through the cases Kovic had been working on, compiled a list of names of people we thought could be possible suspects, but he never came up. There's nothing linking Polmar and Kovic. I'd never even heard of him until a few hours ago, and I doubt Kovic ever had any contact with him either.'

Blix brought his hands together and rested them on the table in front of him. Thought about his brief encounter with Polmar, before he'd shot him. That unstable, bewildered look in his eye. But there was something else. Something about him that didn't quite fit with the image Blix had formed of Kovic's murderer, and yet he couldn't quite put his finger on what that was.

His thoughts returned to Iselin. What if she didn't make it?

Cold sweat dripped down his neck, making his shirt stick to his back.

Brogeland continued. 'After Hikes was arrested then – what did you do? Did you go back to A&E, to Iselin?'

Blix shook his head. 'I went to the station,' he answered. 'Gard Fosse had called a meeting.'

❄

The command room, where Homicide's larger meetings were held, was on the sixth floor of police HQ and had more people crammed into it than Blix had thought possible. Not even when a bomb had gone off outside Oslo City Hall, and the entire country thought it had been hit by a targeted terror attack, had there been that many people in the room. So many, in fact, that they were lined up along the walls in rows several people deep.

They had lost colleagues before, but not like this. Not in what could only be described as an outright execution. It messed with your head. Around him he saw the faces of a number of his colleagues he knew were meant to be off work or on holiday. Blix could see on their faces that none of them would bat an eyelid about the amount of overtime they would be doing, or how little sleep they would be getting in the days to come. All that mattered to them now was finding the person responsible.

Some of them stood with their arms folded across their chests. Others simply stared ahead, hands clasped around their coffee cups, not focussing on anything in particular.

The clock had just turned half past seven. Kovic had been dead for three hours, maybe a little less.

'Good evening,' Gard Fosse announced, already struggling to keep his voice steady. Blix felt that he wasn't putting on an act for once. 'It's...' Fosse paused. Cleared his throat. 'It's days like today that...' Again, he had to stop and compose himself before continuing. '...That nothing makes sense. That the world has been completely knocked off its axis. That a deep abyss has opened beneath us. Luring us in.'

Blix was reminded of what he had said to the audience at his own talk in Sandvika earlier that day. How processing grief always began with a phase of feeling utter despair. Followed by anger. And then, maybe, hatred. Until the bottomless pit of emptiness drags us in entirely. Into its nothingness.

'It is at times like these that we need something to hold on to,' Fosse said. 'And, luckily, dear colleagues, we do have something to hold on to: our memories of Sofia Kovic. The laughs we shared...' He raised his hand to cover his mouth for a moment. '...And her smile that lit up every room.'

Fosse had kept his eyes fixed on the table in front of him. He eventually lifted his gaze and looked into the faces of his colleagues.

'It is these memories that we must keep in mind while we work on this case. While we do our jobs. While we find the person who did this.'

He said the last sentence with such force that there wasn't a single person in the room who didn't have their eyes on him.

'Let's get started.'

The crowd began to disperse. Fosse gave a sign to indicate that he wanted the core, most experienced investigators to stay behind: Alexander Blix, Tine Abelvik and Nicolai Wibe.

He lay a hand on Blix's shoulder. 'How's your daughter doing?'

Blix responded with a quick shrug. 'She's been checked over at the hospital, but all things considered, she's doing okay,' he added. 'I've booked her in to see Eivind Neumann, the psychiatrist. He's made room to see her first thing tomorrow.'

'Sounds like a good plan. Has she said anything about what happened?'

'She's giving her formal statement as we speak, but I'm not sure how much she'll manage to recount today.'

'We'll take what we can get,' Fosse said with a nod. 'Normally, I'd ask you to lead the investigation, Blix, but seeing as your daughter is wrapped up in this case, I'd like Abelvik to take this one.'

Blix turned to face her. She looked just as surprised as the others.

'Can you handle it?' Fosse asked her.

Abelvik seemed unable to speak for a moment.

'Yes... yes, sure,' she said eventually. 'Of course.'

'Great. I've got to go prepare for the press conference.'

Fosse turned and left. Abelvik stood motionless for a few more seconds, staring into the distance. She looked uncomfortable in this new, unfamiliar role she suddenly found herself in.

Wibe shifted his weight impatiently from one leg to the other, wanting to get started. Abelvik walked up to the whiteboard, grabbed a marker and yanked the lid off.

'Okay,' she started. 'As I see it, we've got three possibilities.'

She turned to the board and wrote a large *1*.

'Personal motive,' she said, bringing the pen up to the board again to write *private life* in her neat, slanted handwriting. 'A partner, ex-boyfriend, any other relationships ... we'll have to take a close look at all her close contacts.'

Blix cleared his throat. 'She had just ended a relationship,' he said.

Abelvik turned to look at Blix.

'With whom?' Nicolai Wibe asked.

Blix swallowed. 'A thirty-two-year-old plumber from Drammen,' he explained. 'Jo Inge Fjellvik, I believe. I've just started gathering information on him.'

'Good,' Abelvik nodded, as she turned to the board again to write the figure *2*. 'Kovic could have been a random victim. Even if Hikes was a dead end, there's still the possibility that this was a burglary that went wrong, or something else where she just happened to be in the wrong place at the wrong time.'

'Unlikely,' Wibe piped up. 'The way she was killed suggests the perpetrator knew what he was doing. He went there to kill her. But by all means, we should look into every possibility.'

Abelvik nodded again, placing the pen back to the whiteboard for a third time.

'And as for the third motive, it could be work related,' she said.

Blix nodded. That's exactly where he would begin. Looking into whether she had been threatened, who could have wanted to target her.

'What cases was she working on?' Wibe asked. He turned so he was facing Blix. 'You worked with her the most.'

'I've started compiling an overview of the cases she was investigating from the last six months. I'd say Thea Bodin's murder is probably the one she spent the most time on. The unsolved hit-and-run case – we still have almost nothing to go on. Other than that, she was working on a few domestic-violence cases, and was generally helping out with other investigations when needed.'

'Do you know if there were any conflicts in any of those cases?'

'I mean, there's always some sort of conflict,' Blix said. 'But I don't think there was anything specific.'

'Could she have come across something that could've landed her in hot water?'

Blix had already considered that angle. Being an investigator meant uncovering all sorts of secrets and lies, things people would rather not be made public.

He shrugged. 'I hadn't been in touch with her for the last few days. She did try to call me twice this afternoon though, but didn't leave a message. The last attempt couldn't have been more than an hour before she was killed.'

Abelvik fiddled with the pen in her hand. 'I'll get a team together,' she said. 'We'll need to go through all the cases she's worked on since joining the department. Find out who she's put away, who's been released.'

'We will also need to carry out a door-to-door operation,' Wibe added. 'Include the entire St. Hanshaugen area, and not just restrict it to residents either. We need to talk to everyone who's been in the area, who passed through on their way to or from something.'

Blix agreed. The murder had been committed at a time that would be favourable for the investigation – the middle of the afternoon on a Friday. There would've been lots of people out and about. Yet, that could've been a calculated decision on the part of the perpetrator too. They would blend into the crowd, become one among many.

'We need to get our hands on all the CCTV footage we can,' Abelvik continued.

'Already under way,' Blix informed her.

'And we'll have to invade Kovic's privacy as well,' she added with a sigh. 'Read her emails, phone log, social media, look into her relationships with friends, neighbours, family. We'll need access to her computer, phone, laptops. We'll have to go through everything. Track her final movements. Her bank activity. See if she took public transport – and where.'

'I'll talk to her mother,' Blix said. 'Once the initial shock has subsided.'

'Good,' Abelvik replied. 'Anything I've left out? Anything else we need to look into first?'

No one answered. She put the cap back on the marker and gave them a brief nod, indicating that the meeting was over.

Wibe immediately headed towards the door. Abelvik grabbed Blix's arm and held him back.

'This feels a bit weird...' she began.

'What does?'

'This. Me – taking your role. I'm sorry, I didn't know anything about it.'

'Don't worry about it,' Blix smiled. 'It's fine, I agree with Fosse; it's the best, and right, decision.'

She stared at him for a moment, as if she didn't fully believe him, but seemed to accept his answer in the end.

'There's something else I'd thought about,' she said. 'Could Iselin have been the target?'

Blix stared at her, asked her to elaborate.

'The perpetrator turns up almost immediately after she gets home,' Abelvik explained. 'Kovic becomes an obstacle between him and Iselin. He eliminates her and continues towards his target.'

It felt like the temperature in the room had suddenly plummeted. Blix had to steady himself on the back of the nearest chair. He hadn't looked at it that way.

'Why would anyone be after Iselin?' he asked.

'I don't know, but I don't know why anyone would want to kill Kovic either. Regardless, Iselin's our only witness. The perpetrator could see her as a potential threat. She might be in danger.'

Blix nodded.

'I recommend we implement a few security measures,' Abelvik added. 'Organise some protection, police presence outside your flat, or alternatively have her stay at a secret location.'

'I'm taking her back to mine after she's done giving her statement,' he explained. 'It's safe, familiar. But I'm sure she'd feel better with a patrol car stationed outside.'

'That'll be up to Fosse,' Abelvik said. 'As for what you do and don't want to be involved in here over the next few days – that's up to you. You can choose what contribution you make, how much time you can spend on it.'

Blix hadn't considered anything other than coming into work as usual, hadn't even thought that he should stay at home.

'Thank you, Tine,' he said anyway.

8

It was a long time before Iselin was done giving her statement. They questioned her for more than two hours. Blix knew it would be difficult, trying to remember every detail. Not just from the events that had happened earlier that day, but from their interactions in the days, weeks before Kovic's death. That was where you usually found the answers, the key to solving a murder.

Now sat in his desk chair, Blix rolled himself over to Kovic's workstation. Their desks had been opposite each other for as long as she'd worked in Homicide. Almost three and a half years. Her desk was still covered in loose sheets of paper. There was a phone charger and a set of headphones too. She had stuck a Post-it note with a reminder to 'call mum' to the edge of her computer monitor. She had scribbled keywords all over the large desk mat. A pack of chewing gum was poking out underneath a pile of documents. Everyday objects that made it that much harder to face the fact that she would never sit here, opposite him, again.

Blix leant back. His gaze moved across to the window, out into the darkness.

His father had been dead for so long that he could barely remember exactly how it had felt, how he had dealt with the grief. A few other friends and acquaintances had passed away over the years, but he couldn't remember ever feeling a similar level of despair. Heightening that, he was worried about Iselin too. Every time he thought of her, it felt like something had stuck its hand in his chest and wouldn't let go. It made his forehead sweat, made him want to yell out. Hit something.

And yet it also gave him the fuel he needed to find Kovic's killer.

There were two case files lying in her letter tray. One was the Thea Bodin case. The hit-and-run murder. Kovic had been the lead investigator. The case had become quite convoluted, but as far as Blix knew, there was nothing to suggest that she'd been any closer to naming a suspect. The other folder was a copy of a rape case Kovic had been assisting with, mainly by interviewing the victim's friends. The perpetrator had been known to the victim, had belonged to the same community and had the same group of friends, but Kovic hadn't had any contact with him.

He put the case files aside and began to sort through the rest of the documents in the tray, filtering out what seemed irrelevant. There was a circular explaining the new case-processing procedure, a letter from HR outlining their occupational health services, a page with information about a change in legislation and various other random documents that were of little use to the case. He started transferring everything into a cardboard box. He gathered up all the loose documents and notes, and filed them into plastic wallets. They mainly consisted of names and telephone numbers, a case number here and there, and a few notes she'd underlined for things she needed to remember. Nothing stood out to him yet, but he'd still have to go through it all. Call all the phone numbers, check out the case files. But first and foremost, he would need to get an overview.

He pulled out the top desk drawer. Several pens and pencils, a stapler, a few paper clips, some lozenges ... nothing of interest.

The next drawer down contained the notebook she always had with her. The contents were essentially the same as his own – a mix of keyword-based summaries from conversations and interviews, and various to-do lists. When she had completed a task, she would draw a line through it.

She'd included dates with most of the notes too, even adding a time alongside some of them.

Blix flipped through to the last page. Last Friday. Three jobs had been crossed out, but one remained.

~~Call T. Klevstrand~~
~~Archives~~
Meeting – PF
~~Meeting with the interpreting service~~

Thobias Klevstrand was a lawyer working as the Bodin family's counsel. She would naturally get in touch with him to let him know she was taking a week off. 'Archives' most likely referred to the case archives located in the basement of police HQ. The meeting with the interpreting services must've meant she had to interview a witness whose first language wasn't Norwegian, so she'd had to arrange for someone to assist with the questioning. And the job that remained, was to meet with PF. The Police Federation, most likely.

Kovic had never been that involved in the union though, and as far as Blix was aware, she'd never had any problems that she'd needed them to settle for her. He'd have to have a chat with their union representative, but it didn't really seem like it could be all that relevant. Blix opened the bottom drawer and found an old class photo from the Police University College. From 1998, long before Kovic had even started her training. Blix recognised a few of the faces. Petter Falkum was on the bottom row, easily recognisable with that thick moustache of his. Several of the people looking up at him had also ended up becoming investigators, while others chose to continue working in the patrol unit. A few of them were no longer in the force, having gone on to better-paid jobs in the private sector. One or two of them were dead. Cancer, suicide.

He turned the photo over and looked at the back. Nothing. He couldn't understand why Kovic would have it, but then again, it could have easily been left in there by whoever had used the desk before she had. Petter Falkum, maybe.

There was another case file underneath the photo. The sight of it made Blix frown. It was one of the most talked-about cases of the past six months, but Kovic hadn't been working on it. It was a closed case and should've been filed away in the archives.

Blix knew it well.

One day early last spring, financier Aksel Jens Brekke had barricaded himself inside a bank located on Aker Brygge, along with four of its employees. His ex-girlfriend had been one of the hostages. The ordeal went on for six hours before finally escalating, resulting in a Delta sniper having to shoot and kill Brekke.

Although the incident ended with a fatality, it was an open-and-shut case. The bank's CCTV system had captured all Brekke's movements on camera. The four hostages had provided concurrent statements. Brekke had been acting erratically, like a desperate man, with no other goal than to confront his ex-girlfriend. The interaction had quickly developed into an argument. Tensions escalated, and Brekke had pulled out a gun.

Blix leafed through the documents, keeping an eye out for any notes Kovic may have written in the margins or for any labels she may have added. He hadn't come across anything by the time Wibe called him over.

'The plumber's in interrogation room two,' he informed him.

Blix dropped the file back in the drawer, stood up and followed Wibe into the observation room. A young officer was stationed behind the control panel with all the recording equipment. There was a screen showing what was going on in the interrogation room. The investigator on one side of the table, Kovic's ex-boyfriend on the other. His name was displayed along a strip at the bottom of the screen: *FJELLVIK, Jo Inge*.

Petter Falkum was conducting the interview. He was known as Columbo around the office, simply because one of his eyes had the same trademark squint as the actor with almost exactly the same name – Peter Falk. Kovic hadn't understood the reference. She was too young to be familiar with the old TV crime drama.

'They've just started,' the officer informed them, before turning the sound up.

'It never turned into anything serious,' Fjellvik explained. 'I wouldn't even call it a relationship really. We just hung out for a few weeks. Went on a few dates before I stayed over at her place. I think we both knew there wasn't any more to it. It just kind of petered out.'

'Who ended it?'

It looked like Fjellvik had to think about it.

'She did. But I agreed.'

Blix leant closer to the screen. Kovic's ex was an attractive man. Slim but muscular. Dark hair, dark eyes. Still had a tan from the summer. His body language was difficult to interpret. He was restless, couldn't sit still. It looked like he was finding it hard to decide what to do with his hands. Blinked a lot. Swallowed every now and then, eyes searching the room.

He looked nervous, but anyone who had been called in to talk with the police after finding out their ex had just been murdered would have trouble staying calm. There was no guidebook on how to behave in such a situation.

Falkum requested that he elaborate on various aspects of their short-lived relationship, before asking Fjellvik to recount his movements that day.

Fjellvik explained how he had stopped by a wholesale warehouse to pick up a few parts he needed for that morning, before driving out to attend the jobs that had been booked for the day. First to fit a pipe for a bathroom renovation in Bekkestua. That had taken up most of his time. Then he had headed back towards Oslo to install a washing machine and replace a few taps in an old house in Ullern.

He took his phone out. 'I've got the times logged here,' he said.

He swiped across the screen and took a minute to find what he was looking for.

'I arrived at the last job at half past two and finished at five,' he said. 'A bit later than usual, but I'd promised to get everything done before the weekend.'

They'd estimated the preliminary time of death to be 16:45.

'Were the owners home?' Falkum asked.

'No, they had one of those new doors with a code lock. I let myself in with a code they'd given me.'

Petter Falkum asked for the address and the name of the homeowners.

Wibe jotted the information down as well. 'I'll check that out,' he said, but remained where he was to watch the rest of the interview.

The conversation turned into an attempt to map out Kovic's circle of friends. She had never mentioned the plumber to any of her colleagues, and there could've been other people in her life that none of them knew about. People who were a part of Kovic's life outside of work.

'We've had more information start to trickle in,' Wibe said without taking his eyes off the screen. 'Kovic used her bank card yesterday morning. Bought something at a shop down the road and spent just under two hundred kroner. That corroborates with a statement one of her neighbours gave, having seen her coming home at around eleven o'clock. There was another charge on her account about an hour later, a purchase made on zalando.no. Otherwise, there was very little activity on her social-media accounts over the last twenty-four hours. Next to nothing really, other than liking a few photos and status updates on Twitter, Facebook and Instagram.'

Blix nodded, mainly just to show that he'd heard what Wibe had said. 'Have you heard anything from the team analysing the surveillance footage?' he asked in a low voice.

'Spoke to them fifteen minutes ago,' Wibe answered. 'Doesn't look good. No CCTV cameras on the street outside. None in St. Hanshaugen Park either.'

'What about the door-to-door inquiries?'

'A man in the same building heard a racket out on the scaffolding,' he continued. 'He said that at first he thought it was just the builders, but then he remembered he'd already seen them knocking off work for the weekend. So he looked out, and saw a half-naked girl running down the street.'

'Iselin,' Blix said as his eyes momentarily darted towards the door to the hallway, back to the room she was being questioned in. It was tempting to leave and listen in to her interview instead, but Blix told himself that his daughter would tell him everything later.

He could see on the screen that Petter Falkum had started going back through everything, summarising Fjellvik's statement.

'The IT team have provided us access to Kovic's emails and the private folders on her server,' Wibe added. 'I've got someone going through them now.'

'Have they manage to get into her laptop yet? Her personal one, I mean?' Blix asked.

Wibe shook his head.

'Come to think of it, do we even have that?' he asked.

The man sitting at the control panel leant forward, his eyes narrowed as he tried to concentrate on what was going on in the interrogation room.

Blix nodded to Wibe that they should leave and followed him into the hallway. Once there, he pulled his phone out and called Ann-Mari Sara, the lead forensic technician who he knew would still be working in Kovic's flat.

'Have you got Kovic's laptop?' he asked when she picked up.

Sara said she needed a minute to check her records, returning half a minute later.

'We've not found a laptop or anything like that here, no.'

Blix and Wibe exchanged a look.

'I know she had one,' Blix said, as much to Wibe as to Sara. 'Can you double-check in her bedroom, all her handbags, rucksacks, under the sofa...'

'We've done all that already,' Sara replied, a little peeved. 'There's no laptop here, Blix.'

'Is there anything else in the flat that the perpetrator might have stolen as well? A TV, maybe? She had quite an expensive camera somewhere.'

'Both of them are here,' Sara reported back.

'What about money? Bank cards, cash?'

'I've not found any cash, but that doesn't necessarily mean anything. Everyone uses cards these days. And all Kovic's cards were still in her purse. There's nothing to indicate that this was a robbery.'

'Okay, thanks,' Blix said.

He hung up and looked at Wibe. 'Her laptop's missing.'

✻

'So what you're saying,' Bjarne Brogeland began, 'is that you didn't really make much progress on the first day?'

'I wouldn't say that,' Blix rebuked. 'You know just as well as I do that the first phase of an investigation as extensive as this one, with an unknown perpetrator, is all about mapping everything out and drawing up an overview, doing the sorting and systematising. We built a good foundation.'

'But you didn't get any further than that?'

Blix looked down at the table. Stared at his hands, one resting on top of the other.

'No,' he admitted.

9

Emma wasn't really someone who got nervous, usually. Looking back on the other times she'd had to explain herself to the police, she'd never broken into a cold sweat or felt as restless as she did now. That, she thought, was primarily due to the fact that she had always been sure of her role in whatever investigation she had managed to get tangled up in. The answers had given themselves.

This time was different.

She could justify why she had become involved, but she still felt hesitant – unsure whether she should be careful about what she told them, for both Blix's sake and her own. That was why she could feel the beads of sweat forming on the back of her neck; that was why her hands were suddenly so clammy.

The woman sat on the other side of the table – specialist investigator Hege Valle – was known for being thorough, but Emma had never had anything to do with her before now. Valle was in her early fifties and was wearing her police uniform, the tie of which was knotted so high up her neck that it almost looked as if it were choking her. She had short, spiky, red hair – a colour Emma was pretty sure wasn't natural, but that nonetheless worked well: matching her red lipstick and contrasting nicely with the blue shirt. Valle sat directly opposite Emma, back straight, practically on the edge of her seat, as if she couldn't wait to get started. She was tapping her fingers lightly against the stack of documents on the table in front of her.

'Before we begin,' Emma piped up. 'Could you ask for an update on Iselin?'

Valle looked up. 'We're receiving regular updates about the situation,' she answered in her sharp, nasal voice.

'And what was the last you heard?'

'That...' Valle looked as if she were trying to choose her words carefully. 'We don't know anything concrete yet,' she said. 'But the surgeons know what they're doing. Best in the country, so I've been told. We're all hoping that they can save her.'

Emma swallowed. She could still see the sight of Iselin's lifeless body on the floor. Could still hear the deafening sounds of the gunshots that followed.

Emma had experienced more than her fair share of grief over the last few years. And, in a brief moment of selfishness, she thought to herself that she must be cursed, considering the amount of people she had loved or been close to who had wound up dead. But her pain was nothing in comparison to what Kovic's mother would be going through right now, over the next few days, months, years.

'Are you ready to start?' Valle was watching her. There was no warmth or friendliness in her gaze.

Emma had started to feel like a suspect, as if she had done something wrong. *You have though*, she thought to herself, before clearing her throat and answering:

'Yes, I'm ready.'

'Good.'

Valle glanced up at the red light in the corner, checking to make sure the audio and video recording had started as well, before proceeding to state who was present, what the time was, and what case the interview was connected to.

'Age?'

'Twenty-six.'

'Address?'

'Falbes gate, in Bislett.' She gave the building number and floor.

'Civil status?'

'Single.'

'Profession?'

'Journalist. But I'm currently writing a book about how relatives and survivors deal with losing a loved one as a result of extreme violence.' Emma could hear how fast the words were tumbling out of her mouth.

'Is that something you've been tasked with doing?' Valle asked. 'Like an assignment?'

'No,' she answered, inhaling deeply to try and regulate her breathing, to calm herself down. 'But I have a contract with a publisher.'

Valle jotted down a few notes as she spoke, before lifting the pen from the paper again and letting her eyes rest on Emma.

'How do you know Alexander Blix?'

Emma felt a sharp pain in her chest as it suddenly tightened.

'He saved my life when I was five years old,' she began, taking another moment to exhale slowly. 'He shot and killed my father. Seconds before Dad was going to shoot me.'

Emma paused again, her memories taking her back to that moment.

'After that, we didn't really have anything to do with each other, until our paths crossed again a few years ago – once I'd started working as a journalist.'

'Are you lovers?'

Emma laughed. 'You're joking, right?'

'Just answer the question.'

'No,' she scoffed.

'And he's never made any advances?'

'Blix? No. Christ, he's old enough to be my father. And I do kind of see him like a father figure, in many ways. Why do you ask? How could that possibly be relevant to...'

'It's just one of several angles we're looking at,' Valle replied.

'Angles? What do you mean?'

Valle didn't respond. Instead she said, 'Timo Polmar – who's that?'

Emma needed a few seconds to gather her thoughts.

'A man who I'd imagine is currently lying on the autopsy table, even though it's pretty clear how he died. That's all I know.'

Emma could feel herself burning up.

'What do you mean?'

'I don't know who he is.'

'But you were right there in front of him when he was shot, were you not?'

Emma nodded. 'Doesn't mean I know who he is though,' she retaliated.

Valle stared at her.

'You were in the same room as him,' the investigator stated. 'What were you doing there?'

'I ... was with Blix,' Emma answered.

'Why?'

'Because...' She lowered her gaze. 'Because I've been involved in this investigation from day one.'

'And by *investigation*, you mean...?'

Emma raised her shoulders before quickly dropping them again. 'Sofia Kovic's murder ... and everything that happened after that.'

Valle's gaze remained on Emma for a while longer, before looking back down to her notepad and writing something else.

'Can you tell me about your relationship with Sofia Kovic?'

The sound of a telephone ringing down the hallway reached them in the interrogation room.

Emma looked down at her lap.

❄

Her friendship with Kovic had begun one evening when Emma had had to stay overnight at the police station. Kovic had come to find her early the next morning, with a warm smile and a piece of toast in her hand. They'd never really said all that much to each other before that point, but they were only a year apart in age, and seeing as Emma and Blix were so close, she'd got to know Kovic quite well too.

They had a lot in common. And even though they had eventually become close friends, Emma still always referred to her as Kovic, never Sofia.

Kovic had wanted to take Emma to visit Trogir, the Croatian harbour town she was originally from, just a fifteen-minute drive from the airport in Split. The way she had described the port – the boats, the colour of the ocean, the warmth of the water in the summer...

They could rent an apartment, Kovic had suggested, close to Okrug Gornji – one of the largest and most beautiful beaches in the area. They could take one of the water taxis over to the city centre one evening too. The last time they'd spoken about the trip was only two weeks ago.

Emma felt a lump in her throat. Her bottom lip began to quiver. She still hadn't spoken to Kovic's mother.

She had invited Emma to join them for dinner at her house one warm evening last August. She had served *ćevapi* – a traditional Balkan dish of minced-meat sausages, grilled and served with salad, raw onions and pita bread. They had cooked them on a charcoal grill in her back garden, and they'd tasted incredible.

❄

'But you are still a journalist,' Hege Valle stated. Her voice startled Emma out of her reverie. 'And you published a few articles about the case as well.'

'Yes, even though I knew Kovic personally, I didn't have a problem writing about her death.'

'You did seem to set the tone for most of the media coverage though...' Valle scanned through her documents, as if she had printed copies of Emma's articles. 'You were the first to release certain information, were you not?' she added.

'Yes, that...' Emma thought back to how some of the articles had come about. 'That's my job.'

'So it had nothing to do with your close relationship with Alexander Blix?'

Emma didn't like the question. Yet again, she felt like she was being asked to explain the exact nature of her friendship with Blix, but she let it slide.

'All good journalists have their sources,' she said instead. 'I'll never reveal mine.'

Her statement made Valle smirk, like she saw right through Emma anyway.

'But, based on what you knew about Kovic's life at the time of her death, did you come to any conclusions regarding who might've killed her?'

'Besides Jo Inge Fjellvik, you mean?'

Valle answered yes with a nod.

'No one came to mind immediately after, no. But I did remember something later that evening: someone had threatened Kovic once.'

'Oh?'

'This guy she'd arrested. Dennis Skofterud. There had been an altercation, and she ended up with a pretty gnarly black eye. He threatened to kill her as she was putting him in the police car. Kovic told me about it on a bike ride a while back – we happened to be passing by the spot where she'd arrested him.'

Valle nodded, as if she already knew everything Emma had just told her. 'Did you tell Blix about this person? That incident?'

'Not immediately.'

'Why not?'

'Because I wanted to find out more about him myself first, before telling anyone else.'

'And did you find out more?'

Emma nodded. 'It turned out he had served some time for murder, a little over twenty years ago.'

'And *that's* when you went to Blix?'

'I tried, but he was busy. Seeing as the death threat had been included in the report for his last arrest, I'd presumed that Blix and the others would connect the dots and go after him without my input.'

Valle scribbled a few notes down.

'So what *did* you do next?'

Emma looked away. Found a spot on the wall she could stare at.

'I set up a meeting with him.'

10

It had just turned 22:30 when Blix received a message telling him that Iselin had finished giving her witness statement. She had also given her DNA and fingerprint samples.

Blix found her waiting for him in one of the meeting rooms. She was sitting back in her chair, cup of tea in hand and her phone on the table in front of her, flipped over so it was screen-side down. A female officer sitting at the other end of the table looked up at him as he entered, but Iselin didn't acknowledge his arrival.

He pulled out a chair and sat next to her. Gently lay his hand on her forearm. Lightly stroked her arm a few times. Searched for something to say. He noticed a heap of papers stapled together on the table in front of her.

'Is this a copy of the interview?' Blix asked, directing the question at the officer.

She nodded. Blix pulled the documents towards him, skimmed their contents. It was a detailed statement, going as far back as when Iselin and Kovic first met. Any mention of what had happened after she had arrived home a few hours prior didn't come up until page three. Descriptions of how she had spoken to Kovic, how she had then gone upstairs to her room. The gunshot, the fight with the perpetrator, her escape. Efficiently recorded by an experienced investigator. Short sentences, objective descriptions. Nothing that gave away how they really felt – their shock, anguish, horror.

Iselin picked up her phone. 'Can we go?' she asked meekly.

Blix hadn't finished reading, but he put the documents down immediately.

'Of course,' he answered. 'Let's go home.'

❋

Twenty-five minutes later, Blix was guiding his daughter upstairs and into his flat on Tøyengata, double-checking that he had locked the door behind them.

Fosse had rejected the idea of using extra resources on any security measures, or having Iselin stay at a temporary address. He had, however, organised for a patrol car to pass by a few times during the night, but that was the extent of it.

Iselin had lived with Blix for a short period before starting her studies at the Stavern campus of the Police University College, so she already knew where everything was. Blix had never taken the time, or had the means, to do anything about the drab, shoebox flat he had owned for almost four years now.

Iselin took her shoes off, hung her jacket up and walked into the bathroom. Before closing the door, she turned back to face him.

'Have you spoken to Mum?'

Blix had contemplated calling Merete, but it was late in Norway, which meant it was the middle of the night in Singapore.

'I'll call her in the morning,' he said.

He made them both a cup of tea and turned the TV on, making sure to avoid all the news channels. Knowing his daughter's tastes, he flicked through the guide to see what was on the Discovery Channel or National Geographic. The latter was showing a programme about emperor penguins.

They sat in silence and watched as the camera panned across the breath-taking Antarctic landscape, complemented by the warm, calming voice of Sir David Attenborough. Iselin drew in a deep breath, as if to remind herself that she did, in fact, require oxygen. It seemed to Blix that she was slowly coming round.

'So what now?' she asked after a while.

'We'll find who did it,' Blix said.

'That's not what I meant,' she said. 'I meant, what about *me*.'

Blix waited until she looked at him.

'We have a psychiatrist we often go to, in the force,' he said. 'I've arranged for you to see him tomorrow.'

Iselin looked exasperated. 'There's nothing wrong with me, Dad.'

'You need to talk to someone,' Blix said. 'A professional.'

'A psychiatrist makes it sound like I'm sick or something.'

'We go to him specifically because he specialises in trauma,' Blix continued. 'He can help you process what you've been through. It's best to meet with him sooner rather than later, so you can start the process and try to move on.'

She sighed heavily.

'You need it,' Blix insisted. 'And it might be beneficial to the investigation. He might be able to help you remember certain details a bit more clearly.'

She didn't respond straight away.

'Will you be taking me?' she said eventually.

'If you want me to.'

'I don't want to go by myself.'

'I understand. I'll go with you, my darling. No problem.'

'Won't they need you at work?'

'Probably,' he said, sending her a quick smile. 'But you're more important.'

'But isn't it important that you go in?' she said. 'You're the best investigator there.'

'That's not true, Iselin. We've got more than enough capable investigators. They'll manage just fine without me.'

'Yeah, but maybe they shouldn't.'

Blix was about to object, but Iselin was quicker.

'Were you planning on staying with me here until they arrest the guy? So you can keep an eye on me?'

'If needs be.'

'What if that takes weeks? What if it never happens?'

'Then we'll take it one day at a time. Let's just get through this evening, and we'll see where we stand tomorrow. Okay?'

They sat in silence for a moment.

'What about Emma? Couldn't she come over?' Iselin looked at him pleadingly. 'I don't think anyone will be out looking for me,' she continued. 'And Emma ... I like Emma. And I know you trust her.'

Blix had a 'no' waiting on the tip of his tongue, but Emma had already offered to help just a few hours beforehand.

'I can check with her. How does that sound?'

Iselin smiled and nodded gratefully.

'Could you...' he began. 'I would find it helpful if you could try and tell me what happened this evening. I know it'll be hard. I know it'll be painful.'

She looked into his eyes. 'If I do – does that mean I can get out of seeing the psychiatrist tomorrow?'

The corner of her mouth twitched slightly. The hint of a smile. It warmed his heart.

'I think it's a good idea that you talk to him regardless, my darling. But neither he nor I will pressure you to talk about it if you don't want to. That's up to you.'

Iselin looked down at the cup of tea in her hands. She was gripping it tightly. He watched as she lifted her shoulders up to her ears and slowly released them, breathing out.

'I got home at four o'clock,' she began.

11

The lock was being funny again. Iselin had to jiggle the key around a bit so she could turn it and get the door open.

Kovic's flat was split over two floors, but she only used the lower floor. Iselin had been renting the loft space for the last six months or so.

She smiled at the thought. Almost twenty-five square metres all to herself, including a little ensuite. She felt like she had so much more freedom here than back when she was living with her dad.

She kicked her shoes off in the hallway and walked into the kitchen.

Kovic was leaning on the table, scrutinising a few documents she had in her hand. She didn't seem to have noticed that Iselin was home.

'Hey,' Iselin said.

It took Kovic several seconds to drag her eyes away from the paper.

'Hm?'

'Got a lot on?' Iselin asked.

'Oh, yeah...'

Kovic tucked the sheets back into one of the green folders the police used as case files before she started clearing the table. She picked up the dirty plates and glasses and put them in the sink.

'Aren't you off this week?' Iselin asked.

Kovic closed the lid of her laptop. 'This is what time off looks like,' she said with a sigh, her hand making a sweeping gesture across the kitchen table. 'You never really have time off with this job. Especially not now, when...' She stopped herself. 'You'll see what I mean,' she said with a tired smile. 'That's just how it is, mini-Blix.'

Iselin smiled, but wondered if she should say something. She wasn't all that keen on the nickname Kovic had given her. It was already a well-known fact that she was following in her father's footsteps; she didn't need everyone at the station referring to her by a name that only emphasised the relationship between the two of them.

It did make her wonder whether it had been a stupid idea to enrol at the Police University College in the first place. She had applied to study at the campus in Stavern to get a bit of distance from the general police environment in Oslo, but no matter what she did, she would always be compared to her father. She couldn't do anything about sharing a surname, something that made it abundantly clear that they were related. She just hoped she wouldn't do anything to embarrass him.

Kovic usually enjoyed having company. Whenever Iselin got home, she'd meet her with a wide smile, a warm hug and a barrage of questions about what they'd been studying that week. Recently, however, it seemed as if she would rather be by herself. Have time alone. To think. Iselin didn't need to be a trainee police officer to see that something was troubling her.

'Need any help?' she asked, nodding in the direction of the kitchen table. 'I'm quite good at problem-solving.'

Kovic shook her head. 'Thanks anyway,' she said, following it up with another smile.

Iselin felt as if it were a 'you aren't experienced enough to help me with this' kind of smile.

'What I really need to do is to talk to your father.'

'Can't you get hold of him?'

'No, he's giving a talk today, or at least I think he is. Either way, he's not picking up. He's a busy man, your dad,' she said, sitting down at the table.

Iselin nodded. 'And there's no one else you can talk to?'

Kovic silently held Iselin's gaze for a few seconds.

'Abelvik, Wibe ... Fosse?' Iselin suggested.

At the last suggestion, Kovic wrinkled her nose and shook her head slightly, but she still didn't offer a response.

'I'll stop snooping,' Iselin said, holding her hands up. 'I'm going upstairs to relax a bit. I'll be heading out later with Ida and Cecilie.'

She carried her things up to her room and spent the next few minutes unpacking her toiletry bag and organising the textbooks she'd brought home to read over the weekend. The room felt a bit stuffy, so she opened a window, taking a moment to look out at the renovation efforts. The entire front of the building was decked in scaffolding.

She sent off a couple of messages to some friends before taking a long shower. After drying off, she stood in front of the bedroom mirror in her underwear for a bit, sorting her hair out – using her curling tong in an attempt to give it some volume.

She heard the doorbell ring downstairs.

The sound of a kitchen chair scraping against the floor as Kovic got up. Followed by the sound of her footsteps walking through the hallway, opening the door. A man's voice. Iselin smiled. It hadn't been that long since her last relationship.

She was just about to twist another strand of hair around the curling tong when a yell reached her from the floor below.

Iselin span round to face the door. The sound of things falling, hitting the floor, shattering. And then a faint *pff*.

Iselin intuitively associated the sound with a gunshot, but muffled, like a gun with a silencer. The sound that followed was like a body collapsing to the floor.

She put the curling tong down. Tried to convince herself that she hadn't heard what she thought she'd just heard. She must have misunderstood.

Reaching down, she groped around for the closest clothes she could find, picking up a pair of trousers from a pyjama set she'd left on the floor. She stood there, listening.

The sound of someone moving about downstairs, but otherwise nothing else. No voices. She quietly stepped into the pyjama bottoms and tugged them up. Took a few cautious steps over to the door to the staircase, wondering whether she should shout down to see if everything was okay. Instead, she turned her head slightly, ear to the door, trying to hear better.

Silence.

No.

Footsteps. Slow. Deliberate. A *click, click, click* – the sound of heels meeting the parquet floor. Curtains being drawn, a plug being pulled out of the socket. A rustling of papers.

Iselin had her phone in hand, readying herself to ring the emergency services, when the footsteps got louder. The sound of a person striding towards the front door. The footsteps stopping abruptly.

She thought of her own shoes that she'd kicked off in the hallway. The jacket she'd hung up.

Iselin held her breath, and without realising it, found herself backing slowly across the room. Her elbow came into contact with the pile of textbooks on her bed. She spun round, but it was too late – she couldn't stop them, could only watch as they tumbled to the floor. The loud thump as the first one hit the ground made her gasp.

She listened, strained her ears.

The sound of footsteps again.

Near the staircase.

On the staircase.

Heading upstairs.

Towards her.

Fear seized her. She contemplated throwing herself under the bed, hiding in the wardrobe, but she had no time. Instead, she searched for something she could defend herself with. The chair was all she had time to grab. Picking it up, she positioned herself – behind the door, back against the wall, chair raised above her head. She listened as the footsteps approached.

The sight she was met with momentarily paralysed her. A man in a balaclava – the only parts of his face that were visible were his mouth and dark eyes. On his hands, a pair of black gloves. He was holding a pistol.

With all her might, she brought the chair down.

The intruder had seen her, but hadn't managed to avoid the blow. The legs of the chair came crashing down onto his right arm, making him lose grip of the gun, which tumbled to the floor. He launched himself after it. Iselin raised the chair again and hurled it across his back. She then used it to shove him away from the gun.

The man grabbed hold of the chair legs. He roared, tore it out of her hands and threw it across the room. Seizing hold of her shoulders, he cast her aside and charged at the pistol again.

She collided with the desk and felt one of her ribs snap. The force of the impact made the mirror hanging on the wall beside it fall and shatter.

Gasping for air, Iselin threw herself to the floor to scramble after the gun, shoving aside the clothes, textbooks and make-up now strewn across the room.

He was on top of her now, pushing her down as he stretched out above her, fingers nearing the pistol. Iselin thrashed around beneath him, using her arms, legs, knees. She could feel his breath against her skin. Could smell his heavy, spiced cologne.

Her left arm jolted as she came into contact with something. Something hot. The curling tong. She grabbed the handle and drove the rod into the man's chest, managing to find a patch of bare skin in a gap between the balaclava and his jumper.

He screamed in pain. His body twisted round. Wrapping his hand around the cable, he tugged the curling tong away from his chest and hurled it across the room.

Iselin reached for the pistol, but couldn't quite get her fingers around it. Throwing her arm out instead, she managed to slide it further under the bed, out of their reach.

The man hit her. A clenched fist against her jaw. Her lip burst open. The taste of blood filled her mouth. He jumped up and stormed across to the bed.

She managed to push herself up slightly and looked back.

Watched for a second as the man pushed the bed aside. Crouched down. Hand stretching underneath, towards the pistol.

Iselin got to her feet. The intruder was blocking her way to the door.

The window.

The scaffolding.

She was across the room in three steps. Threw the window fully open. Didn't look back, didn't dare take a moment to stop moving. Took one step out onto the rickety scaffolding, then another...

And then, behind her:

Pff.

12

'Jesus Christ.'

Blix couldn't think of anything else to say. Instead, he just pulled Iselin in close. Held her there for a long time.

It had been a battle of life and death. It must have been a matter of millimetres, milliseconds.

Iselin moved away, using both shaking hands to lift the cup of tea to her mouth. Blix watched her. She was pale. As she had recounted the events of that afternoon, the skin on her neck had become steadily more inflamed.

'Did he only shoot once?' Blix asked.

'I believe so,' Iselin said.

He tried to visualise the situation from the perpetrator's perspective. Perhaps he had followed her to the window to complete his mission but had decided that shooting blindly down an open street, without being sure if there were any witnesses nearby, would have posed too great a risk.

Iselin had been resourceful, but she'd also been lucky.

What I really need to do is talk to your father.

'Kovic did try calling me while I was giving my talk,' he began. 'Did she mention what she was calling about?'

Iselin shook her head. 'I didn't ask either,' she answered. 'It seemed like something she only wanted to share with someone she could trust.'

Blix thought about that damned talk. Thought about how everything could have been so different had he only picked up the phone. He wondered why she hadn't tried calling anyone else – the others.

He slowly got to his feet. 'I just need to make a quick phone call,' he said. 'I'll be back in a second.'

He walked into the kitchen and grabbed his phone from where he'd left it on the countertop. Found Ann-Mari Sara's number. He was counting on her still being at the crime scene.

'Me again,' he said once she answered. 'There should've been a case file in Kovic's kitchen. I don't think I saw it when I was in there. Have you got it?'

Blix could hear her moving around. Flipping through some papers. Followed by Sara's heavy, northern Norwegian dialect:

'Nope, doesn't look like it.'

Blix took a moment. Thought through what that could mean. But there was really only one thing it could mean.

The perpetrator had taken it.

He must have taken her laptop too. There might not have even been anything incriminating on it, but he probably didn't want to take that risk.

'Right, okay,' he said. 'Thanks.'

Blix hung up. His thoughts moved to Thea Bodin, the twenty-nine-year-old who had been killed in a hit-and-run on Maridalsveien, a road Kovic often cycled herself. The car had hit Bodin at high speed from behind. The collision had broken her neck, and she had most likely died instantaneously. Her body had been launched onto the side of the road, onto a rocky bank, where she was eventually found. They hadn't found any signs of braking on the road. No signs that the driver had even contemplated stopping.

He remembered a conversation he and Kovic had had a few weeks ago. She'd mentioned wanting to take the investigation in a bit of an unconventional direction – look at things from a different angle.

'What do you mean?' Blix had asked.

'Just … I don't know exactly,' she'd responded. 'I'm not saying that I think we've got a serial killer on the loose or anything, driving about, running people over. The risk of being exposed, killing people in that way, would be far too great.'

'But you want to look into it anyway?'

'I want to see if Thea's murder might be connected to something else, another case we've investigated in the last few years.'

Blix remembered reacting to her proposal with scepticism. 'You don't have much to go on other than the fact the driver *might* have been driving a dark car,' he said. 'Sounds like a bit of a shot in the dark.'

'Maybe it is,' she admitted with a sigh. 'I'm just so frustrated at not getting anywhere.'

'That's the nature of the job I'm afraid.'

'I know that. But I still feel like I need to be doing something,' she continued. 'See if there are any profile similarities, for example. If there was something about Thea, what she did, who she was, that might have had something to do with her death. Like her job, what she did for a living. Or if there was something going on in her neighbourhood, or something about her past, where she went to school or university, where she went shopping, what websites she visited – that kind of thing.'

'We've done a fair bit of that research already,' Blix reminded her.

'I know, I know. I just want to look deeper.'

Blix remembered studying her for a few seconds, impressed by her zeal. Her determination, work ethic.

'By all means,' Blix said. 'And it's your case. Just remember that there are other cases you need to focus on as well.'

'I can look into it in my spare time.'

Spare time, Blix thought, returning to the present. She would've had plenty of spare time while off work this week.

He turned his attention back to Iselin and headed into the living room. Watched as thousands of emperor penguins huddled together on the TV screen, side by side, protecting their young from the bitter whip of the polar wind. It struck him that they must be in the coldest place on Earth.

'I've texted Emma,' Iselin said, without taking her eyes off the screen. 'She'll be over at eight o'clock tomorrow morning.'

13

'So Blix wanted you to babysit?'

Emma lifted her head. It looked as if Hege Valle was trying to hold back a laugh.

'Iselin is twenty-three,' Emma retorted, a little more curtly than she had intended. 'And I don't think Blix actually wanted me to go over, but he seemed to come round. Realised it was a good solution. A practical one, at least. For everyone.'

'So you just happened to be available then? Free to help out at such short notice?'

'I'm lucky I've got such a good boss.'

'Anita Grønvold.'

Emma nodded. She had reduced her hours to part-time at the news agency while working on the book. Stepping in to help out every now and then when they needed her.

Valle smiled. 'I like Anita,' she said. 'She's one hell of a woman, as we say where I'm from.'

The glare from the ceiling light reflected off her white teeth.

'Blix thought you were qualified to look after his daughter then, did he?' The sarcastic tone in her voice made Emma shuffle uncomfortably in her chair.

'I think all he cared about at that point was that someone was there to keep her company,' she replied. 'Just sit with her.'

'And you weren't worried that whoever killed Kovic would potentially come looking for Iselin too?'

Emma considered the question.

'Not really.'

Valle stopped for a moment. Used her finger to wipe away a touch of spittle that had collected in the corner of her mouth, before continuing:

'What was the plan, exactly? Were you going to spend the entire day there, until Blix got back?'

'Initially, the plan was just to be there,' Emma responded. 'And then take her to her appointment with the psychiatrist.'

❋

'I don't want to go.'

Iselin and Emma stared at each other. They were sitting at the kitchen table, each with a cup of tea in front of them.

'Your dad said you'd say that,' Emma said, with a slight smile.

'What else did he say?'

'That I can't let you out of my sight.'

Iselin nodded.

'What is it you're most nervous about?' Emma asked.

'I don't even know,' Iselin replied, looking down. 'Having to relive it, probably. Even though I'm doing that all the time anyway. Up here.' She tapped her forehead.

'I get it,' Emma said, leaning over to hold Iselin's hand. 'But your dad will hunt me down if I don't take you, so if you won't do it for your own sake, can you at least do it for mine? Please?' Emma winked.

Iselin looked up and smiled.

'Get yourself ready,' Emma said, patting the top of her hand. 'And I'll go and see if there are any assailants waiting outside.' She pushed her chair out and stood up.

'You don't really think there's anyone out there, do you?' Iselin asked. There was a slight panic in her voice.

'No, no,' Emma assured her. 'But I take my job as a bodyguard *very* seriously.'

Iselin laughed.

Twenty-five minutes later and they were downstairs, waiting on the pavement outside Blix's apartment building. It was a bitterly cold morning. A powerful gust of wind forced them both to pull their scarves more tightly around their necks. Emma had wanted to spend as little time outside as possible, so she'd booked them a taxi. It was a short drive, and they pulled up outside Oslo Cathedral just before nine o'clock.

They hurried across the tramlines and onto the busy pedestrian street, Torggata, on the other side of the junction, where they passed two men handing out that day's edition of the left-wing newspaper *Klassekampen*.

Eivind Neumann's office was on the fifth floor of the building right on the corner of Torggata. Emma searched for the psychiatrist's name on the buzzer and entered the passcode – 604 – to ring up to reception. Emma pulled Iselin in towards her, so both of them were visible on the little doorbell camera above the buzzer. After a few seconds' wait, they were let in.

When the lift doors opened, a well-dressed man in his mid-fifties was waiting in the hallway to greet them.

'Good morning,' he said in a warm voice. 'You must be Iselin.'

He extended his hand to shake hers, taking a moment to study her. 'You look like your father,' he said, followed by a short laugh.

Iselin shook his hand, responding with a rather weak 'hi'.

Neumann then addressed Emma: 'And you are...?'

'A friend,' she said. 'Here for support. Thank you for agreeing to see Iselin at such short notice, and on a Saturday as well.'

The psychiatrist had a penetrating gaze that rested on her for a few seconds longer than she appreciated.

'I know how important it is to get started with such matters as soon as possible,' he answered, taking Emma's outstretched hand. 'Much easier to get back to normal that way.'

He returned his gaze to Iselin, sending her a quick smile before saying to Emma:

'Sorry, but you will have to wait outside.' He pointed towards a small, empty waiting room. 'There's coffee if you want some,' he said.

Emma turned to Iselin, who was suddenly looking peaky.

'It's all going to be okay,' Emma assured her. 'And I'll be waiting right here.'

❄

A fluorescent light in the ceiling of the interrogation room started flickering, making Emma glance up.

'But you didn't wait for her, did you?'

She lowered her eyes again to find Hege Valle staring at her, scrutinising her. The sudden crushing sense of guilt made Emma divert her gaze.

'No. I'd planned to meet Dennis Skofterud at a café down the street. Iselin's appointment was meant to last an hour and a half. I thought I could use the time productively. I didn't think it was something Iselin needed to know about.'

'Because you didn't want her to worry?'

'Exactly.'

'Did you clear that with Blix first?'

Emma took a moment before answering:

'No.'

Valle wrote something down. 'How did you convince Skofterud to meet you?'

'I told him I was working on a project about extreme violence, a book documenting what it's like to be a relative of a murder victim, and I wanted the perspective of someone who had actually killed someone.'

'And he agreed to that?'

'Well, he agreed to meet me.'

'And you didn't think that was stupid?'

'What do you mean?'

Emma and Valle locked eyes.

'Meeting a man who had been convicted of murder and who had also threatened Kovic? Were you not worried that he was the one who killed her?'

Emma took a moment to work out how to explain it.

'It was in the back of my mind,' she answered. 'That was why I asked if we could meet in a café, in public. But that case, the murder conviction, was different.'

'How exactly?'

'Well, it was drug-related, some internal conflict. He owed someone money, and they'd been threatening him. His lawyer argued that it had been self-defence. The jury was divided. And anyway, it was twenty years ago. He served his sentence and was released years ago.'

Valle stared at her in silence for a moment.

'Didn't he shoot the victim in their own home?'

Emma nodded and threw her hand out. 'I mean, yes, he fit the bill as a potential suspect, but I didn't see him as an immediate threat.'

14

The morning meeting concluded with Ann-Mari Sara's report on the forensic examination of Kovic's flat. They had managed to lift solid footprints from the perpetrator's shoes from both the kitchen and the staircase. Her account was supplemented with photos of the crime scene, displayed on the large screen behind her. The footprints measured in at 29.4cm long, so a men's size ten. They still needed to identify the type of shoe he'd been wearing.

Various fingerprints had been collected as well, but they didn't think they would be of any use seeing as the intruder had been wearing gloves. Some of the items needed further testing for DNA traces, such as the curling tong Iselin had used to defend herself.

'So we're looking for someone with burn marks on their chest?' Petter Falkum commented.

Sara nodded and summarised: 'Looking at the crime scene, then, it began with Kovic opening the door. The situation escalated quickly. We should be getting the autopsy report later today, but she was shot at close range on the left side of her forehead.'

'Point-blank execution,' Wibe mumbled.

'We believe he might have used a nine-millimetre calibre pistol,' Sara continued. 'The bullet was secured during the autopsy, and we found two shell casings inside the flat.'

'Two?'

Sara nodded and pointed at the image on the screen. 'One was found inside a shoe in the hallway, and the other upstairs,' she clarified. 'From the shot fired at Iselin.'

They all sat in silence. Sara clicked on to the next image.

'The kitchen table,' she said, looking over at Blix. 'According to Iselin's witness statement, Kovic's MacBook had been there. As was a case file. Both are missing.'

'Are we able to trace the laptop?' someone asked.

'IT are working on it,' Sara nodded. 'It should be possible if it connects to the internet.'

'Surely the case file is of greater concern?' Wibe suggested. 'She was meant to be off this week, so she must've taken it home with her. It could be directly connected to her murder.' He turned to face Abelvik: 'Is it possible to find out which file she had?'

Tine Abelvik responded with a doubtful grimace. 'That would mean accounting for every physical copy of our case files until we're left with whichever one's missing,' she said. 'And we don't know if it's an archived or active case. It would be a particularly resource-intensive task.'

'But we can start on the cases she was involved in,' Wibe proposed.

'That might not provide any concrete answers either, though,' Falkum interjected. 'There could be several missing case files.'

Blix sat and listened. He was torn. Everything that had happened had nothing to do with Iselin. It all pointed to Kovic's work. The intruder had targeted Kovic. Iselin had simply been in the wrong place at the wrong time.

Abelvik stopped to jot down a few notes before turning to Petter Falkum:

'What's the situation with Martin Hikes?'

'We found stolen goods from eight different cases in his flat, so he has been arrested, but there's nothing that connects him to Kovic. He's also extremely short-sighted and can't see a thing without his glasses. And the perpetrator wasn't wearing any. Hikes doesn't match the build of the man Iselin described in her statement either, he's far too weak.' Falkum opened the folder on his lap. 'He *was* in the area around the time of the murder, though, but left when he heard the police sirens. However, he did make an interesting observation. He'd spotted a man wearing gloves walking up and down Geitmyrsveien. When the sound of the sirens got closer, he saw the man make off down Ullevålsveien.'

'Did he give a description?'

'Said he was wearing a cap, either black or blue. Dark jacket, dark trousers.'

'What do you mean, he was walking up and down Geitmyrsveien?' Blix queried. 'Like he was looking for someone?'

'I don't know,' Falkum shrugged.

Abelvik nodded as she wrote a few more notes. They ended the formal meeting but stayed in their seats for a while, throwing various theories and hypotheses around the table. They discussed their options and distributed tasks.

'Right,' Abelvik announced eventually, closing her notebook. 'Let's get to work.'

15

Brogeland drained his glass and refilled it from the jug of water on the table between them. He held it up to Blix, as if to ask if he wanted any.

Blix shook his head. Brogeland checked his notes.

'Did you figure out which case file Kovic had taken home with her?'

Blix shook his head. 'Not as far as I know. Abelvik had two people looking into it, but it's time-consuming work.'

Blix was about to say something more, but held it back. Brogeland noticed his hesitation.

'But...?' he enquired.

'There was another case file in the bottom drawer of Kovic's desk,' he said. 'A closed case. A case she had nothing to do with. And no reason to look into.'

For the first time in a while, Brogeland picked up his pen and jotted something on his notepad. 'Which case was that?'

'The Aker Brygge hostage case.'

Brogeland raised an eyebrow. 'The one with Aksel Jens Brekke?'

Blix nodded, tempted to point out that there hadn't been any other hostage incidents on Aker Brygge.

'Why would Kovic be looking at that case?' Brogeland speculated.

'I've been wondering that myself,' Blix replied.

'And she hadn't been involved in the investigation at any point?'

'No. It was Petter Falkum's case.'

'What did you do with the file?'

'I kept it so I could talk to Falkum about it later. After I'd been to see Kovic's mother, that is.'

※

Maria Gade lived in a two-bedroom flat at the end of Holmestrandgata, in an Oslo neighbourhood characterised by its greenery and what used to be working-class housing. Blix had always liked this part of the city and had been close to moving to the area a few years ago, if it hadn't been for the fact he had been royally outbid.

Opening the door for Blix, Maria Gade had had to use her other hand to steady herself against the door frame. A slight woman, she had brunette hair and was always impeccably dressed. Her eyes were bloodshot. She had a tissue clasped tightly in the hand she used to keep her balance.

'Hi,' she said feebly. 'Come in.'

It was all she could bring herself to say.

Blix stepped into the flat. He closed the door behind him and turned to face Kovic's mother again:

'My deepest condolences.'

She thanked him, her eyes filling with new tears.

'This won't take long,' Blix assured her. 'But it's important that we talk.'

'I understand,' Gade said. 'Come on in. Don't worry about taking your shoes off.'

Blix took them off anyway, but kept his jacket on.

'I've got some coffee brewing,' she said. 'Can I get you a cup?'

'No, but thank you,' Blix answered.

They walked into the cramped living room and sat down on either side of the coffee table. It was dark – the curtains were drawn. There were three vases of flowers dotted around the room. One was from the police – he could see the card from where he sat.

Maria Gade wept silently. Her tears flowed – she was unable to stop them.

'I'm sorry,' she said. 'I just...'

'Don't apologise,' Blix said, instinctively looking away, up at the walls, at the photos of Kovic's family. There was one of Kovic as a child, standing beside her Croatian father, who had died in a workplace accident when she was just eleven years old. A wedding photo caught Blix's eye. Gade, years ago. The resemblance between mother and daughter was undeniable. The short distance between the eyes. Their defined cheek bones. Narrow lips.

Gade sniffed. Blew her nose before clenching her hand tight around the tissue again.

'She always spoke fondly of you,' she said.

'Sofia?'

Gade nodded. 'She really looked up to you. Was glad you were her boss. She often said so.'

Even though Kovic had never said this to his face, Blix knew how she had appreciated him. Still, hearing it now, after her death, brought a lump to his throat that was difficult to swallow.

You need to get better at giving people praise, he told himself. The people you care about. Before it's too late. It takes so little, but could mean so much.

'Sofia was an excellent colleague,' he said, forcing himself to swallow. 'And a great friend, even if we didn't share much of our personal lives with each other.'

A heavy silence descended around them.

'When was the last time you talked?' Blix asked after a while.

'Yesterday,' her mother said. 'No. The day before that. She came over for lunch.'

'How did she seem, to you?'

'Distant,' Gade responded without having to think about it. 'Her mind was elsewhere.'

'Any idea where exactly?'

Gade shook her head. 'I asked, but she didn't say. Just waved it off, as she always did.'

'Was she often like that, then? Distant?'

'Not really. I mean, she was always deep in thought, when she was here at least. I always thought she was thinking about work or a boyfriend. And she couldn't talk about work, so I rarely asked. Not that she said all that much about any boyfriends either. Not voluntarily anyway.' Gade smiled at her own comment.

'So you weren't aware that she had been dating someone until fairly recently?'

'No, no, I knew that,' she replied. 'I always asked regardless.'

'Did you ever meet him? Jo Inge Fjellvik?'

'No,' she said, shaking her head. 'I only ever met one or two of her suitors over the years.'

'Were there ... many?'

'No,' she answered quickly. 'She wasn't like ... *that*.'

Blix held his palms up. 'That's not what I meant.'

'You're looking for potential suspects,' Gade said. 'I realise that. But I didn't get to know any of the men she dated.'

She sniffed, mindlessly rubbing one thumb over the other.

'I've been trying to think about that too,' she said after a while. 'Because I knew you'd ask. But I can't think of a single person who would have anything against Sofia. Everyone liked her. That was the impression I always had, anyway.'

'That was my impression too,' Blix agreed. 'And I think we're both right.'

He sent her a weak smile.

'Can you think of anything about your daughter's life that you think we should take a closer look at?' he continued.

Gade straightened up a little, looking directly at him. 'What do you mean?' she asked.

'Anything at all: what she had been up to recently, who she might have seen, things she would've told you about,' Blix elaborated. 'Or anything she said about where she had been in the last few days or weeks, or where she was planning on going. Absolutely anything could be significant.'

Gade looked back down at her hands, thinking it through. She took a while, before saying:

'She didn't really say much about ... anything. She worked. She was so committed to her work. And she exercised, liked to look after her health.'

Blix studied Gade – it looked like a thought, a memory, had suddenly popped into her mind.

'I think something was troubling her though,' she continued. 'Something she didn't want to talk to me about. Or with you either, perhaps?'

'What makes you think that?'

'She ... was seeing a psychologist. Were you aware?'

Blix lifted his chin slightly.

'I only found out by accident – a calendar notification popped up on her phone. She'd left it on the table while we were eating.'

'What did it say?'

'Just "therapy", I think.'

Blix took a moment to think about what Gade had just said.

'Did you ask *why* she needed to see a therapist?'

'Yes, but she wouldn't tell me.'

'Did you notice *when* her appointment was?'

'Not exactly,' Gade replied. 'But I think it was meant to be right after she'd been here. She had to leave to be somewhere, anyway.'

Blix felt a vibration in his jacket pocket.

'Did she say anything about *who* she was seeing?' he pressed.

'No.'

Blix paused to gather his thoughts. His phone continued to ring. He fished it out of his inside pocket and saw Emma's name on the screen. He cast a quick glance up at the clock on the wall. Iselin must have finished already.

'I'm sorry,' he said as he stood up. 'I'm going to have to take this.'

'That's quite alright.'

❄

Blix paused. Clasped his hands together. Released them again. Wiped the sweat from his forehead. Felt the urge to stand up, leave the interrogation room, get some fresh air.

'Everything okay?' Brogeland asked.

Blix buried his head in his hands for a few seconds.

'No,' he answered. 'Not at all.'

16

Emma checked the time on her phone, took a sip from the tall latte glass. Dennis Skofterud was five minutes late.

She had chosen a seat facing the door and found herself surrounded by mothers with young children, as well as pensioners, couples and a group of students. Scrolling through her phone, she saw that the nation's news sites had named Sofia Kovic as the victim of yesterday's murder.

Anita had published the article Emma had spent the night putting together about Kovic. It painted a good picture of who she was, both as a person and as a police officer, but Emma hadn't included any speculation about what might have led to her death.

Ten minutes had passed. She only had forty-five minutes left before needing to head back to the psychiatrist's waiting room. Emma wondered whether she should message Skofterud, but decided to give him a little longer. Maybe it would be for the best if he didn't show up. She could still cobble together another article – about a man, previously convicted of murder, who had recently threatened to kill Kovic. It would've been better to include a quote or two from the man himself, but that wasn't the main reason she had wanted to meet with him. She wanted to get an impression of whether he seemed capable of having anything to do with Kovic's murder.

She waited five more minutes before picking her phone up again and messaging Skofterud's number: *Are you nearly here?*

No reply.

The waiter came and placed a pastry in front of her.

'Sorry for the wait,' he said.

Emma had forgotten she'd even ordered anything. She should really go get lunch with Iselin when she was done. She put her phone aside, and tore off a piece of pastry, but she'd lost her appetite.

A man in his late-forties appeared in the doorway. He looked around, searching the room for someone, but he didn't really bear any resemblance to the photos she'd seen of Skofterud. The man noticed someone behind her, waved and walked over to them.

Emma pushed her plate aside, turned her phone over and came to the conclusion that Skofterud wasn't coming.

The phone buzzed in her hand. A text from Iselin: *I'm done. Took the lift down and am waiting outside. Needed some fresh air. Where are you?*

Emma shot up and grabbed her jacket. Started to type out a reply while walking towards the door.

Sorry. I'll be there in three. Everything okay?

As she passed the counter, she bumped into a man holding a particularly full cup of coffee.

'Oh god, sorry about that,' she said.

The man grimaced, a look of irritation on his face as he shook the hot coffee off his fingers. She apologised again and eventually got a sulky 'it's fine' in return.

She walked out and hurried over Karl Johans gate, back to Torggata. No reply from Iselin yet, no sign that she'd even opened the message.

A tram blared its horn at a black car that had come to a stop on the rails just outside the cathedral. The sudden noise made the driver jump into action, the tyres of the car screeching as it sped away, with the tram continuing to trundle along after it.

Emma turned the corner onto Torggata and scanned the area. She couldn't see Iselin waiting anywhere near the door to the psychiatrist's building. Maybe she'd gone into a shop, Emma reasoned, what with it being so cold out. Iselin hadn't eaten breakfast that day either, so she had probably nipped into the corner shop opposite, or one of the other cafés or take-out places. There were several dotted along that street.

Emma checked her phone again. No new messages. She sent another: *I'm here. Where are you?*

Nothing.

Emma looked around. There was a fast-food restaurant packed full of people on the other side of the street. She rushed over and pushed open the door, immediately hit by the heavy aroma of lamb and spices, and the din of people talking and laughing. But no Iselin. Emma wove her way through the crowd, into the toilets and shouted:

'Iselin, are you in here?'

Silence.

Emma had her phone in her hand, but the screen was still black. A growing sense of unease had started to take hold of her. She rang Iselin again.

Straight to voicemail.

Emma ran outside and looked frantically up and down the street. Still no Iselin.

There was a clothes shop next door. Emma ran in and darted up and down the aisles. Asked the shop assistant behind the counter if she'd seen a woman in her early twenties come in during the last few minutes.

'Don't think so,' the woman answered absent-mindedly, without looking up.

Emma tried the next shop, and the next, before running back down the other side of the street. She went in every shop that was open and asked, but none of them had seen Iselin.

She tried phoning her again, but was met with exactly the same result as before. Voicemail. Now she was scared. And annoyed – if Iselin had gone home without letting her know...

But Iselin wouldn't be that irresponsible.

She would know to give her a heads-up, to tell her. Would know that Emma would be worried. Think, she told herself. What could've happened? What natural explanation could there be for why Iselin wasn't picking up, for why she wasn't standing outside the office waiting for her?

Maybe she'd bumped into a friend, Emma reasoned, and ended up going with them somewhere or other. Someone she knew well, someone who would make her turn her phone off...

Emma shook her head, feeling the panic seize her now. She had to force herself to stop and think rationally.

Maybe Iselin had gone back upstairs, to wait inside the psychiatrist's office? That would be the most logical answer.

Emma ran back to Eivind Neumann's building. Hoping he was still in. There was a lot resting on it. She was allowed back in almost instantly. On the way up to the fifth floor, she sent Iselin yet another message, asking where she was and begging her to call as soon as she read it.

Emma took a deep breath. She's just in the toilet somewhere, she told herself. She's just been distracted by ... something, someone.

This time Eivind Neumann was not waiting for her when the lift doors opened. Instead, she found him in his office, behind a closed door with *Dr Neumann* engraved on it in gold lettering.

'Oh, hello,' he said, taking off his horn-rimmed glasses.

'I ... had hoped that Iselin was still here,' Emma said. Her voice was shaking.

'Sorry,' Neumann answered, with a glance up at the clock. 'Iselin left about fifteen minutes ago.'

'I can't get hold of her.'

A worried wrinkle formed across Neumann's forehead. He picked his own phone up and looked at it, as if weighing up whether or not he should try and call her himself, but he put it back down.

'Maybe her battery died?' he suggested. 'Or maybe she got tired of waiting...?'

The latter suggestion made Emma feel uneasy, but she nodded anyway, trying to compose herself. Her mind was racing.

'She'll turn up,' Neumann tried to reassure her with a smile.

It had started to rain. Cold, heavy raindrops hit Emma's burning cheeks as she emerged onto the street. She scanned the area one more time. It felt like something with sharp claws had taken hold of her chest, clutching on to it tightly. She looked at her phone again and decided to wait for a few more minutes. If Iselin didn't call or text back by then, she would have no other choice but to call Blix.

17

Her back ached. Iselin was lying at an uncomfortable angle on the back seat, her feet hanging down into the footwell behind the driver's seat. Body curled round beneath the window, head resting partly on the car door and partly on the back of the seat.

She glanced at the man sat beside her, certain she'd never seen him before. He was so tall his head grazed the roof of the car. His neck was sinewy, the skin on his face taut. His eyes were dark. He didn't look at her, but she could feel the tension emanating from his body. As if he were ready to react if she tried anything.

'What are you going to do with me?' she asked. Her voice trembled. 'Who are you?'

Neither he nor the driver answered.

She tried to swallow, rid herself of the dryness in her throat. The panic washed over her in waves. Her body was reliving the events of the day before. The exact same fear coursed through her body – but this time, she couldn't move. She couldn't escape. The panic hammered against her chest.

Did what happened yesterday have something to do with what was happening to her now?

Iselin regretted not screaming back there, not acting out, not having done something. She should've resisted, tried to get people's attention. But she'd just been so confused, so startled that this man was threatening her.

'I'll kill your father if you don't do as I say,' he'd said.

She'd simply stared at him at first, unsure whether she had even heard him correctly. But the look in his eye had quickly convinced her.

'I'll kill your mother as well, when she's back from Singapore. I'll kill Cecilie. Your best friend.'

Iselin had stood there, paralysed, unable to say a word.

'Give me your phone.'

She had been holding it, seeing as she'd only just sent Emma a text a moment before he approached her. When she didn't hand it over as ordered, he yanked it out of her hand and turned it off.

He had then grabbed hold of her upper arm and led her back down Torggata. It had all happened in less than a minute, and the next thing she knew, she was being shoved into a car and told to lie down on the backseat. Don't get up, don't say anything, don't do anything – just lie there.

The man in the driver's seat had spun round, the expression on his face one of shock. 'What the fuck?'

'Drive!'

'But...'

'Drive, I said. Just act normal. We'll talk after.'

A loud horn from the tram behind them had startled the driver, forcing him to put the car in gear and race away.

'What the fuck have you dragged me into?'

'You owed me...'

'Yeah, I was going to find you a car, not ... You're insane! Fucking hell, they never should've let you out.'

They hadn't bound her hands together, but she'd noticed the man had a gun tucked away inside his jacket and had his other hand resting on it, ready. The car would stop every now and then, but with the position she was lying in, she knew that if she tried to turn to open the door, he would put a stop to it immediately.

She thought of Emma. Of her dad, of ways in which she could let them know she had been taken. Think of what you've learned, she told herself. Use it. In that moment, though, it didn't feel like she could do all that much.

Their speed increased. The buildings disappeared. Iselin tried to sit up a bit, to ease the dull ache in her back, but every movement involving the muscles around her stomach and ribcage, no matter how slight, would send a short, painful spasm shooting through her torso. She tried to hide her grimace.

The man would occasionally send her a piercing sideways glance, but wouldn't keep his eye on her for long. Iselin noticed that a few beads of sweat had formed on his upper lip. The skin on his neck was inflamed. He was bouncing his leg the entire time, up and down, up and down.

From her position below the window, all she could see was the tops of trees flying by as they drove. The man behind the wheel drove calmly, without saying a word. He turned the radio on at one point, flicking through the channels until he was shouted at from the backseat to turn it off. Concentrate on the road.

'What are you going to do with her?' the man in the front seat asked.

He didn't get a response.

Iselin swallowed, tried to think – not a single rational plan came to mind. They drove for a while with neither man saying anything. It wasn't long before they turned off the main road and made their way down a narrow, gravel side road. The sound of stones crunching beneath the tyres. They were surrounded by trees on both sides now. Iselin discreetly lifted herself up a touch, straining to peek out of the window.

They were on a forest track.

But there wasn't a single cabin in sight.

She had to think of something.

It took a few minutes before they reached the end of the track, emerging into a large car park. There was a barrier at the other end. The driver parked up beside a black panel van. They were the only people there.

He turned off the engine. The man in the backseat took a deep breath, raising his shoulders up to his ears as he did. Blinked rapidly.

'Out,' he barked at Iselin.

She looked down at the gun he was now aiming at her. A pistol. Black, with a short barrel.

'Out,' he repeated, this time with a nod at the door. 'Get out.'

Iselin pushed herself upright. Opened the door. Put one foot on the ground, then another. There was nothing but forest. She could hear the gentle flow of a river nearby. Even though it was a Saturday morning, it didn't look like there was anyone out walking. She wondered whether she should shout out anyway, or take the opportunity to just leg it – she would probably have a few seconds, tops, while the gunman climbed out from the other side of the car – but it was quite a way to the closest trees, the only place she would be able to hide. There was a footpath about ten metres away, a red-painted signpost behind the road barrier pointing the way, but that was too far as well. She would be an easy target.

She turned to face the man with the pistol. And gasped.

He was attaching a silencer. Iselin froze. Panic rose from deep within her, up from the pit of her stomach. She felt it latch on to her chest, sit in her throat. She couldn't bring herself to say anything, couldn't bring herself to move. Couldn't force herself to look around again, search for escape routes.

The driver was out of the car now too.

'What the fuck are you doing? You can't seriously be thinking of—'

'I ... have to,' the gunman said, inspecting the pistol to ensure the silencer was attached correctly. He let the hand holding the weapon hang down by his side. Nodded to Iselin, indicating that she should move closer to the black van.

She couldn't bring herself to do it. A single tear had escaped and was making its way down her cheek. She couldn't even protest.

'Come on,' the man said, gesturing with the gun and taking a step closer. He gripped hold of Iselin's upper arm, exactly like he had done back on Torggata. The sensation made her snap out of her paralysis, made her remember her lack of resistance last time. It triggered something in her, made her instincts kick in, and this time, she tried to break free, to fight, using her legs and hands. But the man was too strong and dragged her over to the panel van regardless.

'No!' Iselin screamed at the top of her lungs. He grabbed her face, covering her mouth with his sweaty hand. She bit him, just managing to trap a small fold of skin on the palm of his hand between her teeth, making him yell and release her. Iselin screamed another 'no' as loud as she could, but he had clenched his hand into a fist and punched her in the same second, just below her nose. There was a loud crunch as it came into contact with her mouth. Her scream was cut short. Her surroundings disappeared for a moment, and it took a few seconds before she realised she could taste blood.

He shoved her down into the ditch behind the back of the van. Iselin could barely stay on her feet, and again felt a sharp pain shoot up through her body from her ribs as she hit the hard, dense gravel.

'Seriously...'

'Shut up!'

Iselin tried pushing herself up, to get to her feet, to try and escape again, when she looked up and found herself face to face with the barrel of the gun. She stopped, held her hands up in front of her and managed to whimper, 'No, please, don't shoot.' But she knew her words would have no effect. This was it. The end. This was the moment she would die.

She closed her eyes.

And waited.

18

'Your daughter disappeared on Saturday morning around 10:20. Is that correct?'

Bjarne Brogeland had been reviewing his notes, but now lifted his gaze to look at Blix. Blix nodded, before remembering he needed to answer out loud.

'In broad daylight,' Brogeland clarified, as if he thought it were an unlikely scenario.

Blix had thought the same, that Iselin had maybe disappeared of her own free will, but he had dismissed the idea as soon as it had come to his mind.

'I drove to Torggata to search for her myself, of course,' he said.

'You were on duty when you got the message,' Brogeland pointed out. 'But you didn't tell anyone else? Request the help of any colleagues?'

'I wanted to get an overview of the situation first.'

'What do you mean?'

'I thought there had to be a sensible explanation. I wanted to make sure she was actually missing. That Emma had tried everything, thought of everything.'

'But you then used police resources to track her phone?'

Blix nodded. 'It was an emergency.'

'But you didn't get authorisation from the public prosecutors to do that first?'

'I was getting desperate. It felt like every second was vital. It didn't help much, anyway. Her last recorded location was in the city centre. On Torggata. An outgoing text to Emma Ramm. After that, her phone was cut off from the network.'

Brogeland took another sip from his glass of water.

'So at that point, you were more or less starting from scratch. Iselin was missing, and you had no solid leads to follow. What did you do next?'

❉

Blix hung up and turned to face Emma. They were standing in the centre of Torggata. People rushed past them in every direction.

'Her phone was disconnected from the network thirty-seven minutes ago,' he told her. 'It's off.'

He could see Emma begin to well up.

'This is my fault,' she said, on the verge of tears. 'I shouldn't have left her. I should've stayed in the waiting room. None of this would have happened if I'd just stayed.'

Blix had been thinking the same thing as he drove into the city centre.

'I had requested certain protective measures,' he said, looking away. 'Security. Gard Fosse said no.'

But I shouldn't have trusted you, he said inwardly, turning back to Emma. He could just as easily blame himself, though. He could've chosen not to go into work. Could've taken Iselin himself.

Blix took his phone out again and, as he walked in the direction of Eivind Neumann's office, called the psychiatrist. He didn't give him a chance to talk, just quickly explained the situation the second he picked up.

'I could see her friend was worried,' Neumann said. 'I hope she hasn't—'

'Are you still in the office?' Blix interrupted him.

'Yes, I had a few things I needed to—'

'I'm on my way.'

A few minutes later, Emma and Blix were standing in the psychiatrist's room.

'Explain,' Blix said. 'What happened?'

Neumann stood up, a quizzical look on his face.

'How long exactly was Iselin in here for?'

'I didn't look at the time when she left,' he began, walking round to the front of his desk. 'I had initially set up a ninety-minute consultation, but it didn't last more than forty-five. An hour, tops. She responded well, but she was getting visibly tired. And it was her idea to stop for the day too, even though we had plenty of time left. We agreed to talk again on Monday. And I escorted her out.' He looked at Emma. 'She was surprised when the waiting room was empty. I got the impression she was upset, but I think she felt like she had to prove that she was strong. That she didn't need any help or sympathy. Prove that she was fine by herself.'

'Did she tell you that?'

'Not as such, but she said she was going downstairs to wait for you outside.'

Blix looked at Emma again. 'Where were you?'

'Erm, in a café round the corner. Iselin sent me a message when she was done, but by the time I got here, she was gone.'

They held each other's gaze for a while. He felt a growing desperation within him, more intense than anything he'd felt before. He pulled one of the visitor chairs out, sat down and called Tine Abelvik.

'We have a situation,' he began, concentrating hard on keeping his voice stable, trying to sound calm. 'Iselin is missing.'

'What do you mean?'

Blix couldn't keep his voice from cracking, but he still managed to get through the sentence and explain what had happened.

'I'm sending all our available patrol units,' Abelvik told him.

Blix nodded. He knew they had already wasted precious time.

'Her phone has been disconnected from the network,' he informed her. 'But there might be some CCTV cameras in the area.'

'I'm on it,' Abelvik assured him. 'I'm sending out a team to collect and analyse it now. Stay where you are.'

19

Emma had searched for a photo of Iselin on her phone. She approached people on the street, walking person to person the length of Torggata and back, showing them the photo and asking if any of them had seen her, but they all shook their heads and pressed on, battling against the powerful autumn wind.

She approached a bearded man standing on the side of the street, handing out free copies of *Klassekampen*.

'Have you seen this woman?' Emma asked him.

The man leant closer, squinted at the screen. He shook his head.

'How long have you been standing here?' Emma continued.

'Since nine.'

'The woman in the photo may have been abducted,' Emma said. 'Here,' she added, pointing to a spot on the road running perpendicular to the pedestrian street. 'Sometime between quarter past and half past ten.'

The man looked as if he doubted it.

'Did you see anyone behaving oddly?' she asked.

The sound of a police siren wailing in the distance was growing more intense, getting closer. Emma was about to move on, ask someone else, when the man leant in to look at the picture once more.

'Actually, I think I might've seen her,' he said. 'If it is her, a man was holding on to her arm, like this,' he continued, demonstrating by gripping Emma's upper arm. 'Looked like she didn't like it.'

'Did you notice what he looked like?'

The man took a moment to think it over.

'Tall, short, fat, thin...?'

'He was taller than she was,' he said eventually. 'By quite a bit.'

'By how much? A head taller?'

'Yeah, at least. I don't think he had a beard either. I tend to notice when other people do.' He instinctively stroked his own.

'Anything else you remember?'

Again, he took a few seconds to reflect.

'He might've been wearing a leather jacket,' he said. 'A black one. But I could be wrong.'

Emma nodded. 'Did you see which way they went?'

'I...' He paused. 'I think they got into a black car, parked over there.' He pointed towards the road.

'By the tram stop?' Emma asked.

'Yes. I remember because a tram came along just after and beeped at the car.'

Emma swore inwardly. She had also heard that. She had seen the same car even, which Iselin may have been abducted in.

'Did you notice what time the tram went past? Which one it was?'

'Sorry,' the man replied. 'The trams pass by here constantly.'

Emma knew that already.

❄

'What did you do after that?'

Hege Valle watched Emma.

'Well, all the alarms were raised, naturally. Blix drove back to the station. I continued searching for Iselin by myself. Went round all the local shops that had windows looking out onto the cathedral and road, and asked all the employees if they'd seen or heard the tram around 10:20. Other than one or two having seen the black car, no one had seen anything else. Hadn't noticed its licence plate or anything. But there was another possibility. The tram driver. He drove right up behind the car, so would've had plenty of time to notice details like that. So I called the company that operates the trams and asked them which one passed the cathedral at 10:20, give or take a few minutes. Three did. It was just a matter of getting the drivers' phone numbers then. Luckily, the operator I spoke to was pretty helpful.'

'And you called all three?'

'No, I only had to call two of them. The driver for the number thirteen tram remembered the incident. And he remembered part of the licence plate number too – something like AV88. It was enough for Blix and the others to locate the car on some of the CCTV footage and toll stations around the area.'

'And the footage confirmed that Iselin had been abducted?' Hege asked.

'I don't think she was visible on any of the videos,' Emma responded. 'But it was all we had at that point.'

20

The nausea suddenly hit him. Blix skirted past his colleagues and out into the hallway. He tore open the door to the toilets, threw himself onto his knees in one of the cubicles and vomited. Coffee and bile.

He fumbled around behind himself for a moment, eventually managing to close the door. He knelt there for quite some time, hanging over the toilet bowl. The heaving made his whole body shake. He retched, but nothing more came out.

Someone entered the toilets and headed into the other cubicle. Blix waited for him to finish before moving. He dragged himself to his feet and trudged over to the sink. Avoided looking at himself in the mirror. He let the water run until it was ice cold, cupped his hands together beneath the tap and splashed his face. He dried himself with one of the rough paper towels and walked back into the office to join the others.

Ella Sandland was working on analysing the CCTV footage over in a corner of the open-plan office. She was a particularly talented analyst. Blix trusted her. She had acquired her expertise when training with the Manchester police, and had helped find conclusive evidence in a number of major cases. A deep furrow had settled across her forehead as she sorted through the footage, adjusting the contrast and sharpening the resolution – but it didn't look like she was getting anywhere.

'One of the cameras must have picked up their faces,' Blix groaned. 'Load the next one.'

She moved the cursor across the screen, opened a new file and loaded the images they had sourced from one of the other surveillance cameras.

Blix paced back and forth. Occasionally glancing at the screen to see how she was getting on. She had the recording set to fast-forward, stopping it once it reached 10:20. She let the video run at normal speed.

Four minutes later, they watched as a black BMW appeared. The car stopped for a pedestrian, before heading in the direction of the city courthouse. The thought that Iselin might have been held hostage in that car made Blix clench his fists so hard that his knuckles turned white.

'Fuck's sake,' he said as the car drove out of view.

The angle was too high for them to catch anything other than the licence plate, the grille and the polished black bonnet.

Tine Abelvik was walking towards him, a few papers in hand.

'Found anything?' she asked.

Blix shook his head and folded his arms across his chest.

'The owner of the car was not aware it had been stolen,' Abelvik informed him, handing him the document.

Ella Sandland looked away from the screen momentarily. 'So it was stolen today?' she asked.

'Can't say for sure yet,' Abelvik replied. 'The registered owner said they'd only just sold it to a car dealership in Helsfyr. It was left in the car park with all the other used cars. The keys must've been stolen from the office at some point during the week. We're working on finding out when exactly.'

Sandland had uploaded a file from another camera. It looked like it was located on the wall of the courthouse, giving them an image of the car's windscreen for the first time – but only from a distance. Abelvik stood watching.

'Zoom in a bit,' she requested.

Sandland paused the video and drew a rectangle over the centre of the screen. The software did the rest, automatically enlarging the section around the windscreen. The morning sunlight was reflecting off the glass, but it was still possible to just about see a face behind it, and a black knitted hat.

Blix leant in closer. 'Who the hell is that?' he asked,

'Well, it's a man, we know that much,' Abelvik said.

Sandland scrolled back to the start of the recording, adjusted the speed to a much slower rate and pressed play. It didn't help – they couldn't get a better picture. It was impossible to discern who was sitting in the backseat too.

The car drove out of shot.

'It's the best we have,' Sandland said.

'Keep going,' Abelvik said. 'There has to be more footage. Other cameras.'

It felt planned, Blix thought. Orchestrated. As if whoever was responsible for the abduction knew that Iselin had an appointment with the psychiatrist. The most logical explanation for kidnapping her was that it had something to do with Kovic's murder. That Iselin knew something, or that she could, either directly or indirectly, expose the perpetrator.

His thoughts drifted back to what Kovic had said to Iselin. That she wanted to talk to *him* about something she had discovered. She hadn't trusted anyone else.

Blix took a few steps back and leant against the wall of the office. His gaze swept across the room, over colleagues he had worked with for more years than he could remember. People he trusted.

His phone rang. Blix tore it out of his pocket and looked at the display, hesitating for a moment when he saw who it was. He had sent Merete, Iselin's mother, a long text message in the early hours of the morning, explaining what had happened in Kovic's flat the day before. He had deliberately not included the details concerning Iselin, but had promised to call her sometime later that day. He hadn't had a chance to yet. He had no idea how he was going to break *this* news to his ex-wife.

'I have to take this,' Blix told the others, disappearing into one of the adjacent meeting rooms. He unlocked his phone and sat down. Raised it to his ear.

'Hi, Merete,' he said. His mouth was dry, his voice reluctant.

'Hi,' she responded, the word rising at the end, as if wary at the sound of his voice.

It had been a long time since they'd bothered with any small talk. Blix felt the urge to engage in it now, to delay the inevitable for just a few more seconds.

'How's Iselin doing?' Merete asked first.

'Are you sitting down?' Blix asked.

'No, I'm in the bathroom. Heading to bed soon. Why, what's happened?'

'I need you to sit down, Merete.'

She hesitated, only for a second.

'What is it? What's going on?'

Blix still couldn't bring himself to tell her. He was finding it hard to breathe.

'Iselin is missing,' he managed to force out before his voice broke.

'What do you mean?'

Blix swallowed, taking a moment to compose himself before continuing:

'Someone has taken her.'

He closed his eyes and felt his heart slamming against his chest. He could hear it too, in his throat.

'What the hell are you saying?'

Blix tried to explain what had happened. It was hard finding the right words, but Merete let him speak. When he was done, he was met with silence. A long silence. He was unsure whether Merete was still on the line, until she said:

'Do you think she's ... dead?'

'It's impossible to know, it's still...'

'Why...?' Merete began, but changed course. 'Whoever's taken her ... Have you heard from them?' she asked instead. 'Have they made any demands?'

'No.'

'Do you know who it is then?'

'Not yet.'

'So...'

It sounded like she was struggling to gather her thoughts.

'But I don't understand,' she said eventually. 'How could this even happen? Was no one looking after her? Weren't *you* with her?'

Blix closed his eyes again. He knew she would blame him for this. And rightly so. He should've handled this better. He should have taken every possible precaution.

Blix stammered, searching for an answer. Steeling himself for a tirade that never came.

'I'm coming home,' she said instead.

'When?' he asked, mainly just to say something. 'How long will that take?'

'Anything from fifteen to twenty hours, I suppose, depending on which flights are available,' she said. 'Why? Isn't it important? Could anything possibly be more important than finding our daughter and holding those who ... abducted her, responsible?'

There was a fierce edge to her voice now. Blix could tell she was bordering on tears.

'No,' he said quietly.

'So find her, then,' Merete said, sobbing now. 'Just find her!'

Blix swallowed, holding his forehead with his hand.

'I will,' he said. 'I promise.'

21

Iselin felt the pressure as he pushed the barrel of the gun into her forehead, just above her left eye. Hard, cold steel. Silence engulfed them.

The driver protested. 'Fucking hell, Timo! You can't. Not here, at least.'

Iselin opened her eyes a fraction. Tried to meet those of the man pointing a gun at her. His index finger was curled around the trigger.

'Please...' she whispered.

The man's jaw twitched. The other man appeared over his shoulder. Looked down at Iselin. Swore again. Above them she noticed a plane flying overhead, leaving a vapour trail in its wake.

The tension from the gun eased as he removed it. Instead, he traced the curve of her head, towards her ear. The man let the barrel of the gun rest against her temple, before sliding it further down the side of her face and nestling it in her neck.

She could no longer see the gun, but could feel the steel vibrating against her skin. As if the hand holding it was shaking. His breathing was strained, as if he was fighting with himself, trying to force himself to go through with it. Iselin felt a rush of adrenaline. She managed to reposition her legs beneath her slightly. She pushed herself up a bit more, preparing to take off along the ditch.

The man pulled the gun away in one swift movement.

'Put her in the van!' he barked at the other man.

'I—' the driver protested.

'Do it,' the man holding the pistol interrupted. 'I can't do it here. They'd find her.' He took a few steps back. 'And we've walked around too much anyway. There are tracks.'

'Can't we just go?' the driver suggested. 'Forget it? Leave her here?'

The gunman removed the silencer. 'It's too late,' he said, shoving the weapon into the back of his waistband. 'She's seen our faces. Get her in the van.'

The driver took the few steps towards her, grabbed her arm and hauled her up. His breath smelled awful. He guided her back between the vehicles, opened the doors to the back of the panel van and shoved her inside. The other man threw a bundle of white cable ties at him. The driver held her hands together and fastened the hard plastic around her wrists. Did the same with her ankles, without Iselin doing anything to resist. She was just glad she was still alive. For now.

The van doors slammed shut. Iselin was lying on her back. She listened as they both climbed in the front. The engine started and they drove away. The van sped up almost immediately. They hit a pothole.

Her head was thrown into the air, and there was nothing she could do to stop it slamming back down against the floor.

It didn't take long for them to reach the main road. The tyres rolled smoothly onto the asphalt. The men were talking between themselves in the front, but she only caught fragments. She managed to pick up a few words – they were short, blunt.

Something about an assignment.

The man who had held the pistol to her forehead had been given a job. He was hired to get rid of her. The driver tried to argue with him, but the discussion came to an abrupt end when the other turned the radio on and drowned him out.

It felt like an eternity before the car stopped again. The engine fell silent. She heard the men get out. Their voices. Something about taking her inside.

The driver opened the back doors. He grabbed hold of her feet and dragged her towards him. In the short amount of time it took the man to carry her in, all Iselin registered was that it had started to rain.

22

It was almost 15:30. The rain lashed against the windscreen. Blix pulled out of the station car park and turned right, heading further into the city centre. Wet autumn leaves sailed through the wind, pasting themselves to the glass and getting trapped beneath the windscreen wipers.

Eivind Neumann lived in the Frogner borough of Oslo, in a large, red-brick house with just one name above the doorbell.

'Any news?' he asked, holding the door open. 'Have you found her?'

Blix shook his head. 'But I have a few questions for you,' he said.

A look of confusion spread across Neumann's face. 'I've only just got back from the interview,' he said. 'I told them everything I knew.'

Blix nodded. He'd already read the transcript from the psychiatrist's formal statement.

'I have some additional questions,' he said, without clarifying that they were about matters he'd rather keep separate from the official investigation.

Neumann showed him into his old-fashioned study. They sat on either side of the grand oak desk. The psychiatrist leant back into the tall desk chair, while Blix leant forward, perching on the edge of the visitor's chair.

'Who knew that Iselin had an appointment with you today?' he asked. 'Did you mention it to anyone?'

Neumann pressed his fingers together lightly, so his hands formed a triangle.

'Not that I can recall,' he answered. 'But I added the appointment to our online system as usual. In our office, we've got two psychiatrists, including myself, three specialist psychologists and our secretary. So in principle, any one of them could have seen the appointment if they'd logged in to check the shared calendar. Eva, one of the psychologists, was in the office today. Eva Brattum. As was Hans Welde, the secretary. I guess they are probably the only people who would've known about it.'

Blix nodded, repositioning himself in the chair. 'I have to ask,' he said.

'I understand,' Neumann answered. 'But there must have been several people in your own ranks who would've been aware that she was coming to see me?'

The chair was hard. Uncomfortable. Blix changed positions again. 'Yeah, maybe.'

'Do you think the abduction might be connected to Kovic's murder?' Neumann asked.

'It's too early to say,' Blix answered.

The words fell out of his mouth automatically, as if they were rehearsed. But someone must've been willing to take the risk of abducting Iselin in broad daylight, in full view of a busy shopping street. It felt like something someone desperate would do.

'Sofia Kovic,' he started again. 'Was she one of your patients?'

Neumann stared at Blix for a moment.

'I ask, as I know she was seeing a psychologist,' Blix continued. 'And because you're the natural choice, when it comes to police officers seeking help.'

'I'm not a psychologist,' Neumann corrected him. 'You know that.'

'They all mean the same thing to most people. Psychologist, psychiatrist. But people at the station tend to come to you, specifically, when they need to talk.'

Neumann rubbed his neck for a moment, adjusted his shirt collar.

'I am bound by a duty of confidentiality regarding all my patients.'

'So she was one of your patients?'

Neumann didn't respond. Just returned Blix's gaze, as if waiting for the next question.

Blix sighed heavily. 'My daughter is missing,' he said. 'Her abduction may be connected to Kovic's murder. If nothing else, the killer may believe that Iselin has either seen something, or knows something. And if Kovic came to see you the day before she was killed, whatever she said may be relevant to the case.'

'I don't see it that way,' Neumann said.

'You'll have to leave that assessment up to us,' Blix replied, vexed. 'The other option would be for you to obstruct the investigation. Which I'm sure you know is a criminal offence.'

Neumann looked pensive.

'Fine,' he said eventually, holding his hands up. 'I suppose the situation is a little different if the patient is no longer with us. So yes, I can confirm that Kovic came to see me two days ago. And on a few other occasions before that as well.'

'And you didn't think this was important enough to mention to the investigation at all?'

Neumann considered the question.

'When I spoke to you yesterday evening,' Blix continued, starting to get worked up, 'I told you that Kovic was dead, that she had been murdered, to be exact.'

'Kovic was suffering from insomnia,' the psychiatrist responded. 'I didn't see any reason to believe that *that* would have anything to do with why someone would want her dead.'

His remark made Blix hesitant. 'Still,' he said. 'Would it not have made sense to at least mention it?'

'Maybe,' Neumann answered. 'But I thought, as far as I was concerned, Kovic was still entitled to my confidentiality.'

Blix tried to calm himself down, think clearly.

'She was having trouble sleeping, you say,' he started again. 'Did she say why?'

Neumann took a while to deliberate what he'd been asked.

'I ... consider that confidential information,' he eventually said.

Blix felt his anger peak. He had the sudden urge to storm out, but forced himself to stay sitting.

'I can get a warrant,' he said. 'It would be better if we were able to avoid even more obstructions and delays to the investigation though, as things are.'

Neumann stood up, crossed his hands in front of him.

'Sorry,' he said. 'But you'll have to come back with a warrant. The health board carry out regular checks to ensure all laws and regulations are being complied with. If I don't follow the rules, in the worst case, I could lose my licence.' He held his hands out and shrugged apologetically. 'I hope you understand,' he concluded. 'I'm not trying to be difficult.'

Blix sighed.

'Thanks for cooperating,' he said bitterly.

23

The droplet of water that fell from the ceiling landed in the exact same place as the last. The spot, less than a metre from where she was sitting with her back pressed up against the wall, was slowly growing, the damp spreading across the floor.

Iselin swallowed.

She was alive, but knew it was only a matter of time until she wasn't. Yet she also knew that in the end, the man who had accepted the job couldn't go through with it. She'd heard of that happening to hunters. They could be decked out in their kit, guns locked and loaded, but once the animal comes into range, they can't bring themselves to pull the trigger. They'd touched on it in one of the modules for the Police University College's firearms training course. Humans had an inherent resistance to taking the life of another living being. The first time soldiers serving in a war zone have to actually shoot at someone, eighty-five percent of them deliberately aim to miss. The next time is different.

Still bound at the ankles, she pulled her legs up to her chest. Even with the cable ties keeping her wrists together, she was able to slide her arms around her knees, hugging them in tight. She tried to retain her warmth by making herself as small as possible. There was a draught coming from further inside the dark building – an open window or a hole in the roof somewhere. The air was heavy with the overwhelming stench of solvents. And tobacco. One of her captors smoked.

The sound of a plane flying overhead made her lift her gaze to the ceiling. It wasn't the first time she'd heard one. It sounded like it was ascending, as if it had only just taken off. She sat and listened to see if she could hear any more, soon realising they were passing over constantly. Wherever they were keeping her couldn't be far from Oslo Gardermoen Airport. Meaning she wasn't far from Oslo either, she reasoned. From her father. The police.

A door slammed somewhere down the hall. Not long after, she heard voices, but she couldn't quite catch what they were saying.

Her chest constricted.

The men exchanged a couple more words. She managed to pick out a few. Something along the lines of completing the job.

The cable ties were starting to slice into the skin of her wrists. It wouldn't be long before they bled.

'You can sort this out yourself. I'm out of here.'

The driver.

'You can't leave now,' the other voice retaliated. 'You're just as involved in this as I am.'

Timo. Or at least that's what the driver had called him. He was the one with the gun, but he wasn't the same man she'd fought with at Kovic's. That man had been shorter, stockier, his build more ... dense.

Flashbacks from the fight rose to the forefront of her mind. She could hear the man's panting as he held her down, smell his body, his cologne, see his dark eyes boring into hers, that calculating gaze behind the balaclava. She wanted to shake the memory out of her head, but a sudden wave of realisation crashed over her. The revelation made her gasp, made her eyes shoot wide open.

She knew who he was.

But couldn't understand why. Or how.

I need to tell Dad, she thought, looking down at the cable ties preventing her making any attempt to escape. Iselin knew they were difficult to get off. But not impossible.

24

'Let's talk more about Dennis Skofterud.'

Hege Valle flipped to the next blank page of her notepad, looking up to focus on Emma again. 'When did you tell Blix about him?'

'A few hours later,' Emma replied with a sigh. 'As I said, Skofterud never turned up, and I wondered why, obviously. Thought it might have something to do with Iselin, so I tried to track him down.'

'And did you?'

'Yes. He hadn't tried to hide his address or anything. I was waiting outside his workshop when I called Blix.'

The Kripos investigator glanced down at her papers. It looked like she had a list of times and phone numbers.

'And that was at 15:54?' she asked.

'Sounds about right,' Emma replied. 'He didn't pick up the first time I called.'

'What did you tell him?'

Emma thought back. It was a little complicated. When Iselin went missing, all she had told Blix was that she'd gone to a café, but hadn't mentioned anything about meeting anyone.

'I told him the truth,' she answered.

Valle nodded slowly. 'Did you think Iselin was being held hostage in Skofterud's workshop?'

'I mean, it was something I thought we should check out, anyhow. And Blix agreed. He drove straight over to meet me there.'

Valle took a few notes.

'And he came alone?'

'Yes.'

'And you went in together?'

Emma rested her hands on her lap. She couldn't tell them everything that happened, just what was necessary.

'Yes,' she answered.

❆

The door to the interrogation room opened and a young plainclothes officer stepped in. He passed a note to Brogeland and disappeared into the hallway again, not once looking at Blix. Brogeland read the message and put the paper aside with the rest of his notes.

'Is that an update about Iselin?' Blix asked.

'We'll let you know as soon as we hear anything,' Brogeland answered.

He picked his pen up and continued the questioning:

'Why did you drive to Alnabru – to Skofterud's workshop – alone?'

'I was already in the car when Emma rang,' Blix answered. 'I'd just left Neumann's house.'

'But Emma Ramm thought there was a possibility that Skofterud was holding Iselin hostage there, right?' Brogeland questioned. 'Shouldn't you have called for back-up?'

Blix straightened up. 'I don't think you understand,' he said. 'Kovic had been conducting her own, internal investigation. She had obviously uncovered something in an old case that she felt she couldn't talk to anyone else about. She didn't trust anyone – just me. And that put me in a difficult position.'

'So you chose to operate on your own?'

'I drove there by myself, at any rate.'

'Because you trusted Emma?'

'What do you mean?'

'She left Iselin alone in the psychiatrist's office,' Brogeland reminded him. 'And didn't tell you that, rather than staying there with her, she had organised to meet with a convicted murderer.'

It wasn't a question. Blix chose not to comment.

'So, what happened in Alnabru?'

25

Emma climbed into the passenger seat of Blix's car. Her wet hair was plastered to her face. She brushed it aside, out of her eyes.

The windscreen wipers scraped back and forth. Blix had pulled over opposite a fenced-in area holding a car park and a flat-roofed brick building with a company sign mounted above the front door: OptiTune. Two large garage doors faced onto the asphalt. Based on the company logo, it looked like it specialised in tuning car engines.

'Where's Skofterud?' Blix asked.

Emma pointed to a door at the far end of the building. 'There's got to be an office in there or something.'

'How did you find him?'

'This was where Kovic arrested him. She mentioned it once when we were cycling past.' She nodded at her bike, which she had propped against a tree on the side of the pavement.

'He was doing something outside when I got here.' She pulled out a folder she had been keeping dry in her jacket. 'Have you found any footage of the abductors from the CCTV cameras yet?'

'Some,' Blix said. 'They're working on finding more now.'

She held out the photos of Dennis Skofterud for him. 'These are the ones I found in the online photo archives,' she said. 'You've probably got more recent ones at the station, but he looks more or less the same.'

Blix took one of them. Two men had taken Iselin. One abductor, one driver. The surveillance footage they'd collected so far was pretty poor. It was hard to tell if either of them could've been Skofterud.

He turned the steering wheel and drove through the gates.

'We should talk to him,' he said.

'What? Just like that?' Emma protested.

'*You* should talk to him,' Blix corrected himself, pulling into one of the parking spaces. 'Ask him why he didn't turn up earlier.'

They got out and walked to the door Emma had pointed at. A sign on the wall told them the workshop was closed on Saturdays. Emma reached out for the handle anyway. It was locked. She knocked on the mottled glass window. They waited, but no one came.

Blix strode over to the closest garage door and banged his fist against it. The shutter clattered and creaked as someone behind lifted it up. A man with long, scraggly hair ducked underneath and pushed it all the way up.

Dennis Skofterud.

'We're closed,' he said.

'I waited for you at the café earlier,' Emma started. 'Where were you?'

Skofterud stared at her, his eyes shifted to Blix, then back to Emma.

'You're the author?'

'Yep,' Emma replied. 'Why didn't you come?'

'I changed my mind.'

'Right, well I tried calling you,' Emma added. 'You could've told me you weren't coming.'

Skofterud tilted his chin at Blix. 'Who are you?' he asked.

'He's helping me with the book,' Emma answered, before Blix had a chance to respond.

Blix took a few steps towards the man. 'It's raining,' he stated.

Skofterud made no signs of inviting them in. He glanced suspiciously at Blix again and then over at the unmarked police car. That's when it seemed to click. He took a step back and slammed the shutter down –

Blix just managed to shove his foot underneath in time. He yanked the shutter back up with his right arm, but Skofterud was already careening round the counter, knocking over a pile of leaflets in his haste, and through a door at the far end of the room.

Blix raced after him, through a hallway, emerging into a larger workshop. Skofterud was heading towards a black BMW, but changed course, over to a door that looked like it led back outside. It was locked, and he fumbled around trying to get the door open long enough for Blix to catch up with him. He rammed his forearm into the back of the man's neck, pinning him to the door, and used his free hand to check he wasn't carrying a gun.

'I've not done anything,' Skofterud gasped.

Neither of them spoke for a moment, the sound of metal clinking filled the silence as Blix handcuffed the man.

'You didn't answer her question,' he said. 'Where were you this morning? Between ten and eleven o'clock?'

Skofterud twisted round to try and look at Blix, answering him over his shoulder.

'I was picking up a car,' he said. 'Why? What's this about?'

Blix grabbed his arm and spun him round to face him, looking him in the eye. 'Where?'

'In Vestby.'

'Is there anyone who can confirm that?'

'Confirm?'

'An alibi,' Blix snapped. 'Do you have an alibi?'

'I don't need...'

'Just answer the question.'

'No, I don't know. Maybe...' he said, looking off into the distance for a moment.

'Did you talk to anyone?' Blix asked. 'Did anyone see you on your way there, or back?'

'I stopped to get some things at a petrol station,' Skofterud answered. 'They'll probably have CCTV there.'

'What did you buy?'

'Something to eat ... A hot dog. And a Coke.' It seemed as if he suddenly remembered something, and his eyes lit up. 'I have a receipt,' he said, almost contorting his body to bring his arms round to one of the front pockets of his jeans, stretching his fingers to reach inside.

Blix watched him struggle. He pulled out a hundred-kroner note, a few coins and a pack of chewing gum. He tried in the other pocket, but found nothing there either.

'It must be in the car,' he said with a nod towards the BMW parked behind them.

Blix pushed him towards it.

'Between the seats.'

Emma climbed in and fished it out.

'10:27am,' she read aloud, holding her phone out in front of her to take a photo of it.

Blix had to see it for himself. He would have been at the petrol station mere minutes after Iselin was abducted.

'What about yesterday afternoon?' he asked. 'Where were you then?'

'Yesterday...?'

'At four-thirty,' Emma said.

'At the gym.'

'Where?'

'In Furuset. The one in the shopping centre.' There was a fervour to his voice now. 'The owner can confirm that. Lars, he's called. Lars Vikse. There's cameras there too. Not in the gym itself, but outside. Around the centre.'

Blix let Skofterud stand there, hands cuffed behind him.

'I've not done anything wrong,' he insisted.

'Is that your car?' Blix asked, climbing into the driver's seat of the BMW.

'No, belongs to a friend,' Skofterud answered.

Blix flicked the sun visors down, checking behind them before stretching over to the passenger seat and opening the glove box. He rummaged through the contents. A pair of gloves, the service handbook and a couple of pens.

He turned his attention to the backseat, lifting up a jacket and throwing it on the floor, out of the way. He pressed a button to open the boot, got out and walked round.

'Don't...' Skofterud started.

There was a small, black rucksack in there. Blix unzipped it and pulled out a jumper and a pair of joggers. At the very bottom of the bag, he found at least a dozen small parcels rolled up tightly in layers of cling film.

He took the bag to a workbench and, using a pair of wire cutters, tore one open. White powder scattered across the counter.

'Keep an eye on him,' he told Emma.

Blix looked round and spotted a door with a sign nailed to it: WC. He dragged the bag off the counter, walked inside and poured the contents of the parcels into the toilet without bothering to see what kind of drugs were in the rest. He flushed, waited, and flushed again to make sure it was all gone. He walked back into the workshop, chucked the bag aside and removed the handcuffs from Skofterud's wrists.

'Aren't you going to arrest him?' Emma asked.

'Don't have time,' Blix replied.

26

A trolley loaded with old computer monitors had been left in the hallway. Blix squeezed past two colleagues, charged towards Fosse's office and let himself in without knocking.

Fosse looked up and immediately put the pen he'd been using down on the desk.

'Kovic was seeing a psychiatrist,' Blix announced. 'Neumann. She had an appointment with him the day before she was killed, but we need a warrant to access his patient notes. Neumann won't hand them over.'

Fosse stared at him. 'I've spoken to Abelvik ... You need to leave this to her, Alexander. It's not right for you to be here, in the middle of all this, right now ... as the situation stands.'

'Well I am in the middle of this, regardless of whether or not I actually want to be,' Blix retorted.

'Have you been in touch with the colleague support scheme?'

Blix waved his hand as if to dismiss the notion. 'Don't need to,' he said. 'I need to find Iselin. And find out what happened to Kovic.'

He crossed the floor to one of the visitors' chairs, but didn't sit down.

'Patient confidentiality is difficult to navigate,' Fosse started.

'The patient is dead,' Blix reminded him. 'I want to know what was going on with her. You need to get one of the lawyers into court and get that warrant as soon as possible.'

Fosse hesitated, before nodding eventually. 'I'll get Pia Nøkleby to see to it,' he said. 'She'll need a report to substantiate why it's relevant though.'

Blix sighed. 'I can do that.'

'And then go home,' Fosse ordered. 'There's nothing else you can do here now.'

'There's *a lot* for me to do here.'

'Regardless,' Fosse said. 'You have another role. You're not just an investigator anymore. You're the relative of someone wrapped up in a case. Having you in the office is only stopping the others from doing their jobs properly. They don't know how to act around you. They're unsure, self-conscious. They refuse to work while you're here.'

A vein started pulsating behind his temple. Blix could feel it, beating away. He clenched his jaw, but couldn't stop himself:

'This could've been avoided,' he seethed.

'What do you mean?'

'Abelvik recommended that Iselin be given extra security,' Blix said. 'You said no.'

'It became clear early on that Kovic was the target,' Fosse responded calmly. 'We understood as such from Iselin's own statement. The perpetrator was after Kovic. Iselin was in the wrong place at the wrong time.'

'But then she became a key witness.'

'She didn't see him,' Fosse objected. 'She said it herself: she wouldn't recognise him even if she saw him again.'

'He can't know that. And anyway, she heard them talking.'

Fosse stood up. 'I understand why you would see it that way,' he said. 'But we took everything into consideration.'

Blix took a few steps towards Fosse, felt the rage welling up inside him. He was getting ready to argue back when Fosse's phone rang. Fosse instinctively turned to it. It was clear from the expression on his face that he needed to answer it.

'Go home,' Fosse repeated. 'Let us handle this.'

Blix spun round and strode out of the office, slamming the door loudly behind him. He headed over to his workstation, passing his colleagues, who all avoided looking at him, busying themselves at their desks.

Fosse was right. He was a distraction. But sitting at home, twiddling his thumbs, wasn't an option. This was where he belonged, where he could do something.

It took him ten minutes to write the report that should grant them access to Kovic's patient notes. They wouldn't be able to submit the application until Monday morning, and the process of getting it through the legal system would probably take a full day at least.

He pushed himself away from the desk, but stayed in his seat, staring at Kovic's empty chair. Her desk.

Her notebook was still there, next to the three case files. It made sense that she had the hit-and-run case there. It was an active investigation. She'd also had a few tasks left to complete on the rape case as well. But she'd kept both of those files in the letter basket. The third had been tucked away, hidden in the bottom drawer of her desk.

A closed case Kovic hadn't had any involvement in. He couldn't understand why she had it in the first place. But that was what made it interesting. He always looked for things like this in an investigation. Discrepancies. Things that didn't quite fit.

Blix looked round at the sound of raised voices – they were coming from a nearby office. Through the glass wall, he could see a group of people huddled around a computer. Nicolai Wibe's voice could be heard above the others. Blix couldn't catch what was being said, but it was obvious he was pleased about something. Wibe grabbed his laptop and emerged back into the open-plan office.

Blix pushed himself out of the chair and walked over to him. 'Any news?'

'The car used to abduct Iselin,' Wibe began. 'We may have photos of the guy who stole it.'

He stopped. Perching his laptop on one hand, he opened the lid with the other and explained:

'The people who worked at the dealership weren't even aware the car had been stolen. So, if the abduction *is* connected to Kovic's murder, the perpetrators would've probably stolen it on Saturday morning, which means they realistically would've only had a few hours to steal the car – from whatever time the shop opened that day. It made sense to start there, anyhow.'

Blix nodded, eager to get a look.

'We've had someone looking through the CCTV footage from the dealership with two of their employees,' Wibe continued.

A few images appeared on the screen. A man in a black jacket, a jumper with a high-neck collar and a knitted beanie was standing in the middle of the room. The salespeople's cubicles and offices could be seen behind him.

'The keys were being kept in a cabinet over here,' Wibe explained, pointing at an office in the right-hand corner, at the back. 'There isn't a camera in there though, so this is the closest shot we've got. However, they only had six people booked in for Saturday morning. The employees can account for everyone, except this man.'

He moved his finger to the man in the centre of the image. The still was of far better quality than those sourced from the city-centre surveillance cameras. The hat and his general build matched that of the man who'd been driving the car Iselin was abducted in.

Blix held his phone out and took a photo of the screen.

'We've issued an internal bulletin to all patrols, so they know he's wanted and what he looks like,' Wibe added. 'And we should have his name within the hour.'

Blix glanced at the clock. It had been more than eight hours since Iselin disappeared. His thoughts raced – it was impossible to keep his mind from wandering to the worst-case scenario. On average, seventy-five percent of victims were killed in the first three hours of being abducted.

'Where are you going?' Wibe asked.

'Out,' Blix replied. 'Home.'

He glanced back at the case files on Kovic's desk.

'I just need to grab something first,' he added, waiting until Wibe had walked back to his own desk.

27

'Should we take a break?' Brogeland suggested.

'I'd rather not,' Blix answered. 'I want to get this over and done with.'

Brogeland seemed somewhat irritated, but didn't say anything.

'Let's do a quick run-through,' he proposed. 'At 16:57 on Friday, you were informed that there had been an intruder in Kovic's flat, and gunshots had been heard.' He glanced down at his timeline. 'You arrived at around 17:15, and Kovic had been pronounced dead. Your daughter, Iselin, was then taken to A&E, having fought with the intruder. You go to her, but then leave her there a short while later, before having heard her account of the events. After she's given her witness statement at the station, you take her back to your flat.'

Blix nodded. Sounded about right.

'The following day, you ask news blogger Emma Ramm to look after Iselin and accompany her to her appointment with the psychiatrist, Eivind Neumann, while you go to work. Around 10:30 that morning, Ramm notifies you that Iselin is missing. Over the next few hours, it's established that she was abducted in a black BMW stolen from a dealership in Helsfyr. Later that same day, you and Ramm pay a visit to a man previously convicted of murder, and who had recently threatened Kovic. Dennis Skofterud. You rule him out as a suspect by yourselves, without informing the head of the investigation.'

Blix couldn't do anything other than nod to confirm.

'Just as your colleagues are on the verge of identifying one of the abductors, you tell them you're going home.'

'Fosse had ordered me to stay out of the department,' Blix said.

'But you didn't go home?' Brogeland prodded.

'No.'

'What did you do?'

'I went downstairs and took out my handgun.'

✻

Blix eased the small rucksack, in which he had tucked the Aker Brygge hostage case file, off his back and placed it at his feet. He rooted around in his locker in the firearms room and found his shoulder holster. He fastened it around his torso, ensuring it sat tight against his chest. His service pistol was locked inside a plastic case. He unlocked it and lifted out the gun. The metal felt cold against his sweaty palm.

Holding it in his right hand, he released the magazine from the grip and caught it with his left hand. He slid the gun into the holster and searched around for the ammunition box. Plucking out nine cartridges, he momentarily weighed them in his hand, before feeding them into the magazine. The spring's resistance increased as each round was loaded.

He pulled the handgun out of the holster again and slipped the magazine back in place, knowing it was locked in at the sound of the metallic click. He triggered the release and the slide moved back smoothly, inserting a cartridge into the chamber.

He lifted the gun, cocked his head to the side, closed one eye and focussed on the sight. Felt how firmly he gripped the gun. He flipped on the safety, positioned it back into the shoulder holster and concealed it beneath his jacket.

Heading back down the corridor, away from the firearms room, he walked past colleagues and either nodded at them or increased his pace and strode by without making eye contact. Just as he was approaching the exit doors, he paused, turned, and jogged back over to the lift. He wanted to make sure he had one of the portable police radios as well, so he could be kept in the loop via the internal communication system.

The lift transported him back up to the sixth floor. The copy room, where the radio-charging station was located, was almost directly across the hallway from the lift doors. He slipped into the room and picked up one of the radios that was flashing green.

Out of habit, he glanced over at the wall of in-trays. They were each labelled with a black sticker. *A. Blix* was printed on his in white letters. A couple of brown envelopes and a few loose documents were poking out, but he couldn't be bothered checking to see what they were. Not now. They could wait. Everything could wait.

Kovic's was on the row below his. A thick envelope filled the entire tray. He pulled it out and saw it had been sent from the south-eastern police district.

He stood there for a moment, feeling the weight of it in his hands. Its size would suggest the envelope contained a case file.

He tore it open and eased the file out. The key details had been stamped on the green cover: *Penal Code § 275 – Murder. Suspect – Tore André Ulateig.*

The case had been processed by the police in Drammen. They'd sent a short distribution letter with it as well, listing the number for any phone enquiries regarding the loan of such case documents.

The file was unusually thin for a murder investigation, but it looked like everything that should've been included, was. It also contained external reports by expert witnesses and documents from the health services and other public bodies that hadn't been attached to the electronic version.

He skimmed through the first few pages. Ulateig's ex-wife had been the victim. The case was straightforward. Ulateig was already serving his sentence. Blix skipped through to the final verdict, finding Ulateig's confession. There had been no appeal, and there seemed to be no doubt of his guilt.

Skimming through the rest of the file, nothing stood out or would even suggest why Kovic might have been interested in the case. He couldn't see a connection to the Aker Brygge hostage case either.

He slid the papers back into the envelope.

They were going to have to expand their efforts when trying to figure out which case the perpetrator had stolen from Kovic's kitchen table. There was a distinct chance it might not have even been from their own police district. He considered putting the envelope back into Kovic's in-tray and notifying Abelvik, but ended up dropping it into his rucksack alongside the Aker Brygge hostage case file instead.

28

Her head was pounding. The pain was coming from somewhere around her temple, travelling along a neural pathway until it culminated in a throbbing behind her right eye.

Emma squeezed her eyes shut tight in an attempt to drive the headache away.

She knew what was causing it. Her back, shoulders and neck had become one massive knot of tense muscles. She hadn't eaten anything all day either. Nor had she had a drink, other than a few sips of the latte she'd ordered while waiting for Skofterud. While Iselin was abducted. More than eight hours ago.

She pushed the laptop away, stood up and walked over to the kitchen counter. She didn't look for anything to eat, opting to rummage around for a pack of paracetamol instead. Grabbing a glass, she moved to the sink to fill it with water. She swallowed two of the tablets while thinking back on the last conversations she'd had with Kovic. The bike ride they'd been on the day before she was killed; all of the other bike rides they'd taken together. Thought back on whether *anything* had ever come up in their conversations, something that had passed her by then, but which she could hold on to now.

Kovic was a private person in many ways. She wasn't one to mention if she was worried about anything, never brought up what was bothering her; she would only ever show the positive side of her life. If she did talk about men or whoever she was dating, it was only ever comments about them in general, just surface-level details.

Emma walked back over to the kitchen table, grabbed her phone and opened their messages – a conversation that stretched back months. Texts to see whether the other one wanted to do anything, if they would work out, where and how long for. They'd discussed various cycling routes, whether or not they would have time for a coffee or a glass of something else afterwards. Emma had tried to pry into the cases Kovic was working on as well, attempts that Kovic would usually dismiss with a 'Ha-ha, nice try, hun'.

Emma swallowed hard.

'Hun' had been Kovic's pet name for her. While Kovic had always been Kovic to Emma.

She rang Blix. Didn't really expected him to pick up, but he did.

'Any news?' she asked.

'Maybe,' he answered.

'What does that mean?'

She sensed Blix's hesitation.

'I'm calling because I'm worried,' she said, pacing back and forth across the kitchen floor. 'Not because I'm snooping around for something to write about.'

Blix cleared his throat. 'They've found photos of the man who stole the car she was abducted in.'

'Do they know who he is?'

'Not yet, but the photos are good. It looks like the same guy who was driving at least.'

'So what are you doing now?'

The line went silent for a while, before Blix answered:

'Nothing.'

'Nothing?'

'I'm waiting.'

'For what?'

'For them to identify him.' There was an edge to his voice, a bitterness. Something didn't quite sound right.

'Them?' she asked. 'Aren't you at work?'

'They don't want me there.'

'Are you at home then? I can come over.'

'No,' Blix said. 'I'm not home.'

She could hear the crackling of a police radio in the background, the sound of a bulletin coming through. Another unit answered.

'Where are you?' Emma asked. 'What are you doing?'

'I'm waiting,' Blix repeated.

She had to drag it out of him. He was sitting in his car outside the police station, waiting for his colleagues to make a move.

'Are you planning on tailing them?'

'I can't just sit at home,' Blix answered. 'I can't leave it to the others.'

'I'm coming down,' Emma said, hanging up before Blix could protest.

She swung her bag onto her back, hopped on her bike and was down at the police station in ten minutes. She spotted his car parked beneath the canopy of one of the chestnut trees. A handful of wilted autumn leaves were pasted onto the bonnet and windscreen. Blix was sitting behind the steering wheel, slumped down in his seat slightly.

She locked her bike to the bike rack and walked over to him. When he caught sight of her, he looked somewhat irked, but leant over to the passenger door and pushed it open regardless.

There were two case files on the seat. He moved them into the back to make room.

'What're they?' she asked, nodding at the files.

'Some cases Kovic had been working on,' Blix answered, moving his gaze back to the rear-view mirror so he could keep an eye on the traffic leaving the station.

'Anything related to what happened?' Emma asked.

'Don't know yet.'

'Can I look?'

Emma had expected him to say no, but the impression she got from his body language was one of resignation. He shrugged without moving his eyes from the mirror.

She twisted round and leant over the backseat, reaching for the files.

'The Aker Brygge hostage case? I wrote a few articles about this one.'

There was a stamp on the front cover – *Dropped* – with a signature that was difficult to decipher. There was a code as well. It looked like it read *101*.

'What does that mean?' Emma asked.

Blix sat up slightly and adjusted the rear-view mirror. A marked police car passed them and drove out of the car park.

'The case was dropped because the suspect is dead,' he answered.

Emma leafed through the documents and stopped at a page about halfway through – a document with images taken from the bank's surveillance cameras. She recognised Aksel Jens Brekke. The financier had forced four hostages into one of the bank's glass-walled meeting rooms and pulled the blinds shut. The last pages showed the moments he had opened them again, before pressing one of the hostages against the glass. Most likely his ex-girlfriend. He'd raised the pistol and held it against the side of her head. The final photos showed a hole in the meeting-room wall, the cracks in the glass surrounding it. Blood spatter. Brekke falling to the floor.

The sniper who had shot and killed Brekke was only questioned as a formality. He'd been asked about the assessments he had made that day, and how he'd gone about addressing the situation.

'Does Kovic know the guy who shot him?' she asked. The thought had suddenly come to her. 'Sigvard Hoff? Or any one of the others who were involved?'

'I don't know,' Blix replied. 'I doubt they had anything to do with each other. She was an investigator; he works for Delta.'

'But why was she looking at this case?' Emma asked. 'It's closed, done and dusted, right?'

'I don't know.'

'What else was Kovic working on?'

'She had just the one active investigation. A hit-and-run case.'

Emma was familiar with it. 'Thea Bodin,' she said. 'Killed after a car hit her bike.'

Blix nodded. 'Neither the car nor the driver have been found,' he added.

'Could the cases be connected at all?' she asked. 'Could Brekke have hit Thea Bodin? That's what caused him to snap?'

'There's no evidence to back that theory up,' Blix said. 'Not that I'm aware of, anyway.'

Emma continued to read through the file. Interviews with Brekke's ex-girlfriend, his former colleagues and business partners. She skimmed through most of them. They all generally described Brekke as depressed and heading towards a breakdown. The business wasn't doing well, he'd been hit by several major financial losses, and after the incident, it was discovered that he had been misusing client funds. But his girlfriend leaving him seemed to have been the main factor that pushed him over the edge. Otherwise, the rest of the investigation looked like it had been dedicated to documenting how the police had shot and killed Brekke, and how their actions were correct. That it had been justified, to prevent him from killing one of the hostages.

Blix spun round to look directly out of the back window.

'They're coming,' he said, turning back and sliding further down into the seat.

Two unmarked police cars were on their way out of the car park. As the first car drove past them, they caught a glimpse of the man in the driver's seat – Nicolai Wibe, still in the process of putting his seatbelt on.

Blix let the cars get about thirty metres ahead, before turning on the engine and pulling onto the road behind them.

29

Brogeland glanced up at the red light above the camera, checking to make sure that what Blix had just said had been recorded.

'You followed your colleagues?' he asked.

Blix nodded.

'I knew they'd have found out where one of the abductors lived and would be going over there.'

'To Odd-Arne Drivnes' flat in Enebakk?'

'I didn't know who he was at that point,' Blix replied. 'But there was a chance that Iselin was there, or at least someone might've been there who could help us with information about where she might be. So I wanted to be there too.'

'And you were armed?'

Blix reached for the glass of water on the table between them. 'I assumed that Wibe and the others would be,' he answered, lifting the glass up to his mouth.

'The difference being that they were on duty,' Brogeland pointed out. 'You were not.'

Blix drank, choosing not to comment.

Brogeland continued: 'And you had a journalist in the car with you?'

'Emma's more than a journalist,' Blix commented.

Brogeland shook his head. 'What could possibly have been going through your mind?'

'Iselin.'

Blix put the glass down in front of him.

'Listen,' Blix said. 'I'm telling you exactly what happened, as it happened. I don't need to hear your opinion. That's not your job.'

Brogeland let the rebuke hang between them as he turned to the next blank page of his notepad.

❋

Their pursuit of the two unmarked police cars took them through the city, heading north via Groruddalen and out of Oslo. They drove at high speed, but didn't turn on the lights or the siren. Blix kept a distance of two cars between them.

It started raining again. The windscreen wipers squeaked as they scraped across the glass, leaving it blurred after each swipe.

After about half an hour, they pulled off the main road at Gjelleråsen and drove into a residential area. The sun was setting and the darkness had begun to settle.

Blix hung back, watching as the brake lights suddenly lit up ahead. A patrol car was parked in a gravel lay-by at the side of the road.

'The patrol unit got here first,' Blix commented. Emma nodded.

The two unmarked police cars pulled over. Blix was forced to drive past them, watching as Wibe climbed out and jogged over to the patrol car. Before losing sight of them in the rear-view mirror, Blix pulled over to the right, into the empty driveway of a house with no lights on. He turned off the engine and twisted round in his seat.

He watched as Wibe walked back to his own car. The police radio resting in between the seats scanned for frequencies in the area and crackled as an update came through.

'Kilo 4-0 arrived at location. No observations made at the address. We're going in.'

'Kilo 0-1 notice received.'

The team sprang into action. The cars drove past on the road behind them. Blix turned back to the wheel, ready to reverse out and follow them, but the first unmarked police car swung off the road fifty metres away, into the driveway of an old, detached house with a fading blue façade and a white-painted stone foundation. The second unmarked car continued on a few metres ahead, letting the patrol car pull onto the drive ahead of them. Three officers immediately jumped out and positioned themselves around the house.

It looked like the basement was being rented out as a flat. The rain running down the car windows made it difficult to see what was going on. Everything was distorted. Blurred.

Two men stood either side of the door to the basement and knocked. No response. Blix expected them to start preparing their tools so they could break the door down, but one of the uniformed officers looked like they'd been upstairs and retrieved a key.

Holding their weapons out in front of them, the officers unlocked the door and entered the flat.

Blix picked up the police radio and rested it in his lap. He could feel his heart rate increasing.

Almost three minutes passed before anything happened.

'Kilo 0-1, this is 4-0,' the radio crackled.

'This is Kilo 0-1. Go ahead.'

'Initial scan of the residence complete. Negative. November 2-1 returning, Kilo 4-0 staying on location to carry out an extensive search.'

'Received.'

Blix ran a hand through his hair. He didn't know what he'd been expecting. If he'd even hoped that Iselin was in there.

The phone in Emma's hand lit up the car interior.

'Odd-Arne Drivnes,' she said.

Blix turned to face her.

'There are four phone numbers registered to this address,' Emma explained. 'Three of them with the surname Olsen, and one under Odd-Arne Drivnes. Drivnes must be the tenant.'

Blix said the name aloud. It didn't ring a bell.

'Can you find out more about him?' Emma asked.

'Not from here,' Blix answered. 'I'll need to go back to the station.'

'Isn't there anyone you can call, who could check for you?'

'Maybe,' Blix said.

He took his phone out. The operation in Drivnes' flat was a classified case led by Kilo 0-1 from the command room of the investigations unit. The unit leader back at the station was probably the only person who had a full overview.

He called the operations centre directly, gambling on the fact that whoever received the call would be unaware of his situation.

'This is Blix, calling from Homicide,' he said, knowing that the operator would be able to confirm this automatically as his name and department popped up on the screen with his phone number.

By the sound of the operator's voice, Blix would've guessed he was quite young. Someone who would be unlikely to ask a lot of questions or object.

'I don't have access to any of the registers at the moment,' Blix continued. 'Could you do a quick criminal record check for me?'

He gave the operator Odd-Arne Drivnes' full name and address, and listened to the man's fingers tapping away at the keyboard.

'Born the twenty-second of November, 1982?' he asked.

Blix took a chance, hoping it would be right, and confirmed.

'It's a long list,' the man on the other end informed him.

'What's he been involved in?'

'Car theft, narcotics, burglaries ... An accessory to crime in most cases. Looks like someone who's generally employed to do the dirty work for someone else ... Hang on.'

'What is it?'

'He's come up in two new cases today. A car theft from yesterday, and another case classified under an imprisonment code, from today. It's confidential, I can't access it.'

'That's okay,' Blix answered, hurrying to end the conversation. 'Thank you for the help.'

The patrol car was backing out of the driveway. The two unmarked police cars remained. All of the lights were now on in the basement flat, illuminating the search operation.

Blix turned to face Emma, looked down at the phone in her lap.

'Can you publish anything with that?' he asked.

'It's a bit fiddly, but yeah. Why?'

'Release his name,' Blix said. 'Publish an article, say the police are looking for him.'

'It's not that easy,' she explained. 'Releasing someone's name and photo is something Anita has to approve first, if we're doing it without official confirmation from the police, that is.'

'Can't you do it anyway? Just publish it?'

'Yeah, I could, but ... if I don't have confirmation from the police, Anita will delete the article within fifteen seconds of my publishing it and then chew me out afterwards. Regardless, we need a photo.'

'I *have* a photo,' Blix reminded her.

He brought up the photo he'd taken of Wibe's computer screen, of a still from the car dealership's CCTV footage.

Emma nodded, delved into her bag and pulled out a laptop. 'I can call Fosse,' she suggested.

'You're better off calling Abelvik,' Blix said, finding the number for her. 'She's the lead investigator.'

Emma punched in the digits and put the call on speaker phone. The sound of the dialling tone filled the car. Tine Abelvik answered on the fourth ring.

Emma introduced herself.

'We've received information that Odd-Arne Drivnes has been named as a suspect in the abduction of Iselin Blix,' she said, but corrected herself: 'Iselin Skaar.'

Silence. Blix had expected Abelvik to ask where Emma had sourced the information from.

'Can you call me back in ten minutes?' she asked instead.

'Is he a suspect then?' Emma asked.

'We're working on that now,' Abelvik responded.

Emma had already opened a new document on her laptop and had started to type.

'So he is?' she said again.

'That's not what I said.'

'You said you were working on it,' Emma pointed out. 'That must mean you're working on locating Odd-Arne Drivnes. I presume that's why you're searching his flat in Gjelleråsen?'

All they could hear was the sound of Abelvik breathing on the other end.

'You aren't denying it?' Emma asked.

'I'm going to have to call you back,' Abelvik said.

The call ended.

But Emma had what she needed.

30

Iselin listened as the steps got louder. She folded her hands, rested them on her knees. Hung her head, unwilling to meet the eyes of the man currently standing on the threshold, choosing instead to stare at the cold, hard floor.

Would he do it now?

Was this when she would die?

She'd had the same thought each time one of them came in. Wondered if they'd managed to come to an agreement – what they were going to do, and how they were going to do it. They had guns. They only had to pull the trigger. Then the assignment would be complete, and they could leave. Continue their lives. Most likely several thousand kroner richer.

Iselin held her breath as she felt the man's eyes on her. As if he were considering what to do. She could hear his laboured breathing. Heavy. Rasping. The smoker, probably.

He turned and left.

She trembled as she listened to the steps disappearing.

She had been allowed to live for a bit longer.

'Shit. Fucking hell.'

'What?'

Iselin could distinguish between the men's voices now. The first voice had been the driver's.

'The police are looking for me. They've released my name online.'

'Just you?'

'Yeah. They've got photos from where I stole the car. Fuck!'

The sound of a door slamming. The voices got louder, but the words were impossible to discern. They were arguing. The sound of something crashing, hitting the floor.

The door opened again.

'I've got to get out of here.' The driver again.

'You can't leave now.'

'Like fuck I can't.'

'You can't take the car.'

Iselin concentrated hard, trying to catch what they were saying. She heard one of them pull up a zipper.

'It's my car.'

'I need it.'

'That's your problem. All of this is your problem. You tricked me.'

Silence. Iselin turned her head so she could hear better. A laugh of incredulity reached her.

'Oh yeah, sure. You're going to shoot me, are you?'

Iselin tried to suppress a gasp. She heard movements. Shoes against the concrete. Steps, walking away.

'I'm off.'

'I'll shoot.'

'No you fucking won't.'

This was followed by a *pff*, which was subsequently followed by a piercing scream and the sound of a body hitting the floor. The shrieking continued, growing in intensity until it seemed as if he ran out of air. Then he let out a long string of profanities – the shot hadn't been fatal.

Iselin had been handed an opportunity, but she had to act quickly. She looked down at the cable ties. Her shoes. Tried to recall details from a documentary she had watched a while back, an American true-crime TV series that summarised criminal cases and showed reconstructions. There had been an episode about a security guard who had been tied up using cable ties, and who'd managed to use their shoelaces to escape.

She bent forward and loosened the lace from one shoe, all the while listening as the wounded man groaned and swore.

'You have to take me to the hospital,' the driver moaned.

'Forget it,' Timo answered.

'I'll bleed to death...'

'Relax, I only shot you in the foot. It's just bone.'

'I need a bandage or something.'

'Here,' Timo said. 'Use my scarf.'

Iselin leant forward for as long as her body would allow. The darkness of the room made it difficult to see what she was doing – she racked her brains to remember exactly what the security guard had done.

She tried to thread the lace between the plastic of the cable tie and her wrist, but couldn't quite manage it on the first go. She cursed inwardly. Tried again and managed to coax it into place, panicking momentarily that the sound of her efforts had travelled into the neighbouring room.

Footsteps. Nearby. She let go of the lace and bent forward again. Let her head rest on her knees. Held her breath.

'What are you doing?' Timo asked.

Iselin lifted her chin to look up at him.

'What am I doing?' she repeated, trying to use her most innocent voice, but not entirely sure if she had succeeded. 'I'm not doing anything.'

He studied her. It didn't look like he believed her. The shoelace lay on the ground between her legs. He might not be able to see it there in the dark, but she couldn't be sure.

He continued to stare at her for a few more seconds, until turning and leaving.

Iselin exhaled and continued her efforts, weaving the lace through the cable tie again and using her teeth to tug on the end and pull it all the way through. It felt easier this time.

She eased the lace back into the top hole of her shoe and tied a hefty knot so it wouldn't slip out. Holding the other end between her teeth, she thrust her head back. The lace coasted through the cable tie. While tilting her head back, she shoved her legs out at the same time – using the lace and her body together to act as a saw. She made sure it was rubbing against the same part of the plastic each time, back and forth, back and forth. She managed to get some momentum, maintaining a solid pressure on the strip. And it worked. The plastic was fraying, but so was the lace. She continued with all her strength, worried that the lace wasn't thick enough, that it would fall apart before it broke through the plastic. She was sweating, her breathing hard and heavy.

And then, with a pop, the cable tie snapped. Her hands were free.

She suppressed a *'ha!'* – happy and relieved she had actually managed it. She quickly rubbed her hands over her sore wrists, before applying the same technique to the cable tie around her ankles. It was easier now she could use her hands to cleave the lace over the plastic. It didn't take long before her ankles were free too.

She jumped up.

And lost her balance. She'd gotten up too fast. Iselin cupped her hand to her forehead and waited a few seconds for the room to stop spinning. She looked around.

The floor was concrete, the walls a mixture of concrete and brick. Thick steel beams criss-crossed the slanted ceiling. A faint yellow glow shone through a skylight, probably from a streetlamp.

Through the wall, she could hear the wounded man moaning.

'Sorry,' Timo said. 'But I couldn't just let you leave. That's the only car we've got.'

'Fucking prick,' the other spat.

Iselin crept over to the wall, making sure she stepped carefully. Even the slightest sound could give her away, alert them to the fact she was on the move. She knew she would only be able to sneak out while the two men were occupied with something else. How that would happen, she had no idea.

'I need a smoke.'

The voice was close, just the other side of the wall.

She tried to get her breathing under control. Easier said than done. It felt as if her heart were about to jump out of her chest. She forced her lungs to inhale more slowly. To breathe in deeply. It helped her calm down, but only slightly. She heard the click of a lighter.

Centimetre by centimetre, she edged closer to the door frame. Peeked round. There were several bulbs hanging from the ceiling, but only one was on. There was a table in the middle of what was a large hall. Just one desk chair tucked under it. A plastic hose stretched along the length of the hall. There were more damp spots dotted about the floor in here too, and it smelled of mould. There was a pinboard on one of the walls, covered with sheets of paper, postcards and posters. Behind the table, further into the hall, was the skeleton of a car – most of its body had been removed. The hall was split over two levels, one of which was an open walkway running above the ground floor. There was a spiral staircase at both ends of the hall, so the walkway was accessible from either side.

Iselin stretched her neck a little further, and managed to glimpse the man lying there, clutching his shin, hugging his leg into his body. Timo was standing with his back to her. It looked like he was distracted by something on his phone. The smell of the cigarette smoke hit her nostrils.

She pulled her head back slightly and looked the opposite way. She could see another wall a few metres from the door – the other side of a corridor. It was her only option. Timo was still facing the other way, but obstructing her escape route. He shifted his weight from one leg to the other, glanced at the other man, before returning his gaze to his phone.

There was a pool of blood on the floor now. Under and around the driver's foot. He looked pale, like he was still in a significant amount of pain. He reached over to his jacket and fumbled about for something in one of the pockets. When Timo looked over again, the man retracted his hand and leant back on his elbows.

He'll see me, Iselin thought. He would either have to look the other way or black out before she could make her way down the corridor.

Timo took a few steps towards the man on the floor. Iselin lurched back behind the wall quickly, scared that the driver had seen her. When she dared peek around the doorframe again, she saw Timo was kneeling over the man. It looked like he was helping him with the bandage.

Perfect.

He had his back to her, and was hiding her from the driver's line of vision too.

She took one step out, entirely exposed now. It took all her strength to force herself not to run. Step by step, closer and closer, towards the opposite wall, the corridor ahead. She moved as cautiously as she could, but the light in the room was so sparse, she could barely see where she was treading. She was so close now, she started to reach out, to touch the wall, when she kicked a small piece of loose concrete. The sound of it rolling across the floor was so loud that she might as well have shouted to them that she was escaping. No point in trying to get out quietly now. There was a second of silence, followed by the sound of Timo shouting, charging after her.

Iselin darted down the corridor, one of her shoes starting to slide off – she hadn't had time to lace it up again – but she had no other choice but to keep moving.

She saw a door up ahead and, stifling the urge to scream, tore towards it. She could hear Timo coming after her, footsteps slamming against the concrete, the sound of him panting, but she didn't dare turn round, she just carried on, towards the door. Only a few metres away now. She launched herself at the handle.

Luckily for her, it was unlocked.

Once outside, the sharp autumn air struck her. It was dark now, but she had no idea what time it was. A line of trees and bushes bordered the edge of the open expanse around the building. There was a green shipping container to her left. The road was about twenty metres further behind it.

Iselin shouted as she ran, as loud as she could, towards the container, the road. Her shoe fell off entirely with the force of her foot hitting the ground. She booted it off, but didn't have time to stop and pull the other one off. She just kept running, yelling at the top of her lungs.

In the next moment, she felt a pair of strong arms grabbing her from behind. She let out a scream at the same time, a 'no' that erupted from deep within her. Timo said nothing, just lifted her up and turned her round as she frantically lashed out. Iselin tried to squirm, kick herself free, but his grip was too tight. He carried her back, step by step, the same way they'd come, while Iselin continued to scream and fight.

Once they were through the open door, he put her back on her feet, grabbed her round the neck, and forced her further inside. Only now did Iselin realise that she must have stepped on something. A sharp pain was shooting through her foot.

Timo shoved her into the workshop.

The empty workshop.

The driver was gone.

A few seconds passed by before they both heard a car engine on the other side of the building.

'Christ,' Timo barked.

He let go of Iselin and ran at the open door. He pulled the gun out, stopped in the doorway, and aimed it straight ahead.

He fired one shot, then two, three, in quick succession, but the sound of the car's engine became more and more faint as it sped away. Timo fired two more shots. Iselin heard one hit a window, glass shattering, but it didn't seem to have done anything to halt the driver.

Timo remained standing there on the threshold for a few seconds longer. He came back into the hallway and let out an almighty roar.

31

Twelve minutes had passed by the time Abelvik called back. Emma had already published the article, but Abelvik seemed to be unaware of the fact.

'Have you spoken to Blix?' she asked.

Emma glanced at Blix. He sat with his gaze fixed on the rear-view mirror, which he had angled at the house, following the action playing out in Drivnes' flat.

'Yes,' she answered. 'But you've excluded him from the investigation. Gard Fosse sent him home.'

Abelvik chose not to comment.

'We're releasing a press release in the next half hour,' she said instead. 'We will be giving the name and photo of a man we are currently searching for. You already have the name. I would appreciate it if you could wait to publish anything until after we have done so. It would also be the smart choice, considering your own safety, and Blix's too.'

Emma ignored the last remark and asked instead: 'Have you established his motive yet? Is there any link between him and Kovic?'

'I have no further comments,' Abelvik replied and hung up.

Emma turned in her seat, glanced behind her, at the house the investigators were searching.

'Is there any point in us staying here?' she asked.

Blix leant forward, as if he were about to start the engine, but stopped and leant back again.

'We'll stay just a little longer,' he said.

Emma twisted round and reached into the backseat, picking up one of the case files. A murder investigation in Drammen.

'Tore André Ulateig.'

She vaguely remembered the name from a case that the media had repeatedly referred to as a 'family tragedy'.

She leafed through the file. 'Killed his wife with a hammer,' she read aloud. 'They had three children.'

Blix nodded.

Emma checked when the case dated back to. 'Nearly two years ago. What was Kovic doing with this?'

'I've not had time to look at it properly yet,' Blix answered.

Emma flipped through until she found the transcript of the killer's interrogation. A statement at the top clarified that the husband had confessed and admitted his guilt. She skimmed the interview. Read the illogical explanation he'd given for reason and motive.

'His wife had left him,' she commented. 'For a woman.'

Blix faced her. 'Hm?'

Emma placed her finger on one of the lines of the murderer's statement. 'His wife was a lesbian. She'd met a woman and moved in with her. Took the kids.'

Blix didn't say anything.

Emma read on.

'Looks like he couldn't handle it,' she summarised. 'He went to therapy to deal with the shame of his wife leaving, and for anger management as well, but it seems like he just concluded that killing her was the only option, the only way to make things right again. He thought she was evil and that she was having a negative impact on their children. Killing her would be best for everyone. It was the only rational solution, in his eyes.'

'*Crime and Punishment*,' Blix commented.

'What?'

'Dostoevsky,' Blix explained. 'The Russian author.'

Emma had read parts of it, but it hadn't made much of an impression on her.

'The protagonist – Raskolnikov – devises a scheme to kill an evil pawnbroker,' Blix continued. 'He steals her money and ensures she can't harm anyone else again. He convinces himself that he's acting morally, doing the right thing, and because of that, he considers himself above the law. So his own evil act is balanced out by all the good that will inevitably come from it.'

Emma tried to follow the reasoning.

'He thought he was an extraordinary person who could take people's lives without remorse,' Blix added, with a nod towards the documents lying on her lap. 'Raskolnikov, I mean. In the book.'

Emma sat there, contemplating what he'd said. She unlocked her phone. Her article had been picked up by various other news outlets and had been shared across social media. It was only a matter of time before other journalists turned up.

'I should take some photos,' she said.

She opened the car door to climb out. The light inside the car came on automatically.

'Wait!' Blix urged, grabbing her arm.

A car had appeared, driving down the road behind them at high speed, but slammed on the brakes and came to an immediate stop. Emma closed the door again. The car, a black panel van, rolled slowly towards them. It was difficult to see much in the dark, but it looked like there was just one person inside.

The van passed beneath a streetlamp. The pale light fell across the driver's seat. The man behind the wheel was wearing a black beanie and black leather jacket.

'Drivnes,' Blix uttered.

A moment later, the van had swung into another driveway and made a sharp U-turn. Blix threw the car into reverse. It leapt backward as the gravel shot out from under the wheels and he jerked the steering wheel round. The tyres spun as they met the wet asphalt. And then they gained traction.

32

Blix soon caught up with the dark panel van. He drove up right behind it, flashing his headlights in an attempt to make it pull over. It only sped up.

Emma grabbed the door handle.

'Shouldn't you call someone for back-up, to help stop him?' she asked. 'For a road block, or a spike mat or something?'

Blix clenched his jaw and concentrated on the road. He didn't want to involve the others. Didn't want to waste time taking Drivnes to the station, going through the whole interrogation process, getting the photographs, taking his fingerprints, registering and cross-referencing his DNA. Didn't want him having access to a lawyer, or having some other investigator sat opposite him, questioning him. He wanted to talk to him himself, no unnecessary delays. No formalities.

The road was dark, the surface wet. They rounded a corner and emerged onto a long, straight stretch of road. An oncoming car passed by, leaving the other lane open. Blix pulled out, slammed his foot on the gas pedal and accelerated, so the cars were side by side.

The man in the black van swerved towards them, forcing Blix to yank the steering wheel down and pull onto the side of the road. The tyres met the edge of the asphalt, jolting the car off course. The steering wheel jerked in Blix's hands. Lamp posts and trees shot by mere inches from the window. A branch whipped the windscreen. Blix forced his foot down on the brakes, letting the van get ahead again before hauling the car back onto the road. The tyres screeched against the slippery ground as he, again, slammed his foot down on the accelerator.

Blix continued his efforts, driving up close behind the van. Bumper to bumper. The sound of metal scraping. Emma yelled out in the seat next to him.

The road curved ahead. The van suddenly swerved off onto a narrow side road. The tyres squealed as Blix changed direction at the last second, attempting to follow the van off the main road. The rear wheels lost grip and the car spun. He braked hard and tried to straighten up, gaining control again as they lurched forward.

He let the van get a few cars' lengths ahead of him, before speeding up and ramming it.

Crunching metal. The van jolted forward, but the collision hadn't been powerful enough for the driver to lose control of the vehicle.

Blix moved his foot over to the brake pedal, allowed the car to get ahead slightly before making another attempt. He pulled the car all the way over to the other side of the road, before wrenching the steering wheel back, ensuring that they hit the back corner of the van. Their seat belts constricted immediately. He was worried the airbags would deploy. The van spun across the road. It skidded sideways, continuing for a short distance before disappearing off the side of the road, down a slope. Chunks of grass and soil flew into the air before its journey came to an abrupt end against a tree trunk. The headlights flashed briefly before cutting out.

Blix threw the car door open, stormed down the slope, towards the van. He tore open the driver's door and dragged the man out. Drivnes protested, shouting out in pain. Blix slammed him against the side of the van.

'Where is she?' Blix exploded.

Spit landed on the man's face.

'It wasn't me,' he said, trying to turn away. 'It wasn't me!'

'Where is she?' Blix roared.

The man tried to string a few words together, his speech incoherent.

'It's Timo. Timo has her. Timo Polmar. I don't know anything. I was just told to get him a car, but he's mental. He shot me...'

Emma had climbed out of the car now, but was waiting up on the roadside.

'Check the van!' Blix shouted to her.

She slipped as she made her way down the bank, but steadied herself and got to the back of the van, opening the doors. The rainwater from the roof washed over her face.

'Empty!' she shouted back.

Fists clenched, Blix tightened his grip around the man's jacket collar.

'Where is she?' he repeated, pulling him up once more and driving him into the side of the van.

He didn't answer.

Blix took his pistol from out of his shoulder holster. Took the safety off and held the mouth of the gun so it was resting under Drivnes' chin.

'Blix...' Emma spluttered. 'Don't...'

'I can show you,' Drivnes stammered. 'It's not far.'

Blix stared at him for a few seconds, before tucking the gun back into his holster and dragging the man back up the slope, onto the deserted road. They slipped on the wet grass but Emma helped them get back to their feet.

'You're driving,' he told her, forcing Drivnes into the backseat before any other cars appeared.

33

Iselin was on the floor again, leaning against the wall, her hands bound behind her back this time. A few metres away, the driver's blood had turned a dark crimson as it started to dry. She tried to avoid looking at it, but it was hard to ignore.

The sight of blood had always made her queasy. A bit stupid for an aspiring police officer, but she'd thought she would get used to it with time.

Time.

She lowered her head, resting it between her knees.

She was only twenty-three. Some people lived until they were well over a hundred. Her father was forty-eight, and her mother forty-six. They'd both lived more than twice as long as she had ... had both experienced so much. Iselin wasn't sure whether she would even survive the evening.

She thought about her father, what he would be doing now. Thought about whether her mother had been informed that she was missing. She thought of all the things she wished she'd done, everything she'd do if she made it through this.

She would talk to her mum more often. She would be a better friend. Travel more. Read more. Learn more.

Live more.

She would definitely live more.

The click of a lighter made her look up. Timo had yet another cigarette hanging from his mouth. He inhaled, held the smoke in his lungs for a few moments, before releasing it in one large plume of smoke.

'Have you got a spare?' she asked.

She had only tried smoking a few times before, but was sure she could force down a few drags if he offered her one.

He looked over at her, kept his eyes on her as he plucked something off his tongue.

'That was the last one,' he said.

She nodded.

'What's your name?' she asked. 'It can't just be Timo.'

The man stood there, eyes fixed on her.

'Don't mess with me,' he said, bringing the cigarette to his lips again.

Iselin shuffled. 'My name's Iselin,' she said. 'Did you know that?'

The man didn't answer.

'You don't really want to do this,' Iselin continued.

'You don't know anything about me,' the man retorted.

Iselin changed the direction of the conversation. 'So what happens next?' she asked in an attempt to drive home how futile their situation was.

He stared at her, a look of contempt etched across his face.

Iselin nodded towards the blood on the floor. 'With that kind of injury,' she said, 'he'll have to go to the hospital. It won't be long until the police find him. And he'll tell them everything. Put all the blame on you.'

Timo ran a hand over his head, strode over to the window and stood there, staring out into the dark.

'You can get a head start,' Iselin suggested. 'Everything would be so much easier if you just let me go.'

He turned to face her again, tugged the cigarette out of his mouth and flicked it at her. He took the few steps to close the gap between them and stepped on it, demonstratively grinding the cigarette into the concrete floor, all the while maintaining eye contact. There was a cold determination in his eye.

34

Blix reached for the glass of water, downed a good mouthful. Could feel the beads of sweat resting on his skin. He could've adapted his statement. Probably should've. Made up a story that would get him off by hiding behind various legal terms regarding necessities, self-defence and justified action.

He glanced up at the camera, the recording light flashing above it.

What he'd told them could cost him his job, result in him being charged and sentenced. Sent to prison. But it was the truth, and it would've come out anyway. He had always stood by his decisions.

'Let's go through it one more time,' Brogeland said.

The clock on the wall told him it was 01:58. Blix closed his eyes, let them rest for a moment.

'Why did Drivnes head home?' Brogeland asked. 'If he already knew the police were looking for him?'

'I asked him the same thing,' Blix answered, sliding down a little further into his chair. 'He had some cash stashed away in the garage. Euros. He wasn't sure whether the police had been to the flat yet, if they'd found it. He took the risk and drove there to check.'

'And you saw him there, but didn't tell anyone?'

Blix nodded, and walked Brogeland through his subsequent actions again, how he had pushed Drivnes off the road and taken him into his own car.

'So Odd-Arne Drivnes just volunteered to show you where Iselin had been held hostage?'

Blix nodded.

'What injuries did Drivnes have when you put him in your car?'

'He had been shot in the foot,' Blix repeated. 'Timo Polmar had shot him. He also had a few minor cuts and scrapes, probably from the crash.'

'Did you have your service handgun out?'

'Yep.'

'Did you use it to threaten him?'

'I made it clear I was armed,' Blix nodded, without going into detail.

Brogeland looked like he wanted Blix to elaborate, but let his statement lie.

'What did Drivnes say about Polmar?' Brogeland asked instead.

'He said Polmar was unstable, and that he was the one who abducted Iselin. The agreement had been that he would source a car for him, but he wasn't aware of Polmar's plans. He'd provided a few services for him previously. And vice versa.'

'What did he mean when he said Polmar was unstable?' Brogeland asked.

'That he imagined things, and that he'd only recently been discharged from the psychiatric hospital.'

'And you also had Emma Ramm accompany you to what was now a new, armed situation with someone who was mentally unstable?'

'She was the one driving,' Blix explained. 'But I confronted Polmar alone.'

❉

They were heading in the direction of Jessheim, to a closed-down car repair workshop. Blix sat in the middle seat, pressing Odd-Arne Drivnes up against the car door. He had fastened Drivnes' seatbelt through his own, and then handcuffed him to it for good measure.

Emma left the motorway when he instructed her to, taking the first exit at the next roundabout. They drove down a road with hotels dotted along each side, across one more roundabout and past a petrol station with a McDonald's. They continued down a straight road with warehouse after warehouse looming over them. The lights from a plane not long since taken off from Oslo Gardermoen Airport could be seen shooting across the dark sky above.

They approached yet another roundabout.

'Left here,' Drivnes said.

Emma slowed down. A bus braked behind them, stopping just inches from their bumper, but continued straight on once Emma had turned left, onto a narrower, less-used road. A forest lined their right side. The other looked like it had once been home to a forest too, but was now a barren plot of land. Gigantic, slanted grey roofs of various warehouses could be seen just ahead.

'Turn here,' Drivnes said, jerking his head to a car park on the left.

'Drive on a bit,' Blix told her. 'You can let me out up the road instead.'

Emma continued. Drivnes pointed out a large, multi-storey building towards the back of the plot. A faint light illuminating the interior could be seen through some of the windows, otherwise the building's façade was only partially lit by the glow of the nearby lamp posts.

Blix scanned the area. Noted all the doors and windows, the areas in light and those shrouded in darkness.

'Okay,' he said once there was enough space between them and the building. 'Stop here.'

35

Timo Polmar walked purposefully over to the workbench. He pulled out a drawer and rummaged inside, then closed it and opened the next one down. He stood there, staring into the drawer for a minute before smacking his forehead with the palm of his hand and walking off, further into the spacious workshop, to another counter. There, he delved into a box and found what he was looking for. A roll of duct tape.

He inspected it, unrolled a few inches and tore a strip off. He looked satisfied. Iselin stiffened – she felt a sudden twinge of pain coming from her bare foot. She moved a touch, trying to find a more comfortable position on the hard concrete floor.

Timo strode over to the other side of the room, opened a cabinet and pulled out a rope, which he coiled into one large loop and hung over his shoulder.

The lights of a car driving by on the road outside flashed through the high windows. Iselin could see how they bathed the nearest trees in light.

Timo crouched down, crept over to the window and peeked out. It was the first time she'd registered any movement outside. It gave her hope.

'You know they'll find where we are,' Iselin said. 'It's just a matter of when.'

He glanced back at her.

'You should go,' she continued. 'Before it's too late.'

She stretched her neck up and wriggled a little to try and see what was going on outside as well.

'If you leave now, you'll have the advantage.'

The car lights disappeared. Timo turned and walked back over to her, grabbed her under the arm and hoisted her up. Iselin tried to pull away from him, but with her hands tied behind her back, she had no way of resisting.

He shoved her ahead of him. Her body felt heavy, her legs numb. She fell, but was heaved back onto her feet again. And that was when she saw what he had made with the rope.

A noose.

36

'So you found where Iselin and her captor were,' specialist investigator Hege Valle stated, keeping her gaze on Emma. 'And you didn't notify anyone else?'

Emma paused before answering.

'Do you have children, Valle?'

The investigator pursed her lips. '*I'll* be the one asking the questions,' she replied.

'For those of us who don't have children, I think it's impossible to imagine what it must have been like to be in Blix's situation. He saw an opportunity to save his daughter. He took it.'

'Without even considering what was right or wrong.'

'Oh, no, I'm sure he thought about it, but I reckon he was focussed on saving Iselin, first and foremost.'

Valle's mouth stayed as one tight line.

'He killed a man,' she said.

'Yes ... he did.'

'He shot him four times.'

'That may be. I wasn't counting.'

Valle leant back in her chair. 'That wasn't the first time he'd shot someone either,' she pointed out.

Emma stared at her, felt a flame of anger erupt inside her.

'He shot your father,' Valle stated.

'That was over twenty years ago,' Emma rebuked. 'And it was the only solution. In fact, they use it as an example at the Police University College. As a justified use of deadly force.'

'It's not been that long since he was involved in another shooting,' Valle continued. 'In Nydalen. Which also ended in a fatality.'

Valle stared at Emma, as if waiting for her to answer. Emma decided not to rise to it. The investigator shuffled a few documents and returned to the case at hand:

'And the plan was for Blix to go in alone?' she asked.

Emma suddenly felt very aware of herself.

'That was the plan, yes.'

❄

Emma turned in her seat, glancing over her shoulder at Odd-Arne Drivnes in the back.

'What do we do with him?' she asked.

'You stay here and keep an eye on him,' Blix answered.

Emma shook her head. 'You can't go in alone,' she said. 'I'm going with you.'

'Too risky.'

'I don't want to stay here alone,' Emma said, with a nod into the back. 'With him.'

'You've got to take me to the hospital,' Drivnes moaned.

'After,' Blix said, climbing out.

He bent down to the driver's window and looked Emma in the eye. 'Call Abelvik,' he said. 'Tell her where we are. *Do not* follow me in there.'

She nodded reluctantly.

Blix turned and disappeared into the shadows.

37

Blix had to concentrate on regulating his breathing. Tried to draw the oxygen deep into his lungs as he approached the building where Iselin was likely being held captive. There was a chill in the air, but Blix was sweating.

The building was formerly used as a car-repair workshop. There were heaps of scrap metal and rogue car body parts on the asphalt in front of it. Behind a caravan and a white trailer, sparse forest lined the edge of the car park.

Blix crept round to the back of the building and came to a locked door. He carried on, passing a green shipping container. There was a pile of spray-paint cans on the ground beside it. A little further on from the container, Blix caught sight of one white trainer. It had no laces and looked suspiciously clean against the brown autumn leaves covering the black asphalt. It can't have been there for long.

It looked like Iselin's.

He left it there and, now crouching slightly, hurried to the next door. Also locked, but this one had a mottled window.

Blix looked down, scanning the ground around his feet, and found a stone with a particularly sharp edge to it. Pulling the sleeve of his jacket around it, he paused, trying to estimate the force and strength he would need to use, then knocked it against the windowpane. The sound of the glass cracking rang out into the night. He hoped it hadn't alerted anyone inside. Blix stood still, listening intently. No footsteps, no shouting. Nothing to indicate that anyone had heard him.

He eased the shards of glass out of the frame and laid them down carefully, trying to avoid making any more noise. It didn't take long until the hole was big enough for him to slip his arm through and turn the lock.

He tip-toed inside, onto the concrete floor, carefully shutting the door behind him and pulling out his gun. The combined aroma of numerous chemicals grew almost overwhelming as he crept down a corridor, finding his way by the only light, which came from the green emergency-exit sign on the wall.

The rain drummed against the roof, drowning out the sound of his movements. He suddenly heard a noise coming from deeper within the building. A loud, metallic clang.

There was someone there.

Blix followed the sound, eventually reaching a curtain of transparent plastic. He used the barrel of the gun to move the sheet aside and peek through. No sign of Iselin or her captor.

Blix carried on, into another room with a single fluorescent lamp dangling from the ceiling, and then through another door. He emerged into a large hall. A workshop. He could hear someone whimpering, the sound of stifled sobs. Fast, nasal breathing.

He stopped in his tracks.

Lifted his gaze.

And felt the air leave his body.

Iselin – standing on the edge of the narrow walkway above. She had a thick strip of duct tape plastered tight over her mouth. Her hands were bound behind her back. A noose hung around her neck. The rope was fastened to a hook, which was itself connected by a chain to a hoisting device dangling from a pulley on the high ceiling of the workshop, presumably used for lifting engines out of cars, or moving large car parts around the room.

A tall man stood on the other side of the railing behind her. He had some sort of device in his hands – a large, mechanical remote control. The chain clattered as he pushed various buttons. The rope twitched.

'Armed police!' Blix shouted, pointing the gun at him. 'Stay where you are!'

Iselin's wide, petrified eyes found his.

Blix concentrated on the man holding the device.

'Easy now,' he said, keeping the gun aimed at him. 'Don't do anything stupid.'

He began to move towards the spiral staircase leading up to the walkway.

'Don't come any closer,' the tall man warned him.

'Put the control down!' Blix shouted back.

The metal shook beneath his feet as he took the first few steps up the staircase.

He could hear the rattling of the mechanism above them again. The rope gave a violent jerk as the pulley began to move away to the other side of the room, taking the rope with it, making it tighter and tighter, centimetre by centimetre. It would eventually tug the rope far enough across the room that Iselin would lose her footing and be dragged off the walkway. She would hang there in the middle of the room, the slip knot choking her.

Blix stormed up the rest of the steps, leaping up two at a time. The sound of the metal quaking beneath him thundered around the room.

He heard Iselin's muffled scream behind the tape. The pulley continued to roll away. The rope stiffened. She fought against it, but there was nothing she could do. In a few seconds, she would be hauled off the walkway.

38

Emma stood beneath the canopy of a particularly dense tree, staring at the building – at the spot where Blix had disappeared into the shadows. She didn't want to wait in the car, even though the man in the backseat was still handcuffed to the seat belt.

Some of the rain found its way through the foliage, forging a stream through her hair and down her face. She wiped it away with her hand. It had been seven minutes since she'd called the police. A lorry had backed into a port in one of the other buildings at the far end of the industrial estate. Aside from that, there had been no other traffic. No movement.

She glanced back at the car, checked the time on her phone again and made her mind up. She didn't necessarily need to go into the building, but she could move closer. Be closer to Blix if he needed any help.

She crouched down slightly, trying to make her body smaller, and ran, head bowed, towards the closest part of the building, aiming for an old caravan. She hid behind it for a moment, but couldn't hear anything. She should find somewhere closer.

Her phone started to vibrate in her hand. It was Anita Grønvold, her boss and editor at news.no. She let it ring. As soon as the buzzing stopped, she moved, creeping around the back of the building. The light from a nearby lamp post reflected off the windows.

She spotted a door with a shattered pane of glass and inched over to it. She stood and listened. The only thing she could hear was the rain.

She tried the handle. It was unlocked. There were wet footprints on the concrete floor, heading further in.

She closed the door slowly behind her and followed the footsteps down the corridor, until a sudden sound made her stop dead.

A sharp, hard bang echoed through the building.

A gunshot, Emma thought.

The same sound rang out again.

And then two more times, in quick succession.

39

Timo Polmar sprinted to the other end of the walkway. The mechanism worked ruthlessly without him. The rope was now taut. Iselin was being pulled by her neck. Closer and closer to the edge.

Blix leapt up the last steps and threw himself towards Iselin. He stretched his arm out, but she lost her footing. She fell from the walkway, hanging from the ceiling, kicking her legs out wildly. Blix groped into the air after her, but couldn't quite reach.

He yelled incoherently.

The pulley continued to move towards the other end of the workshop.

The electric hum of the motor suddenly cut short. The pulley stopped. Iselin hung there, in the centre of the room, swinging from side to side like a pendulum. All that could be heard was her muffled gurgling.

Polmar was halfway down the spiral staircase, getting further away with every second, and the remote control with him.

The sounds coming from Iselin died down. Stopped entirely.

Blix lifted his gun, tilted his head to the side slightly, closed one eye and followed Polmar through the sight.

He pulled the trigger. Registered one of Iselin's feet making a convulsive movement out of the corner of his eye.

There was no time.

He wouldn't be able to stop the man, get the remote and pull Iselin back. He shifted his focus. Lifted the gun and aimed it at the rope. Fired once and watched, desperation filling him as only a few of its fibres frayed. He fired again. The sound echoed around the vast workshop, but the impact was equally ineffective.

He kept his finger hovering over the trigger. Blix followed the swinging movement of the rope. He took a deep breath, pulled it and fired two shots in quick succession.

The impact frayed the final few fibres and the rope split apart.

It was like everything happened in slow motion.

Iselin fell.

And fell.

And fell.

Blix stood paralysed, watching from the walkway. Eyes following her body with each centimetre as she neared the floor. Falling from that height, her body started to rotate, forcing her to spin mid-air. The entire time she fell, Blix kept thinking to himself: I was too late, I was too late!

She hit the floor.

The sound of her head meeting the concrete below...

Blix held his breath. Hung over the handrail.

Iselin lay there.

Motionless.

40

A door separated Emma from the room where the shots had been fired. The light coming from the other side shone through the cracks in the door frame. The only other light illuminating the dark corridor was coming from the sign marking the emergency exit.

The shots were followed by a deafening commotion. A booming, as if from distant thunder. She associated the sound with a memory from somewhere deep in her subconscious: the wheelchair ramp they had at school. The shaking of the steel as the pupils all ran up it.

She should get out. Go back down the corridor, back outside, or run through one of the side doors. Find a place to hide, somewhere out of the way. Yet she approached the door instead, and slowly opened it.

The hinges creaked. She closed her eyes to try and block out the sound of its high-pitched grating against the frame, but opened them again almost immediately.

There was a body in the middle of the room, sprawled in an unnatural position on the dirty concrete floor.

Iselin.

Emma opened her mouth, but nothing came out. Her vision blurred. Her legs felt like they were about to give out – she had to use the door frame to steady herself.

A tall man was running across the room. He curved round Iselin and was heading right at her. He made a movement with his hand, as if trying to wave her out of the way. The other hand moved to his back.

Emma couldn't quite grasp what happened. She heard a gunshot, but couldn't figure out where from. Four deafening shots. The sound reverberating around the concrete walls almost made them sound like one, unified shot – one massive explosion.

The noise made her instinctively throw herself to the ground. The man who had been charging at her was now suspended in mid-air. Back arched. Chest forward, shoulders and head flung backward. A pistol drifted out of his hands. He crashed to the floor in front of her and lay there on his stomach, head to the side.

Someone shouted. Emma looked up to see Blix on the walkway above. He screamed his daughter's name. A cry of complete despair. Trembling, pained.

Iselin hadn't moved.

Emma pushed herself up, looked down at the man below her. His eyes were wide open, glassy. His jacket was torn apart at the back. Blood seeped through the wounds where the bullets had hit him.

41

The echo from the gunshots rang round Blix's head. Polmar's body had collapsed into a pile on the floor. Blix stood there, gasping for breath. His face was cold, his hands clammy. His chest constricted. He registered every heartbeat, couldn't get his brain to think clearly. His vision flickered in and out. He concentrated, focussing on Iselin. On the concrete floor, lifeless.

He called out her name. Forced his legs to move. Rushed towards the spiral staircase, but hit his head on something protruding from the wall. He fell back and lost grip of the pistol. Warm blood streamed down his head and into his eyes. The gun tumbled down the metal steps before sliding across the concrete and coming to a stop on the ground floor below him.

Blix pushed himself to his feet again. Jumped down the steps, taking several at a time. The construction shook violently beneath him.

Emma was already hovering over Iselin. Kneeling beside her, she had ripped the strip of duct tape off her mouth and removed the noose from around her neck, but moved aside once Blix reached them.

'Iselin,' he whispered, taking hold of her shoulders. 'Can you hear me? Dad's here. Dad's here.'

A deep gurgle forced its way up her throat.

Blood trickled out of the corner of her mouth, seeped out of one of her ears.

He lifted an eyelid. Her eye was bloodshot, the pupil unresponsive to the light.

He clasped a hand around her limp hand, lifted her chin up with the other so that she could breathe more easily, but he was scared of moving her any more than was necessary.

'Iselin,' he howled desperately and turned to Emma. She was standing behind him now, phone to her ear, already explaining the situation to an emergency operator.

'Is she breathing?' Emma asked, moving the phone away from her ear slightly.

Blix rested his ear on Iselin's chest. He could hear gurgling, but was unsure whether she was trying to breathe or if it was the sound coming from her damaged internal organs.

'I don't know.' His voice broke on the last word.

He held two fingers to her neck and waited. Registered a faint pulse. Emma relayed instructions from the emergency operator. Blix pulled Iselin's chin down and blew twice into her mouth while pinching her nose. Her ribcage expanded, rising and sinking.

He pushed himself onto his knees again, interlocked one hand on top of the other and placed them on her chest. With his arms held out straight, he pushed down. Tried to find a steady rhythm, but knew he was doing it too quickly. He tried to compose himself, while his eyes still frantically searched Iselin's face for signs of life.

Nothing.

He counted out loud, stopping at thirty, bending down to blow twice more into her mouth before returning to the chest compressions.

'Come on,' he told her. 'Breathe. Breathe.'

He registered the sound of sirens in the distance. He glanced at Emma, knew that the ambulance couldn't be here already. Abelvik must have deployed all units to their location.

'Go outside, show them where we are.'

Emma protested, but Blix interrupted her.

'Out!' he ordered. 'Tell them that the building is secure.'

He nodded at Timo Polmar's body. The first unit to arrive would need to be informed that the threat had been eliminated.

Emma ran back the way she came in. The sirens got closer. Blix had lost his rhythm. He performed three more chest compressions and two new mouth-to-mouth insufflations, before continuing with a steady rhythm. His eyes were fixed on Iselin's face.

Happy memories flashed before him. Her first day at school, her confirmation, the time they'd gone to a carnival, one of her volleyball matches. The images were replaced with a vision that would be forever etched into his memory. The fall.

The sirens died down. He could hear the vehicles pulling up outside. Car doors slamming. Someone shouting out commands.

They entered from both ends of the building. Two teams of armed officers. Even though Emma had passed on his message, they still came in according to procedure, securing the building on their way towards them. Blix could hear them clearing each room, until two officers emerged into the workshop and stopped in front of Polmar. One stood above him, his gun aimed down at the body, while the other kicked the pistol aside, flipped the visor of his helmet up, and, crouching down, checked for a pulse. Another officer came in and offered to take over from Blix.

Blix shook his head and continued trying to resuscitate Iselin.

'Get the ambulance here!' he shouted.

The man checking Polmar's pulse stood up and shook his head. One of the radios crackled. And silence descended around them.

42

'Do you need some air?'

Brogeland's voice was suddenly softer. Blix realised that his hands were clamped onto the armrests, gripping hard. He closed his eyes. He couldn't hold back the tears, just let them roll down his face. He sobbed helplessly. Sat there for a while, unable to control his body's convulsions, the anguished thoughts fuelling his desperation, his fear.

He finally got his breathing under control. Dried his eyes.

'Sorry,' he mumbled.

'Don't apologise,' Brogeland said.

'But no,' Blix answered. 'I don't want to take a break.'

Brogeland paused for a moment, before nodding and redirecting his gaze down to the papers in front of him.

'So, you shot Timo Polmar in the back.'

A few seconds passed by.

'Yes,' Blix said at last.

'From the walkway?'

'Yes, he ... would have killed Emma.'

'How could you tell?'

'He was armed and had already demonstrated that he was capable and willing to use the gun.'

'He had shot his friend in the foot,' Brogeland specified. 'But he hadn't shot Iselin, and he didn't seem like a particularly proficient gunman either. So what made you come to the conclusion that Emma was in immediate danger?'

Blix tried to reconstruct the situation in his head. Search for the words to describe it. But he couldn't find them.

'The fact is ... you shot him four times. In the back. Without him having fired a single shot at anyone with the intention to kill.'

Blix couldn't verbalise a response to that either.

'Did he say he was going to kill Emma?' Brogeland enquired.

'No,' Blix answered weakly.

'Did he aim his gun at her at all?'

Blix closed his eyes and tried to visualise the scene, but all he could see was the sight of Iselin.

'He must have done,' he replied, rather than admitting his uncertainty.

Brogeland waited for him to continue.

'You can ask Emma,' Blix continued. 'She was the one facing him. She can explain.'

Brogeland leant back, considered Blix.

'It is very unfortunate for both of you, and the investigation as a whole, that we can't get Timo Polmar's version of events,' he said. 'We might have been able to establish a motive, taken his statement for Kovic's case, asked him if he had actually intended to kill Emma Ramm. But we can't, Blix. We can't do that, because you shot and killed him.'

Blix lowered his head.

'Did you pull the trigger because of what he did to Iselin?'

'No.'

'So it had nothing to do with revenge?'

'I had to stop him.'

'And that's why you fired four times?'

'Yes ... it was a justified use of lethal force. I had reason to shoot.'

'There will be mixed opinions about that.'

'Maybe among those of you who weren't there,' Blix contested. 'People who have never had to make a split-second decision and act accordingly.'

Brogeland carried on:

'Whatever the case may be, let me remind you that you have broken every single one of our protocols,' he said. 'First, by not staying out of the investigation as you were told to by your superior. You then armed yourself, without permission. You didn't alert anyone to the fact you were also pursuing a suspect. You forced him off the road, without knowing whether or not your actions would kill him. Threatened him, took him against his will and neglected to alert anyone to the fact that you had found the location where Iselin was being held hostage.'

'I just wanted to save her,' Blix said. 'I wasn't thinking of anything else.'

43

'Why do I get the feeling that you and Blix have coordinated your versions of what happened tonight?'

Emma looked up and met Valle's scrutinising gaze. 'We didn't have time to do anything like that. Besides...'

'So you think it was something you should've done?'

'That's not what I meant. Don't put words in my mouth. I didn't talk to Blix at all afterwards. He went straight to the hospital, I believe. With Iselin.'

Valle nodded slowly, as if she didn't entirely believe what Emma had said. Emma thought of Blix. Could still see him in that moment – his eyes, how he'd looked at her as he got into the ambulance. How she had tried to approach him, but he had just turned away.

'What do you think about Blix shooting a man four times in the back?'

Emma blinked a few times. Shrugged. 'I mean, what should I think? He did what he thought was necessary.'

'From an objective point of view, it looks like an act of revenge.'

Emma took a few seconds to process that angle.

'He ... did it to save me.'

'Did he?'

'Yes, he ... Polmar was coming towards me. He had a gun.'

'Was he pointing the gun at you?'

'Yes,' she said, followed by a painful swallow.

'And you're sure of that?'

Emma paused. She hadn't actually seen the gun before it fell out of Polmar's hand.

'Yes,' she answered, nodding quickly. Registered that her voice shook. She glanced up at the camera, shifting uncomfortably in her seat as the room suddenly felt much warmer, the air heavier.

'Is there anything else you want to tell us?' Valle asked as she flipped back and forth between a few pages of her notepad.

Emma exhaled slowly. She had chosen to cooperate, had done so from the moment the police had picked her up. What she had been involved in was far too complicated, too significant for her to not contribute without reservation. But she was regretting having not asked for a lawyer. The questions had only become more critical, and it had gradually become harder to verbalise what had seemed rational in the moment, but could be perceived differently in hindsight.

'Anything you might have held back or failed to mention?' Valle enquired.

Emma straightened up and shook her head. 'No,' she answered.

But that wasn't true. She hadn't told them that she'd kept Kovic's case files.

❄

The flashing lights atop the police cars coloured the industrial estate blue. The sound of updates coming through one after the other on all the radios filled the air. More and more armed officers swarmed the area. Tine Abelvik approached Emma and asked her to explain.

The words got jumbled in her mouth. She composed herself and managed to explain the most important events of the night. Enough for Abelvik to get a general understanding of what had taken place.

Abelvik's radio crackled, followed by a metallic voice: '*All clear.*'

Abelvik looked Emma in the eye.

'You wait here,' she commanded before turning to run in to find Blix.

The sound of more sirens reached them from the distant motorway, all blending in with each other.

'Wait!' Emma yelled. 'The car.'

Abelvik spun back round. 'What?'

Emma was still struggling to form a coherent sentence.

'Blix's car,' she managed. 'There's a man in there. The other abductor. Drivnes.'

Abelvik halted a couple of officers on their way into the building.

'Where is it?' she asked.

Emma turned to point, failing to orientate herself properly.

An ambulance finally raced into the car park.

One of the officers Abelvik had stopped took hold of Emma. 'Show us,' he demanded.

Emma went with them. She turned to see two of the ambulance personnel running towards the building. A third was pulling a stretcher from the back of the vehicle.

She had Blix's car keys in her pocket. Once they were close enough, she pressed the button to unlock it. The lights flashed a few times, accompanied by a little beep.

They could see Drivnes' silhouette in the backseat. One of the officers held his gun in front of him while removing a torch from his equipment belt. Drivnes jerked and shouted something incomprehensible when the beam of light hit him. His eyes were barely open.

The other officer approached the car and took hold of the door handle. Once given the signal, he opened it.

Odd-Arne Drivnes was noticeably paler. Sweat was streaming down his face.

Emma kept her distance. Her adrenaline was working overtime. Her body trembled. She tried to gather her thoughts, to consider her own role in what had happened, think about what would happen next.

The officers unfastened Drivnes, carried him out of the car, laid him on the ground and called to request another ambulance. Emma walked towards the car, opened the passenger-side door and took her bag out.

Kovic's case files had slipped off the seat, the documents had fallen out and were loose in the footwell. She picked them up quickly, shoved them into her bag, closed the door and threw the bag onto her shoulder.

Drivnes screamed in pain as one of the officers eased his shoe off to check his wound. Another ambulance drove towards them at high speed. Emma moved back, taking a few steps at first, before turning entirely and hurrying back over to the building.

Two of the paramedics were wheeling Iselin out of the warehouse on a stretcher. With a hand on either side of her, they rushed towards the ambulance. A third was running beside the stretcher, holding the oxygen mask.

Blix was right behind them. He tore himself away from Abelvik and followed his daughter.

They lifted the stretcher into the back of the ambulance. Blix climbed in through the side door. Emma ran over to him.

'Blix!' she shouted.

He turned. Their eyes met. He leant forward to grab the door and slammed it shut behind him.

44

Blix intertwined his fingers, clasping his hands together tightly to try and stop them from shaking. It didn't help. They moved up to his face instead, to touch the bandage on his forehead.

'I've told you everything,' he said. 'Can't we finish now?'

'Soon,' Brogeland answered. 'There are just a few things I need to clarify.'

'Can we check on Iselin first?' Blix requested. 'We've been in here for hours, and I haven't had a single update.'

Brogeland stared at him for a few seconds.

'We can call them, surely?' Blix continued when he didn't receive an answer. 'Instead of just waiting for *them* to call?'

He could hear the desperation in his own voice. Brogeland collected his papers.

'I'll see what I can do,' he said, getting up. 'Stay here. I'll be back soon.'

The sudden silence felt suffocating. Blix couldn't stay in his seat any longer. His legs felt like jelly as he got to his feet. He tried to take a deep breath, but the rigid knot in his chest made it difficult. There wasn't much space to move around, but he paced across the room regardless. Back and forth, back and forth.

He was facing the other way when the door opened. Brogeland came back in.

'They're calling them now,' he told him.

He pulled his chair out and sent Blix a disapproving look, nodding towards the chair opposite him. Blix sat down again, resting his palms on his thighs.

'Let's go back to Kovic's murder,' Brogeland said. 'In the half-day you spent searching for your daughter, did you get any further in the murder investigation?'

Blix thought about the case files Kovic had requested, but decided not to mention them. They might still be in the car.

'No,' he said, 'I was otherwise occupied.'

Someone came to the door. Two hard knocks. Brogeland shouted 'come in'. Blix turned in his seat and was met by a young female officer who glanced down at him quickly before motioning with her head to Brogeland, as if to request he come out into the hallway.

'What is it?' Blix asked. 'Have you heard from the hospital?'

Brogeland held a hand up to quell him.

Blix stood up anyway. 'Say it,' he urged her. 'Just say it!'

'One moment,' Brogeland told him more forcefully, getting up and walking to the door.

It was as if all of the air in Blix's body had caught in his throat. The images flashed before him again – her battered face, the bloody hair, how still she had been, no signs of life in her face or her body. Just say everything went well, he prayed inwardly. Say that she's okay, that everything will be fine.

A clock on the wall idly ticked by. It was nearly quarter past two in the morning. He watched as half a minute dragged by, then a full minute, before someone pushed the door open.

Brogeland entered.

The smile Blix had been praying for was nowhere to be seen.

Just the same pale face as before, the same sturdy body, standing there with one hand on the door handle.

'That ... erm, that was the hospital,' Brogeland informed him. 'There ... there's no easy way to say this, Alexander, so ... I'll just come out with it. I'm so sorry. They couldn't save your daughter.'

FOUR DAYS LATER

45

The rays of the early-afternoon sun crept through a gap in the curtains, painting a yellow line across the wall. The light shone across a drawing Iselin had done for him back when she was in nursery. It was supposed to be the two of them. Him and her, hand in hand, on the way to or from that very same nursery. It was a colourful drawing – even after years of fading, the sky was still a bright, clear blue. It was curling at the corners, the yellow paper folding in on itself slightly, with clear strips of tape across its edges just about helping it to hang on to the white wallpaper behind.

Blix blinked.

Inhaled deeply through his nose. Stretched towards the bottle on the coffee table in front of him and poured a new glass. His back ached. He took a large gulp and felt it scorch his taste buds, felt the burning sensation as it travelled down into his chest. It did nothing to diminish the screams of anguish he was trying to suppress within him.

He had never been particularly fond of vodka. Or any spirits really, but it's all he had in the cupboard – the remnants of a get-together he'd organised with a few colleagues one evening many, many years ago.

The sound of a car door slamming on the road outside reached his flat. The roar of a powerful engine starting up and racing off. Blix moved his hand up to his forehead, picked at the scab that had formed around the stitches. He sat there with the dark, dry blood underneath his fingernail. He used his thumbnail to pry it loose and let it fall to the floor; it joined a few clumps of dust that had started to gather to form one large dust bunny. As if they were lonely.

The TV remote and a pack of painkillers lay on the table beside the bottle. And a coffee cup. There was a book as well, but that had been there for as long as he could remember. Behind that, another remote. And his phone. Probably dead, he hadn't bothered to charge it. Next to it, a pair of headphones missing one of its rubber pads.

The TV was on, but he barely registered what was on the screen. He downed the rest of his glass and put it aside. Wondered if he should refill it, but sat there instead, staring at the bottle until his vision blurred and he was forced to blink a few times.

The sound of the doorbell gave him a start. Probably just someone who lived in one of the other flats and had forgotten their keys, wanting to be let in the front door. The buzzer went again. One ring. Two, three, four rings.

And then silence.

Go away, he begged inwardly. Please go away.

He reached for the bottle. Filled the glass. Tipped the contents down his throat. Some of it dribbled out of the corner of his mouth. He caught it with his tongue and used the palm of his hand to wipe around his mouth.

The sound of footsteps walking up the stairwell. Light steps. One person, getting closer and closer. Stopping on the landing outside. Knocking on his door. Three cautious knocks. Blix could hear the rustling of clothes, a short sniff. Three more knocks, a little harder this time.

'Blix?'

He closed his eyes. Recognised the voice. Tine Abelvik.

He sat there quietly, holding his breath, hoping she would turn and leave.

'Blix, I know you're in there.'

He sighed.

'I'm not leaving until you open this door.'

Blix rubbed his face with both hands.

Suspended during an ongoing investigation, was all he'd been told. He didn't know what the formal charges against him were, or what to expect, but he knew the chances of him ever going back to work were minimal. Being dismissed would be getting off lightly. It was highly unlikely he would get through this without facing legal consequences. In the worst case, he could be looking at a hefty prison sentence, but he didn't care. Reality felt so distant, insignificant.

Another knock on the door.

He placed both feet on the ground, put his hands on his thighs and pushed himself up from the sofa. Stood there, swaying for a few moments. The room spun around him. A wave of nausea rose from the pit of his stomach, but he managed to swallow it back down.

'Blix!'

He put one foot in front of the other. And again. Stepped over a jumper he'd left on the floor and headed into the hallway. Got to the front door and put his hand on the handle. In one unified movement, he unlocked it and pushed it open.

He was met with the sight of Tine Abelvik, decked out in her service uniform.

Blix could tell she had just been crying. Her cheeks were slightly swollen, puffy. There was a sadness in her eyes.

'Hi, Blix,' she said.

They stood there looking at each other.

'Can I come in?'

Blix opened the door wide for her and walked slowly back into the flat. He could hear her close it behind her, then take her shoes and coat off. He'd thought of telling her not to bother, but then he couldn't be bothered to tell her that either.

Blix returned to the sofa. Turned the TV off.

'Do you want anything to drink?' he asked, picking up his own glass.

'No, thanks,' Abelvik answered, sitting in the armchair at the other end of the coffee table. 'I've just come from the funeral.'

Blix sighed. 'That was today?'

Abelvik didn't answer.

'I should have been there,' he said quietly.

He looked down and rotated the glass in his hand.

'No one expected to see you there, Alexander. Everyone understands why you weren't.'

Blix nodded slowly. 'How was it?' he asked.

'Like any other funeral,' Abelvik answered, exhaling heavily. 'Awful. Beautiful. Painful. And multiply that by about hundred, considering the fact you're having to say goodbye to a colleague. And that colleague was only twenty-six years old. Who you saw lying on the floor with a bullet hole in their forehead.'

'Any progress with the investigation?' he asked.

'The murder weapon has been identified,' Abelvik answered. 'The same weapon Timo Polmar had on him.'

'So it *was* him?'

Abelvik didn't respond immediately.

'Everything seems to point to that being the case.'

She stood up and walked across to the nearest window. Drew the curtains and opened it. A gust of cold autumn air swept into the living room. It didn't take long before Blix started to shiver. He stood up and, on shaky legs, went into the kitchen and grabbed the jacket he'd left hanging over the back of a chair. He sat back down.

'Is there a "but" coming?' he asked.

Abelvik turned to face him again. 'Have you never come across Polmar before?' she asked, folding her arms across her chest.

Blix shook his head. 'Have you?'

'Several times,' Abelvik answered. 'Remember Elise Hurdal?'

Blix searched his memory, but nothing came. He shook his head again.

'A missing-persons case, happened around the time you were teaching at the Police University College. A young girl went missing after school. We dealt with it as a criminal case, as did the media. It received a lot of attention in the news. Polmar, accompanied by a priest, came to the station and confessed to Petter Falkum. Said he'd killed her and dumped her body in Bunnefjorden. We spent several days searching the fjord, before she was actually found over in Nordmarka. She had swallowed an entire pack of sleeping pills. Had written a letter. Everything Polmar told us was a lie. A figment of his imagination.'

'So...' Blix fingered the wound on his forehead again. It hurt just to think.

'He's confessed to being involved in numerous other cases as well,' Abelvik continued. 'Polmar was mentally ill. He's been in and out of treatment for years. There's a gap in his memory that he, for some reason or another, fills with fantasies – convinces himself that he's responsible for whatever case is currently in the media spotlight.'

'I understand,' Blix said, without really seeing what she was getting at.

Abelvik sunk back down into the armchair.

'Polmar was one of Eivind Neumann's patients,' she carried on. 'A year ago he was transferred to Neumann from a colleague who was about to take her maternity leave. Neumann had to cancel Polmar's appointment so he could see Iselin. Which could've put them in the same place at the same time. It is most likely that Iselin was an incidental victim who gave him the opportunity to actualise one of his fantasies.'

Blix took a while to let her logic sink in. It didn't quite hold up. If it really was a coincidence, then Polmar would've needed to be on Torggata at the exact same time as Iselin. He must have taken the opportunity as it arose there and then. Which didn't fit with an abduction that seemed to have been planned.

'What about the DNA?' he asked. 'From the curling tong?'

'They've only found Iselin's on it so far.'

Blix stared at Abelvik, and had to ask her to explain.

'The lab technicians aren't sure whether Iselin had used it in the way she'd explained in her statement,' Abelvik said. 'But it might also be the case that the heat destroyed any cells that would have otherwise been on it.'

'But there has to be something?' Blix protested.

'They're not done testing it yet, but that thing can get up to two hundred and forty degrees. More than enough to sterilise it.'

Blix wanted to ask about the autopsy, whether there had been a burn mark on Polmar's body, but didn't get the chance.

'Regardless, there's no doubt about the fact that he killed your daughter,' Abelvik continued. 'And it's clear that—'

'I killed her,' Blix interrupted.

He looked over at Abelvik.

'Me. I'm the reason she's dead,' he insisted.

'Blix...'

'I couldn't save her.'

'You couldn't—'

'I could, and I should've.'

'There was a chance she could have survived a fall from that height. You couldn't have predicted it going the way it did. You chose the best option. The only option.'

Blix was about to object again, but the words lodged in his throat.

'It is Polmar's fault that Iselin died, and only Polmar's, Alexander,' Abelvik insisted.

A fierce heat spread across his cheeks. His eyes began to well up with tears, and he looked around for something to hold on to, something he could flatten or tear apart. Throw at the wall.

'Don't look at me,' he said. 'Just don't look at me – I can't deal with anyone being nice to me right now.'

'Okay. Sure. Sorry.'

Blix clasped his hands together and rested his elbows on his thighs. Stared at the floor. A tuft of dust had latched on to the sole of one of his slippers.

'I'll ... leave you in peace,' Abelvik said, standing up. 'But Fosse wants to talk to you.'

'Well, I don't want to talk to him.'

'It doesn't sound like you have a choice,' she continued.

Blix made a frustrated movement with his head. Assumed it had something to do with the formalities around his suspension.

'Kripos and the specialist unit assigned to the investigation are still looking into the circumstances surrounding everything that happened at the warehouse, and whatever led up to it,' Abelvik continued. 'And there was something else as well. Something about a report. Or some notes or something, I'm not entirely sure.'

Blix was going to answer, but decided against it. Instead, he said:

'He'll just have to wait. I...' He cleared his throat. '*We* will be burying Iselin on Friday. I don't have the capacity to think about anything else right now.'

46

It was an ice-cold morning the day Iselin Blix Skaar was buried. Just a few degrees above freezing. A grey shroud of fog slowly drifted over the cemetery, making way for the clear blue sky and a blazing sun that blinded those attending the funeral at Ris Church, forcing them to squint and look away.

Emma felt numb from standing out in the cold.

It had only been two days since Kovic's funeral. Two days since she'd had to say goodbye to someone she had grown close to. Two days since she had gone home alone and had spent the next twenty-four hours ignoring her phone, avoiding every single message and phone call.

She thought of Kasper, of his funeral she had flown to Denmark to attend. Before his death, her grandfather had been the last person she'd lost, albeit while she was still in her teens. However, as someone who had grown up without either of her parents, Emma had already had more than enough experience with death by that point. Especially when it came suddenly and without warning. She had watched as people died right before her eyes. There had been several times when she thought it was her time to die too. She'd seen dead bodies, before the police had arrived and dealt with them. Once you had experienced things like that, been forced to know what death smells like, to taste the fear of it too, it becomes a part of you forever. Like a horrible, invisible tattoo.

Maybe you should just go, she told herself as she followed the crowd that was slowly forming a queue into the church. Leave Oslo. Leave Norway. Maybe you should do something else, something that doesn't put you in so much danger, something that isn't so bloody fatal for those around you either.

It was enough now.

More than enough.

She thought of her grandmother, how she should pay her a visit again soon. It was far too long since the last time. Despite everything, that sweet old woman was still alive.

Emma took the order of service handed to her as she entered the church. She looked down to see a photo of Iselin aged about sixteen or seventeen. She was smiling. That was how Emma would remember her. She would always look back on Iselin as a young woman with a strong exterior, a woman who had gone through things that had forced her to put up those walls – walls, however, that were built on a foundation always at risk of crumbling in the face of criticism or a disagreement. Emma had noticed it whenever they'd found themselves with opposing opinions in a discussion – in Iselin's searching, somewhat wary gaze over her cup of tea or glass of wine. And then in the short amount of time it would take her to change her mind and agree with Emma instead.

But what would come to mind first and foremost, when she thought of Iselin, was a beautiful woman, both inside out – someone with a kind soul, who would have certainly become a brilliant police officer, a wonderful partner and mother. An empathetic person who had great compassion for all – the tall and small, the young and old. Who would greet everyone with a smile on her face and a warm, friendly hand.

Emma turned to the first page, recognising the words to a couple of the hymns they would be singing. The names of the choir, the musicians. There was nothing about whether anyone close to Iselin would be saying anything. Emma hoped that Blix wouldn't, and that those who would, would be able to do so without breaking down, without weeping, sobbing.

She looked across the church and found Blix on the very front row. Dressed in a black suit, he sat motionless. He didn't stand up when anyone came over to shake his hand. A woman bent down to give him a hug. He didn't move his arms, didn't acknowledge her embrace, didn't return a comforting hand on her arm. Emma wondered whether she should go over as well, but decided against it. She had tried calling him several times, had sent several texts too, expressing how unbelievably sorry she was. Had told him that if there was anything she could do or if there was anything he needed, he just had to say the word. But she hadn't heard back.

The seats to his left were empty. There was a woman sitting to his right, about a metre or so away – at least a head shorter than Blix, and clinging to the arm of the man on her right. She was resting her head on the man's shoulders. Merete, Emma thought. Iselin's mum.

The rows were full of uniformed officers. She caught sight of Gard Fosse, immaculately dressed in full, freshly pressed formal uniform – black Sam Browne belt buckled diagonally across his white dress shirt and round his waist. He was standing in the aisle, directing the others from his unit, pointing to where people should sit. Emma spotted Tine Abelvik among them. Nicolai Wibe. She had expected to see Kripos' own Hege Valle there as well, but the woman who had spent a good three and a half hours interrogating Emma, and who promised that there would be more to come, wasn't anywhere to be seen. Emma presumed that some, if not all, of Iselin's classmates from the Police University College were present too. Other friends. A man a few rows in front turned round and looked past her, to the back of the church. Emma recognised him from the *Worthy Winner* production team, the reality TV show Iselin had taken part in. As for the rest of those lining the pews, Emma had no idea who any of them were.

The organist, who had been playing a slow, mournful melody, stopped as the church bells began to ring. Emma took a seat at the very end of one of the final few rows, finding herself sitting a little too close to a man who reeked of cigarettes. A kind of calm descended over the church, only interrupted by the sound of quiet whispering, clothes brushing against each other, someone coughing or clearing their throat. And then complete silence.

She lowered her gaze.

Another funeral. Another person she was close to who had left this earth long, long before their time. Even though she had told herself she wouldn't cry – not today – the tears came anyway.

She thought about Blix. How alone he must feel right now, in his grief, his anguish. How difficult his life would be after this. How impossible it would be for them – the two of them – to have any semblance of a normal relationship with each other, after all that had happened. Perhaps. She cried at the thought of all she had done.

The organist began a new hymn. People stood up, getting ready to sing. Emma was glad to have something to focus on.

She wasn't sure which she preferred: graveside ceremonies or having to see the hearse drive away with the coffin. Both were equally grim, and the realisation she'd even had that thought – contemplating which one she preferred – made her shake her head. As if she preferred one over the other.

Iselin was driven away from Ris Church in a long, black Mercedes that had a distastefully flashy company logo plastered across its side. Standing there outside the church, watching it leave, it almost felt like the car was just rolling away. The gravel crunched beneath its wheels. With every metre, every second, Iselin drifted further and further away.

This was the last time they would ever see her.

A car. A few trees. The clear blue sky above them.

The car rolled further away. Houses. A fluffy, milky-white cloud. A faint vapour trail left by a plane that had long since departed.

Even further.

Even smaller.

One more second, then another.

Until the car disappeared round a corner. And Iselin was no more.

47

Even though she had a key, Emma always liked to ring the doorbell, mainly because she wanted her niece to hear her voice over the intercom, so by the time she got up to the flat, she'd be met at the door with open arms and a big, wide smile. Emma needed it today. But Martine wasn't waiting for her when she let herself in, even though her jacket was hanging on the hook in the hallway. The rucksack she usually took to nursery was on the floor next to her shoes.

'She's sick,' Irene explained. 'The nursery called this morning, asked me to go in and get her.'

'Oh dear,' Emma said, hanging her own jacket on the hook. 'How sick?'

Irene tilted her head to the side, contemplated the question.

'Well, she was complaining about a sore stomach and a headache.' She lowered her voice. 'But I think she just wanted to spend some time at home. She's not wanted to go in for the last few mornings either.'

'She's not being bullied, is she?'

'I don't know,' Irene sighed. 'I don't think so.'

Emma took a few steps, and peering into the living room, saw Martine tucked under a blanket on the sofa. She wasn't asleep, but Emma could see her eyelids flicker as she followed whatever she was watching on the iPad resting on her lap. The light from the screen painted bright colours across her small, sweet face.

'Hi, sweetie,' Emma said tenderly, bending down to kiss her.

Her forehead didn't feel particularly hot.

'Hi,' Martine replied weakly, her voice flat.

'So I hear you're sick?' Emma said.

The sentence seemed to make Martine's symptoms even worse. She nodded slowly.

'You know the rule, right? That people who are sick, especially kids who love their aunts, are allowed to eat whatever they want?'

Martine looked up at her.

'Nice treats. Naughty treats. Pancakes.'

'Can we make pancakes, Mummy?'

Emma turned to look at her sister, who sent her a disapproving look in return.

'Is that what you would like, my love?'

Martine nodded.

'See?' Emma said, winking at her. 'Aunts always make things better.'

She pushed a few strands of hair behind Martine's ear, subtly checking her scalp as she did. It didn't look like her hair had thinned any more since the last time she had seen her.

Irene still hadn't told her daughter that she had the same condition that Emma had – *alopecia totalis* – and that she too would eventually lose all her hair, turning completely bald, just like Emma was, underneath the various wigs she would switch between. Emma's own childhood had been plagued by anger, bitterness and rebellious behaviour. More than anything, they just wanted to make sure that Martine didn't end up heading down the same path.

'What're you watching?' Emma asked.

'A series on NRK Super,' Martine explained, pretending to be tired.

Emma glanced down at the screen, at an image of school children in a classroom. Young girls bickering, singularly concerned about being as mean to each other as possible by the looks of it. Exactly how Emma remembered school being.

'I'll be back in a min, sweetie,' she said, getting off the sofa. 'Just going to have a chat with your mum.'

Irene was waiting for her in the kitchen.

'Tea? Coffee?'

'Is that the best you've got?' Emma asked with a sigh.

'You can have whatever you want,' Irene said, opening a narrow cupboard next to the dishwasher.

'The stronger, the better.'

Irene pulled out a bottle of Talisker whisky and held it up for closer inspection.

'Perfect,' Emma said, even though she didn't really like whisky.

She sat down, letting her sister find the glasses and pour them each a dram.

'Are you staying here tonight?' Irene asked.

'I'm not sure yet,' Emma answered. 'I really need to get some work done.'

'Work? Now?' Irene replied.

'I'm way behind on the book. And then there's Kovic's murder. It's been playing on my mind.'

'You can't be working on that, surely? You're, you know...'

Emma looked her sister in the eye.

'Oh, you mean *that* kind of work,' Irene said. 'Not writing about it. Looking into it yourself. Your own covert operation.'

'I've still got Blix's case files,' Emma responded. 'The ones Kovic requested before she was killed.'

'Isn't that illegal?' Irene questioned. 'Keeping hold of police documents, I mean?'

'Probably,' Emma said. 'I'd planned on giving them back to Blix, so he could do it, but he ... won't talk to me.'

'That's not exactly surprising. Given what he must be going through right now.'

'No, I know. But I can't just turn up at the police station with them either, this long after everything. I'm in enough trouble as it is.'

She took a sip of the whisky and winced. Felt it burn as it travelled down her throat.

'So what is it you're trying to find out then?' Irene asked. 'They've solved it, have they not? Timo Polmar killed her?'

'Everything seems to point to that, yeah,' Emma said. 'But I'm struggling to understand his motive.'

'Are you sure you actually *need* to understand it?'

Emma stared at her sister. 'What do you mean?'

'Not everything has to mean something. People do stupid things all the time.'

'That's just not a good enough answer for me.'

'You have to know why.'

'Yes.'

They sat there, drinking in silence for a while.

'So you think someone else killed Kovic?'

Emma nodded.

'And if that is the case,' she said, 'her murderer is out there somewhere.'

48

The soil she was buried beneath was still damp. A temporary cross had been planted at the head of the new grave. Bouquets of flowers, wrapped in bows and adorned with hand-written notes, were piled up around it. Some were wilted, others completely ravaged by the rain. Blix couldn't remember it having rained.

He stood there.

Dropped to his knees.

And when the engraved letters started to blur, and it got to a point that his brain couldn't comprehend that the name he was looking at, on that cross, meant that Iselin was dead, gone forever, he got to his feet and walked away.

Whenever he'd closed his eyes over the last few days, he had thought, prayed, hoped that, when he opened them again, everything would be back to the way it was. When he awoke from each brief period of fragmented sleep, he would find himself in this stage of purgatory, between dream and reality, in which he had forgotten or not been able to understand where he was, until it would dawn on him, and all come crashing down again – the gunshots, the fall, the impact, the lifeless eyes, Merete's scream and her fists, hammering against his chest, the feeling of Iselin's skin, still warm against his own, the taste of blood as he tried to breathe life into her, her chest inflating and collapsing, the rest of her body, completely still ... And then the tsunami of pain and guilt and regret and despair would wash over him, sending him into a dark spiral that would only gain momentum every single time, down, down, down, until he eventually reached some form of rock bottom, a place where he couldn't possibly feel any more pain than he already did, where it couldn't be any darker, colder.

This was his life now.

This was how it would always be. Every day. Every hour. Every minute. After every dream, he had to wake up to the hard, cold reality. Over and over again.

How the hell was he meant to go on like this?

How was he supposed to get through each day, each night, life itself? The plan had been that, when the time called for it and he was old and grey, *she* would take care of *him*. He would spend his days sitting there in his chair, looking forward to when she would come. Maybe she would visit every day, or just every now and then. Regardless, he would always look forward to seeing his own flesh and blood, his own daughter, all grown up, an adult woman, who would certainly have enough to be getting on with in her own life – a husband, children, friends, her job – but who would still come and take care of him, because he was her father, because she loved him. Because it was her turn.

As it should be.

As it should've been.

It had been a few years since Iselin had stopped using his surname. Blix had thought it was something Merete had convinced her to do to begin with, to make him feel even worse about their relationship and how they had drifted apart, but Iselin had made the decision herself. It was more practical, she had said. Shorter, with just Merete's surname. Easier to say. And she wanted to be her own person, she'd said, have her own identity. She shouldn't have to, and didn't want to, just be known as 'Blix's daughter'.

He'd understood her reasoning.

It still hurt.

Yet another thing to be bothered about, he'd thought. A surname. As if removing it somehow made her less his.

He thought about various other stupid things that had upset him over the years. When she didn't respond to his messages or return his calls. When she never asked how *he* was. When she would ask Merete's new partner for help, when she could've just asked *him*, even though it was actually easier to ask Jan-Egil, seeing as she lived under his roof.

Blix had complained about how bad she was at tidying up after herself. Clothes, food, the shoes she would leave in the hallway. How it was seemingly impossible for her to just help out once in a while. Everything should be in its place. But Iselin had blamed him for her bad grades in the first year after he and Merete had separated, and then for the divorce. Everything had been his fault. His, and only his. It had angered him – it wasn't right, or fair. I was never like that when *I* was young, he'd told himself, over and over again.

He had cursed the ungrateful youth of today. He'd complained to friends. Complained to Merete, blamed her for not being more supportive, more helpful. In the worst periods, he had even regretted becoming a father.

As he did now, too.

If he had never become a father, he would never have been forced to feel pain like this.

But all that stupid, misplaced aggression. The bitterness he had held on to. All that time and energy, wasted on things that didn't even matter. Iselin should still be here, so she could do it all again, and then some, if only she were still breathing. If only she had survived. She could have called him now, ordered him to hand over the keys to his flat and demand that he move out, sleep on the street. And he would have done it, in a heartbeat, without hesitation. If only...

Blix wiped away the tears. Registered someone moving out of the corner of his eye – he turned and saw a man walking purposefully through the cemetery. Towards Iselin's grave. Blix took a deep breath in and exhaled. Wished he had somewhere to hide, or that he had seen Gard Fosse before Gard Fosse had seen him. But it was too late.

Blix braced himself. He was unsure whether he could get through the next interaction. Fosse lifted a hand to greet him as he approached. He had a thin folder in his hand.

'I thought I might find you here,' he said, stopping a couple of metres away.

For once, Fosse wasn't wearing his service uniform. Blix stared silently at the man he had attended police college with. The man he had once shared a patrol car with. The man he had once called his best friend.

He seemed uncomfortable. Blix couldn't decide whether that was because of the grave they were standing next to, or whether there was something else making him look so uneasy.

Fosse took a few steps closer.

'How are you?' he asked.

Blix shrugged. He suddenly realised that the cold had settled into his body. Now Fosse was here, he just wanted to get home and wrap himself up in a blanket.

'Have you been eating?' Fosse asked.

He had rested his hand on his back.

'No.'

'Slept at all?'

'A bit,' Blix said. 'Not much.'

'Maybe you should get something for the sleep,' Fosse suggested. 'Something to help you—'

'I don't want any pills.'

Fosse studied him for a few seconds before nodding.

'You know that if there's anything we – the department – or I, personally, can do...'

'You've said that before,' Blix responded. 'Thanks. But I don't need any help.'

He knew he sounded ungrateful, but he couldn't bring himself to soften his words, or stop them either.

'I'm on my way home,' Blix said, starting to walk back towards the cemetery gates. 'What do you want? What're you doing here?'

Fosse looked pale. As if there were something he had dreaded raising.

'Something has come up in the investigation that puts everything in a new light,' Fosse answered, following Blix. 'Something you should be aware of.'

'What's that then?'

Fosse hesitated. He moved the folder from one hand to the other.

'What is it?' Blix pressed.

'Kovic's patient journal,' Fosse explained. 'The psychiatrist's notes you requested the warrant for.'

Blix nodded.

'It's been a few days since they ended up on my desk, but I wanted to talk to you first, before passing them on to anyone else. They're going to have to be included in the investigation.'

'Okay...?' Blix said, glancing at Fosse walking beside him. 'What's in them?'

Fosse took another few seconds before answering.

'Well, she was having trouble sleeping, first and foremost. You might have known that already. But ... she also started seeing Neumann for something else...'

He paused again. Blix was starting to get annoyed.

'Spit it out!'

Fosse stopped and took a deep breath.

'She started seeing him because she might have been having a problem with you.'

The sentence made Blix stop in his tracks.

'She had said that an older, male colleague who she spent a lot of time with had been making inappropriate advances.'

Fosse wouldn't look him in the eye.

Blix just stared at him. 'And you think she was talking about *me*?'

Fosse didn't respond to this.

Instead he said: 'Whoever it was had groped her...'

Blix snorted in incredulity. 'You're being serious?'

'See for yourself.'

Fosse held out the folder. Blix snatched it from him and turned to the first page. The psychiatrist's notes contained detailed information about the patient, including an entry dated to their last session. Blix skimmed each line, until he reached the section Fosse was referring to.

'The patient reports that she has been on the receiving end of numerous types of unwanted sexual contact from a male colleague whom she is often on duty with. She mentions several episodes in which he has put his hand on her thigh while alone together in the patrol car, forced himself on her in the lift, pressing his crotch against her, and made inappropriate comments about her body...'

Blix blinked a few times, shook his head and continued reading.

'From what I have gathered, the person in question appears to be someone who is significantly older and who she has worked with closely since joining the department. The unequal power dynamic in the relationship seems to be making it difficult for her to reject the advances, and she is scared of sharing these extremely negative experiences with others in the workplace. She reports experiencing insomnia and having issues with her circadian rhythm, both of which are biological symptoms of depression and anxiety.

Blix's lips parted involuntarily.

'Bloody hell,' he uttered. 'This is just ... completely, utterly insane. I never laid a hand on her...'

He had to read it through again.

'This isn't me,' he said resolutely. 'There's no mention of a name.'

'The description doesn't really fit anyone else ... other than you,' Fosse responded.

Blix tried to search his memory, to think back on any episodes that Kovic could have misunderstood or misinterpreted, but couldn't think of one single occasion. He'd never even complimented her. Never said anything about her appearance, whether she looked good, or how nice her hair or clothes were. He had never...

No.

Never.

He just wasn't like that. He had always behaved appropriately with members of the opposite sex. So why the hell had Kovic said otherwise? Maybe she had seen something in the way he'd looked at her? Had he been interested in her ... without knowing it himself? And Kovic had realised, figured it out, in one way or another?

After Merete, there hadn't been anyone else for Blix. He couldn't bring himself to go through that again, hadn't even thought of opening that door. And then to consider pursuing a colleague ... a woman young enough to be his daughter...

'This is absurd, Gard,' he said at last.

'It's hard to wrap your head around,' Fosse said. 'But it's a different time now, things are different than when we started out. We can't—'

'I've never touched her,' Blix interrupted.

'You say that,' Fosse nodded. 'But this is what Kovic told the psychiatrist. She hardly would've gone out of her way to make this all up just to hurt you, would she?'

Blix didn't know what to say.

Fosse shook his head.

'I just don't know why she didn't come to me first. Or why she didn't talk to the union.'

Blix didn't respond. His mind was elsewhere. Analysing all the memories he had with Kovic.

They had always worked well together. Had a good rapport. Maria Gade, Kovic's mother, had said the same thing, that Kovic had liked him. Liked working under his wing.

Maybe *she* had been in love with *him*?

And her infatuation had manifested into something unhealthy? It had done something to her psyche, so much so that she had to see a psychiatrist, that she...

No, he told himself as soon as the thought popped into his head. He would've noticed. He was good at observing when someone was interested in him in *that* way. And Kovic hadn't been.

Something must've been going on with her, he concluded. She must have been seriously unwell. In some shape or form.

'You might want to consider getting a lawyer,' Fosse said.

Blix couldn't rein his thoughts in. He could see exactly how the Kripos investigators would interpret the accusations.

'Kovic said she was scared of you,' Fosse continued. 'And a few days later, she's dead.'

Blix gawped at him.

'*Scared* of me?'

'Yes, or...'

'It says that she was scared of saying anything, Gard. That's not the same as being scared *of* me. And, to reiterate – there's no mention of my name in here, she doesn't specifically say that she's talking about me.'

Blix felt as if he were about to explode.

'No, that may be...'

'There's no *may* about it.'

'But maybe she couldn't bring herself to come to me or anyone else in the department because she knew it would cost you your job. Destroy your reputation. Your life.'

A wave of nausea washed over Blix.

'Do you think I killed her?' he asked, his voice trembling now. 'Is that what you're saying?'

'I don't think anything,' Fosse said apologetically. 'But I know how this is going to look from an investigator's perspective. There's a lot that doesn't add up. Or that actually does add up, if we let our minds run wild with it.'

'Is that so?' Blix retorted, hearing the hostility in his voice now. 'Explain it to me.'

Fosse took a deep breath before elaborating:

'Think about it. Forget about your own role in this and try to look at it objectively. An attractive, young investigator experiences unwanted attention from her superior. She's afraid to tell anyone about it because if word does get out, he'll lose his job. She's sitting on the detonator that could ruin his life. Maybe he's aware of that too. So, to stop it from happening, to keep her from ending his career, irrevocably destroying his relationships with colleagues, friends and family ... he makes sure that she can't tell anyone.'

'Jesus Christ,' Blix exhaled.

'Listen, Alexander – it's a motive. You can see that, right?'

He thought back to what Iselin had told him, what Kovic had said to her on the day she was murdered. *What I really need to do, is talk to your father.* And she had tried calling him, twice.

So she could tell him what she had told her psychiatrist?

'I was in Sandvika that day,' he said, clearing his throat. 'Giving a talk, at your request, if you remember.'

'Yes, I know. However – again – if we try to look at this objectively: a man in your position could feasibly – and this is entirely hypothetical – arrange for someone to do it for you. Timo Polmar was a loose cannon. A nutter, a guy with psychological issues. And Iselin wasn't meant to be in the flat that afternoon. She took the earlier train home from Stavern. So she became a potential witness. She even fought with him. For all we know, Polmar might not have even known she was your daughter, and decided that he couldn't take any chances. And then you couldn't take any chances either, so you shot and killed him. That way, he couldn't tell anyone who it was who'd hired him to kill Kovic.'

Blix could see the logic behind the hypothesis. He was used to thinking the same way himself, and had to focus hard to try and find the flaw.

'Why would I request access to her patient notes then?' he asked, shaking his head. 'I hadn't even heard of Timo Polmar until a week ago. And yet I'm supposed to have hired him to kill Kovic?'

Fosse didn't have a response.

'The case file that was taken from her kitchen table,' Blix said, the thought suddenly hitting him. 'The murderer took it. Which case would *I* have needed to take, to make sure that no one else knew what Kovic was working on?'

An elderly woman walking her dog was heading towards them on the gravel path. Fosse stared at the ground.

'I have a meeting with the head of the Kripos investigation in an hour,' he said.

Blix swore.

'It wasn't me,' he said, nodding at the folder with the psychiatrist's journal. 'I've not done anything wrong.'

'Get yourself a lawyer,' Fosse repeated. 'And make sure they're a good one.'

49

The car was emitting a strange noise. Something in the suspension. Probably a result of ramming Drivnes off the road.

Blix glanced down at the dashboard. None of the warning lights had come on. The insurance would barely cover the damage, but that didn't matter.

He drove right up behind the car in front. Flashed his lights and held the palm of his hand on the horn. It eventually pulled over and let him pass.

Rage coursed through his body. His mind raced, and for the first time since the events of that closed-down workshop, something other than Iselin was occupying his thoughts.

A bus in front slowed down for a speed bump. Blix checked to see if it was safe to overtake.

It wasn't.

He swore and honked the horn again. Moved his hand back to the steering wheel and kept both hands gripped tightly around it. Thought of Kovic. Shook his head. None of it made any sense. And there was only one person who might be able to help him understand it.

Just under ten minutes later, Blix had pulled into a parking space on a side street off Bygdøy allé and was walking through the gateposts leading up to Eivind Neumann's old, brick house. Blix rang the doorbell. It didn't take long before he heard footsteps approaching. The psychiatrist opened the door, a look of surprise on his face upon seeing Blix there.

He apologised for turning up unannounced, and on a Sunday.

'I should've called first,' he said. 'But this won't take long. I've just got a few things I need you to clarify for me.'

Neumann stepped aside and invited him in.

'First of all, let me offer my condolences,' he said. 'It was truly, truly awful, what happened to your daughter.'

'Thanks,' Blix said quickly. He didn't want to think about Iselin now. 'I'm here because I read Kovic's patient notes.'

A thoughtful wrinkle formed across Neumann's forehead.

'She can't have been talking about me,' Blix carried on. 'It makes no sense whatsoever. I never behaved like that.'

'It doesn't say anything about who...'

'Everything in that journal points towards me,' Blix interrupted. 'There aren't really any other people it could be referring to. I need to know exactly what she said, to understand who she was actually talking about.'

Neumann shook his head. 'We never really delved that far into the matter,' he replied. 'But she was clearly experiencing things in the office that had quite an impact on her.'

'In the office?' Blix asked.

'Yes, or rather ... at work,' Neumann specified. 'Just a turn of phrase.'

The psychiatrist moved his weight from one foot to the other.

'Didn't you notice anything yourself?' he asked. 'You worked closely with her, didn't you?'

Blix had already mulled it over on the drive there, but couldn't remember anyone ever having given Kovic any unwanted attention.

'Could it be about something else?' he asked. 'Could it all be made up? Something she had convinced herself was true?'

Neumann looked sceptical.

'Her allegations are completely absurd,' Blix continued. 'Can you, with your expertise, say anything about her state of mind, anything that might explain all this?'

Neumann started, but hesitated.

'Please,' Blix begged. 'I know you've got to adhere to your doctor-patient confidentiality and all that. Kovic was your patient, but she's dead now, and the investigators are building a case against me. They think I'm behind her death. They're pursuing the wrong person.'

Neumann scratched at the stubble on his chin. 'Well,' he started. 'Kovic seemed of sound mind to me, I have to say. I didn't notice anything in particular that would suggest she was suffering from a specific mental disorder, at least. One that would make her create such elaborate claims just for the sake of it. She seemed ... unhappy. Depressed. As if just confiding in me about it caused her significant stress.'

Blix breathed out heavily. He would have to try and pinpoint the specific incidents she was referring to, try and figure out exactly when they happened, and who she could've been with.

'The episode in the car,' he started. 'The hand on her thigh. Did she say anything about when that was? What job she'd been driving to or from, anything like that?'

'She mentioned several episodes where that had happened,' Neumann said.

'But did she mention any details?'

Neumann shook his head. 'That wasn't what I was focussing on,' he replied. 'I'm sorry, I don't think I can help you with this.'

Blix thought of Emma, and how she and Kovic had become close friends. Maybe *she* could shed some light on the accusations. But he couldn't bring himself to talk to Emma. Not now, not tomorrow, maybe never. And he had already discussed Kovic's state of mind with her anyway. She hadn't mentioned anything like that.

'You ... look a bit peaky,' Neumann said. 'How are you dealing with everything? The grieving process?'

Blix stared at him.

'If you don't mind my asking?' the psychiatrist added.

He didn't know how to respond. Didn't know if he even wanted to talk about it.

'It's still early days,' Neumann said. 'So it's understandable if you haven't processed anything yet, if you're just taking things an hour, a minute, at a time. But I see it as a positive sign that you're here anyway. That you're doing something.'

Blix wasn't sure whether any of this would help him at all.

'Can I give you some advice?' Neumann asked.

'Is it that I should talk to someone?' Blix replied.

Neumann responded with a hearty laugh. 'That's what everyone says, I know,' he started. 'But it's good advice. It's healthy to discuss your thoughts with someone else, regardless of who that may be. But that's not actually what I was going to say. I was going to encourage you to go back to where it all happened: the crime scene.'

Blix looked him in the eye. The knot that was permanently settled in his chest constricted at the thought of returning to the place where Iselin had been held captive.

'That is the absolute last thing I would want to do. Ever.'

'And that's exactly why I think it might be a good idea,' Neumann went on. 'That place is somewhere you will always associate with the worst thing that ever happened to you. And that gives it a certain power over you.'

Without wanting to be, Blix was transported back to the workshop, through memories of that night. To the fall, the sound of her body smacking onto the concrete floor. Her lifeless eyes.

'That place will control you if you don't do anything about it,'

Neumann continued. 'You'll avoid it, choose other roads north, avoid passing Jessheim altogether, because you won't be able to bring yourself to drive past that specific exit.'

Blix had given that some thought already, that he would never be able to pass Jessheim without thinking of Iselin.

'I ... lost a good friend of mine in an accident not that long ago,' Neumann continued. 'I'm not saying that that's the same as losing a child – not at all – but visiting the place she died had a therapeutic effect on me. It hurt, of course, but it helped. I felt a bit better, afterwards. Or the loss was a bit easier to deal with, at least.'

Blix wanted to leave.

'Regardless,' Neumann added, 'it's early days. You need to do things in the right order. But for the long run – think about it. I can go with you if you want some support. And let me know if there's anything I can help you with in the meantime. If you ever need someone to talk to.'

50

Emma's text arrived the moment Blix got home. He contemplated swiping it off the screen and ignoring it, but he let his thumb slide across the display out of habit, opening the message:

Hi. Just wanted to say that I'm thinking about you a lot. I'm trying to understand what really happened. I've still got the two case files Kovic had from the archives. Trying to see if I can find any answers there. Let me know if you want to talk about this or if you want to go through the case files with me – Emma xx.

As long as he had thought Iselin was still alive – or as long as he hadn't found any evidence to suggest otherwise – he hadn't done anything to stop Emma being involved in the investigation, even though he knew he should have. But now he was looking down at a text from Emma Ramm on the screen, the rage welled up inside him again.

He should never have saved her life back then, more than twenty years ago. The Teisen Tragedy. If only he had been passive like Gard Fosse, if only he had stayed outside and hadn't gone into the house where the father was keeping them hostage, Emma probably would've been killed by her father. And then they would never have ended up in this situation. Someone else would have accompanied Iselin to Neumann's office, someone who would've actually been there for her, and Iselin may have survived.

He closed the message and started browsing through the photos on his phone instead. Most of them were ones he'd taken for work – incidents and evidence that he needed to document, that might end up being useful. Almost no photos of Iselin.

Blix walked over to the bookcase beside the TV, where he kept a few photo albums. Some had photos from his own childhood, while others were for more recent ones. He took one out and flipped to a page with photos of Iselin on her last day of secondary school. He, Iselin and Merete had gone out for dinner together. The waiter had taken the photo. All three of them were smiling up at him. As a family.

The events that took place in Emma's house on that day all those years ago had destroyed his marriage. It had marked the beginning of the end. If the Teisen Tragedy had never happened, his life might have been entirely different. He probably would have taken on another role in the police, and as a result, would never have been Kovic's mentor. All that had gone to hell in his life was related to his relationship with Emma, in one way or another. He knew it was an irrational thought, but he couldn't hold it back.

He took the photo album into the kitchen and sat at the table. Traces of Iselin were still dotted around the room. A glass with dried orange-juice dregs by the sink. Her last drink. A pack of crispbreads left out on the side. A pair of woollen socks she'd slept in on her last night, draped over the back of a chair. Her keys were in the middle of the table.

Blix sat and stared at them. There were four keys in all. Three large ones and one small, as well as a little plastic figurine.

He pulled them towards him. The smallest key was marked with a letter and a number, probably for her locker at the Police University College. And then there was the key to her dorm room in Stavern, and a key to his apartment. And a key to Kovic's flat.

Whatever Kovic had been working on at home, in her own time, was the key to understanding everything that had happened since. The lab technicians were finished in her flat. The crime scene had been examined and released, but had probably been left in the same state.

He sat there for a while longer, before clutching the keys into his fist and getting up.

The temperature outside had plummeted. The people he passed on the street were thoroughly wrapped up. Blix had left the flat without his scarf and gloves, but he couldn't be bothered to run back upstairs for them. Luckily, the car warmed up quickly.

He found a free spot outside Kovic's apartment building, climbed out and jogged over to the entrance. A woman was on her way out as Blix went to unlock the door. He held it open for her and nipped in afterwards.

Standing on the threshold to her flat, he thought he had the wrong key. He had to jiggle it around in the keyhole and struggled to turn it, but it eventually clicked into place.

He hadn't been prepared for the sight he was met with.

The flat hadn't been cleaned. There was still blood and other solidified bodily fluids from where Kovic's body had lain. All of the surfaces were covered in fingerprint powder left over from the forensic team. There were chalk marks and lines, stickers with digits and numbers.

He wasn't sure what he was looking for. Something Ann-Mari Sara and the other technicians had overlooked. There was a plate and coffee cup in the sink, a dusting of fingerprint powder covering both. He opened the cupboard beneath the sink and pulled the bin out. It was half full and starting to smell. An empty can that had once contained pineapple slices was perched on top. The contents of the bin had most likely been examined, the technicians routinely laying each item out on grey paper and photographing one after the other, before putting everything back.

There were two pens on the kitchen table. That was all.

He wondered whether Abelvik and the others had managed to trace the whereabouts of her laptop or if they'd worked out which case files Kovic had taken home with her.

His thoughts drifted to Emma; she must've taken the files he had had with him in the car that night. And then there was the one that had been stolen from Kovic's kitchen table. Three files in all. And Abelvik and the other investigators weren't aware of two of them. He should tell them. It might help them see the whole picture.

He walked into the living room. There was nothing to suggest that the perpetrator had been in there, but there were still traces of the fingerprint powder on the door frame and armrests.

There were three remotes on the coffee table, as well as an empty glass and a bowl of raisins. Several books were stacked in a pile on the shelf underneath the tabletop. Blix took one of them out – a biography of Charles Manson with a photo of the American cult leader on the cover. The blurb described him as one of the USA's most brutal serial killers. She had taken it out from the library. And it had a four-week loan period. Which meant that it must've been a topic Kovic had found a recent interest in.

He flipped through it, but couldn't see how it had any relevance to the cases she had been working on.

There was also a newspaper and a few magazines on the shelf. The paper was a few weeks old. The pages were turning frail and discoloured. A page with an article about the hit-and-run case she had been investigating had been dog-eared. A group of Thea Bodin's friends had gotten together to talk to the journalist about what happened. They had described the person who had hit her and driven off as a heartless monster.

Several online articles had also been tucked into the newspaper. Kovic must have printed them off at work. She didn't have a printer at home.

One of them was about the German philosopher Friedrich Nietzsche, exploring his view that he who fights monsters should see to it that he himself does not become a monster. A warning of what coming face-to-face with human suffering can do to a person. If you gaze too long into the abyss, the abyss also gazes into you.

Kovic's pursuit of the killer must have had quite an effect on her. But had she sought out the article because she recognised this happening to herself, or was it something she had come across while trying to comprehend what kind of human being could be capable of doing that? What kind of monster could just leave a young woman on the side of the road, to die?

Blix looked back down at the shelf, scanning the books to find any more she'd borrowed from the library. There were a number of psychology textbooks. All about understanding the human psyche.

One of the other printed articles was about coincidences, patterns and connections. Kovic had underlined various words and sentences, but they didn't mean anything to Blix. He knew that Kovic had been pursuing two theories in the Bodin case. One being that the hit-and-run had been an accident, and that Thea Bodin had been a random victim; the other being that it hadn't been an accident at all, and she was the target. He assumed that was why Kovic had wanted to keep hold of the article. It compared coincidences to winning the lottery. Giving the example that if someone were to place a bucket along the railway line connecting Oslo and Bergen, the probability of you winning the lottery was equal to the likelihood of you throwing a coin out of the window of the train at any given point along the journey, with it still managing to land in the bucket. And yet, someone always won.

He put the articles down and picked up one of the psychology textbooks. Using his thumb, he quickly flipped through it. The pages fluttered, hopping over several at once, with the rest falling after.

Blix did the same again, this time glimpsing a note stuck between two of the pages like a bookmark – she had inserted it into a chapter regarding explanatory models around the psychology of suicide. There was a phone number on the note. He recognised Kovic's slanted handwriting, her doodles. The typical circles and other random shapes she would always end up absent-mindedly drawing while sat on the phone, listening to whatever the person on the other end was saying.

He looked the number up in an online directory, but nothing came up.

The number didn't necessarily have to be anything to do with the case, but the note had been left among the material Kovic had been looking through immediately before her death. It could be the phone number of someone who knew something, someone who could shed light on what happened.

He punched the number into his phone and held it to his ear. No answer.

51

Emma stared at the text she had sent Blix. Read forty-four minutes ago, but still no reply. The same outcome as the other messages she had sent him over the last few days.

She wondered how long she would continue trying, whether there was even any point. Perhaps it would be better to just go to his flat, refuse to move from his doorstep until he opened the door and agreed to talk to her. But she wasn't sure if there was any reason even to do that. What would she say? Sorry?

It could be that they would never have any semblance of a relationship again. The consequences of her actions were irreversible. Impossible to forget. Impossible to forgive.

But there were still so many loose threads. It was all so unclear. She made her mind up. If Blix didn't want to talk to her, she wouldn't force him to, but she could at least tell him what she'd found out – if she had found anything at all, that is. She could speak until they were able to draw two resolute lines under the answer. After that, she would leave him be.

She put her phone down and leafed through the case file about Tore André Ulateig, the Drammen hammer murderer. Some of the documents had fallen out and must still be in Blix's car, but those she did have provided a good insight into the investigation.

In all its gruesomeness, it was a pretty straightforward case. A man had pleaded guilty to killing his lesbian ex-wife and was now serving his sentence in Drammen Prison. Emma wondered whether Kovic had spoken to anyone who had worked on the case, or if she'd met Ulateig herself. For anyone working for the police, arranging a meeting with a prisoner was just a matter of formality, but for outsiders like herself, it was more difficult – her request would take at least a week or two to process. She would have to find another way, one that didn't take as long. And she might have a few options.

She thought of Ulateig's lawyer first. If Kovic had spoken to Ulateig, then his lawyer, Helene G. Gustavsen, was probably aware of it. Emma found her phone number on the website for the Gustavsen, Olsvik & Laberg law firm, and sent her a text, asking whether Kovic had been in touch with her to request a meeting with Ulateig.

Her reply came soon after:

No. But she wouldn't have had to go through me to do that. She could've just visited him. HGG.

Of course, Emma thought to herself. Stupid thought. She typed out a response:

Could I ask you to check with your client to see whether Kovic did meet with him recently? It's tricky, especially as a journalist, to get in touch with an inmate.

Gustavsen replied:

I'm in court for the rest of the day. Why do you ask? Is it important?

She wasn't sure how important it was, or if it was important at all. She was fumbling about in the dark, clutching at straws. She paused, taking some time to come up with an appropriate reply.

She wondered whether it would be possible to get in touch with Ulateig's children. It had been quite a while since the murder. Maybe they would be ready to talk about it. She checked the file. They had been four, seven and nine when their mother was killed, and were now under the care of a legal guardian. Emma closed the folder. They were still children. They shouldn't have to relive it.

Were there other members of the family she could contact? She didn't really know what she would even ask them, but she had to start somewhere. Emma began to search for old newspaper articles. She found out that Tore André Ulateig had a sister called Veronika Falkum, who lived in Oslo and worked as a teacher.

Emma opened a new tab and typed her name into the search bar.

There were several people with the same name, but after cross-checking various social-media profiles, she managed to find the right one. Her phone number was listed too.

She grabbed her phone, began to type in the digits, but stopped before getting to the end of the number. A Petter Falkum was also listed as a resident at the same address.

Emma said the name aloud. 'Petter Falkum.'

It was a name she'd come across recently.

Putting her phone aside again, she reached over for the folder containing the Aksel Jens Brekke case. There weren't many documents in that file either, so it didn't take long before she found what she was looking for.

Petter Falkum had been one of the investigators working on the Brekke case. He had interviewed several of the hostages, including Brekke's ex-girlfriend. And he also happened to be Ulateig's brother-in-law.

Emma searched his name this time and found several photos of the investigator, both in and out of uniform. He was slightly cross-eyed and had dark, curly hair. She clicked on one of the photos of him in his police uniform and sat there, studying it. Although only a minor link between the cases, it was a link nonetheless. The only link. One she hadn't been aware of. Moreover, Petter Falkum worked for the police. According to Blix, Kovic had been reluctant to talk about whatever it was she'd found out with anyone other than him. Which could indicate that someone in the police had been involved, in one way or another.

She got up and walked around the room. Kovic had been deeply committed to solving the hit-and-run case that had resulted in Thea Bodin's death over half a year ago. And yet something had made her check out two other cases from the archives. The Aker Brygge hostage case and the Drammen hammer murder.

Emma only had a basic understanding of the Bodin case, supplemented by what she'd read in other news outlets' coverage of the murder. Enough to have written several articles for news.no.

Searching for more information about the case online, she clicked on a VG article reporting on the lack of answers or movement in the investigation. They'd included a photo of the reconstruction the police had conducted on the road – Maridalsveien. Kovic could be seen in the centre of the photo, standing next to another investigator.

The article included a few words from the family's legal representative, expressing criticism about the level of work the police had done and appealing for the driver of the car to turn themselves in.

There was a photo of the lawyer too. He was rather overweight and had thick, grey hair. Emma recognised him. Thobias Klevstrand. He often took on this kind of case. He was also in the page-wide photo of the reconstruction, a little further from the camera, at the side of the road, his hands on his hips.

Emma leant closer to the screen. None of the people in the photo had been named in the caption, but the investigator standing beside Kovic looked like Petter Falkum. He had the same build, anyway, and the same curly hair.

The discovery lit a fire in her. Petter Falkum was connected to all three of the cases Kovic had been working on before she was killed. It was a tenuous link, and it was, of course, entirely natural that he and Kovic would wind up working on the same case. They worked for the same department, after all. But it was something. What would be really interesting though, was if Petter Falkum had ever had any run-ins with Timo Polmar. But she had no way of finding that out.

She took a screenshot and sent it to Blix. Sending another message immediately after, asking whether it was in fact Petter Falkum in the photo next to Kovic:

His name has also come up in both the hostage case and the Ulateig case, as an investigator and a relative, she added. *Do you know if he has any connections to Timo Polmar?*

She hesitated, but sent it anyway. Got up and went to the toilet, before coming back in and grabbing a crispbread. She didn't bother to put anything on it, just bit into it and stood there, waiting, hoping, for Blix to answer. She picked up her phone, opened her messages and saw that he hadn't read it yet.

What now?

She could call Thobias Klevstrand. Maybe the Bodin family's lawyer would be willing to give her an insight into his thoughts about the case. She could at least ask him if he thought there could be a potential link between the Aker Brygge hostage case and the Drammen hammer murder.

She couldn't find his direct phone number online anywhere, so she called his law firm. A friendly voice answered on the first ring, as if the woman on the other end had been waiting for someone to call.

'Thobias is currently away on business,' she explained after Emma introduced herself. 'He won't be back until next week.'

'Would he be available for a phone call?'

'You'd be lucky to catch him. It might be best if I let him know you've called, and he can call you back if he has the time.'

'Please, that would be great,' Emma said. 'Tell him it's about the Thea Bodin case,' she added, glancing over the table at the two other cases she actually wanted to ask him about.

'Will do,' the woman replied.

Emma ended the call and sat there, gaze fixed on the pages of the Drammen hammer murder investigation. She flipped through the documents until she found what she was looking for – evidence confirming a growing suspicion she had had. Thobias Klevstrand was listed as the legal guardian and representative for Tore André Ulateig's children. Good to know if he did end up calling back.

Emma spent the next hour browsing through old news articles about Thea – articles she had written herself for news.no, mainly covering the status of the investigation, as well as Thea's parents' pleas for help, tips, witness observations, anything that could assist them in finding out what happened. The case was, and remained, a mystery. The police had almost nothing to go off. An observation of a car, supposedly black or dark blue. That was it. Thea was hit and killed along a stretch of road where the houses were few and far between – something that could've been cold-hearted calculation, or just simply bad luck. Maridalen was a popular area for hiking all year round, so Emma leant more towards the latter theory.

Her phone rang.

An unknown number.

'Emma Ramm,' she answered.

'This is Thobias Klevstrand. You requested that I call you?'

'Oh, yes, hello,' she said surprised, and introduced herself properly. 'Thank you for returning the call,' she added. 'I wanted to talk to you about Sofia Kovic. She was the lead investigator for the Bodin case.'

She paused. The lawyer didn't say anything.

'The hit-and-run murder,' Emma elaborated. 'I understand that you're representing the family. I'm looking into the possibility that something Kovic came across during the investigation may be connected to her murder.'

'You're a journalist,' the lawyer said, more as a statement than a question. The arrogance in his voice annoyed her.

'I'm more than that,' she said. 'Sofia Kovic was a good friend of mine.'

'What makes you think that something in the Bodin case might have led to her murder?' the lawyer asked.

'I'm just looking into the possibility,' Emma answered.

'But there must have been something that gave you the idea?' he pressed. He sounded interested.

'Nothing other than the fact it seems like a logical line of thought,' Emma replied.

'Logical?'

'She put a lot of time and effort into investigating the case,' Emma said. 'She could have come across something. Got too close to something else.'

'She must have been working on several cases, though,' the lawyer added. 'The Bodin case hasn't budged for several months now.'

Emma wondered whether she should mention the two on her kitchen table – the hostage case and the hammer murder – but chose to wait.

'When did you last talk to Kovic?' she asked instead.

'She always rang whenever anything new came up in the investigation. Which wasn't often.'

'When was the last time?'

It took a while for him to answer, as if the lawyer was unsure whether or not he should.

'She'd tried getting hold of me,' he replied. 'And left a few messages asking me to call her back, both at the law firm and on my voicemail, but it wasn't something I prioritised at the time. I was working on complicated negotiations with a foreign client. And by the time I could call back, it was too late.'

'What did she want to talk to you about?'

'I don't know. Maybe you have an idea?'

'I don't actually,' Emma answered. 'I know she had been looking at some old, archived cases. I'm trying to find out if there may have been any links between them.'

'Which cases?'

Emma wasn't sure whether she should answer this time.

'One of them is a case you'll know about,' she started. 'The murder of Liv Bente Ulateig. You're her children's legal guardian.'

The lawyer didn't respond.

'Does that tell you anything?' Emma asked. 'Can you see a connection?'

'No,' he replied immediately. 'What was the other case?'

'The Aker Brygge hostage case.'

'The one with Aksel Jens Brekke.' Again, stating it rather than asking. It was clear the lawyer was familiar with the case.

'Yes,' Emma answered. 'Any idea why she would be looking into either of those?'

'Were there any other cases?' the lawyer asked without answering her question.

'Not that I know of.'

'Do the police know about this?'

Emma wasn't sure how to answer that. Blix knew about it, but she couldn't be certain that Abelvik and the others had the same information. She hadn't mentioned it during her interrogation and didn't know whether Blix had either.

'I don't know,' she said eventually. 'Have you spoken to the police since Kovic's death?'

'Not yet,' the lawyer answered. 'I'll give them some time, but they'll eventually have to appoint another investigator to the case, to follow up on Kovic's work.'

It felt like the lawyer wasn't particularly interested in the possibility that a new lead in the Bodin case may have been a factor that led to Kovic's murder. Emma thanked him for his time and hung up. She suddenly felt discouraged. Everything was moving so slowly, or not at all.

She checked her phone again and sighed. Blix still hadn't read her message.

52

Blix wasn't hungry, but he could tell his body needed food, so he grabbed a kebab from the nearest takeaway on his way home – one stuffed with meat, sauce and salad. He felt sick after just a few bites. He put it on a plate and left it on the counter, filling a glass of water instead. He drank the entire glass in three large gulps, forcing him to stop and catch his breath afterward. It had been enough to make the room spin momentarily.

Two distinct buzzes from the hallway made him realise he had left his phone in his jacket pocket. He remembered it going off while he waited to pay at the kebab shop as well. Blix wiped his mouth clean, walked into the hallway and fished his phone out of the pocket. He'd missed a call. It was from Nora Klemetsen, a journalist who had worked for *Aftenposten* for years.

Reporters had been increasing their efforts to get in touch with him over the last few days, but Blix hadn't answered a single one of their attempts. Klemetsen had sent him a text as well, asking him to call her back 'whenever worked for him'.

He'd received two texts from Emma too.

He sighed. Felt his hand clench around his phone at the sight of her name. He waited a few seconds before opening the first one. The contents of the message made him frown.

'Petter Falkum,' he said aloud. Columbo. He was a few years older than Blix, but didn't quite have the same investigative expertise. He had been assigned to the same department after suffering a knee injury that had stopped him continuing on active duty. He'd always been the one to dress up as Santa whenever they'd held a Christmas party for the children of those who worked in the department. The stiff Santa mask had frightened Iselin. She had made Blix accompany her over to him to get her goodie bag.

Falkum had also received a few complaints from some of the trainee investigators at the Police University College. They generally revolved around him not having the necessary professional expertise to work in that kind of mentoring role, but there were a good few complaints about his demeanour and attitude towards the female students.

Blix could remember two occasions when Falkum had taken his place at the lunch table, when he'd had to leave before Kovic was done eating. Falkum and Kovic had been put on several of the same assignments before too, and he'd definitely seen them leaving the lift together more than once. Neumann's journal notes could potentially refer to Falkum.

A thought suddenly came to him about something he had read in Kovic's notebook:

~~Call T. Klevstrand~~
~~Archives.~~
Meeting – PF.
~~Meeting with the interpreting service~~

Meeting. With PF. He had originally thought that would be the Police Federation, but it could also stand for Petter Falkum.

Clasping his phone in his hand, he put his shoes back on and pulled his jacket down from the hook. Seconds later, he was out of the flat and crossing the road, heading towards police HQ. He shook his wristwatch out of his jacket sleeve. It had just turned three o'clock.

Blix recognised the uniformed woman, Siren, monitoring the security desk at the entrance to the police station. She would usually smile at him, but not today. She didn't look up at him either when he spoke:

'I've left my pass at home.' He cleared his throat. 'But I just need to run upstairs and grab something from my desk. Is that alright? I won't be long.'

Siren glanced up at him briefly before nodding and opening a door to the side of the desk.

'Thanks.'

Siren escorted him over to the lift and made sure he was granted access to the sixth floor. Blix thanked her again, but received no response.

As the lift rattled upward, it felt as if the floor was swaying beneath him. He hadn't been to the station since Iselin had died. The days had all blended into one. He hadn't known day from night, night from day – he hadn't known what was what.

It was surreal, being back. As if nothing had happened. As if he was just going to work, would just go and grab a cup of coffee, sit down at his desk and gradually let the day begin. He would check the news, talk to Abelvik and Wibe whenever they arrived, get a quick update on what was going on out there in the capital, and then start to think about the imminent morning meeting. The day ahead. What they would prioritise.

But everything was different now. *He* was different. The others were too. He felt it the moment he walked into the office, how everything and everyone was still plagued by what had happened.

Ella Sandland was the first to notice him. Blix saw her lips part in surprise. As if he were the last person she had expected to see.

'Blix,' she said, almost as a gasp.

He took a few steps towards her and asked, 'Do you know if Petter Falkum's in today?'

'Petter?' she repeated. 'No. What...'

'I need a word with him.'

'But...'

Blix was already walking away. Scanning the rest of the room. Watched as faces popped up over their computer screens, looked up from their notes, telephones. Felt as the silence descended, as if every sound had suddenly been sucked out of the room.

He and Tine Abelvik spotted each other at the same time. She strode over to him, a look of deep concern etched onto her face.

'Blix,' she said. 'What are you doing here?'

Blix looked round. Everyone was watching. He felt himself start to sweat.

'Petter Falkum,' he said. 'Where's Petter? It's him, he's the one who...'

He stopped himself. Saw as Abelvik narrowed her eyes a fraction, as if she were trying to figure out what he meant.

'Petter's off sick,' she said. 'He's not been in for days.'

'Off sick,' Blix repeated sarcastically. 'Petter Falkum is PF. Maybe. In Kovic's notebook. I need to talk to him. He's the common denominator. In the Aker Brygge hostage case, and the Drammen hammer murder case too. And with Thea Bodin.'

He took a step to the side to peer round Abelvik and blinked a few times.

'Blix, what are you talking about?'

He had to run through his train of thought one more time before realising he was the only one who knew about Kovic's notebook and the two case files.

'Petter Falkum worked on the Aksel Jens Brekke case, the hostage case,' he explained, cupping his hand to his forehead. 'And he was Tore André Ulateig's brother-in-law, the hammer murderer from Drammen.'

'Ulateig ... what does he have to do with the case?'

'He ... I ... I need to talk with...'

All eyes were still on him. Everyone's faces had the same look of disbelief, as if they were all in shock.

It was rare for investigators or officers to be suspended. It was usually just a matter of formality. Colleagues supported colleagues – unless it was obvious that a violation or offence had been committed.

They know, he thought. They know about Kovic's confidential sessions with Neumann, the contents of his notes.

'Believe what you want.' The words came out louder than he had planned. 'I never laid a hand on her,' Blix continued. 'Kovic. Never. It was never ... I ... We ...'

Blix saw the confused expression in Abelvik's eyes, and could feel the eyes of everyone else in the room, like a strong spotlight had suddenly been turned on him.

He headed back to the lift. Heard Abelvik call after him, but he didn't turn round. Walking away, he realised he couldn't feel the floor beneath his feet, and everything around him seemed out of focus.

Abelvik caught up with him, grabbed hold of his arm.

Blix stood still.

'There's someone in here,' he said between gritted teeth. 'Someone Kovic worked with, someone higher up ... There's someone here who ... I don't know if it's Petter Falkum,' he said, meeting her gaze. 'Or if it's you.'

Nicolai Wibe appeared by her side.

'Or you. Or someone else here who ... who...'

He started pointing at people, everyone, at the faces of those watching him, eyes wide open.

'Alexander,' Abelvik started. 'Everyone knows how hard this has been for you.'

Wibe took a step towards him, laid a hand on Blix's shoulder. 'Come on,' he said gently. 'Let's go into one of the meeting rooms, we can talk a bit more in there.'

Blix let him lead him away. Taking in everything around him as if through a kind of filter. All the sounds in the room were suddenly loud, ringing in his ears, fighting for priority. He could hear the photocopier at the other end of the room just as well as he could hear the phone ringing on the desk right beside him. He could hear the sound of his own footsteps. The ceiling light seemed much sharper than usual, piercing his eyes. He blinked, had to stop for a moment. He looked up to see Gard Fosse at the other end of the room. The disapproving expression on his boss's face made Blix snap.

'Did someone go and get him?' he asked, incredulously. 'So my humiliation could be complete?' Blix smiled broadly. 'Come and arrest me, Gard,' he shouted down the hall. 'It was me, I did it! I killed Kovic! And then I tried to kill Iselin afterwards. And I managed it in the end too!'

Spit flew out of his mouth as he seethed.

'Please,' Wibe begged him. 'Come with us. Just come this way.'

Blix wanted to continue raging at Fosse, but it was as if his tongue and lips wouldn't let him. The tears erupted from his eyes. His cheeks reddened. He could hear as the sob burst out of him. The floor beneath him felt soft and wet. It felt as if he were swimming, his head under the water while Abelvik and Wibe stood either side of him.

Everything went dark.

Cold.

He couldn't breathe.

53

It felt like he was falling.

Like he couldn't open his eyes.

When he finally did, he managed to blink a few times and realised that he was standing in a lift, with Tine Abelvik beside him. She was watching him in the mirror. Holding his arm. As if she were afraid he would run off.

Come and arrest me, Gard!

His own words came back to him like an echo.

Jesus Christ.

Blix caught sight of himself in the mirror. Pale, unshaven, unkempt. He was thinner. There were stains on his trousers. He knew he smelled. Old sweat mixed with fresh.

The lift doors slid open. A cacophony of sounds hit him. Abelvik held onto his upper arm as she manoeuvred them both towards the doors. The foyer of the police station had a high ceiling, but it felt like the walls were caving in on him, trapping him. He could feel people's eyes on him – he tried to block them out.

He welcomed the cold October air against the hot skin of his face. The evening was starting to set in.

'I ... don't know what I was saying up there,' Blix said, glancing at Abelvik quickly before fixing his eyes on the ground. 'But if I ... if I...'

'Don't think about it,' she said. 'You're not yourself right now.'

'I didn't mean it.'

'I know that.'

'And I never did anything to Kovic.'

'I know that too.'

'How can you know that?' Blix could hear how despondent he sounded. He lifted his gaze to look at her.

'Because I know you,' she replied. 'There probably isn't anyone else up there who knows you as well as I do.' She said this with a nod up to the windows on the sixth floor.

Blix agreed, even if he couldn't say the same about her. But what did it matter, really?

'What ... do the others think?' he asked, anxious about what she might say.

'Obviously I can't speak for everyone,' she began. 'But I haven't heard a single officer, lawyer or investigator accuse or suspect you of doing anything.'

'It must have been one of us,' Blix responded. 'Who Kovic...'

He wanted to explain how he had come to the conclusion that it was Petter Falkum, but realised he had nothing to back up his accusation. He had jumped to a conclusion built on random coincidences. He had overreacted, acted too quickly. Too soon.

Abelvik put a hand on his shoulder. 'Have you spoken to Merete?' she asked.

Blix shook his head. 'I saw her at the cemetery recently. She wouldn't come over to Iselin's grave while I was there, so I ... left. Let her be there with her in peace.'

Abelvik nodded. 'She'll come round, understand that it wasn't your fault.'

Blix was about to object – he knew Merete.

'She'll eventually recognise that you did everything you could.'

Blix couldn't bring himself to respond.

'She'll go back to Singapore after a while anyway, I think,' he said after a moment's silence. 'If she can bring herself to go. To leave Iselin, I mean.'

'Maybe a little distance will do her some good,' Abelvik added.

'Maybe.'

He felt her watching him.

'Do you want me to walk back home with you?' she asked.

He shook his head. 'You've not got your coat.'

'I can go get it,' she answered. 'It's not a problem.'

'I'll be fine,' he said, forcing a smile. 'I can escort myself off the premises.'

She opened her arms and embraced him. He bent down. Let it happen. Felt the warmth of her skin. Her hair. She gave him a quick pat on the back and pulled herself away.

'Just call me if you need anything,' she said. 'Anything at all. Anytime.'

Blix thanked her, and she headed back to the doors. She looked back over her shoulder at him before going inside. Blix lifted his hand to wave, turned and walked away. He inhaled the crisp air deep into his lungs, making the decision to shower once he got home. Eat something and get some sleep. But his thoughts wandered to Iselin. And Neumann, and his advice to return to the crime scene, so he could move on. Process the grief in the very place Iselin died, where his memories were at their strongest, at their most painful.

Pain.

He was in pain, but he deserved so much more. To shout at his colleagues like that, to accuse them of ... Blix shook his head. Couldn't bring himself to think about it anymore, couldn't bear the thought of all their eyes on him.

He bent his head against the autumn wind and shoved his hands into his pockets, brushing against something cold and metal.

His car keys.

54

The thought of going there, to the place where it happened, made him feel sick. He got into the car anyway, and pulled out onto the road. He could hear a scraping sound coming from the undercarriage, and one of the headlights was clearly crooked. He turned the radio on, but turned it off almost immediately.

He wanted to sit in the silence. The loneliness.

He wanted to think of Iselin, feel her presence there with him.

He could see her in the passenger seat. Earphones in as usual, listening to music, even though it was just the two of them in the car. Phone in hand, constantly messaging someone or other, completely uninterested in anything besides what was going on in her own world. He asked her a question. Asked her again after she had removed one of the earbuds. He watched her answer. But didn't hear what she said.

The motorway.

The darkness.

The lights of oncoming cars blinded him. It felt like he'd been drinking. Like he was swerving over the road. The yellow line in the centre of the tarmac wriggled across his vision. He was forced to blink quickly, focus his eyes, as he caught up to the red taillights of the cars in front. Thoughts he had never had before crept into his head. That there was nothing more for him in this life. He could understand the reasoning of those who had left him. Felt the temptation of just letting the darkness seep in, take him over, completely and absolutely. How easily he could do that, here and now. He would just have to put his foot on the accelerator, and let everything disappear. The mountain side was just on the right, he could find an opening in the guard rail, or wait until he crossed the part of the Nitelva river that ran past the Olavsgaard Hotel, not long after the turn off to Skjetten and Lillestrøm.

There were fields on the way to Jessheim as well, both before and after Kløfta. Trees he could drive into. But there would always be an element of uncertainty – he might survive. But maybe it was best to take the chance anyway. See if he was lucky or unlucky, depending on how you looked at it.

The road came back into focus. Blix was seconds away from driving into the back of the car in front, forcing him to brake abruptly, hold on to the steering wheel with both hands. He felt his heart suddenly slam against his chest – like it was pounding away all the way up in his throat. A train whistled by the roadside in the direction of the airport. Like a swift, neon snake.

Blix approached Jessheim. The fields flew past. He thought about the last time he'd driven here, with Emma beside him. On the way to save Iselin. To find Polmar. His vision blurred again. All he could see was the noose around her neck, all he could hear was the sound of the motor, the pulley rolling across the ceiling. He watched as the rope tightened, pulling Iselin off the edge, the sound of her gurgling, the groaning that filled the hall, Blix's own breathing, the decisions he had to make, then and there. The gunshots. The fall. The impact. The traces of life still in her when he raced over, while he tried to save her. The life that was no more.

A plane was coming in to land at Gardermoen Airport, illuminated in the sky by its navigation lights. Blix wiped the sweat from his face and blinked a few more times. Put the full beam on and took the next exit. His heart was beating in his chest like a tight fist pounding against his rib cage, as if it were trying to break free. His knuckles tightened around the steering wheel.

He turned into the warehouse car park a few minutes later.

The car rolled to a stop, and he turned off the engine. He sat there, staring ahead for a few minutes, into the trees, into the darkness. You won't be able to do it, he told himself. You'll never be able to go in. Just start the engine and leave. Go home. But without even realising it, he had opened the door. Put one foot down on the cold ground. Then the other.

He could see the blue flashing lights in his mind's eye. The oxygen mask over Iselin's face. The lifeless body. He took a full step away from the car and closed the door behind him. The sound thundered through his head, making his temple throb.

He looked around.

It was like nothing had ever happened.

No police tape. No traces of blood. He looked up. Stars in the night sky. His eyes searched for a thin arrow of light shooting across the black, in the hopes he could make a wish. But nothing appeared.

Blix put one foot in front of the other, headed round the back of the building. A car passed by on the road. Blix arrived at the door and grabbed the handle. Pulled it towards him, hard.

It was locked. Of course it was locked.

He walked round to the other side of the warehouse. A wooden plank had been bolted across the entrance he used the last time he was there, barring entry.

He felt relieved. He didn't have to go in after all, didn't need to see the crime scene again. And yet, at the same time, it frustrated him. Exactly like the psychiatrist had told him it would, he felt an urge to confront it, in a way.

He could break in, like last time. Smash a window. But he wouldn't. Couldn't bring himself to.

He would have to postpone it. Man up, convince himself to do it again some other time, come back.

With slow, heavy steps, he walked back to the car. He did a lap around it before getting back in, inspecting the damage caused by the collision. Adjusted the headlight, so it would be aiming straight ahead again, and tore off a strip of rubber that had been flapping against the side of the car. He opened the car door but stood there for a moment, considering the dark building in front of him. A closed-down car-repair workshop.

What had made Polmar bring her here?

He must have been familiar with the place, Blix reasoned. Known that it was here, known it was empty. He must have had a key.

A dog barked somewhere nearby. Blix climbed back into the car and slammed the door shut.

55

Maridalen had its own unique serenity at this time of day, when the sun hadn't risen yet and a layer of mist hung over the frosty fields, when you could see the smoke rising from the chimneys of silent farms nearby. If you were lucky, you might even spot a wild animal or two among the rolling, foggy hills, on the hunt for breakfast. It was a time of day that could have you convinced that the whole world had stopped, that all was calm, and there was nothing to worry about.

Emma inhaled the sharp early-morning air into her lungs. A quick glance down at her smartwatch told her it had been twenty-three minutes since she had left her city-centre flat, that her heart was toiling away at 145 beats per minute, and that she was travelling at 24.2 kilometres an hour.

Starting the day like this had become part of her routine, but it had been a while since she had last seen 6:00am, since she had last dragged herself out into the pitch-black of an autumn morning. An occupational therapist who had once convinced her to go on a date had, at some point between the third and fourth glass of wine, looked deep into her eyes and asked her what exactly she was cycling away from. Amateur psychologists, Emma had answered. And cellulite. The fact that he'd just squandered any chance of getting some that night was something she had waited to tell him until after she'd finished her fifth glass of wine, because she certainly hadn't been looking for pillow talk or any sort of meaningful exploration of her psyche.

She pushed her thoughts aside and concentrated on her technique, keeping her knees close to the frame of the bike so her muscles worked more efficiently. She accelerated to twenty-eight kilometres an hour, her heartrate rising steadily, but she had plenty more in her yet. The sun would come up in about an hour, dressing everything around her in a warm glow, a few minutes later than it had done the day before. Everything would gradually warm up, losing the morning's bewitching otherworldliness. It was worth getting up early to see the sun come up over the surface of Maridalsvannet.

Emma cycled past the large car park at Brekke, reducing her speed to 26.4 kilometres an hour. She would often take the bus there in the winter and head up into the mountains to enjoy a long, refreshing day skiing. Usually up to Kikut or Kobberhaughytta. It always amazed her how little time it took to get from the centre of a capital city, out into nature, where you could spend days wandering about without ever bumping into anyone else.

Today's trip took her steadily closer to where Thea Bodin's murder had taken place. She gradually reduced her speed, eventually coming to a complete stop when she thought she was at the right spot. She took her phone out and found the photos of the reconstruction that had been published in the newspaper article. She realised she had stopped in the same place the lawyer Klevstrand had stood, with his hands on his hips.

She knew the case well now, having read almost every article that had covered the investigation. The most likely explanation was that it had been an accident, and that the perpetrator had panicked and driven off. According to routine procedure, though, the police had still investigated those closest to her, scrutinising her circle of friends to find any possible motives. The police had also interviewed people who lived near the crime scene. The investigators had examined their cars and had contacted local garages to enquire about any vehicles they might have repaired recently with damage that could've been caused by a collision. Everything they would usually check had been checked and double-checked.

Emma leant over the bike's handlebars. She felt more and more certain that the Bodin case had been Kovic's starting point for whatever she was trying to pursue. The core of which everything else revolved around. Somewhere or other along her quest to find the perpetrator, she had found a link between the Aker Brygge hostage case and the Drammen hammer murderer. A fatal link.

The only thing Emma had managed to find herself was Petter Falkum. But she didn't have any of the other pieces to solve the puzzle. There was a fourth case. According to Iselin, Kovic had taken another case file home with her. A fact that made Emma feel like she was groping around in the dark.

She had no idea whether Abelvik and the other investigators were thinking along the same lines as she was. Regardless, she should return the two case files she had kept. She could take copies of them and push them through Blix's door so that he could return them himself.

On the other hand, all the documents had been printed off from the police's computer system, so they technically had the same information she had. The question was whether they were even aware of the cases Kovic had taken from the archives.

A car with a trailer hurtled past. There was a bouquet of withered flowers on the side of the road up ahead. She swung her leg off the bike and walked over to them. Took a photo.

It could all end at any time, Emma thought.

Thea Bodin was just out cycling. Bam, game over. She might not have even seen or heard the car. As for Kovic: someone had rung her doorbell, and a minute later, her life had ended.

Emma hopped back onto the bike and turned round to cycle home. She pedalled rhythmically, felt her face warm up as the sunlight hit it. Her heart rate rose steadily.

Kovic had managed to see the connection, Emma thought. Found a lead. She would just have to do the same.

56

It was quarter past nine when Blix pulled up outside the small storage facility in Kjeller. For the first time since Iselin's death, he had managed to sleep uninterrupted for a few hours during the night, and had even forced himself to eat an entire piece of toast and a soft boiled egg at breakfast. He had also swallowed a tablet that, according to the advert, would give him more energy. Thus far, there did seem to be a correlation between theory and practice. He felt better. Fitter.

A man around Blix's age was standing at the entrance to the building. He was wearing a dark-blue beanie and a thick winter jacket. Stepping out of the car, Blix watched as he inhaled a long drag of his cigarette.

'Gunnar Sundby?' Blix asked, walking towards him.

The man nodded, flicking his cigarette away but not bothering to stub it out.

'Alexander Blix. Thank you for meeting me at such short notice.'

'Absolutely awful, what happened,' Sundby started. 'I was in complete shock when I heard about it.'

They shook hands. Blix hadn't mentioned anything about his own role in what had happened at Jessheim, he just let the former owner of the repair workshop believe he was carrying out routine investigations.

'This way,' Sundby said with a nod backward, to the building behind him.

They started walking.

'Can I ask what this is about?' Sundby enquired. 'I mean, I understand it's about Timo Polmar, of course, and everything that happened in my old workshop. But, like I said on the phone, it's been a good while since he worked for me.'

Blix nodded.

'He stopped working for me a fair while before I closed the place down and moved,' Sundby continued. 'So I don't really get why you need to look at my accounts.'

Blix didn't like using the phrase 'gut feeling'.

'Just routine procedure,' he said.

Sundby looked sceptical.

'Why did you close your business?' Blix asked, trying to redirect the conversation.

Sundby sighed. 'The same reason why anywhere closes down really. It wasn't profitable enough, so when the contract for the rent expired, I packed up and moved everything here instead, while I tried to figure out what to do next.'

'How long has it been since you closed down?'

'About two and a half months.'

'And how long did Timo Polmar work for you?'

'I've been through this with the other investigators,' Sundby said, sounding a little exasperated. 'Seven or eight months, I believe. But, again, like I said on the phone, he never gave me the keys back. The owner of the property should've changed the locks, but they clearly weren't in any rush to find new tenants.'

'When did he stop working for you?'

Sundby pulled his keys out and inspected them while answering, 'It would've been sometime last spring.'

They had arrived at a door. Sundby found the right key and unlocked and opened the door in one swift movement. They entered the storage building.

'It's a good space, this,' Sundby explained. 'You can come and go as you want. And all of the rooms have steel walls and doors, so no one can see what you're keeping in here.'

He quickly glanced at Blix, as if suddenly nervous that he would think he was involved in some sort of dubious activity.

'What was he like?' Blix asked.

'Who?'

'Timo Polmar.'

'Do you mean as a person, or as an employee?'

'Both, preferably.'

Sundby's keys clattered against each other as they walked through the building.

'I mean, he was an odd one, that Timo. A tricky guy to figure out, but I never thought he was capable of doing what they said he did on the news. To abduct a girl and...'

'Odd in what way?'

'It's hard to explain. He was trained as a car-body repairman, and he was a good one too, but it was almost like he was never fully aware of himself, or reality, if you get what I mean? Like, he'd laugh at the strangest things, and then wouldn't laugh at things normal people found funny. I always had this feeling that he had a couple of screws loose, you know?'

'But you still employed him?'

'Yeah, I believe in giving people chances,' Sundby said. 'He looked as if he needed it as well, the day he turned up for the interview. And he knew his stuff, as I said. That's the most important thing. He always came to work too. I'll give him that. He had a very good work ethic.'

'But he only worked for you for about seven, eight months, you said?'

Sundby stopped outside a door with 032 written above it. Put a different key in the lock and turned it.

'As I said, it wasn't easy running that business.'

He pulled the door towards him. Inside the narrow storage unit were shelves upon shelves of boxes full of spray-paint cans, office supplies, packs of light bulbs, books and binders. In one of the boxes, Blix caught sight of a candlestick and two remote controls.

'I never throw anything out,' Sundby said apologetically. 'But it was receipts you wanted to see?'

'Yes. I'm mainly interested in seeing your accounts from last May.'

Sundby turned to look at Blix. The expression on his face now a little more suspicious.

'This wouldn't have anything to do with that case in Maridalen would it? That girl, the hit-and-run?' he asked. 'Do you think Timo might have had something to do with it?'

Blix thought about how to respond.

'You've already spoken to us about that,' Sundby continued. 'My wife takes care of the paperwork. She found the documents from all the jobs we had in the months after that happened, or at least all the jobs that involved car-body repairs. A man came in and went through it all. I believe all of the other car workshops in the area were investigated as well.'

'Do you know who she spoke to?' Blix asked. 'What the name of the investigator was?'

Sundby shook his head. 'I wasn't there, but she joked that he looked like Columbo, if you remember him. The only thing missing was the coat.'

Blix felt his heart rate increase. 'Petter Falkum?' he asked. 'Could that have been his name?'

Sundby had started rummaging through the shelving with all the binders.

'I really don't know,' he answered, taking some of the boxes down and stacking them on top of each other on the other side of the room.

Blix's phone vibrated in his jacket pocket. He took it out and saw that Emma was trying to call him. Again. He shoved it back in his pocket.

'Here,' Sundby exclaimed, pushing himself up from the box he had been searching through on the floor, wiping away some moisture that had settled on his forehead as he did so. 'Here are all the jobs we did in May last year.' He handed Blix the binder.

'Thanks.'

Blix opened it. They were filed chronologically. He quickly flipped through them until he reached the day after the hit-and-run, and then continued to scrutinise the documents slowly from there. There was no mention of a black or dark-blue car in the first few days following Thea Bodin's murder. Nor in the days or weeks after either. In fact, there were no receipts concerning a dark car of any size at all in May.

Blix turned to Sundby. 'Do you know whether the investigator took anything with him?'

Sundby shook his head.

'Can you ask your wife?'

'I think she would've said if he had,' Sundby responded, taking his phone out anyway. 'I spoke about it with the boys who'd worked for me afterward as well. None of them recalled any cars coming in with damage caused by a collision. It had been a few months by that point, but they would've remembered. And we'd have recognised if it had, we kind of have to know what different types of damage look like.'

Blix nodded at his phone. 'Can you check anyway?' he asked.

He had thought that if the perpetrator had taken the car to a workshop, they might have tried to camouflage the damage. Might've hit something else to hide the original scrapes and dents.

Blix looked through the folder one more time while Sundby called his wife. The answer she gave sounded negative.

'Ask if the investigator could've taken something without her seeing,' Blix said.

Sundby relayed the question to his wife and ended the conversation.

'She left him to look through the documents by himself,' Sundby explained. 'But he should've said if he had taken anything. Can't you ask him?'

Blix nodded, closed the binder and handed it back. 'Do you document all the jobs you work on?' he asked.

'What do you mean?'

'Do your employees ever work on private jobs?' Blix asked. 'Favours for friends, that kind of thing. Could they use the workshop like that?'

'Not for paid jobs,' Sundby answered forthright. 'Just on their own cars.'

'What about Timo Polmar?' Blix asked.

Sundby hesitated. Blix watched him.

'Look, I don't care if you broke the rules every now and then,' he told him. 'It happens everywhere, all the time, in workshops just like yours. I'm looking for a possible murderer. Answer honestly, and I promise there won't be any consequences: Did you do any work off the books?'

Sundby didn't answer immediately, but Blix could tell he was thinking about it.

'Now that you mention it...'

He stared at the wall for a moment.

'Timo did. A couple of times. It was one of the main reasons I had to let him go, actually.' Sundby folded his arms across his chest. 'I'd had a word with him about doing that once or twice before, and gave him a strict talking to about not doing it again. But there was one Saturday when I came in to grab something I'd left in the office, and Timo was here. He was working on an SUV. A Mercedes, I think. Anyway, it was a job that hadn't gone through the company. He said it was for a friend, but that wasn't the first time he'd said and done that.'

'What repairs was it in for?'

'I think cosmetic mainly. It had a dent on the side, a few scratches. I believe it had hit a brick wall. I told him I didn't want to see the car there on Monday, so I think he must've dealt with it over the weekend. He would've corrected the dent, plastered it, cleaned it up and then painted it. I've always run a clean business. Always had a zero-tolerance policy: no corruption, no nonsense. Just want to put that out there.'

'I believe you,' Blix replied. 'So when was that?'

'I don't remember the precise date,' Sundby answered. 'But it was one of the last things he worked on here. He didn't work his notice period, so it must have been around the middle of May last year.'

Blix stared at him. Thea Bodin was hit and killed on the fourth of May.

'An SUV, did you say?'

'A GLE, if I'm remembering it correctly. A 350. Standard model, but not the latest one.'

'Colour?'

'Dark blue. So dark it was almost black, actually.'

Blix felt a surge of adrenaline.

'Do you remember the licence plate number?' he asked, but knew it was probably futile to ask. 'Anything at all? Any of the numbers, letters?'

Sundby shook his head.

'Did he say anything about who owned the car?'

'No.'

'Did you have a look at the car at all?' Blix pressed. 'Was there anything inside?'

The former workshop owner shook his head again.

'But it didn't have anything to do with the girl who was killed in that hit-and-run, if that's what you're thinking,' he stated. 'The damage didn't fit that kind of accident. The owner had hit a wall, like I said. You could see the residue of the brickwork on the car.'

Blix didn't respond. An uneasiness in the pit of his stomach told him he was onto something. He was convinced he'd found the car from the Bodin case. If he could find the owner, he might be able to find Kovic's murderer. And that person could be found somewhere in Timo Polmar's circle of contacts.

57

Blix got back in the car and took his phone out. Noticed Emma had called – again. But when he didn't pick up, she'd not left a text this time – she'd recorded a voicemail.

He ignored it and started driving towards Oslo city centre, fired up by this new discovery. He was getting closer, he could feel it.

He pulled into the fast lane and overtook a lorry while fumbling around on his phone. Tine Abelvik was one of the last numbers he'd called.

She took a while to pick up.

'I might have found something,' he said.

'What's that?'

'The car,' Blix answered. 'The one used to kill Thea Bodin.'

'Where?' Abelvik asked. 'What do you mean?'

Blix didn't want to explain over the phone.

'Are you at work?' he asked.

'Yes.'

'I'm coming in,' Blix said.

A quarter of an hour later and he was standing in the police-station foyer, waiting for Abelvik. He could tell she wasn't happy with the situation.

'Can we do this here?' she asked.

Blix looked round. 'I'd rather not.'

'Okay,' Abelvik said. 'Let's go up.'

They waited for the lift.

'Is Petter Falkum back?' Blix asked.

Abelvik shook her head. The lift doors opened and they stepped in along with two others. No one said anything.

Blix followed Abelvik through the department to her workstation. He sat in the spare chair.

'Go on,' Abelvik said. 'What do you mean you've found the car?'

Blix told her what he'd just discovered. Abelvik listened without interrupting. He could tell she was sceptical, and disappointed. She had clearly thought he'd found the car parked in a garage somewhere.

'Have you analysed Timo Polmar's phone?' he asked, nodding towards her computer screen.

'It's under way,' Abelvik answered.

'But you have his list of contacts?'

'Yes.'

'We have to see if there are any names of interest on there,' Blix said.

Tine Abelvik made no sign that she was going to log on to her computer.

'We have to find whoever it is in Timo Polmar's circle who owned a dark SUV at the time of Thea Bodin's murder,' Blix continued.

'I'll get someone to look into it,' Abelvik responded.

A few investigators walked by.

'How are you doing?' Abelvik asked. 'In general?'

'Better,' Blix responded.

It was true. He did feel better.

'I have something for you...' Abelvik began. 'I don't know...'

'What is it?'

'Iselin's belongings.'

'What belongings?'

Abelvik looked uncomfortable. 'We found her phone in the workshop in Jessheim,' she said. 'And a purse with her cards and cash. We also took her laptop from Kovic's flat.'

Blix nodded. Abelvik stood up, walked off somewhere and came back with a cardboard box and a release form.

'I need you to sign this,' she said.

Blix nodded, took a pen from Abelvik's desk and signed his name, before lifting Iselin's phone out the box. It was inside a transparent evidence bag. A yellow Post-it note had been stuck to the screen, with four digits scribbled across it: *1 2 3 4*. The investigators who had unlocked the phone to check its contents must've generated a new passcode. He didn't know how they'd managed to unlock it in the first place. Iselin used the facial recognition option. Maybe they'd taken it to the hospital with them and held it in front of her face. Maybe that was how they'd gotten into Timo Polmar's phone as well.

He put it back down and saw the same kind of note on top of her laptop, this time with a combination of letters and numbers.

'Is there anything I can do for you?' Abelvik asked.

Blix shook his head.

'Or, actually, there is one thing,' he said, taking out his own phone.

He thought about the phone number he found in Kovic's flat, but didn't want to tell her that he'd been there.

'I keep getting a call from this unknown number,' he said. 'It's not registered, and no one answers when I call back. Can you find out who it is?'

Abelvik turned to her computer and logged on.

Ann-Mari Sara appeared at the other end of the room. She was walking quickly, and in their direction.

'What's the number?' Abelvik asked.

Blix began to read it to her, but before she could press enter, they were interrupted by Sara.

'DNA match,' she announced.

Abelvik looked from Sara, to Blix, and back to Sara. Blix could tell that she didn't want to have this conversation in front of him, but Sara continued.

'On the curling tong,' she said. 'But it's not Timo Polmar's DNA.'

'Whose is it then?'

Sara shook her head. 'Unknown,' she answered. 'Unidentified.'

'But you said there was a match?'

'A match with an unknown profile in the crime-scene register,' she explained. 'From material Kovic submitted a few weeks ago for another case.'

Abelvik and Blix quickly glanced at each other.

'The Bodin case?' Blix asked.

'No.' Sara's facial expression shifted from fresh enthusiasm to sober professionalism. 'Walter Wiik,' she said.

Blix leant forward.

Walter Wiik had been an investigator in the Rape and Serious Sexual Assault unit, and had taken his own life the year before. It was a well-known fact that he had been battling with depression, had trouble sleeping and had been struggling with prescription drug abuse.

'What did you say?' Abelvik asked.

'Walter Wiik's suicide,' Ann-Mari Sara answered. 'There's a DNA match found at the scene...' she said, looking down at the papers in her hand.

'"From a glove, right hand – internal",' she read.

'Internal?' Abelvik repeated.

Blix didn't know the details of the case, he just knew that Walter Wiik had driven to his cabin, put a pistol to his temple and pulled the trigger.

'Was he wearing gloves when he shot himself?' he asked.

'I didn't deal with the case myself—' Sara began.

Abelvik interrupted her, holding up the palm of her hand. 'Wait. Wait a second,' she said. 'Let's take this to Fosse.' She turned to Blix: 'You have to go.'

Blix protested. Abelvik cut him off.

'Sorry, but you can't be here right now.'

Blix sighed, but agreed: 'Fine.'

He stood up. This new information added a whole new set of complications to the case. The suicide could have been faked. The murderer might've been the one wearing the gloves, that they had then put on the corpse afterwards, so Walter Wiik would have gunpowder and blood splatter on the glove. It meant that the murder of another police officer had been written off as suicide. If it was this that Kovic had discovered, it would put everything in a new light, would make everything easier to understand. The same person who killed Kovic had killed Walter Wiik.

'The file on her kitchen table,' Blix said suddenly. 'The one the perpetrator took. It must have been the Walter Wiik case.'

'Blix, you have to go,' Abelvik repeated.

She grabbed her phone, scrolled until she found a number, put the phone to her ear, and walked off in the direction of Fosse's office. Ann-Mari Sara followed her.

Blix stayed in his seat, trying to process all the information he had just been presented with. The office was almost empty today. On Abelvik's computer screen, the phone number he had read out to her a few minutes ago was still waiting in the search bar. She'd walked away without logging out.

Blix glanced around, pulled himself closer to the desk and pressed enter.

The police didn't have access to private telephone numbers, but the case-processing system did contain the names, addresses, birthdays, emails and telephone numbers of everyone who had been in contact with them for one reason or another.

There was a hit.

The number belonged to a Hans Vidar Hovland – he lived in the Sagene borough of Oslo.

Blix jotted the name and address down on a scrap of paper and clicked onto the profile to see which cases Hovland had been involved in. Just the one. Registered as a witness in an investigation. The system provided the case number, but in grey letters, meaning it had been closed and archived.

Blix moved the mouse up to the number and clicked on it. Before a new window filled the screen, a dialogue box popped up first warning him that another officer, Ann-Mari Sara, was looking at the same case.

Walter Wiik's suicide.

Blix peeked over the screen, over at the door to Gard Fosse's office, wondering if he should call Abelvik back to tell her what he'd found. To tell her there was a direct link between a phone number he had found in Kovic's flat and a case that now looked like the murder of another investigator.

He decided against it, and sat there for a while instead, taking in the information on the screen in front of him.

Petter Falkum was named as the lead investigator. The case was opened on the seventh of May last year, with Walter Wiik's date of death registered as the fourth of May.

The same day Thea Bodin had been killed.

In the box giving the location of the crime scene, it just read: 'Cabin, Nordmarka'.

The hit-and-run had taken place on Maridalsveien, on the road between Nordmarka and Oslo. That must be the link Kovic had found having moved in circles around the case. She must've looked at what else had happened the same evening Thea Bodin had been killed. What might have made the driver carry on without stopping, even if it had been an accident. What had made him not want to be seen? Why was it that no one could know he had been there, on that specific stretch of road?

Blix had another quick glance at Fosse's office. It wouldn't be long before they logged in to the same case and received a notification that Tine Abelvik was already looking at it. They would know it was him.

He opened the document with Hans Vidar Hovland's witness statement. It was three pages long, more than he would be able to get away with reading right now. He pressed print and as soon as all three pages had been sent to the printer, he logged out.

He knew he should get up and leave, but he sat at Abelvik's desk for a short while longer. He leant forward, opened the search bar again and typed in Kovic's name.

One hit. The murder investigation in which she was registered as the victim.

He opened it and was shown a list of the other investigators who also had the case open on their computers.

The number of documents attached to the case had grown exponentially since he'd last looked at it. It took some time for him to filter through everything and find what he was looking for. The folder containing the contents of Timo Polmar's phone. Who he'd called, who'd called him, and who was saved in his contact book. It was too long to have a proper look at. Instead, he opened Abelvik's emails, composed a new one to send to his private email address, and uploaded the files from Polmar's phone. As soon as the email had sent, he clicked on the folder of sent emails and deleted it, then went to the deleted emails folder, and erased it entirely. He logged out of the Kovic case, stood up and, folding the freshly printed papers in half, left Abelvik's workstation with them in hand.

The door to the department was just about to close behind him when something suddenly occurred to him. He managed to shove his foot in the doorframe before it shut. He had a quick glance around and briskly walked back over to his own workstation. Opposite, Kovic's desk had been left in the same state as before.

He bent down and pulled out the bottom drawer, where she had been keeping the Aker Brygge hostage case file. The old class photo from the Police University College was still there too. It was Petter Falkum's year group. Blix had originally thought it must've been in there because he had worked at that desk at some point or another, but knew now that there must have been another reason. His gaze swept across the rows of young, uniformed police officers. And, in the third row, came across another pair of eyes he knew far too well.

Bjarne Brogeland, standing there, a wide smile on his face.

Blix continued scanning the faces and found what he was looking for, the reason why Kovic must've had the photo – Walter Wiik. The late police officer was standing in the second row, third from the right.

58

Fifteen minutes later, Blix had parked outside a block of flats. The walls either side of the entrance were covered in indecipherable graffiti. It was a cold, grey day. Drizzly.

He found the door entry panel and pressed the button with Hovland written beside it. He hadn't actually expected anyone to answer, but a croaky voice responded.

'Hans Vidar Hovland?' Blix asked.

'Yes?'

Blix leant closer to the intercom and introduced himself. 'I work for the police,' he added.

'What's this about?'

'Walter Wiik, and a few other things.'

There was a moment of silence before Blix heard the electronic click of the door unlocking behind him.

'Third floor.'

Blix took the staircase two steps at a time. A tall man with tousled hair was standing in the doorway.

'Sorry, but you won't be getting a handshake from me,' he said, holding up the palm of one of his hands.

Blix could see it was bone dry and covered in sores.

'People usually think it's a bit gross,' he said with a weak chuckle. His smile was fleeting.

'I mean, it *is* gross,' he added. 'It's ichthyosis. I've had it for as long as I can remember. Tends to get worse whenever it starts to get cold out, like now.'

Blix responded with a nod, and Hovland led him into the kitchen. A cat rose from the floor and darted into another room.

'I tried to call,' Blix said.

The man gestured to a chair on the other side of the table.

Blix sat down.

'I don't usually pick up if it doesn't say who's calling,' he said. He had his phone in hand, and pointed to the display. 'If I've not got the number saved,' he clarified. 'I get so many nuisance calls these days.'

'I understand,' Blix said.

Hovland took a seat as well. There was a cup and pot of coffee on his side of the table.

'Did a colleague of mine called Sofia Kovic get in touch with you recently?' Blix asked. 'She was murdered last week.'

Hovland coughed. His voice was a little croaky when he answered. 'Yes, I've been following the story. It was horrendous, what happened to her.'

'Your phone number was written on a note found in her home,' Blix continued, without elaborating.

No reaction.

'Why did she have your number?' Blix asked.

'I guess ... she ... I don't know. She turned up at my door a few weeks ago.'

She must've tried calling as well, Blix thought. Like he had. She hadn't got through, and that was why Hovland hadn't cropped up anywhere in the investigation.

'What did she want?' Blix continued.

'She wanted to talk to me about ... Walter.'

'Walter Wiik?'

'Yes.'

Blix could feel his heart in his throat. 'Why was that?' he pressed.

'She wanted to talk about his suicide.'

'What about it?'

'She asked a lot of questions, about Walter. Pretty much the same questions I was asked in the interview after I'd found him.'

Hovland shuffled in his seat slightly – he looked uncomfortable.

'They documented them, my answers. They'll be saved somewhere.'

Blix had read the witness statement in the car. Hans Vidar Hovland and Walter Wiik had been lifelong friends. Hovland had become a commercial driver, while Walter became a police officer. Neither were married or had family of their own. In his statement, he'd described how recently, Walter Wiik had gradually become more depressed and despondent. Hovland hadn't been able to reach him by phone, so had gone to check up on him. When it was clear he wasn't home, the cabin in Nordmarka had been the next place he thought to look.

'But was there anything in particular Kovic was asking about?' Blix asked. 'Did she mention anything?'

'It seemed to me that she wasn't entirely convinced it had been suicide.'

'What makes you think that?'

Hovland thought about it for a moment, before answering:

'Well, I found him, of course,' he started. 'Lying there, with the gun. There was no doubt about what happened.'

'Were you surprised?'

Hovland moved a little in his seat again.

'I was actually,' he admitted. 'I didn't think things had gotten that bad. Everyone said that though, that he was melancholic. Down most of the time. Walter liked to listen to sad music and things like that, but...'

'You didn't think he was sad?'

Hovland shook his head.

'It would make him happy, actually, listening to that kind of music. It would make him feel something. He often said that. Insisted that we believe him too.' He put his hand on his heart. 'And I said that to ... what was her name again?'

'Kovic.'

'That was it, yes. I told Kovic that it certainly looked like he had that kind of personality, from the outside ... to those who didn't really know him, if you know what I mean. From when he was just a child.'

Blix thought he understood what Hovland was getting at.

'But he was on sick leave, wasn't he, before he ... died?' Blix asked.

'Yeah, but ... I don't think he really used it, to be honest. But there was something bothering him. He was seeing a psychologist, and he had been put on some sort of medication. So he was probably going through it worse than I was aware at the time.'

He waited a moment.

'But...?' Blix pressed.

'But there's something not quite right about it all. A feeling I can't quite shake off. I feel like none of it really adds up. And then there's the fact he did it *there*, in that way.'

'What do you mean?'

'That cabin was his sanctuary. He drove there to switch off. It was heaven on earth to him. And he chooses to shoot himself there? That wasn't like him.'

'You thought if he was going to take his own life, he would've done it differently? Somewhere else?'

'Yes, at least not in a way that was so ... messy. I remember him telling me one time that he thought it was particularly gruesome, inconsiderate even, when people who wanted to end their life, chose to shoot themselves. Think of whoever has to find the body, he said. It's bad enough finding a dead body, let alone having to see the contents of their skull too.'

Blix thought about Hovland's interview, running through everything he had told Petter Falkum.

'You didn't mention this in your first statement?' he told him.

Elbows on the table, Hovland clasped his hands in front of him, rubbing the palms against each other so that small flakes of dry skin drifted down to the surface below.

'Did I not?' he asked. 'I had wanted to speak about him positively, I suppose. Make it clear that he wasn't...'

His sentence trailed off. Blix would have to read the statement again, but the impression he'd got was that Walter Wiik had been severely depressed. Or at least that was the side of him that Petter Falkum had emphasised in the report.

The cat sauntered back into the room. It walked under the table and rubbed against Blix's legs.

'Did Walter ever invite anyone else to the cabin?' he asked.

'I don't think he had any company up there for quite some time. He was with a woman for a few years, and another one sometime before that. So they would go with him every now and then, I believe, but Walter liked to spend his time there alone.'

Blix wasn't sure how far he should push with his questions, so he felt his way forward intuitively.

'If there was someone who wanted to make it look like suicide,' he began, 'can you think of who that would be?'

Hovland didn't answer.

'Can you think of any reason why someone would want him dead?' Blix asked instead.

'Nothing other than what I already told the woman, Kovic,' Hovland eventually answered. 'That it must've had something to do with his job. He knew something or other about someone, and they didn't want to be found out.'

59

The bitter wind swept in from the sea, carrying small granules of salt with each gust and scattering them across the quay. Emma hurried over to the café and pushed open the door. She turned to close it and, coming face-to-face with her own reflection in the glass, patted her hair down, tidying the wild strands that had been blown about by the wind.

She'd had an early start.

Monica Nesset had agreed to meet with her that morning. They were getting coffee just a stone's throw away from her workplace, the very one where she had been held hostage – an ordeal that had gone on for more than six hours.

The café was practically empty. The interior looked something like a mechanic's workshop, apparently inspired by Aker Brygge's shipbuilding days. There was exposed brick between the steel beams, and various bits of machinery from the maritime industry decorated the walls.

Emma found a table from which she could keep an eye on the door. She pulled her laptop and notebook out of her bag.

For the majority of the time she had been held hostage, Monica Nesset's ex-boyfriend had kept a revolver pressed against her head. He had been shot and killed by one of the Delta snipers in the end. The bank's CCTV system had caught it all on camera. Stills from the footage were included in the case file. In one of the last images of the ordeal, Monica Nesset could be seen standing alone in the middle of the room, covered in her ex-boyfriend's blood.

A waiter came to the table. Emma ordered a bottle of Farris water and a prawn sandwich before popping her earphones in.

The final few hours of the drama had been transmitted directly to the VGTV and Nyhetskanalen news channels. The broadcast was still available in the programme archives. The news reporters and their cameras had stationed themselves outside as soon as they had caught wind of the situation, and had captured the most comprehensive coverage. Emma had watched most of the broadcast already, but wanted to see the rest before Monica Nesset arrived.

The footage that had aired on TV primarily captured the entrance to the bank. Emma knew that the meeting room the hostages had been held in was on the first floor, with windows looking onto a side street. The broadcast would occasionally turn to focus on the police presence and ambulance personnel who were waiting on standby, or on the curious spectators. Now and then, the reporter would pop back on screen to update the viewers. He would invite various eyewitnesses to join him as well. People who had seen the armed man enter the bank, employees from the neighbouring buildings who had been evacuated. The commander of the task force also appeared and made an announcement, giving a sober report explaining how the police were negotiating with the perpetrator. After a while, it became clear that they had identified the man. They didn't release his name, but had started to refer to him as the 'thirty-two-year-old financier'.

The waiter arrived with her food. Emma thanked him and continued watching the broadcast as she ate. There was a clock in the top-right corner of the screen, displaying the time of the broadcast – 14:32. Emma knew that Aksel Jens Brekke was shot and killed at 14:54. She would be able to finish watching by the time Monica Nesset was scheduled to arrive.

Images from a different surveillance camera appeared on the screen, one located in the foyer of another building, where an armed police officer stood waiting outside. On the wall was a list of the various company names that had offices in the building, as well as an overview of which floors they could be found on. The reporter explained that this was where the thirty-two-year-old worked.

'He left his office around five and a half hours ago and made the hundred-or-so-metre walk across to the bank, where he took four hostages,' the reporter said as the camera panned along the walls of the buildings, following the route Aksel Jens Brekke had taken. 'His motive and demands are not yet known, but from what we understand, the thirty-two-year-old had suffered major financial losses over the last six months.'

The camera zoomed in on the dark windows of the bank in an attempt to capture whatever was going on inside. The clock read 14:34. Aksel Jens Brekke had twenty minutes left to live.

Emma put her sandwich down and rewound the broadcast by thirty seconds. The camera swept from the bank, across the building façades and back down to the barricaded area around the bank's front doors.

She paused the recording. The name and logo of one of the companies was visible through the frosted windowpanes on the ground level of one of the other buildings: *Klevstrand & Partners*.

That had to be the lawyer Thobias Klevstrand.

She typed his name into the search bar and confirmed that the office for the Bodin family's legal representative was on Aker Brygge. In between Aksel Jens Brekke's own office and the bank.

That didn't necessarily mean anything; it could easily be a coincidence. Regardless, Thobias Klevstrand was turning out to be a common denominator in all three of Kovic's cases.

The recording continued, the seconds ticked down. A fat seagull landed on the top of a bronze statue outside the bank. It sat there for a moment, head tilted, before taking off again.

The police suddenly leapt into action.

'Something's happening,' the reporter announced.

A team of tactical police officers stormed forward and entered the bank. Two ambulances drove right up to the front doors. More officers charged over. There seemed to be a moment of confusion and chaos, until the ambulance personnel were granted entry.

The reporter relayed to the viewers that gunshots had been heard inside the bank. It was not yet clear whether the captor had been serious about his threats, but it seemed most likely that the police had taken action first.

Emma continued watching the broadcast for another ten minutes, up to the moment the viewers received confirmation from the police that the ordeal was over, and that none of the hostages had been hurt.

A woman with curly blonde hair who looked like she was in her early-thirties walked into the café. Emma recognised her from the photos in the case file. She stood up and waved her over.

Her handshake was quick, to the point.

'Would you like a drink, something to eat?' Emma asked.

Monica Nesset smiled. 'Just a latte, thanks,' she replied.

'I'll get one too,' Emma said, and walked over to the counter.

She ordered, subtly studying Monica Nesset as she waited. A petite woman with a rather narrow face and a chest slightly too large to be natural on such a slender body. She was sitting with her back straight, looking rather prim and proper. Looking like she was aware of the fact too, Emma thought, without being able to put her finger on why she felt that way – other than her own prejudice. Maybe it was the elegant, clearly expensive clothes she was wearing. Or the necklace perched on her collar bone, one that screamed exclusivity, and probably cost an obscene amount of money. At first glance, there was nothing that would indicate that, just under five months ago, Monica Nesset had been through something traumatic that had very nearly resulted in her death. She didn't look particularly tormented by it.

Emma took the two coffees back to the table and smiled as she sat down. 'Thank you for coming to meet me.'

'I'm the one who should be thanking you,' Nesset replied, smiling back. 'Sick leave is so boring. I thought it would be like a *holiday*, you know? But six days in and you're already pretty sick of Netflix.'

Emma laughed. 'You're still off work then?'

'I'm on active sick leave now,' Nesset answered. 'So I can come and go when I want. I've just come from work actually.'

'How is it?' Emma asked. 'Being back at work, in the same place where it all happened?'

Monica Nesset took a sip of her latte.

'I was dreading it to begin with,' she said. 'But I've been seeing a psychotherapist, and they encouraged me to go back as soon as possible. And it felt good in the end. Like it gave me a kind of control, ownership, over what happened.'

Emma nodded and had a quick glance down at the questions she'd jotted down in advance.

'As I said when we spoke on the phone, I'm ... working on a book about what it's like for people to carry on with their everyday lives having been exposed to extreme trauma, but I wondered if I could start by asking you something else first? The name Sofia Kovic – does that mean anything to you?'

Nesset had a more watchful look in her eye when she heard Emma's question, and shuffled in her chair a little, straightening her back even more.

'Yes,' she said. 'That's the policewoman who was killed, right?'

Emma nodded eagerly, encouraged by Nesset's response.

'I met her,' Nesset continued. 'A few days before her murder, actually. It was awful, hearing what happened to her. She was a nice woman.'

'Very,' Emma agreed. 'Do you mind if I ... ask why she wanted to talk to you?'

Nesset scrutinised Emma, narrowing her eyes slightly, as if waiting for an explanation. Emma didn't want to volunteer any extra information: *Let the subject talk.*

'She wanted to talk to me about Aksel and our relationship and...' She looked down at the table. 'She was mainly interested in Aksel – how he had changed while we had been together. Or ... well, how he changed afterwards. As in, after I broke up with him.'

'In what way?'

'She asked about his behaviour. If he messaged me a lot, stalked or tried to manipulate me ... if he threatened me...'

She swallowed. A hint of pink had appeared in her cheeks as she spoke, just visible beneath the layer of foundation.

'And did he?'

Nesset collected herself before answering:

'Aksel was the kind of guy who couldn't stand losing,' she said, pulling the latte glass closer to her. 'It hit him quite hard, my not wanting to be with him anymore. Took a toll on his self-esteem. He thought I'd found someone else, of course, which I hadn't. I just didn't have those feelings for him anymore, and he couldn't handle it. He always wanted to be the best. The biggest. The strongest. The most attractive. Have the prettiest woman on his arm.' She quickly looked at Emma. 'I mean, I don't mean...'

'Don't worry,' Emma said, holding her hands up. 'You were his trophy. It's easy to see why,' she added with a disarming smile.

'I think he might have been a bit blindsided when I ended it, even though I feel like all the signs were there.'

She paused. Emma didn't ask any follow-up questions, just waited for her to continue.

'But, yes,' Nesset said after a while. 'There were a few red flags. Pretty much straight away, actually. First he was going to kill himself. Then he decided he wanted to kill me instead. Then he wanted to kill us both.'

'Did you believe him?'

Nesset thought about it.

'Not really,' she replied. 'It's what that kind of person tends to say if they've been rejected or they're depressed. But then people kill their partners all the time, everywhere. So, I was a bit worried in that respect, yes.'

'Did you tell anyone? The police, for example?'

She shook her head. 'I didn't know he had a gun, and I didn't believe he would actually go through with it, his threats.'

'Why not?'

'I thought he was too much of a coward to tell you the truth,' Nesset replied. 'But he got what he wanted in the end.'

'What do you mean?'

'He was shot. By the police.'

Emma picked up her pen and clicked the top with her thumb, ready to start writing.

'You think that was his plan then?' she asked. 'He wanted the police to shoot him?'

'Yes. Or ... maybe. It's the most rational explanation, I think. In hindsight anyway. He wasn't demanding money or anything.'

Emma waited for her to elaborate. Something else must have contributed to her having come to that conclusion.

'Aksel would call me at all hours of the day, even after the relationship had ended. When he'd been drinking, usually. He would go from begging for us to get back together to blaming me for everything that had gone wrong in his life. He threatened to kill himself, but I never thought he meant it. I thought he was just saying it to scare me or make me feel guilty and regret leaving him, and that it'd make me want to take him back. But ... he called me again the day before the whole ordeal. He seemed sober, for once, and very calm. Happy, almost. But he repeated his suicide mantra. I didn't think any more of it at the time, and I told him that – that he had to stop with the empty threats. I can clearly remember what he said to me.'

'What was that?'

'That he didn't need to do it himself.'

Emma put the nib of the pen to paper, but still didn't write anything.

'Again, it didn't mean anything to me at that point,' Nesset continued. 'But I understood what he meant afterwards. I think he had already decided, when he called that day – he sounded content, like he had this serenity about him, in the knowledge of what he was going to do.'

Emma nodded. 'Did you tell the police this? Afterwards?'

'Yes. I've spoken to my therapist about it as well. We'll never know what he was thinking, but the whole time he was in the bank, holding us hostage, he seemed so calm. As if he knew how it was going to end. Like he was prepared for it. Didn't close the curtains or anything, didn't try and make it difficult for the police.'

'What about Kovic? Did you tell her this?'

Monica Nesset nodded. 'Suicide by cop, she called it. And it's definitely a thing. When someone deliberately acts in a threatening way to provoke a deadly response from the police.'

Emma took a sip of her coffee. Wiped the foam from her upper lip.

'Why are you asking about all this?' Nesset asked.

'First and foremost because Kovic was asking the same questions,' Emma answered. 'Your case has been closed for months now, of course. There aren't really any major questions left either, regarding what happened that day. Yet Kovic came to talk to you in her spare time, investigating what happened, and she did the same for a few other cases too, just a few days before she was killed herself.'

'Why?' Nesset enquired.

'That's what I'm wondering,' Emma responded. 'I'm just splitting hairs so far. But maybe there's *something* about this case that links it to another investigation. Or any of the other cases. I know she was working on solving a hit-and-run murder, and she was looking at a few more.'

'But what could that "something" be?'

Emma shrugged and glanced down at her notebook, where she had written *Thobias Klevstrand*.

'Do you know the lawyer Thobias Klevstrand?' she asked on a whim. 'Or do you know if Aksel knew him?'

Monica Nesset leant back in her chair. It was clear from the expression on her face that Emma had unearthed something,

'He was a friend of Aksel's,' she said. 'They studied together.'

'And they both worked in offices on Aker Brygge too,' Emma pointed out.

Monica nodded. 'Thobias...' she began '...helped Aksel, with various things.'

'What kind of things?'

She considered Emma for a few seconds.

'You're a journalist?' she said. 'That's what you do, usually?'

'A news blogger,' Emma nodded. 'But I'm not writing anything about this. I'm just trying to understand what happened. Trying to get to the bottom of whatever Kovic had been working on in the days before she was killed.'

The woman on the other side of the table didn't look convinced. She sat there, eyes staring into Emma's, as if she were assessing whether it would be right to tell her anything else.

'Thobias helped Aksel with his will,' she said.

'He had already written a will then?'

Monica Nesset nodded. 'He had no one else,' she explained. 'He left me everything.'

'You were the sole beneficiary?'

'He didn't leave much,' Monica Nesset explained. 'He'd lost most of his money through various failed investments. There was minimal profit after selling his flat, so most of it came from the life insurance.'

Emma was trying to think through how to word her next question, but Monica Nesset continued herself:

'I received almost eight million kroner in total. It's not something I go round telling people, but I feel like I deserved that money, in a way. It was mainly the fact he actually had a will and had taken out insurance that made me certain he had planned everything he did that day.'

'In what way?'

'He wrote the will ten days beforehand. Signed the insurance the same day too.' She smiled weakly. 'With us,' she added. 'At the bank.'

Emma nodded.

'There was a standard exemption in one of the clauses,' Monica carried on. 'In the case of suicide, the insurance only applies if it was taken out a year in advance.'

Emma fiddled with the pen, but still didn't write anything. She would remember it all anyway.

'Did you tell Kovic about this as well?' she asked.

Monica Nesset shook her head. She looked troubled. She drained the tall latte glass and glanced at her watch.

'I have to get to another meeting...' she said.

'Of course,' Emma replied. 'Thank you for taking the time to meet with me though.'

Monica Nesset stood up. 'You should talk to Thobias Klevstrand,' she said. 'I've been wondering if he knew anything. If he could have said something to him about the small print in the insurance contract.'

Emma nodded. 'Thank you,' she said again.

The sound of Monica Nesset's high-heeled shoes clicking across the floor echoed around the café as she walked out.

Emma took the case file from her bag and read through it again. Who she really needed to talk to, she thought, was the lead investigator for the case, scribbling his name down in her notebook. Petter Falkum. First and foremost though, she needed to talk to Blix, and she knew exactly what to do to get him to talk.

60

Blix got into the car and put one hand on the steering wheel. Tried to summarise all the information he had just been presented with.

A clear picture was starting to form.

A probable scenario, at least.

Someone killed Walter Wiik in his cabin up in Nordmarka, and had tried to make it look like a suicide. On the way home, momentarily distracted, the perpetrator had hit Thea Bodin as she was cycling through

Maridalen. Everything seemed to indicate that *that* had, at least, been an accident. The damage to the car was significant enough to warrant a repair job. And the perpetrator knew Timo Polmar, so took the car to the workshop he worked at, only after having further dented it so they wouldn't be able to tie the damage on his car to the one the media had described in an appeal for more information. Regardless, he got Polmar to carry out the repairs as a favour, so neither the licence plate number nor his name would be registered anywhere.

Kovic must've found out who that was, Blix reasoned, and that was what had made her a target herself. And Iselin had only been involved because she'd been in the wrong place at the wrong time, and seeing as she may have been able to identify the perpetrator, became another victim who needed to be taken care of. A man who had been close to being exposed several times but, by ingenuity, luck, or a mix of both, had managed to get away every time.

The feeling of unrest coursing through Blix's body was too strong for him to just go straight home. He drove towards St. Hanshaugen instead, to Kovic's flat. Iselin's keys were still sitting in the cupholder between the seats of his car.

A gust of wind swept an empty plastic bag and various other pieces of rubbish across the road in front of the car. Blix pulled over, parked, and took Iselin's laptop in with him.

The key fought with the lock, just as it had done last time. It was cold in the flat. It didn't look like anyone else had been there since the last time.

He walked around the flat, once again looking at the aftermath of what had happened, and ended up in the living room. There, he took his jacket off and sat down with Iselin's laptop perched on his knees. It automatically connected to the Wi-Fi. After a few strokes of the keyboard, Blix had logged into his emails and was able to download the files he'd sent himself from the station.

The books Kovic had been reading were on the table in front of him. The corner of the note with the phone number of Walter Wiik's childhood friend was poking out of the book Blix had found it in. A psychology textbook. He pulled it towards him and opened the front cover. He hadn't put much thought into it last time, but she had left the note in a chapter about psychological explanatory models for suicide. She hadn't just slotted it in on any page. Kovic had been on to something.

Walter Wiik triggered a long chain of events. The investigation had taken Kovic all the way back to him. And now there was DNA evidence providing a direct link between the two cases. The same person who had faked Walter Wiik's suicide had taken Kovic's life. He was counting on Tine Abelvik coming to the same conclusion, which would force the investigation to take a step back, re-evaluate. Thus far, it had been about finding a motive for Kovic's murder, but they now had to work out who had murdered Walter Wiik too. There was a short-cut, however – find the owner of the car that hit Thea Bodin.

He returned his focus to the laptop and began with the data from Timo Polmar's phone. His activity was listed chronologically. The last time he had used it was a quarter of an hour before abducting Iselin. He had called Odd-Arne Drivnes. Prior to that, there had only been one other instance where they'd called each other.

He had also received a call from Eivind Neumann shortly after eight o'clock. Which made sense, given that the psychiatrist had to cancel his appointment on the same day, so he could see Iselin instead.

Blix sat there, staring at the entry on the list in front of him. That had been the start. It had changed everything. It had taken Iselin from him and destroyed his life.

There were just two calls recorded on the day before. An outgoing call to the job centre, and an incoming call from a telephone sales company.

He scrolled further down the list to get a general overview before processing it all. Nothing stood out, nothing grabbed him.

Polmar's list of contacts consisted of one hundred and seven saved numbers. Most were stored under the contact's first name, some with just initials or nicknames. A few entries included keywords indicating their relation to him. Some of the first names were the kind of car the person owned, some were a location. Several of the numbers were people from various public-sector institutions, such as social services, the job centre and the health services. There was also a priest, two doctors and a lawyer. One of the contacts stood out from the rest: 'Petter Police'.

Odd-Arne Drivnes' number was saved under 'Odd', while the psychiatrist was written phonetically as 'Noymann'.

Blix was convinced that the number of Kovic's murderer would be somewhere in his contact list, but he felt helpless without access to his usual tools. Without the software to identify who the numbers were registered to, without being able to search for the owners on the motor-vehicle register and align each contact with the type of car they owned, until he was left with just one of them. If he were at work, he would have managed it in about half a day. But now, he was groping around in the dark.

He leant forward to grab his phone so he could ring Abelvik. It was vital she understood how important this was, and how close they could be to the answer. It rang three times before the call was declined. Not long after, he received an automatic text telling him that she was busy and would call back later.

Blix chucked his phone onto the sofa beside him and sat there, considering the pile of library books under Kovic's coffee table. The book at the very bottom was the one about Charles Manson.

He eased it out from under the others and stared at the cover, looked down at the face of the notorious serial killer, still unable to grasp what made Kovic think someone like this was behind Bodin's death. The cases Kovic had been looking into didn't have much in common. No connection regarding method or type of victim. A staged suicide of a police officer, a hit-and-run, a spousal homicide committed out of jealousy, and a hostage situation that ended in a police sniper shooting the captor.

Blix stared into Charles Manson's eyes. There was something wild and unrestrained about them. He was commonly referred to as a serial killer, but he hadn't actually killed a single person himself. He'd always made others do it for him, similar to how the Aker Brygge captor had forced the police to kill him.

A gust of wind suddenly whipped the rain against the windows. Blix leant back into the sofa and closed his eyes. He could see the connections and a number of potential scenarios. He composed hypotheses and formed theories. But all he had in the end was speculation.

He continued sitting like that for a while, eyes closed. Realised he quite liked the darkness. He contemplated never opening his eyes again.

61

Half an hour later, Blix had pulled into a space just down the road from his flat on Tøyengata, exhausted after a day that had felt like an eternity.

He went to grab his phone from its holder on the dashboard but fumbled and lost his grip, making it tumble down into the space between the cupholder and the passenger seat. He leant over, trying to wriggle his fingers into the tight gap to fish it out, but couldn't quite reach.

He swore, got out of the car and walked round to the passenger side. Opening the door, he bent down and shoved the seat back. A few loose sheets of paper were lying under the seat. A few rogue reports, statements and interview notes from the case files Kovic had either requested or checked out of the archives. From the Aker Brygge hostage case and the Drammen hammer murder.

Blix collected the pages together and had a look through them on his way into the building and up to his flat on the second floor. Just a few steps away from his front door, something stopped him in his tracks, and he looked up.

'Hello.'

Emma was sitting on the floor, legs stretched out, back against the wall, gazing up at him. 'I'm glad you're here,' she continued. 'It's bloody freezing.'

From her spot on the floor, she demonstratively blew into her hands and rubbed them together.

Blix stared down at her.

He had thought about this moment, imagined that he would feel an instant spark of rage upon seeing her again, but a whole tsunami of other, unexpected emotions overwhelmed him instead.

And it hurt.

Deep, deep inside him.

Emma Ramm, whose life he had been secretly keeping up to date with ever since she was five years old, after making her fatherless. Someone who, for the same reason, he had always felt so much guilt about, and who he had tried to protect, help, when their paths crossed again. Someone he had trusted, appreciated, and who he had practically treated as his own daughter.

'Emma,' he said, despondently. 'Why are you here?'

'I'm waiting for you,' she answered. 'I'm tired of sending texts and getting nothing back.'

He sighed and made an exasperated gesture with his hand.

'I've brought these for you,' she said, sticking her hand into her bag. 'Kovic's case files.'

Blix took the two green folders from her and slipped the loose papers he'd just found in the car back inside.

'Thanks,' he said, staring down at her, standing where he had stopped moments earlier, having not moved in inch.

'We need to talk,' she continued.

'Do we?'

'Yes. We do.'

Blix inhaled deeply through his nose, and slowly exhaled through his mouth. With his eyes closed, he began:

'I know that...'

He stopped. Opened his eyes and blinked a few times. Looked up at the ceiling. Tried to stop the tears that were threatening to escape.

'I know that...' he tried again, but the words didn't want to come.

Emma pushed herself up. Her lip was trembling too.

'What I know,' she said, 'is that it's cold as hell out here.'

She lay a hand on his shoulder. It looked like she was trying to smile. She made a movement with her head, a nod towards the door.

'Let's go in, we can talk in there.'

It felt like all the air had left Blix's body. He couldn't fight it anymore. He looked into her face, blinking away the tears that had already broken free. He nodded and unlocked the door.

❋

Emma took her boots off and hung her coat on the hook. She left her bag on the floor in the hallway and followed Blix in.

'Have a seat,' he said, nodding towards the sofa opposite the TV. 'Do you want anything? Tea or something?'

'We can get to that in a bit,' she said.

Blix put the case files on the coffee table. Picked up the grey blanket draped across the sofa, folded it, hung it over the back of the seat and sat down. Emma sat in the armchair at the other end of the table. It looked like Blix had been living on the sofa for the last week. There was a pillow on one end. A woollen sock turned inside out. An empty bottle of some sort of spirit was peeking out from under the sofa.

Blix shuffled in his seat slightly. He had stopped crying.

'There's … quite a lot I've been wanting to say to you,' Emma said. That wasn't exactly true. She had spent a lot of time *thinking* about what she wanted to say, and how she would say it, but had never landed on anything that felt right, or meaningful enough. She wanted to say she was sorry, that she should've taken better care of Iselin, that she should've stayed out of that warehouse, as Blix had told her to do. It all sounded so obvious, and yet so futile. So meaningless.

'You don't have to,' Blix said quietly.

'Okay, but—'

'It doesn't matter,' he continued. 'It won't bring Iselin back.'

Emma tried again, but couldn't find the words.

'Will it make you feel better?' He looked directly at her. 'If you apologise or whatever, will that make everything alright again? For you?'

Emma looked down. 'It'll never be alright,' she said, subdued.

'So what's the point then?'

Neither of them said anything for a while. It felt like the walls were starting to close in around them.

'Maybe there is no point,' Emma said quietly.

Blix didn't respond.

'What *I'm* afraid of,' he said after a few moments of silence, 'is that I'll never be able to look at you without thinking about what happened. I'm worried that every time I see you or hear your voice, my mind will go straight to the absolute worst thing that has ever happened to me, and it makes me want to...'

He stopped himself. Paused for a few seconds before carrying on:

'And I'm not sure I can put myself through that,' he finished.

'I understand,' Emma said. 'I don't know if I can either. See you, be around you, call or text you without feeling the grief and sorrow, the guilt and...'

'So—'

'What's the point?' Emma interrupted him. 'I don't know,' she continued. 'Should we just go our separate ways, each go to the opposite end of the earth? Avoid any form of contact, any kind of experience or interaction that might remind us of what happened?'

Blix didn't respond.

'We won't read any newspapers in that case then? Won't watch the news? Are you going to say to hell with being an investigator, because that's what you were when Iselin died, that was the profession that got Kovic killed, that was what Iselin was training to be herself...?' She stared at him. 'Should we just avoid every single place we've been to together, all the places you and Iselin visited, and everywhere *I* went with her too?' Emma threw her arms out to the side. 'Should I stop being a journalist, seeing as that's how I got involved in all this? Should I go and sign up to be a bus driver or something instead? A yoga instructor?'

Blix clasped his hands together, his knuckles turning white.

'Will any of that solve anything?' Emma finished.

Blix ran a hand through his hair. 'I don't know,' he said.

Emma let out a heavy sigh. 'Me neither.'

After another long stretch of silence, she said: 'Maybe we both need to go to therapy.'

The corner of Blix's mouth twitched. 'Yeah, maybe.'

Another long silence descended around them.

'Someone once told me that time heals all wounds.'

Blix looked at her. 'I don't believe that. But I do believe that it gets *easier*, even though the wound never disappears. And maybe it'll be easier for the two of us too, but I don't know if that means we'll ever be able to be a part of each other's lives again.'

'I guess we'll just have to see,' Emma said. 'And out of the two of us, you're the one who's going to need the most time, so ... I think I'll just go, and erm, we'll ... see each other around.'

Blix looked down at the floor.

'Yeah, maybe we will.'

Emma looked at him. Put her hands on her knees and pushed herself up.

'We will.'

62

Blix stayed in his chair, aware of the immediate emptiness of the flat after Emma had let herself out. The urge to whet his palate with something suddenly took hold, but he didn't want anything strong, didn't want to numb the pain this time. He needed to keep his head clear. Needed to think.

He leant back into the sofa and shut his eyes. Emma's perfume – a light, sweet fragrance – hung in the air.

She was strong. Much stronger than he was. With everything she had been through in her life ... All Blix could say was that he admired her.

He thought about the interrogation at Kripos; it would surely have to resume sometime soon. He thought about Emma, who was probably going to be charged with something too. Because she'd tried to help him.

Blix shook his head, ashamed of the thoughts he'd had. Ashamed of how he had behaved. Life wouldn't be any easier if he continued to push her away. But it wouldn't be any better either. So what would help?

Finding the perpetrator.

Find him. Slam him against the wall. Hit...

He savoured the thought, allowing all the conversations he'd had over the last few days to run through his head, the connections he'd unearthed and explored, allowing them to mix, float back and forth.

Until something clicked.

A line of thought made his eyes shoot open, made him sit bolt upright. A hypothesis, a possible scenario.

He stood up and fetched Iselin's laptop. Opened the lid. The copy of Timo Polmar's contact list was still loaded on the screen.

Neumann.

Petter Police.

Odd-Arne Drivnes.

Petter Police.

Petter Falkum?

Blix got up and started pacing. Surely there was another Petter who worked in the police.

Ideas came at him from all directions. He thought through each one, looking for a way to confirm the suspicion that had just struck him. A way he could prove it. Something like...

The case files.

He walked back into the hall and grabbed them. Kovic had probably scrutinised every single page of each investigation. Standing there, Blix began with one of the documents he had retrieved from the car. Petter Falkum's report summarising the Aker Brygge hostage case.

He read it with growing eagerness. It was as if the words leapt off the page, throwing themselves at him.

He paused.

Quickly flipped through the rest of the documents until he reached the Drammen hammer murder case. He examined the murderer's confession, following each line with his finger as he read. His eyes darted back and forth across the page.

He stopped again.

Needed just one more piece of evidence, one last confirmation.

His phone was in the living room. Walking back into the room, he swiped it off the table and called Abelvik. Gave up after the fifth ring and tried Wibe. No response from him either.

The operations centre. They always picked up. If he was lucky, like last time, he would be put through to an operator who wasn't aware of his current predicament.

He swiped the phone log off the screen and tapped the operations centre number. A woman answered. He introduced himself and requested help with an inquiry regarding the motor-vehicle register. Told her it was urgent, to avoid any further questions.

It went just as smoothly as last time. He repeated the answer she gave him, whether aloud or just in his head, he wasn't sure: a Mercedes GLE 350. An SUV.

Colour: dark blue.

That was it.

When he thought it all through, everything made perfect sense.

'Was that all?' the operator asked.

'Hm?'

'Can I help you with anything else?'

'Oh, no, thank you,' Blix replied. 'I have everything I need.'

63

The intensity of the wind had picked up, as had the rain. Emma was glad she had chosen not to cycle there, opting to borrow Irene's car instead.

When she had called Petter Falkum, at first he had seemed distinctly indifferent. He was off work for a while, and besides, he wasn't interested in discussing police matters with a journalist. She didn't know exactly what she'd said to make him come round, but he must have realised that she was on to something. Something he might have been dwelling on too, perhaps.

The windscreen wipers squealed each time they swept from side to side. Emma leant over the steering wheel. Trying to figure out how to get through Filipstadkaia. Petter Falkum had told her that he was restoring an old boat he kept moored in one of the area's central jetties. He had detailed the route for her so she would be able to drive all the way up to the end of the dock.

Passing warehouses, containers and tarpaulin halls, she knew she was in the right place. She spotted a fishing boat with two masts lying somewhat tilted in the water, just as Falkum had described. It had sprung a leak, and he was in the process of draining it.

Driving as close as she could, she parked up next to a large car. There was a hose draped over the boat's railing, taking the water from the deck back into the sea. She could hear the hum of the pump working in the cabin below.

Petter Falkum emerged from the pilothouse and waved at her. The cold rain pummelled her face, assaulted her eyes and cheeks.

Falkum helped her on board.

'Is it safe?' she asked, trying to find her sea legs on the slanted deck.

'She's stabilised now,' Falkum replied. 'But I was worried I was going to lose her. A cooling pipe in the engine had burst. Took in a few thousand litres of water before I managed to turn it off, but I'm nearly done. She should be upright again in no time.'

Emma followed him into the pilothouse. 'Quite a project,' she commented as she looked around.

'The plan is that she'll be fully restored in about three years,' Petter Falkum said. 'I'll be fifty-seven by then and can retire.'

'And you'll head off somewhere, get away from it all?'

He smiled. One of his eyes met hers, while the other remained fixed on the deck.

'As far as she'll take me,' he replied. 'Somewhere south, at least. Warmer climes. Norwegian winters are far too cold for me.'

The wind whipped against the masts outside, making them whistle. The rain bombarded the windows.

'By yourself?' Emma asked.

The ageing policeman glanced at her.

'I found your number online,' she said. 'It was registered to the same address as a woman.'

'Oh, I see. No. It's been a while since she set sail herself,' he said with a smile, pleased with his own comment.

Emma smiled back. Falkum sat in the revolving chair in front of the helm, and spun it round so he had his back to the bow. He gestured for Emma to take a seat opposite him.

'I've not been in work since last Saturday,' he said. 'Off sick at first, then I decided to take some of my annual leave. I don't know much more about Kovic's murder, other than what I've read and seen on the news.'

Emma thought about the Drammen hammer murderer, Tore André Ulateig, but didn't want to bring that up just yet.

Her phone went off in her jacket pocket – someone was calling her. Emma reached in to turn the sound off without looking to see who it was.

'I'm glad you agreed to meet with me, anyway,' she said, aware that her phone continued to vibrate. 'You worked with Kovic on the Bodin case, right?'

'Initially,' Falkum nodded.

Emma tried to reposition herself on the bench. It felt hard and uncomfortable.

'I'm trying to understand what happened,' she said. 'I think she may have come across something while she was investigating that case.'

Falkum leant forward slightly. 'What was that then?' he asked. 'What have you found, exactly?'

Emma was unsure where to begin.

'You know who Thobias Klevstrand is, right?' she asked.

'The lawyer,' Falkum stated with a nod.

'Are you aware of his role in the Aker Brygge hostage case?' Emma asked. 'That he helped Aksel Jens Brekke a few days before the incident?'

'Helped him? With what?'

Emma told him all she knew. Falkum folded his arms across his chest as he listened.

'I don't get what that has to do with the case,' he said when she was done.

'There must have been a reason why Kovic had started digging into a closed, archived case,' Emma proffered.

She felt her phone start buzzing in her jacket pocket again. She fished it out this time to decline the call, but froze. It was a video call. A FaceTime request.

From Iselin.

64

The call ended before Emma had time to answer it.

She suddenly realised that she was trembling.

'Sorry about this,' she said, looking up at Petter Falkum. 'I think I need to call someone back...' She held her phone up. 'Do you mind?'

'Not at all, go ahead.'

Emma stood up. 'I'll just go out to the car and take it there,' she said.

'Sure, no problem,' Falkum replied.

Emma went back up to the deck, holding her phone tightly in one hand as she used the other to climb onto the jetty. As soon as she was behind the wheel, she called Iselin's number back.

'Blix?' she said the moment the video call was picked up. 'Is that you?'

'Hi,' he whispered.

'You've got Iselin's phone?' Emma asked, but received no explanation.

'Can you record this call?' Blix requested.

'What's going on?' she asked.

'I've not got much time,' Blix said, looking around. 'Can you record this call or not?'

'Er, yes, I can. I think.'

'Do it,' Blix said. 'Now.'

'Now?'

'Yes. Right now.'

Emma did as Blix asked. She probed around on her phone for a bit until she figured it out.

'Sorted,' she told him. 'Why though?'

'I can't get a hold of Abelvik or any of the others. None of them answering. Or returning my calls.'

Blix's colleagues must have been trying to distance himself while he was suspended, Emma thought.

'You need to get hold of them,' Blix continued. 'Warn them.'

The windscreen had started to steam up. Emma glanced over at the tired fishing boat. Petter Falkum was out on the deck again.

'About what?' she asked Blix.

'I don't have time to explain,' he answered. 'You'll understand soon enough.'

'Where are you, though?'

It didn't seem like Blix had heard her. His face disappeared from the screen and was replaced with a chaotic blur, with Emma only managing to catch fragmented glimpses of his surroundings. She tried to figure out where he was, but it was hard to tell with the phone moving around so much. Blix came back into focus again, a little further away this time. The phone was still now. He looked like he was checking to see if it was steady, making sure the camera was facing the right direction. He took a few steps back, reviewing how much could be seen on the screen, then approached the camera again.

'Where are you?' Emma repeated. She squinted at the screen, trying to identify the room Blix was calling from. And then it hit her.

'In Jessheim,' he answered. 'The workshop at Jessheim.' He glanced around. 'Is it recording?'

'Yes.'

'Great,' Blix replied. 'I've got to run.'

'Wait!' Emma shouted after him.

She had so many questions, but Blix hadn't heard her. He must've muted the call on his end.

'Blix!' she yelled anyway, but he had disappeared somewhere out of shot.

65

Blix left the workshop and went to wait outside, standing under the eaves of the warehouse to keep out of the rain. There was a biting chill in the air.

He was glad he had come back to the warehouse once before, since Iselin's death. The memories that came rushing back, whether he wanted them to or not, weren't quite as excruciating as they were the last time he was here, but he thought that might have been because of what he was here to do. He wasn't sure which emotion was currently more powerful – the sadness, the anger, or the fear of what the next few minutes might hold. Of what was going to happen. He was tense. Anxious to get started. The combination of all of this at once made him feel nauseous.

He looked up at the sound of a car coming down the same road he had a short while earlier. A large, white Porsche sailed into the car park and swung round to the spaces in front of the building. The car's headlights swept over Blix, blinding him.

He remained where he was, squinting as he watched it roll to a stop, listened as the humming of the engine died down. The man behind the wheel took a few seconds to check his phone before opening the car door and stepping out. He was wearing a dark, elegant coat that fell effortlessly from his broad shoulders. He was wrapped up well against the cold, a grey scarf around his neck and a pair of black gloves on his hands. He removed one as he walked over to Blix.

Blix shook his outstretched hand. 'You found your way alright then?' he remarked.

Eivind Neumann smiled. 'Yes, no problem,' he answered, putting his glove back on. 'What would we do without mobile phones?'

'Thank you for coming at such short notice.'

'Don't mention it,' Neumann replied. 'If I can help in anyway at all in an emergency like this, I'll naturally do it. It's my duty.'

Blix forced himself to nod in response.

Neumann continued watching him for a few seconds.

'Have you been having these thoughts for a while?' he asked.

Blix felt his hands clench into fists in his pockets. 'What thoughts?'

'The ones you mentioned in your message,' Neumann said. 'The thoughts about you wanting to ... end it all?'

Blix considered his question.

'They come and go,' he answered, then coughed. 'More and more frequently, actually. I'm scared of what I might do right now. I don't like the darkness that has taken over me. I've never been like this before.'

'Well you've never been in a situation like this before,' Neumann responded. 'So it's no surprise to hear you're feeling that way. When you're going through something like this, what you're going through now, it's normal to feel like you want to end it all. And if you wanted to come *here*, now, while you're in this state...' he inhaled sharply '...this might suggest that you want to inflict more pain on yourself. And, speaking from a psychiatrist's point of view, even though being here might help you move on, I don't think it's a good idea for you to be here alone. So I'm happy you got in touch. And that you actually asked me to come – that tells me that you recognised the signals, the danger you pose to yourself, and decided to take precautions. It tells me that you are a strong person. A person willing to admit that you need help.'

Reluctantly, Blix acknowledged how the psychiatrist's words made him feel, how they gave him a sense of pride.

'There's a saying about hiding skeletons in a closet,' Neumann said. 'Even if you lock the door, they'll still be in there.'

'You could always just set the closet on fire though.'

Neumann stared at him. 'Yes, that would be the easiest solution, of course.'

'And probably the best one in some cases, no?'

Neumann looked like he was trying to choose his next words carefully: 'That's true, not everyone can bring themselves to live with those skeletons, whether they leave them out in the open or not. For many, especially those left behind, suicide is actually the easiest option. A way out. It sounds wrong to say it out loud, but with that option, you don't have to suffer anymore, and those around you don't have to feel so anxious, on alert all the time, always dreading that every call, every text might be awful news. A lot of families actually tend to do much better afterwards, even though their grief and sorrow will always be there, of course.'

'I don't have much family left.'

'Do you not?'

Blix shook his head. 'My father died a long time ago,' he explained. 'And my mother...' He looked down. He hadn't thought about her for a long time.

'It's a complicated story,' he said instead.

They stood in silence for a moment.

'Have you got a new car?' Blix asked, nodding towards the Porsche.

Neumann looked surprised at the sudden change of topic.

'No,' he said hesitantly. 'I got this one last summer.'

'What were you driving before?'

It took him a moment to answer.

'A Mercedes.'

Blix nodded. Let the response go unanswered.

'So it happened here?' the psychiatrist asked, his voice softer. He looked around while he asked.

'In there mostly,' Blix said, with a nod back towards the workshop.

'We probably need keys to get in I'd imagine?'

'No, it's open,' Blix replied, without explaining how he knew. Neumann scrutinised him, as if he thought it a bit strange, but didn't comment on it.

They walked round to the back of the warehouse. Blix opened the door and gestured for Neumann to go in first. The psychiatrist took a few wary steps inside.

Blix followed him in, leaving the door open.

'I have actually been back here once already,' he said.

Neumann turned his head slightly to look at him. 'Oh?'

'Not inside, just outside,' Blix explained. 'A few days ago. Or was it yesterday? I'm not sure. The days all blend into one. But it was then that I realised that Timo Polmar must have worked here, seeing as he brought Iselin *here*, to an empty warehouse of all places. He knew there wouldn't be anyone here because he knew that his boss, Gunnar Sundby, had filed for bankruptcy and closed the place down. And Polmar still had his keys as well.'

Neumann carried on, further into the building. It was pitch-black ahead.

'Just continue straight on,' Blix told him.

Neumann reached the door to the workshop and pushed it open. His shoes made a dull thudding sound as the heel came into contact with the concrete floor. Blix walked over to the control panel on the wall.

'I'll see if we can get a little light in here,' he said.

The hall was suddenly bathed in a blinding white light.

66

The windscreen wipers made long, sweeping arcs as they swiped the rainwater off the glass. Emma drove close up behind the car in front, flashing her lights and forcing it to pull into the other lane.

She had placed her phone in the cupholder between the seats, the screen tilted towards her, but she couldn't see anything. The lights were off in the room, leaving the display a dark grey. As long as she was recording the video call, she couldn't use her phone to notify the others. She hoped that Petter Falkum had understood what she had shouted to him before driving off. That he had to warn Abelvik and the rest of the department, and where he should send them.

There was no movement on the screen. Luckily, her phone was almost fully charged.

She checked her rear-view mirror in the hope of seeing blue flashing lights, desperate for Blix's colleagues to be on their way there already, but all she saw through the rain-washed window were the white headlights of the cars behind.

The speedometer flickered just below 130 kilometres per hour. The wheels charged through the surface water covering the road.

Something on the screen caught her attention. She glanced down. A light had come on, illuminating the spacious workshop.

She picked up the phone with one hand, turned up the sound and held it in her eyeline beside the steering wheel, using the other hand to drive.

The wheels on one side hit a puddle, jerking the car to the left. Emma managed to straighten the car and slowed down, while simultaneously trying to follow what was happening on the screen. Blix came into shot, followed by a man she recognised immediately.

Emma gasped.

'Have you ever been to a crime scene before?' she heard Blix ask.

Emma swallowed. Had to strain her ears to hear what was being said.

'Depends on what you mean by crime scene,' Eivind Neumann replied. 'I've not been to an active crime scene, to put it that way – as in, a place you can clearly tell has recently *been* the scene of a crime. But I've been in buildings and homes where people have died, yes. So in that respect, I have.'

'I've been to a lot,' Blix said. 'Both active and inactive.'

'Naturally, considering your job,' Neumann replied.

Emma listened intently.

'You think you'd get used to it,' Blix continued. 'But ... you don't. And when it's someone you know, or someone you loved, it festers – up here.' He tapped his finger to the side of his head, simultaneously taking a few steps back, positioning himself so that Neumann would follow and stand closer to the camera.

'You've probably had your fair share of officers come and talk to you about the same issue?' Blix continued.

Neumann didn't respond.

'I know, I know,' Blix said, holding his hands up. 'You can't say anything about individual patients, but in general?'

'I have certainly spoken to a number of officers who find it difficult to cope with the things they've seen and experienced while on the job,' Neumann said eventually. 'But that is the nature of the profession.'

'Walter Wiik,' Blix said. 'Remember him?'

Emma didn't know who Blix was talking about. Walter Wiik must've been a policeman, but she'd never heard the name before. Neumann didn't seem to be following Blix's train of thought either.

'He shot himself in his cabin in Nordmarka last year,' Blix clarified. 'In early May.'

'Wiik, yes,' Neumann said, as if it had just clicked. 'Yes, I remember him, of course, he came to see me a few times.'

'I don't know what exactly he came to see you about,' Blix said, 'but I'd always thought of him as a seasoned policeman, experienced. After that though, it was easy to jump to the conclusion that perhaps it had all become a bit too much for him. The problems had all been bottled up. The cork was ready to shoot out.'

Neumann folded his hands behind his back, not offering a response.

'The officers investigating the case, who analysed Wiik's life, saw what they wanted to see,' Blix continued. 'A lonely man battling with his personal demons. An easy conclusion to come to. But Sofia Kovic saw something else.'

Emma was confused now. She truly had no idea what Blix was talking about.

'Kovic had the evidence re-examined,' Blix carried on. 'Someone else's DNA was found inside one of the gloves Wiik had been wearing when he supposedly shot himself.'

Neumann took a step towards him now. 'What are you saying?'

'Someone murdered him,' Blix said. 'That person was wearing the gloves when they shot him, and they placed them on the body afterwards.'

'You say that. But who?' Neumann asked.

'The department are figuring that out,' Blix replied. 'Should have an answer in a day or two.'

He made a dismissive gesture with his hand, as if to wave Neumann's question away, like it wasn't important. He then tilted his head back and stared up at the ceiling, where Iselin had been hanged.

67

'She never woke up,' Blix said.

He lowered his gaze. Stared at the concrete floor, the place Iselin had landed.

'We didn't get to say another word to each other.'

He glanced back up at Neumann and started pacing, walking in a curve around the same spot, while trying to ensure they were both still in view of the hidden camera.

'Timo Polmar died there,' he said, pointing to the dark stain made by his dried blood. 'You knew him,' Blix continued. 'He was one of your patients.'

Neumann didn't comment on the statement. Instead, he asked: 'Can I ask how you felt when you shot him?'

Blix considered the question, tried to recollect how he had felt, what had gone through his head at the time, but couldn't quite put his finger on anything concrete.

'I wasn't thinking about anything other than Iselin,' he eventually answered, followed by a long exhale.

The silence of the warehouse settled around them. All that could be heard was the rain pounding against the roof. He closed his eyes. He couldn't keep them out – the thoughts, the images of that night. The gun, the rope, how he had aimed at it, shot at it, how it had frayed, fibre by fibre, so slowly, too slowly. The fall, how her body had rotated, its weightlessness, the eternity it took for her to hit the ground, the sound of her slamming against the concrete, her head as it hit the floor...

'Have you reflected at all since then – on what happened?' Neumann continued.

The gentleness in his voice made Blix open his eyes, transporting him back into the present.

'Reflected on the fact that I killed a man?'

'Yes?'

'No, there's been more than enough to reflect on with...'

He had to shut his eyes again. Push her away, he told himself. Focus on what you're here to do.

'What are you thinking about right now?' Neumann asked, taking a few steps further into the room. 'Now that you're here?'

The psychiatrist looked around, taking in his surroundings. As if he were trying to absorb all its details. Blix waited a moment, before answering.

'I'm thinking that he got what he deserved.'

Neumann turned to him and cupped his hand to his chin, like he was contemplating Blix's statement.

'Polmar was only being used as a kind of mercenary though,' Blix added. 'He wasn't acting on his own accord, but he was still the one who put the noose around her neck. If he hadn't done that, if he hadn't forced her off the edge up there, Iselin would still be alive.'

'So you assumed the role of executioner.'

'In a way,' Blix agreed.

Neumann nodded slowly. 'That *is* something you can do though,' he said.

'What do you mean?' Blix asked.

'You *can* end someone's life – because your job permits it.'

'In some cases, yes.'

'Does that make you feel powerful?'

Blix fixed his gaze on one of the cracks running along the concrete floor. It was an odd question to be asked, but he tried to think about it.

'I don't know if "powerful" is the right word,' Blix replied.

Neumann crossed his hands behind his back again.

'Ultimately, it's your decision whether someone lives or dies,' Neumann said. 'A lot of people would describe that as a powerful position to be in.'

'Maybe,' Blix said. 'I've never thought of it that way. But that applies just as much to your profession as well, no?'

'What do you mean?' Neumann turned to face Blix.

'I would imagine that the people coming to you are those struggling with their own thoughts to such an extent that they could even find themselves on the brink of suicide. What *you* say or do could also have a huge impact.'

'To a certain extent,' Neumann agreed. 'It is a considerable responsibility. But you know that from your own line of work.'

Still gazing at the crack in the floor, Blix followed it with his eyes. It disappeared beneath one of the workbenches.

He had often felt the weight of that responsibility. The split-second decisions that were his to make. Actions that would have major consequences for everyone involved, often irreversible. Like whether or not to pull the trigger.

'It leaves a mark,' he said, pointing to his head again. 'Eats away at you. Manifests as wounds that never heal. That only cause more pain.'

Neumann took a step closer. 'Do you think that might be why you chose to come here?'

Blix shrugged.

'You felt the urge to take your own life,' Neumann speculated. 'Just a few days after taking someone else's.'

'Yes, but I only feel that way when I think of Iselin.'

'Are you sure about that?'

Blix didn't know how to answer.

'It's only been a year and a half since you were last implicated in another incident involving a shooting. One that had a fatal outcome,' the psychiatrist continued. 'You never came to talk to me about it, or anyone else, did you?'

'No, I...'

'You shot and killed a man a little over twenty years ago too,' Neumann added. 'Emma Ramm's father.'

Blix crossed his arms.

'What I'm trying to say,' the psychiatrist added, 'is that you've never properly dealt with how you really feel about killing someone. And maybe – *maybe* – that's had a deeper impact on you than you realise.'

Blix thought that Neumann might've been on to something.

'I mean, you've shot and killed three people. That's quite a few more than most police officers ever have to deal with, or could even handle, over the course of their careers. At least here in Norway, anyway. It's hard enough doing it just the once.'

Blix looked down. Put in that way, it sounded horrendous.

'I don't know how justified it was, shooting Timo Polmar,' he admitted.

'You don't?'

Blix shook his head. 'He was on his way out. I could have shot him in the leg instead. That would've stopped him from leaving just as effectively.'

'So you reacted rashly?'

Blix deliberated for a moment.

'I acted out of anger, yes. I lost control of myself. Had I not done that, we would've been able to find out who he was working for.' He looked at Neumann. 'Lucky for him,' Blix said. 'Whoever hired Polmar, I mean.'

The psychiatrist stayed silent.

'In the moment though, my thoughts were simply to stop him. That was the reason I shot him,' Blix continued. 'But I acted in a moment of rage too. I shot him because...' He had to stop himself. His vision had started to blur as his eyes brimmed with tears. 'He had hurt my daughter. He'd tried to kill her.'

Blix had to pause again.

'Shit,' he muttered, followed by a deep breath. 'Maybe I shot him because I *did* want to kill him.' He lifted his gaze to meet the psychiatrist's. 'Regardless, I do feel guilty about it,' he admitted.

'Another reason to be here then,' Neumann said with an understanding smile. 'It could help you see things more clearly.'

Blix nodded.

'It's a heavy burden to carry,' Neumann said, his voice taking on that gentle tone again.

Blix wiped the tears away. 'I don't know if I can do this,' he said.

'What do you mean?'

'If I can...' He had to force himself to finish the sentence: 'Live with it.'

'You're scared of what you might do.'

'Yes.'

'You don't know if you can bear living with the pain. The loss of your daughter. The fear of knowing what you're capable of.'

Blix nodded, acknowledging how the psychiatrist's words had worked their way into his head.

'It is a heavy burden,' he said. 'So fucking heavy.'

Neumann took another few steps towards him. 'And now you've started to contemplate taking your own life,' he said in a low voice. 'In what way have those thoughts manifested?'

'How have I thought about doing it, you mean?'

Neumann nodded encouragingly.

'I think about it when I'm driving, for example,' Blix began. 'I've thought about just driving straight into the side of the mountain, or a river or something. But now, now I'm *here*...' He glanced up. At the hoisting mechanism, the pulley on the ceiling. 'I think I should die in the same way Iselin did.'

'By hanging yourself?'

Blix nodded. 'I couldn't save her,' he said, his voice breaking now. 'I want to know what she went through.'

'To punish yourself,' Neumann stated.

'Yes.'

The psychiatrist was standing close to Blix now.

'Do you want to die?' he asked, his eyes boring into Blix's. 'Or do you want to live?'

Blix looked at him. Held his gaze.

'Because if you do want to die...' Neumann continued. 'If you understand that that would be for the best...'

He stopped, raised his eyes to the ceiling. Looked back down again, into Blix's eyes.

It was a surprisingly easy decision to make, Blix thought. To lower the noose around his neck. To do it. To end the suffering and become one with the darkness, for good. Be with Iselin.

Blix closed his eyes.

He could feel a throbbing in his temple. As if the walls of his skull were trying to meet. He opened his eyes again.

'What I want,' he said, taking a step towards Neumann now. 'Is for you to take your shirt off.'

68

Blix moved a few steps to the side, closer to the spot where Iselin's phone was propped up, hidden, so Neumann would follow him, ensuring that everything they said and did would be captured on the recording.

'What did you say?' Neumann asked.

'You heard what I said.'

Neumann furrowed his brow.

'I heard, but ... you want me to take my shirt off?'

'Yes.'

'Why?'

Blix looked him in the eye. 'You know why,' he said.

The psychiatrist stared at him, eyes narrowed, not offering a response.

'Iselin,' Blix said. 'She fought with the man who killed Kovic. Burned him with her curling tong.'

Neumann stood there, eyes fixed on Blix's face. 'And you think that was *me*?'

'I *know* it was you.'

The psychiatrist looked like he was struggling to find the words.

'You have a burn mark on your chest. I want to see it.'

Neumann transferred his weight from one leg to the other. 'I ... don't understand...'

'You don't understand why I want to see it?'

'I ... don't understand what you're talking about.'

Blix locked eyes with Neumann now. 'Were you nervous, that day Iselin came in for her appointment?' Blix asked. 'Were you afraid she would know it was you? Recognise your eyes? Or your body, or your cologne, perhaps?'

Neumann cleared his throat. 'I understand that this is a difficult time for you,' he began. 'But to accuse me of...' He looked away momentarily. 'To claim that *I*...' Neumann shook his head. 'It's ridiculous ... I don't even know what to say.'

'You don't need to say anything,' Blix told him. 'A DNA test will tell us all we need to know. And the DNA on Iselin's curling tong will match that found in Walter Wiik's glove. It won't matter how much you deny it or try to explain your way out of it. I *know* it was you,' he repeated. 'Would you like to know how I know?'

Neumann looked uncomfortable, blinked rapidly a few times.

'Or are you enough of an adult to admit it? Here and now, face-to-face with the father of one of your victims?'

'Blix. Come on...'

Neumann was struggling to formulate a response.

'Drop it,' Blix spat. 'I can *see* how it's all connected. But the thing I'm most curious about, is *why* do it at all?'

Blix took a few steps away from Neumann.

'But I think I may have an answer for that. You mentioned feeling powerful. You asked me how it felt to shoot Timo Polmar. *That* is what I think this is all about. That feeling of choosing whether someone lives or dies, of being so powerful and intelligent that you can control and manipulate others, so they either kill themselves or kill someone else. It's all about that rush you get from it. And yet, it must've gone wrong with at least two of them.'

He turned to face Neumann.

'Walter Wiik,' Blix stated. 'What actually happened? Did he refuse to kill himself? Did your words not work on him?'

Neumann shook his head in frustration.

'Were you worried that he would start talking about your practice?' Blix continued. 'Your methods? Worried he'd tell someone that you'd tried to convince him to kill himself? And that someone would then look into the suicide rates among your patients?'

He took a step closer to the psychiatrist again.

'I think that's what Kovic had started looking into, just from a different angle. She'd found out that Tore André Ulateig and Jens Aksel Brekke had both been patients of yours – two men who had each come to the conclusion that their only options were, respectively, to murder their ex-wife, and to take hostages and behave in a way that was *just* threatening enough that Delta had no other choice but to shoot.'

Blix paused. It felt good to verbalise his accusations. To say them out loud.

'You manipulated Timo Polmar in a different way, though,' he carried on. 'Firstly, you used him to repair that dark-blue Mercedes of yours, after damaging it when you hit Thea Bodin. After that, you encouraged him to live out his wildest fantasies. To abduct a woman. And kill her. The problem with that plan was that, when it came down to actually doing it, he couldn't. He didn't have it in him, couldn't kill her himself, and that's why he brought Iselin here instead.'

Neumann shook his head again, but didn't object.

'Kovic was on your trail,' Blix continued. 'She recognised you for what you were – a kind of Norwegian Charles Manson, convincing others to kill on your behalf. She just had to work out *how* to expose you. That was why she booked those sessions with you. She wanted to see what you were like. See and hear what you would say to her, experience the way you dealt with patients first-hand. If you followed the book, or if you did things your own way.'

Blix paced in a circle around him.

'And it may very well be the case that someone *was* harassing Kovic at work. There are enough pigs and dinosaurs still working in the force for me to believe that ... but I knew Kovic. She was tough, and she would never have let a slap on the arse or anything inappropriate get to her. She would've said something. Chewed the guy out and carried on with her day. You made all that up, in an attempt to make your patient notes look more believable, while simultaneously turning the focus of the investigation away from your own practice.'

Neumann held his palms up. 'I don't have to listen this,' he said, taking a few steps backward.

Blix followed him, taking care not to push him too far, out of shot.

'Relax,' he said, opening up his jacket, turning his pockets inside out and lifting up his jumper, so his bare stomach and chest were exposed. 'I'm not wearing any recording devices. I'm not on duty. I'm here for my own benefit. For answers.'

'You claim to have DNA evidence,' Neumann said at last. 'So you've supposedly got all the answers you need, have you not?'

Blix shook his head. 'The lab reports only point to who's responsible,' he said. 'I want to know the truth. How you got to that point.'

Neumann rolled his eyes, opened his mouth to talk, but didn't get a chance.

'You spoke about *me* and the people I've killed,' Blix interrupted. 'But how many lives are weighing on *your* conscience? It must be a lot, seeing as you saw it necessary to kill Walter Wiik. Do for yourself what he refused to do.'

He took yet another step towards the man before him.

'When did it all start?' he asked. 'How long has this been going on for?'

Neumann clasped his hands together.

'Alright then, when did it escalate?' Blix pressed. 'Did you realise you preferred being face to face with your victims when you killed them? Preferred looking them in the eye? Like you did when you executed Kovic? Was it a different kind of rush, perhaps? And you found you quite liked it?'

Neumann removed one of his gloves and began to unbutton his coat. He kept eye contact with Blix. Reached into the inside pocket, and pulled out a pistol.

The psychiatrist's demeanour changed instantly, as if a cold screen had just been pulled over his eyes. They stood there, staring at each other. Blix glanced between Neumann and the gun.

He swallowed.

'Give me your phone,' Neumann demanded.

Blix hesitated.

'Now,' Neumann ordered. 'Hand me your phone.'

Blix stuck his hand into his jacket pocket and pulled his phone out.

'Unlock it and put it on the floor. Kick it over to me.'

Blix did as he was told. Neumann bent down and picked it up, all the while keeping his eye, and the gun, fixed on Blix. He glanced down at the screen.

Blix knew what he was checking for. Outgoing calls, active audio recordings. Recent texts. Ensuring it was just the two of them, that there was no one else. No one who knew where he was or who he was there with.

Neumann looked at Blix. 'You know,' he said with a crooked smile. 'I had a feeling there was something off about your message ... that it was odd how you all of a sudden wanted to kill yourself. It was just a ruse. A lie to get me here.'

He waved the gun, as if to indicate that he had come prepared.

'I knew you wouldn't be able to just let it lie. And I understand that. Your own daughter...' Neumann shook his head. 'If it's any comfort to you at all,' he continued, 'I never intended for her to get wrapped up in all this.'

'I gathered as much.'

'I'd originally thought of doing the same to Kovic as I did with Walter Wiik,' Neumann added. 'Make it look like she'd done it herself, but your daughter got in the way. Ruined my plan. I had to use Timo Polmar to clean up.'

'Risky,' Blix commented.

'It was a last-minute solution,' Neumann said. 'But Timo was available. He had a session booked in with me the next day, and he was easy to manipulate. All I needed to do to persuade him was press the right buttons. If he was arrested, no one would take him seriously. He was a sick man with sick fantasies, a man who had previously lied to the police on numerous occasions.'

He paused for a moment.

'Besides, I didn't have a choice. And I couldn't say no to meeting your daughter. It was a golden opportunity to find out what exactly she knew, or remembered. When she came in that morning, there was nothing to suggest she recognised me, but I know enough about trauma to see that there was every chance she would connect the dots later. So I let Timo make his fantasies a reality.'

Blix's stomach lurched.

'He was meant to shoot her and dump her body, but he fucked it up,' Neumann sighed. 'I should've known, and I did know really, that when it came down to it, he didn't have it in him.'

He looked up at the pulley.

'But he knew that he had to kill her, seeing as she'd seen his face. So he found an alternative method. A way that meant he could avoid actually killing her himself, keep his distance and control it from afar, so he wasn't directly involved. It was all the same to me, mind, how he did it ... and it would've worked. But then you showed up, and it all went downhill pretty drastically. Even though the end result was basically the same. And best of all,' he said, with a smile, 'was that you spared me from having to clean up myself. I didn't have to take care of Timo afterwards. Neither Timo nor your daughter would be able to tell anyone about my role in all of this. Because they were both dead. And it was all your fault, in both cases.'

The rain outside had become more intense. It was hammering against the roof.

'And everyone understands the effect this has had on you, how depressed you are,' Neumann said, a mockingly compassionate tone to his voice. 'How far gone you are. They'll all understand that you had been getting closer and closer to your breaking point, and that you eventually just ... tipped over the edge.'

'What do you mean?' Blix asked.

'The choice you made,' Neumann answered, wiggling the gun ever so slightly. 'You said you wanted to die like your daughter. I think that's a solid proposal. An apt, almost poetic way to end your life. And I'm ready,' he said. 'Are you?'

69

Eivind Neumann.

The psychiatrist.

All the pieces of the puzzle fell into place as Emma raced down the motorway.

It was obvious now – he was the common denominator in every case Kovic had looked into. As a psychiatrist, Neumann regularly came into contact with people who were particularly vulnerable. It was his duty to help them, but he had pushed them further down a destructive path.

Emma had read through the Drammen hammer murder case files meticulously but hadn't come across any mention of Neumann – he must've been named somewhere in the documents that had fallen out and were left in Blix's car. Rather than helping Tore André Ulateig to accept, overcome and move on from the breakdown of his marriage, Neumann had steered him in the opposite direction. When the police had interviewed those around Ulateig, they had all said the same thing, and it had been included in all the reports: he'd been getting treatment, but he hadn't been getting better. Instead, he'd only become more convinced that his ex-wife was out to hurt both him and their children, and that killing her would be best for everyone.

As was the case with Aksel Jens Brekke. His heartbreak and financial losses had hit him hard. He'd been referred to a psychiatrist because he wanted to take his own life. He didn't have it in him to kill himself, though, but someone had told him how he could make others do it for him.

Neumann's list of patients must have been full of similar incidents. He had been a licensed psychiatrist for almost thirty years. At some point over the course of his career, the opportunity to control and manipulate other people's lives must have consumed him. The authority he had over them, choosing whether they lived or died, must have eventually made him lose control of himself.

Emma's phone started ringing, snapping her out of that train of thought. *Tine Abelvik* flashed across the screen. The call interrupted the recording. Emma couldn't answer, otherwise the video would cut off completely. She would have to leave it.

The recording continued. She could hear Blix playing for time, working his way through the same questions she wanted to ask, enquiring about what had been going through Neumann's mind when he arranged Iselin's abduction.

The psychiatrist had become uncommunicative, as if he just wanted to get it over and done with. He explained in short, blunt sentences how Timo Polmar was supposed to follow Iselin and wait until she was alone. They had never decided to involve anyone else, such as Odd Arne-Drivnes. Polmar, armed with the same gun Neumann had used to kill Kovic, had been instructed to strike as soon as he saw the chance. And the opportunity presented itself the moment Iselin left the psychiatrist's office, because Emma hadn't been waiting outside for her when the appointment ended.

Emma put the phone back into the cupholder, gripped the steering wheel with both hands and pressed her foot down even harder on the accelerator. The noise of the car and the surrounding traffic made it difficult to pick up all that was being said in the workshop. Her thoughts raced.

She glanced down at her phone. On the screen, she watched as Neumann stepped away from Blix slightly. Blix was standing stock-still, arms hanging at his side. He looked resigned. As if he'd given up. As if he knew he was going to die.

70

'I think you already know the answer to that,' Neumann said, answering his own question. 'You know there's nothing left for you here. You know what the best option is – to just end it all, before it gets any worse.'

He backed further away, heading towards a rope coiled up at the edge of the room.

'Can't you see that for yourself?' Neumann asked, quickly glancing down to make sure he wasn't going to trip over anything as he made his way slowly back to the rope. He bent down and picked it up.

'You may think you've hit rock bottom,' Neumann said, his voice calm, level. 'But what you've been through is nothing compared to what's to come. You can't turn back. You're at a point in your life now where nothing will be as good it was before. It will never get better. Only worse. There will only ever be more pain, more hardship.'

Neumann looked around and, finding what he was searching for, leant over to grasp the device that controlled the hoisting mechanism. He tucked it under his armpit, freeing his right hand to tie the rope into a knot and loop. The gun in his left hand complicated the operation.

'You'll find that everyone will eventually turn against you,' he continued, while tugging off one of his gloves with his teeth, letting it hang from his mouth as he continued working on the noose. He was, at last, satisfied with the result. He put the glove back on.

'When the time comes for you to answer for everything you've done, you'll be alone, weak, desperate to avoid your own guilt. But you'll have to carry that guilt yourself, all of it. The murder of Timo Polmar, the responsibility for your daughter's death. No one else will understand. The media coverage will be humiliating. Everyone will agree: you were a failure, a policeman who crossed a line, took the law into his own hands. Who'd shot and killed people before. You'll be seen as some murder-happy copper.'

The thought made Blix nauseous.

Neumann began to slowly approach him again. He put the remote control on the floor in front of him.

'Your prison sentence – it won't change anything,' Neumann continued. 'You'll still have to live with it all – the shame; and it'll never go away. But you can make things easier for those you care about. For Iselin's mother, who will always blame you for not being able to save her daughter. For your own mother. Neither of them deserve to be dragged down with you.' He motioned with the rope. 'It ends, here and now,' he said. 'They'll all understand. The others. They'll be sympathetic, they'll empathise. They'll all remember you with warmth and compassion ... in the end. A man who lost everything, who couldn't go on, and who took the quickest way out.'

Blix was surprised at how tempting the thought was. He was more than halfway through his life, and wouldn't find any enjoyment in the time he had left.

'Do this for them,' Neumann encouraged him. 'One last favour.'

Before arriving at the warehouse, in his head Blix had gone through all the possible ways it could end. One being that he wouldn't be able to expose Neumann at all, but would simply beat the psychiatrist to within an inch of his life. Another being that they would reach this point, where all the cards were on the table, and that Neumann would have to surrender. Or, alternatively, the psychiatrist would take his own life, seeing as it was all over anyway, and maybe drag Blix down with him. Each outcome had been enticing in its own way.

The noose at the end of the rope was now swinging from side to side in Neumann's hands, like a pendulum. The rain lashed against the roof, the sound of it reverberating around the workshop. A steady drumming. It was like standing inside a waterfall.

'You came here wanting to die,' Neumann continued. 'And while I understand that this might have been a ploy to get me here, I do have some experience of judging whether someone has made the decision to go ahead with it.'

He looked at Blix.

'And you have.'

Blix said nothing.

'So...' Neumann flashed him a smile and wiggled the rope a little. 'I'm here to help you,' he said. 'To fulfil your final request.'

Blix blinked. He cleared his throat, suddenly realising how dry it had become.

'Do you want to die like your daughter did?' Neumann asked. 'Or do you want to die in the same way as Sofia Kovic and Walter Wiik?'

Neumann raised the gun so it was level with his head.

In the past, Blix had given a lot of thought as to what he would do if his life was in danger. How he would react in that moment, before everything became completely, utterly silent. If he would be scared. If he would cry. If he would beg for his life ... or if he would welcome death. Now, as he stood there, staring down the barrel of a gun, he neither felt nor thought of anything at all.

Everything was flat.

Quiet.

Empty.

He had got what he came here for.

He had no reason left to live.

He wasn't afraid.

On the contrary.

He was ready.

71

Emma didn't want to watch, but knew she had to.

She picked the phone up again, without releasing her foot from the accelerator. She fumbled, and it slipped out of her hands, but she managed to quickly slam her thighs together, catching the phone in her lap before it fell through her legs to the floor. The car swerved towards the edge of the road. She yanked the steering wheel in the opposite direction, making the tyres screech as the car righted itself. The other drivers blared their horns at her. Emma continued as before, phone in one hand, the other controlling the wheel.

Neumann was in the centre of the screen, aiming the gun at Blix. Desperate tears began to roll down Emma's cheeks.

She passed the exit to Jessheim, aware of the beating of her heart all the way up in her throat. She watched as Neumann took another step closer to Blix. And another.

The screen was so small it was difficult to see any details.

Emma held her breath. She tried to steel herself for what she might witness, the sight of sparks erupting from the mouth of the pistol, Blix's body as it jerked backward from the impact, as he fell to the floor, as he lay there.

But it didn't happen.

Not in that moment, anyway.

The dashboard indicated that she was approaching the next exit at a speed of 153 kilometres an hour. She had never driven this fast before, but she couldn't slow down now – every second was vital.

She sat her phone back in the cupholder and concentrated on the road.

Neumann said something, but Emma couldn't hear what – they were too far away, the sound was too faint.

The slip road appeared. She didn't start to break until it was absolutely necessary. She flew around the next two roundabouts, unsure of what she would even do once she got there. The car raced down the last few hundred metres in a matter of seconds, careening onto the industrial estate and up to the warehouse.

She tore off the seatbelt and snatched the phone from the cupholder. When she looked down at the display, she felt a stab of panic shoot through her chest. The screen only showed a list of her most recent calls. The recording had stopped. She must have pressed something by accident and ended the call.

'Fuck,' she cursed as she shoved open the door.

She had ruined everything.

Again.

72

'Okay then,' Neumann said. 'Which one will it be?'

Of the two options, a bullet would presumably be both the easiest and fastest way out, and if he were only thinking of himself, it was probably the one he would prefer. But Blix thought of what Walter Wiik had said, about how shooting yourself was selfish – an inconsiderate act for those who would have to find the body. In this case, a lot of people would see it on Emma's recording. Emma would have to see it too. But watching him being dragged up by his neck, kicking about until his body became limp, probably wouldn't be any better.

'Shoot me,' he decided.

'Okay.' Neumann raised the gun.

'But I don't want to see it coming,' Blix added, his eyes now filling with tears. 'I don't want to be staring into the barrel of a gun when it happens.'

The psychiatrist looked as if he were giving the request some thought.

'Get on your knees then,' he said. 'Turn around.'

Blix turned and slowly knelt down. With each second, he expected to feel the cold steel of the gun against his temple. Blix could see it out of the corner of his eye.

'Wait,' he said quickly. 'I've changed my mind.'

Neumann sighed. 'You'd rather hang, like your daughter?'

Blix nodded. Looked up.

Neumann waited a moment before replying:

'As you wish. But you can put the noose around your neck yourself. I'm not risking you trying anything.'

Neumann chucked the rope at him. Blix caught it as if he were on autopilot. Stared down at it for a few seconds before slowly lifting it over his head and lowering it to his shoulders.

Neumann bent down and picked the control from the floor. Pressed a button. The sound of the motor coming to life, the pulley rattling along the ceiling, made Blix look up and watch as the hook began to lower, making its way down to where he was standing just a few metres below. Neumann stopped it once the chain was within arm's reach. He fastened the rope to the hook.

Blix blinked. Tears were streaming down his face. The adrenaline was pumping through his body.

Neumann pressed a different button. The hook slowly made its way back towards the ceiling again. The rope became taut.

It started to pull him upward. The noose tightened around his neck.

Blix was hoisted up onto his feet, had no other choice but to obey the rope. He was standing directly below the pulley, which was reeling the chain back to the ceiling, clattering upward centimetre by centimetre. It would be a matter of seconds before he was lifted off the ground entirely. In just a few moments, his air supply would be cut off and he wouldn't be able to speak.

A sudden panic took hold of him.

'The police are on their way,' he was just able to force out.

Neumann snorted derisively.

'It's all been recorded,' Blix gasped, the rope now cutting into the skin of his neck. He quickly pointed towards the shelf where Iselin's phone was propped up, before tugging at the rope again, trying to force a few fingers between his neck and the rope.

'Video...' It was all he was able to say.

But an expression of uncertainty had fallen across Neumann's face.

He pressed a button, stopping the mechanism. Blix was balancing on his tip-toes, struggling with the rope. He tried to talk, but couldn't.

Neumann turned and walked towards the shelves where the phone was hidden, pulled it out, and laughed. He brought it over and turned the screen towards Blix – by forcing his head down slightly to face it, the screen lit up, telling him he would need to enter his passcode to unlock it.

'There's no active video call, Blix.'

Neumann laughed again, before casting the phone aside. Blix tried again to get a few words out, but only managed to splutter. He thought through everything that could've gone wrong, but the only conclusion he came to was that the connection with Emma must've dropped. She might not have seen any of it herself. It might even be the case that none of Neumann's confession had been caught on camera either.

He feverishly tried to dig his fingers underneath the rope, which was now tugging hard against his neck, forcing his chin upwards. The tears blinded him. He blinked a few times. Closed his eyes tight and opened them again.

It was too late.

Then, the sound of metal scraping from deeper within the warehouse reached them in the workshop. As if something had been knocked over and had rolled across the floor. Neumann stopped the mechanism. Blix watched as Neumann's eyes darted from his face to search the space behind him, trying to figure out where the sound could have come from. Blix did the same behind Neumann. He couldn't see anything. But someone could be there. Or it could just be the wind. Blix prayed that it was Abelvik and the others, or better yet – Delta.

The chains rattled as Neumann set the pulley into motion again. Blix felt his feet leave the floor as the rope hauled him upwards.

His vision had already started to fade, the darkness creeping in on all sides.

He couldn't breathe.

He began to rotate around his own axis. Revolving round and round, spiralling. He could hear the motor humming away, hoisting him further and further into the air. A few more seconds and he would pass out. A few more seconds and he would die.

Alexander Blix had thought of death with a kind of longing.

With a desire to let the darkness take over.

And he had wondered what would go through his mind, had wondered whether it were true that you relived the most significant and monumental moments of your life as they played out in your head, or if what you thought about would be random, like the view from a mountain top, the fragrance of an apple tree, the taste of wine. He had wondered whether his life would flash before his eyes, like a film, or if the second his life was snubbed out wouldn't even be long enough for him to witness his very first cry as he entered this world.

But no images came to him.

No memories.

He could only hear a few sounds coming from somewhere in the distance.

Stomping. Footsteps.

And then, a yell.

The room disappeared, and everything became darker and darker.

He felt heavier and heavier.

As if he were falling.

73

And suddenly, they were there.

The sounds, the figures who popped up all around her.

A man aiming his gun out in front of him. Shouting at Neumann to drop his weapon and get to the ground.

But Neumann didn't obey. He didn't move. He just stared up at Blix, who was rotating in the air above him, hanging by a rope from the ceiling.

His legs had stopped kicking.

Tine Abelvik appeared beside Emma.

More followed.

Shouting – loud and intense.

And then everything happened at once, as if in slow motion.

Neumann lifted the gun to his own head. The sound of a gunshot, but who had fired the bullet, Emma didn't have time to register. Neumann fell backward. Both the weapon and remote control flew out of his hands.

The knot around Blix's throat started to unravel.

It fell apart entirely and he collapsed to the floor.

He met the concrete feet-first. The rest of his body crumpled beneath him, his limbs falling into an unnatural position as he came to rest.

Emma rushed over to him as commands were yelled over her head. She knelt down beside him, shoved the hair out of her face and pressed two fingers to his neck.

A pulse.

Just.

She heard someone shouting nearby:

'Police!'

Emma turned to Abelvik. 'Have you called for an ambulance?'

Abelvik nodded. 'They'll be here any second.'

74

Blix opened his eyes slightly.

It was no longer dark.

He was still breathing, but his throat was sore. It was the only thing he could feel. That, and a heartbeat.

Blix wiggled his little finger. Then the next one. An intense pain shot through his arm and into his shoulder. He couldn't move his legs.

The room was out of focus. He blinked a few times, but it didn't help. He sensed movement around him, but he couldn't move his head.

'Blix!'

He felt a cold hand against his cheek. Heard the person's rapid breathing, heard them gasp. He could feel the sensation of the floor shaking beneath him. Footsteps. Maybe.

It was cold.

'Don't move.'

Emma.

'The ambulance is on its way.'

The sounds of the room around him all blended into one, culminating in a loud ringing inside his head. He thought of Iselin, of how she might have awoken in the same way, before the darkness had crept in again. Before she had...

He wondered whether the same would happen to him.

Whether *these* would be his final moments.

More people arrived, piling in around him, surrounding him. It was getting difficult to see again. The pain disappeared. A dark haze began to descend around him, and once more it felt as if he were falling.

He saw Iselin.

Just a few minutes old.

Could see his own face in hers.

Her powerful, piercing cry.

That first toothless smile.

He saw her, standing up, keeping her balance by holding on to one of the speakers in the living room, bopping up and down to a song.

Her first step.

Steps.

Feeding her.

The mess.

Her bib.

Her dummies, which she loved more than anything in the world.

Her baggy clothes, far too big for her. Then too small.

Her first day at school.

Merete's tears as they held each other in the playground.

Their little girl, not so little.

Who grew up.

Who was suddenly an adult.

Who was Iselin.
Who was...
Blix blinked a few more times.
He had stopped falling.
The darkness closed in.

ACKNOWLEDGMENTS

Thomas: So, Jorn.

Jorn: Yes?

Thomas: I just want to say...

(beat)

(beat)

Jorn: Yes, Thomas?

Thomas: See what I did there?

Jorn: No.

Thomas: I just threw in a little cliffhanger.

Jorn: Wow.

Thomas: You know, crime writer and all.

Jorn: Clever.

Thomas: I know, right?

(beat)

(sigh)

(beat)

Jorn: So what is it—

Thomas: Just checking to see if you were still with me.

Jorn: I've been with you for three books now.

Thomas: That's what I want to thank you for.

Jorn: Hm?

Thomas: Thank you.

Jorn: I'm not following.

Thomas: It's simple. It's that time of year again. We need to give our thanks. I thought I'd thank YOU this time.

Jorn: What for?

Thomas: Isn't that obvious?

Jorn: No.

Thomas: Didn't you use to be a policeman?

Jorn: I was, yes.

Thomas: So ... never mind.

(beat)

(sigh)

(beat)

Thomas: Anyway, I thought I'd be original and—

Jorn: Like with the cliffhanger thing?

Thomas: Yes.

Jorn: Clever. I think.

(beat)

(beat)

Thomas: Thank you.

Jorn: I'm lost.

Thomas: So are those who will read this.

Jorn: Explain then. Imagine you're in an interrogation room. The spotlight is on YOU.

Thomas: Like it was for Blix in this book?

Jorn: For instance. ANYTHING that can get you to tell me what the hell you're talking about.

Thomas: I just wanted to thank you.

Jorn: I think we've covered that, thank you.

Thomas: You're thanking me as well? That's sweet, Jorn. Thank you.

(beat)

(sigh)

(beat)

(sigh)

Jorn: So...?

Thomas: Okay, okay, enough with the cliffhangers. I just wanted to thank you for writing these three books with me. It's been a blast.

(beat)

(beat)

(beat)

Thomas: Are you there, Jorn?

Jorn: Yes.

Thomas: You're not wiping your eyes or anything, are you?

Jorn: You really don't know me at all, do you?

Thomas: I'm starting to wonder.

Jorn: I think all those cliffhangers just took my breath away.

Thomas: They left you speechless.

Jorn: Yes. But thank you. Same.

Thomas: Same?

Jorn: We're being original here, aren't we? I'm thanking you now.

Thomas: What for?

Jorn: Oh, come on.

Thomas: Kidding. I'm kidding, Jorn. It's been a blast, right?

(beat)

(beat)

(beat)

(beat)

Thomas: Jorn?

Jorn: Gotcha. You're not the only one who can do hangcliffers.

Thomas: That's really not what they're called.

Jorn: I know. I'm being original. Inspired by you.

Thomas: No wonder we write such good books together.

Jorn: I know, right? And we're not done yet, are we?

Thomas: No, we're not.

Jorn: We need to work a little bit on our cliffhangers, though.

Thomas: Speak for yourself.

(beat)

(sigh)

(beat)

Jorn: We're not done with our thanks, either.

Thomas: Your powers of deduction, Jorn, they know no bounds.

Jorn: I used to be a policeman, you know.

Thomas: I know.

Jorn: So...

(beat)

(sigh)

(beat)

Thomas: I'm going to be very original here and say thank you to everyone I know.

Jorn: Everyone?

Thomas: I might leave out a few. Like...

Jorn: Wow. That's...

Thomas: I know.

Jorn: ...a lot of people.

Thomas: I know.

Jorn: You've had complaints from someone you should have mentioned?

Thomas: No.

Jorn: So...

Thomas: Original, right?

Jorn: Very. Ever thought of writing something?

Thomas: Clever, Jorn.

Jorn: I mean, there's no doubt you're very original.

Thomas: I know all about cliffhangers, too.

(beat)

(sigh)

(beat)

Jorn: My turn: I'm going to thank my family. As always. Beate. Sondre. Marte. My rocks.

Thomas: They rock?

Jorn: Hm?

Thomas: Sorry. Bad joke. Go on.

Jorn: No, that's it.

Thomas: Not very original, Jorn. What happened to your dog?

Jorn: Oh, yes. Thank you. Nothing happened to my dog. Well ... except ... a lot, now that you mention it.... I think he has a problem with his front left paw. But...

Thomas: Interesting.

Jorn: Yes.

Thomas. Cliffhanger material.

Jorn: You don't own a dog, do you, Thomas.

Thomas: I'm allergic, Jorn.

Jorn: Ah yes.

Thomas: I thought policemen had a really good memory.

Jorn: I know quite a few who don't.

Thomas: That's not reassuring.

Jorn: I don't remember their names, though.

Thomas: That's...

Jorn: I'm kidding. I do remember their names.

Thomas: That's ... never mind.

(beat)

(sigh)

(beat)

Jorn: Let's get down to business, then. We have a publisher to thank.

Thomas: We do. Karen Sullivan.

Jorn: Orenda Books.

Thomas: Yes.

Jorn: The one and only Karen.

Thomas: And Megan. We need to thank Megan Turney. Our translator.

Jorn: She's amazing, isn't she?

Thomas: I'm going to be very original here and say yes. She really is.

Jorn: But you already thanked her, didn't you? When you thanked everyone.

Thomas: I even thanked West Camel. Our editor.

Jorn: You did. Wow, you're...

Thomas: Clever. I know.

(beat)

(sigh)

(beat)

Jorn: Did you mention Cole Sullivan?

Thomas: Who's that?

Jorn: Our digital and marketing manager.

Thomas: Of course I did.

Jorn: Have you seen those book trailers he makes?

Thomas: I have, yes.

Jorn: They're amazing.

Thomas: Original.

Jorn: Yes.

(beat)

(sigh)

(beat)

Jorn: I think you should mention your kids, no?

Thomas: I did.

Jorn: I mean, specifically.

Thomas: Like with their names and such?

Jorn: That's a good start.

Thomas: I don't even remember how old they are.

Jorn: You're kidding.

Thomas: I could be a policeman.

Jorn: No you couldn't.

(beat)

(sigh)

(beat)

Jorn: But, seriously, how old are your children?

Thomas: Not nearly old enough.

Jorn: That's...

Thomas: Original?

Jorn: Not what I was going to say, no.

Thomas: Your power with words, Jorn, knows no bounds.

Jorn: I know.

(beat)

(beat)

Jorn: That's it, then.

Thomas: That's it.

Jorn: Thank you.

Thomas: What for?